"Eleano ave to do what's be

She star vith anger and disappointment. She drew in a ragged breath. "That's why you can't take her away from me, Jordon. Surely you must see that. She's beginning to gain confidence in herself. Do you know she wanted to get a job so she could earn enough to pay for her room and board? That's how badly she wants to stay . . . with us." She meandered to the edge of the creek. As he approached, she listened to the sound of crunching leaves, dreading his response.

Jordon came to stand at Eleanore's back. One hand cradled her arm; his other encircled her waist and drew her back against him. He lowered his head near hers, softly stroking his jaw on her silky hair. "You're right. She does belong with you." He kissed her behind the ear and felt her soften.

Also by Deborah Wood . . .

Praise for *Gentle Hearts*,
a Diamond Homespun Romance:

"The folks at Diamond know a gem when they see one. [This] is a real treasure. I enjoyed it from beginning to end."
—*Affaire de Coeur*

"[A] sensitive story of a gentler time with a love strong enough to bear whatever comes its way. Congratulations, Ms. Wood!"
—*Heartland Critiques*

"A touching story . . . entertaining." —*Rendezvous*

Diamond Books by Deborah Wood

GENTLE HEARTS
SUMMER'S GIFT

SUMMER'S GIFT

DEBORAH WOOD

DIAMOND BOOKS, NEW YORK

This book is a Diamond original edition,
and has never been previously published.

SUMMER'S GIFT

A Diamond Book / published by arrangement with
the author

PRINTING HISTORY
Diamond edition / May 1994

ISBN: 0-7865-0006-9

Diamond Books are published by The Berkley Publishing Group,
200 Madison Avenue, New York, NY 10016.
DIAMOND and the "D" design
are trademarks belonging to Charter Communications, Inc.

PRINTED IN THE UNITED STATES OF AMERICA

10 9 8 7 6 5 4 3 2 1

To Laura Taylor with admiration, respect and affection.
Your friendship is a gift I will always treasure.

CHAPTER ONE

August 1866

Glancing around the small wood-framed church in Tuttle, Kansas, Jordon Stone fervently hoped the children employed by these good people would have the kind of life he'd hoped his baby sister would have had. The image of her alone, hungry and terrified haunted him still. He forced the memory to a far corner of his mind where it would stay until he was free of his obligations and miles away.

He stood by the raised sash window and looked at the open doors across the room, willing a breeze to stir, but the sweltering air remained still. If he could only remove his suit jacket. In the heat, it felt like a winter coat.

"Jordon—"

He glanced at Francis Williams, his colleague from the Children's Aid Society in New York City. "Have all the placements been completed?" Jordon had to admire Francis. The man was devoted to the welfare of the children and didn't appear to feel the overwhelming despair that plagued Jordon. On the contrary. Francis was delighted to give the children the tools to become independent, responsible adults. A noble calling but one Jordon no longer felt qualified to answer.

"I would appreciate it if you would speak with Mr. and Mrs. Leah, Jordon. I'll finish talking with the Adamson couple and the placements will be complete, except for Amelia."

Jordon nodded and picked up the notes made earlier by the community evaluating committee and joined Mr. and Mrs. Leah. After introducing himself, he verified the information he had been given.

"I understand you own a general store where Robert would work after school and on Saturdays." The report was favorable, as they usually were. No one wanted to impugn their friends, neighbors or shopkeepers, which Jordon recalled had caused more than one problem for the Society.

"That's right. Me and the missus work the store." Mr. Leah tugged at the front of his coat and shirt collar.

"It is warm today." Jordon loosened his tie. "Do you employ anyone else?"

"I have a boy that makes deliveries, when need be." Mr. Leah cleared his throat and glanced at his wife. "Robert seems like a good lad. He can work after school, use what he learns. Mrs. Leah will make sure he does his homework and chores and see to his manners." Mr. Leah nodded in the direction of Mrs. Leah, who vigorously plied her fan.

"You do understand that the Society believes children who work for their keep, receive an education and reap the rewards of their labor grow to be responsible adults? This doesn't mean Robert will be a slave. I feel children also learn from experience, and that should include free time with other children."

Mrs. Leah lowered her fan and leaned forward. "Mr. Stone, we'll care for Robert like our own. He won't have to work from the time school lets out to sundown. He'll go to church every Sunday and have everything he needs for school, too. We'll do right by him."

They appeared sincere, and Mrs. Leah had stolen several glances at the boy that told Jordon she was taken with the child. Satisfied, he signaled to Robert and the boy approached. "Have you talked with Mr. and Mrs. Leah, Robert?"

"Ya-es, mister." He pulled at his britches and straightened up.

"Are you still in accord with this arrangement?" Robert nervously crumpled his cap with both hands, but Jordon refused to smile. It was his job to make certain that the boy went into this with a good attitude.

"Y-e-s, mister. I be good 'n' work 'ard."

Jordon smiled then. "I'm sure you will, Robert. And be happy. I want you to remember, if you need help, write to Mr. Brice or Mr. Williams. You have the address. They'll be there for you." It takes more than a good scrubbing and new clothes to transform the children, Jordon reflected, and he sincerely wished each child well.

Turning his attention to Mr. Leah, Jordon handed him a card. "This is your agreement with the Society, the same that you signed earlier."

Jordon shook hands with each of them and wished them well, then his attention was caught by a woman sitting at the back of the room. Her floppy bonnet had slipped back, exposing several locks of light hair. Amelia was still sitting by herself, waiting. The woman must have arrived late. He'd let Francis talk to her.

He knew he had finally made the right decision. Heading west was the solution. He'd make a new life. To continue in this work he would need more compassion than he was now able to muster. He felt a hand tug on his jacket sleeve and looked down.

"Yes, Matthew."

The boy stuck out his hand. "Jist want'd t'thank you, sir. Are you goin' t'live with a family out west, like us?"

"I'm too old for a family to take me in. Think I'd make a fair cowboy?"

"Sure, but you'll have t'stop shavin' and git a horse."

Jordon chuckled. The question had been asked with no forethought, but the idea of a solitary life had merit. He shook Matthew's hand and ruffled the lad's sandy-colored hair. "Have a good life. The Lindens seem like nice people."

"I will." Matthew grinned and ran over to the couple waiting for him.

She shouldn't have to wait too long, Eleanore Merrill thought as she watched the children departing with men and women. She had arrived late, missing the opening address, but she had traveled for two dawn-to-dusk days to attend the Children's Aid Society's adoption meeting and had a few questions she wanted answered. If anyone could give her advice on finding homes for orphans, it was the Children's Aid Society—they should have the know-how she lacked.

She stood up, smoothed her faded calico skirt, straightened her damp shirtwaist and removed her limp bonnet. She felt like last week's dish towel, but she wasn't the only one suffering from the heat. Everyone in the room looked a bit bedraggled.

She approached the gentleman who had just finished interviewing the last couple, mainly because he looked more amiable than the man in the fancy suit with the silvery-gray vest, and because she remembered his name.

"Mr. Williams, I am Eleanore Merrill." She held out her hand. After he released it, she continued. "If you have a few minutes, I would like to speak with you about your procedure for finding suitable homes for children."

Mr. Williams glanced at Amelia. "I think Mr. Stone will be able to help you." He waved in Jordon's direction. "If you'll excuse me."

She watched Mr. Stone a moment before going over to him, wondering if he was friendlier than his name sounded or if his name had a bearing on his personality. He did have lovely hair, she mused, thick and brown, the color of rich cocoa, but he looked standoffish.

Again she held out her hand, this time to Mr. Stone, and

stared up at him. "I am Eleanore Merrill. Mr. Williams said you may be able to answer my questions." The man's eyes were misty green but remote, and seemed as devoid of feeling as those of an orphan she had taken into her home after an explosion. He hadn't made a move to take her hand, and she was tempted to lower it. However, she was also stubborn and determined not to be ignored.

Jordon found the woman's penetrating scrutiny more unsettling than the children's. "Mrs. Merrill." He finally shook her hand and dropped his to his side. "If you came about one of the children, you are too late. I believe our flyer stated that you must be interview—"

"Excuse me for interrupting, but I am not here as a prospective employer. And, I am not married. I'm *Miss* Merrill."

Damnation, didn't the woman ever blink? Her eyes were brown and unwavering, her complexion sun glazed, and she had an old-maid schoolmarm's expression. Jordon put down the papers he'd been organizing.

"I apologize, *Miss* Merrill. How may I help you?"

Admiring his firm jaw, she noticed a scar along the right side near his ear. It became more prominent when he clenched his jaw, which he was presently doing.

"I came to see how the Children's Aid Society placement system works. I would like to know how the children are chosen." Was he uncomfortable with her or her questions? Eleanore glanced at the little girl sitting by herself and wondered if this man's manner had anything to do with the child's discomfort.

"Sometimes they're found on the streets. Sometimes they come to us." He ground his teeth. In a few minutes he'd be free—free of responsibilities, free of the innocent reminders of his sister, just the way he wanted. On his own—that is, if he could escape this woman. When he glanced down, he half expected to see her in pants, not a washed-out yellow skirt.

"No, you misunderstood. I would like to know if all the

children are from New York City. Are all of them placed out of the city? Why? How do you choose the children who'll be settled out of the city? Do they have any say in the matter? Are they prepared for the move? Why was Tuttle, Kansas, chosen? What—"

Jordon raised his hand. "One question at a time, please." She stood there staring up at him like a commanding officer. Like a man. "I work at the lodge with the boys as a supervisor, sometimes teacher, and help them find employment. Charles Loring Brice heads the Society and makes the decisions about who goes where. He is responsible for the advance publicity and the flyers describing each of the children. You should write him. If you'll excuse me." He put the records in Francis's old canvas satchel and closed it.

Before he moved away from her, and he certainly seemed to want to distance himself from her, she made one last attempt. "The children have been attending school, haven't they?" He took one step away, but she continued. "They do know how to read and write, don't they, Mr. Stone?"

He paused in midstride, reacting as if he'd been called to attention. "All the children receive instruction until they are placed. Then, Miss Merrill, their employers or sponsors are responsible for their education." He withdrew a card from the breast pocket of his coat and handed it to her. "This is what we give every employer or approved sponsor. It summarizes their agreement with the Society. The address is on the back."

He stepped away from her while she turned the card over. He desperately wanted to continue walking, right out through the open doors, but he wasn't reckless enough to abandon Francis without saying good-bye. He couldn't remember ever encountering a woman like *Miss* Merrill and fervently hoped he wouldn't again. When he thought about women, he envisioned a softer feminine form with a gentle manner. Hopefully, all women in the West weren't as imposing, outspoken and unrelenting as Miss Merrill.

Eleanore sat down on a nearby chair and read the card. Mr. Stone's suggestion wasn't why she had come so far. Then she noticed the little girl swipe at her cheeks with the back of her hand. She hadn't seen the child's face, but her hair was long, almost black and fashioned in braids. The poor dear, Eleanore thought. She reached into her reticule, retrieved her handkerchief and handed it to the girl.

"It's awfully hot in here, isn't it?" The little girl glanced up for a fraction of a moment and accepted the handkerchief. She was pale, but she had the prettiest deep blue eyes and long, dark lashes. Eleanore rather envied the child her inherited beauty. She unfastened the top two buttons of her shirtwaist. It didn't help all that much.

The little girl nodded her head but kept her eyes downcast while she dried her cheeks with the soft cotton square.

Eleanore couldn't help wondering why the child had been left alone. Hadn't Mr. Stone said that all of the children were spoken for? "I'm Eleanore Merrill. What's your name?"

"Amelia Howe," Amelia whispered. She stared at her hands and then held out the handkerchief to Eleanore. "Thank you."

"You're welcome." Eleanore tucked the cloth up her sleeve. "Amelia is a lovely name." Before she said more, Eleanore overheard Mr. Stone and Mr. Williams speaking in hushed tones.

"Who delivered this note?"

"A man on his way to Fort Leavenworth dropped it off. I know you wanted to leave all this behind, Jordon, but would you take Amelia to the James farm? The directions are included. It is north of here, so it shouldn't be too far out of your way. I would take her myself, but I have to catch the train back to New York."

Jordon focused on the unpainted walls of the church. He'd been so close, so *very* close to being free of his obligation to Brice and the children, especially the children. "Has the couple been interviewed? Have you spoken or corresponded with them?"

"The local committee approved them. Mrs. James suffers poor health and requires help around the house. They agreed to settle a small sum on the girl after harvest time each year, and Mrs. James will continue Amelia's education. I haven't any more information beyond that."

Jordon nodded. Amelia had been placed last year and returned to the Society last spring. It was an unfortunate situation, one Charles Brice strived to avoid. The couple had worked Amelia like a field hand and mistreated her at every turn. She managed to get a letter to Brice, which was a heroic act under the circumstances. Jordon wanted to make damn sure the nine-year-old little girl was placed in a good situation this time. She was too much like— No, not now. He wouldn't allow those memories to intrude.

"Of course. Let me see the directions." He read the neatly penned note. "I'll rent a buggy."

"Here." Francis handed five dollars to Jordon. "For the rental and inconvenience. Brice would insist."

As Eleanore listened, her mind raced. Her wagon was out front, and she had to return home to Nebraska. Amelia was frightened, as well she should be, and Eleanore wanted to see for herself that the child was placed with a good family. Not all people were *good,* as much as she would like to believe otherwise.

"Mr. Stone—" She smiled at Amelia and bounded to her feet. "I have a wagon and will be returning to Myles Creek, north of here in Nebraska. I would be happy to give you and Amelia a ride."

Mr. Williams glanced at Stone. "That is a very generous offer, Mrs.—"

"Miss Merrill." Eleanore smiled at him and gazed at Mr. Stone. "I'm ready to leave now."

She forced herself to remain silent, give the man a

chance to think. She wanted to spend more time with Amelia because something about her was disturbing, and Eleanore liked satisfactory resolutions when she sensed a problem.

Jordon's hand closed around the money. Why had his plans gone awry at the last? On the other hand, Miss Merrill was a woman and Amelia would probably feel more at ease with her. The child needed to talk to someone but had said few words to anyone about her recent experience. That bothered him. He could catch a northbound stage from most any town.

He was wasting time.

CHAPTER TWO

As Jordon handed the money back to Francis, he spoke to Miss Merrill. "We can leave when you're ready." The smile that lit her plain face stopped him cold. Maybe traveling with her wouldn't be as tedious as he'd thought.

Eleanore went over to Amelia and held our her hand. "Why don't we make a trip outside before we leave?"

Jordon watched Miss Merrill take Amelia's hand and walk out before he spoke to Francis. "Are you certain you won't need help with the second-day visits? I can delay my leave."

"There's no need. I can make the calls. There aren't that many."

"And you're confident the Jameses are qualified?"

"As far as I know. Have a good journey. I almost envy you." Francis Williams pumped Jordon's hand. "There shouldn't be any complications."

No complications, Jordon thought. Absolutely none, except that *Miss* Merrill was one big complication. He plopped his bowler on his head and picked up his bag and Amelia's smaller one. He found Amelia and Miss Merrill waiting outside by a well-used wagon with a crudely fashioned canvas cover. He shook his head. Something told him he should walk to the nearest livery stable and purchase a horse.

The sky was clear and as blue as Amelia's sad eyes. The road north cut through miles of flat grassland as far as one could see. Eleanore remembered how when she was eight-years-old, riding along a road through wind-whipped grass with her father, she used to pretend the wagon was a ship crossing the sea. Of course she had never seen an ocean, before that time or in the nineteen years since then.

She glanced down at Amelia and wondered what she invented to amuse herself, knowing there was little time to get beyond the protective barrier the child had erected. "You might feel a bit cooler, Amelia, if you unfasten the top buttons on your dress."

Amelia obediently raised her hands and slowly loosened the buttons on her pretty new dress. She tried to be a good girl. She did what she was told. The people from the Society, like Mr. Jordon, were kind, but she knew there were other people who only pretended to be nice. Though she'd been accused of being bad often enough by different guardians, she wasn't sure if what she had done was so terrible.

Accustomed to handling the horse, Eleanore didn't have to concentrate on guiding the animal. She glanced at Mr. Stone. He sat with his coat still in place, his back rigid and his hat slightly tilted down on his forehead.

"Mr. Stone, in this heat, I think we can put etiquette aside and be comfortable. Feel free to remove your jacket and tie. I won't be offended." Actually, she'd had her skirt up to her knees on her ride south. After all, she had been alone on the road, and it was so doggoned hot.

Jordon shifted on the hard bench seat. "I appreciate your consideration, Miss Merrill." He removed his tie and collar, put them in his pocket and took off his coat. He then removed his vest and opened the top of his shirt. His mood improved at once. He settled back and closed his eyes. The hot air felt cool as it brushed across his wet neck. He rested one boot on the rail and savored the idle moment.

At length he jolted to awareness. Had he really dozed

off? He felt stiff and every one of his thirty years. Probably looked them, too, he thought.

"Did you have a good rest, Mr. Stone?"

He stretched and rubbed his neck. "Didn't intend to, but yes." He wiped his forehead and looked around. "Do you know the James farm, Miss Merrill?"

"Mr. Williams said north. This is the main road north, to Middleburg, Nebraska. You do have the directions, don't you?" She pulled back on the reins and brought the horse to a halt—and stared at Jordon. They had been riding for at least an hour, by Eleanore's estimate, and he *just* thought about the directions? Now?

"These are rather sketchy." Maybe it was just as well Miss Merrill had offered to drive him. He'd never been to Kansas before and saw little to recommend it, especially since he wasn't interested in farming. "Are you familiar with Abbyville?"

"That's near the Nebraska border." She flicked the reins, and once again they moved up the road. "We won't get there until morning." A man must have said that men were logical; certainly no woman would have.

"I had no idea it would be that far. I should've thought about buying provisions. I don't suppose we'll go through a town before then."

"Walker isn't too far, but I brought enough food to see me home. We can stretch it. If you're thirsty, there are three jugs of water just behind the seat."

"We'll stop in Walker. I didn't have time for more than a few bites at dinner, and I intend to have plenty for supper."

Eleanore nodded. His gray suit was made of good cloth and fit him well. She had no doubt he could afford several meals and lodging, too. She, on the other hand, had five children in her care and could ill afford any additional expense.

The left wagon wheels hit a rut in the road. Amelia was jostled and bumped Jordon's arm. She righted herself immediately but not before he felt the tension in her. "You must be hungry, Amelia. What sounds good?"

She shrugged, but her stomach rumbled. She instantly pressed her hands on her waist to hide the noise.

He tried to recall what she liked most at mealtime. The fare at the train stops was plain and nourishing, but some dishes were met with relish. Her preference? Blank. Damn, that's why he had to leave. He had nothing more to give. God, he hoped Miss Merrill had packed a coffeepot. Suddenly he was very thirsty.

He climbed over the seat and reached for the water. "Would you like a drink, Amelia?"

She turned her head, licking her lips. "Yes, sir."

Eleanore glanced over her shoulder. "There should be a tin cup in that crate." There was more to the child's withdrawn behavior than normal fear of a new home. Much more, if her instincts were right, and they usually were.

After Amelia drank her fill, Jordon offered Miss Merrill the cup, then enjoyed one himself. While he was in the back of the wagon, he decided to satisfy his curiosity and see just what provisions were there. He found a crate packed with a big old coffeepot, a skillet, three small bundles of what was probably food, and one battered plate.

Out of the corner of his eye he also noticed a shotgun, a wicked knife for a woman to use and some tools. She'd had the good sense to bring protection; he just wondered if she knew how to use the weapons. He watched her—the easy way she handled the reins and her relaxed posture on the bench, with her worn leather shoe resting on the rail—and decided she probably did.

He climbed back over to his place by Amelia. The child hadn't said but two words. He had hoped Miss Merrill would draw her out, but even she was quiet.

"I am curious, Miss Merrill. You said you weren't at the meeting to employ any of the children. Why did you travel so far to attend?"

"I care for a few orphans. I wanted to know how your

Society went about finding homes for their children. I've placed one boy and two girls in the last year, but it's not like giving away pups."

Jordon almost choked. "No, it certainly isn't." He glanced sideways at her. If she had offered him a ride just so he would help her, she would soon realize her error. "The church or community leaders in your town must be willing to help."

It was her turn to look to the side, at him. "There's no church, though several families meet on Sunday morning for prayer. As for community leaders, the business owners make certain decisions, when they must." And they were all eager to leave the children's care to her—which was for the best, to her way of thinking. At least she wouldn't put the children in just any home.

He knew he shouldn't ask, but his curiosity got the best of him. "How did you happen to be the one person in town to take them in? Surely some of the families wouldn't mind another child."

"You mean, why would a single woman be trusted over a family?" She hadn't expected that of him, and it stung.

"No! That's not what I meant. Children are usually sheltered by families, where the responsibilities can be shared."

"I care about what happens to each child." She pursed her lips and inhaled a deep, calming breath. "I understand how it feels to lose parents."

He found he had leaned closer to Amelia in order to hear Miss Merrill's last words. Her voice was tight, the words clipped but softly spoken. She, too, felt the children's pain.

He sighed and settled back. His leave-taking wasn't happening the way he'd planned, but after spending tomorrow night at the James farm, to make sure Amelia would be all right, he'd jump on the next stage. It wouldn't even matter what direction it was headed.

Eleanore recalled Peter, the first child she'd taken in and

the first she had placed in a family. Two years ago last winter there had been a boat accident on the Missouri River and her father had joined the rescuers. He and Peter's parents, the Hawthornes, drowned, and Peter had come to stay with her. She hadn't thought twice about sharing her home with him. He was such a happy little boy, and placing him in a new home three months later had been so very painful.

Her thoughts returned to the present, and she stared ahead. "Isn't that the outline of the town ahead?"

Amelia shaded her eyes. "Yes, Miss Eleanore. I see it too."

Thank God, Jordon muttered, gazing off to the side.

A long while later, or so it seemed to Eleanore, she pulled up in front of the general store in Walker. She stepped down to the ground, shook her faded yellow calico skirt and walked around the wagon to where Amelia stood beside Mr. Stone.

"Ladies." Jordon bowed slightly from the waist and held out his hand toward the boardwalk.

With Amelia just a step behind her, Eleanore entered the store. She passed by a table with shoes, a small display of ready-made dresses, pants and shirts, and several shelves of yard goods. She didn't have a penny to spare, but she suddenly realized that Amelia might like to browse. Eleanore stopped at the counter, feigning interest in the basket of eggs.

"You may look around on your own, Amelia, but please don't leave the store."

Amelia stared at Miss Merrill for a moment. Was it a trick? Amelia wondered. She cautiously took one step away, then a second and another. Her gaze darted around the crowded room. The store smelled funny, like pickles and coffee and kerosene all mixed up. She had never seen a store like this in the city. When she turned to her left, she smelled peppermint, much better than kerosene.

Eleanore swatted at the flies buzzing around her face.

She moved to a display of buttons and thread. She had enough to satisfy her needs for the next months and stepped over to check the price of children's shoes. That was one item she would have to budget for or find something to barter with.

Jordon hung back, watching Amelia's nose twitch and Miss Merrill's gaze wander longingly. He couldn't squander his time. He felt sure the woman would snap to and call him back to the wagon before long. He went over to the counter and caught the storekeeper's attention.

The man came over and smiled. "What can I get for you?"

Jordon pointed up behind the lanky man. "I want that ham, and a pound of bacon." When those items had been placed on the counter, he continued. "Eight fresh eggs . . . do you have any bread?"

"The missus baked this morning. I can part with one loaf."

"Thank you." Jordon smiled. He added six potatoes and three good-size turnips to the counter. "Oh, I'll need a pound of sugar and a pail of milk, if you have any to spare."

The storekeeper laughed. "Where you headin'?"

"Up north, for now." Jordon glanced around to see what else they would need and saw Amelia staring at the jar of candy sticks. "Four peppermint sticks, too."

"Good enough." The man got the items and packed them in a crate.

After Jordon paid the bill, he added his purchases to the back of the wagon. A delicious aroma drifted in his direction. For a moment, he was tempted to take Amelia and Miss Merrill to the diner, but the milk wouldn't last too well in this heat. He dashed back into the store for something they could eat now. He found a jar of peaches and paid for them before he spotted Miss Merrill by the door with Amelia.

Eleanore stared at the jar, then at the almost boyish grin

softening Mr. Stone's strong features. When he paused in front of her, she said the first thing that came to mind. "Will the peaches fill you up?" She hadn't meant to say it just that way. His expression sobered instantly. "I . . ." She unconsciously straightened her back. "I apologize, Mr. Stone."

He opened the door and replied as she passed. "These are for now. The supplies are in the wagon." He followed Amelia and gave her a hand up. "I'll drive, Miss Merrill. You can take it easy for a while."

"I prefer to drive, but thank you for offering."

Eleanore climbed up to her seat and took up the reins. She had assumed the running of her father's house when she was nine and had been driving a wagon since she was eleven, even when she and her father went out together. She saw no reason to turn over to Mr. Stone what she was well able to do herself, as she always had.

Jordon really would have preferred handling the reins to sitting at the other end of the bench with nothing to occupy himself with but his thoughts. He didn't want to think any more. Plan.

That's what he needed. He had only mapped out his westward trip as far as taking the Union Pacific to the end of the line. But he would have to buy a horse, supplies and tack. The heat shimmered on the dirt road. He would follow the trail west, live off of the land for a spell, find a quiet spot.

Amelia lowered the front of her skirt and watched the dry brush fall to the ground. She had never seen anyone make a camp fire before, but she didn't think what she had collected would last long. She wiped her hands on her skirt and went back to the field to search for thicker sticks.

"Wait up, Amelia." Jordon realized his error in assigning the task to her. "I'll do that. You see if Miss Merrill needs help with supper."

Amelia nodded and turned back toward camp. She

didn't know how to cook any better than she could gather twigs for the fire. But she would try.

Jordon watched her start back and shook his head. He feared it would take that little girl a long time to feel secure enough to trust an elder again. He well understood her hesitancy to care about anyone.

Eleanore paused after cutting three slices of ham and glanced at Amelia. "Would you check the turnips?" Part of Eleanore wanted to coddle the child, but experience had taught her otherwise.

"You made a splendid fire, Mr. Stone. How many slices of ham should I cut for you?"

"Two'll be enough." He poked the potatoes with the fork and rolled them over. "I should've gotten a couple forks and plates."

"We'll make do, if you don't mind eating from the skillet." He agreed, as she'd hoped he would. "And I'll start a pot of coffee after I serve the turnips."

He chuckled. "I wondered why you brought that big coffeepot."

"My father used to tease that, in a pinch, the old pot could be used to bathe from."

A hint of a sad smile softened her features, taking several years from her appearance. Her mouth was no longer a straight slash above her stubborn chin; even her eyes seemed to shine with an inner light. Earlier, if asked, he would have said she was about his age. Now he guessed younger. If she'd smile more often and not stare into a person's eyes all the time, she might be considered a fair-looking woman, he thought. That is *if* he were interested, which he wasn't.

A few minutes later she placed the three-legged skillet within his reach. "I'll use the knife, Miss Merrill. And my fingers." He winked at Amelia and was rewarded with a shy grin.

She handed Amelia the fork. "We'll share the plate. Eat

as much as you want. Mr. Stone provided more than enough food."

Amelia accepted the fork and hesitated.

After watching her a moment, Eleanore scooped up a piece of ham with her spoon and ate it. "Go on. It's very good." She gazed at Mr. Stone. "Thank you."

"You're welcome." He'd almost inhaled three bites to her one, plus started on his potato. "You're a good cook. This's the best ham I've had in years."

"I think you were starving."

Amelia forced herself to chew slowly. Mr. Jordon and Miss Eleanore were being good to her. Amelia broke off a chunk of potato with the crispy blackened skin and relished it. She wondered if Miss Eleanore cooked meals like this every day. She didn't look real skinny, except for her face, and that was real pretty, especially when she smiled.

Jordon belatedly remembered the pail of milk he'd set in the shallow creek. "Even that cool water feels hot." He filled the cup and handed it to Amelia. "It may be lukewarm, and I don't think we have any chocolate to mix with it."

Amelia held the cup with both hands and sipped. "It's good."

Eleanore finished her meal. It was decidedly better than her dried beef would have been. With the hem of her skirt wrapped around her hand, she moved the coffeepot from the fire. "You finished the peaches, didn't you, Mr. Stone?"

Jordon gulped the bite he'd been chewing. "I'm sorry. I didn't think you wanted any. Amelia and I ate them."

"No. Just the jar. Is it in the wagon? We can use it for a cup."

"Under the seat." He glanced at Amelia. "Would you like more ham? I'm not sure I can finish this last piece."

Amelia didn't look up. "I'm full, sir." She wiped her mouth with the hem of her skirt, then quickly looked up to see if she had displeased him. Mr. Jordon didn't seem to have noticed.

Eleanore poured coffee into the jar she had just rinsed out and handed it to Mr. Stone. "I hope you don't take it with sugar. I haven't any."

"I bought some." He retrieved the package and came close to smiling when Miss Merrill handed him the spoon she'd just washed. He reached into his shirt pocket and withdrew two peppermint sticks. "This is for you," he said, handing one to Amelia.

She held the candy near her mouth, inhaled deeply and licked her lips.

Holding out the second stick of candy to Miss Merrill, Jordon said simply, "For you." Losing that floppy bonnet had done wonders for her appearance, he decided. Her hair was dark blond, almost brown, and tended to work itself free of the knot at her neck.

Eleanore met his earnest gaze and accepted his offering. "Why, thank you, Mr. Stone." Was it getting warmer? Or was it her? She definitely felt the need to fan herself.

The surprise and confusion in her expression told Jordon much about the formidable Miss Merrill. More than he wanted to acknowledge. They would part company tomorrow, so he needn't wonder if she had never before received small gestures of friendship, or why.

Even though they were camped just off the road, by a minuscule creek, and without benefit of any trees or even a bush higher than her knee for privacy, Eleanore felt an intimacy she had never experienced. Mr. Stone appeared completely relaxed, almost at home, tending the camp fire. She hadn't expected that unsettling feeling.

She had honestly believed the James farm would be only an hour or two from Tuttle, not a day's ride. And she most certainly would not have offered the ride if she'd known it would mean spending the night . . . near him. She had spoken, once again, before thinking or asking questions. Her overriding concern had been for the little girl.

She walked over to the creek and washed out the skillet. She filled it with water to heat and wash the utensils. The ordinary task reminded her of home. Harriet, her longtime friend, had admonished Eleanore not to feel guilty about leaving the children in her care, but she did. She had never left the children with anyone before.

It was getting dark. She really must stop wool-gathering. "Amelia, would you dry the dishes for me?" She handed the little girl a clean towel.

Later that evening, Eleanore spread out her two blankets in the back of the wagon. Mr. Stone's low-pitched, gruff voice carried easily in the still night from where he sat with Amelia. Eleanore straightened the blankets and was about to find out why he sounded so angry, but as she raised her skirt to climb out over the back of the wagon, she heard his words and froze.

"It's all right to be frightened. Everyone is sometime, but I want you to know I won't make you stay with Mr. and Mrs. James if you really don't want to. I'll spend the night there, to make sure you'll be okay."

Eleanore sat back on her heels and sighed. She hoped Amelia had listened to what he said and not the way he'd said it. He really did care, Eleanore realized, and peered around the edge of the canvas.

His expression had softened. He was watching the little girl as a concerned father would, with love in his eyes, his mouth no longer an unswerving line. He wasn't as forbidding as she had first thought. In fact, she decided, she rather liked the curve of his lips.

She stepped over the back of the wagon and joined them near the fire. "Amelia, you look tired. I think it's time for bed, dear."

Amelia nodded.

"We'll share the blankets. I'll come to bed in a little while."

A few minutes later, Amelia lay in the back of the wagon and Eleanore smoothed back the girl's pretty dark hair. "I'll be right here with Mr. Stone. If you need anything, just call." She leaned over and kissed Amelia on the forehead, the way she bid her children good night. "Happy dreams."

Amelia lay very still until Miss Eleanore had left the wagon, then she touched the fingertips of one hand to where she had been kissed. She felt a tear on her cheek and rubbed it off. She would not cry.

Eleanore lifted the coffeepot from the rim of the fire. It wasn't empty. "Would you like a little more?"

"You have some. I'm fine."

She filled the tin cup and sat down. She fluttered the back of her shirtwaist, trying to create a breeze. The crickets must be having a convention, she mused. Mr. Stone rested with his shoulders against his valise, apparently at ease.

"You said you were traveling north. Where are you going?"

"I don't know." When she raised her brows, he chuckled. "I haven't decided yet. My plans only took me as far as heading north a ways and west."

"The west is a large area. Do you have family or friends somewhere out there?" She was teasing, but his carefree expression slipped away as if it had never been, and she knew she had mistakenly said the wrong thing.

He sipped the coffee and willed the image of his sister, Liza, from his mind. She was always there, on the edge of his thoughts. More so since her death, he realized, than during her life. Self-inflicted guilt. A form of atonement. Was that what he was really running from?

"Just curiosity. Haven't you wondered why so many people are moving out there?" He didn't believe in streets paved with gold, but he believed he would discover what he needed there.

"I used to. Papa and I moved several times, and I wondered why he didn't want to search for gold. Evidently he wasn't as adventurous as I used to believe."

"I don't remember my father traveling any farther than Albany, and then only a couple times a year."

Eleanore stifled a yawn and finished her coffee. "Good night, Mr. Stone. Do you need anything from the wagon before I retire?"

He shook his head. "Sleep well, Miss Merrill."

"And you, Mr. Stone." She quietly approached the wagon and climbed in.

She carefully slid in beside Amelia and closed her eyes. Eleanore's mind replayed the day's odd turn of events. One never could tell just what might happen, she thought. That's what makes life so interesting. However, interesting events in her life usually involved other people's children, not a man.

And she had never seen a man with misty-green eyes before.

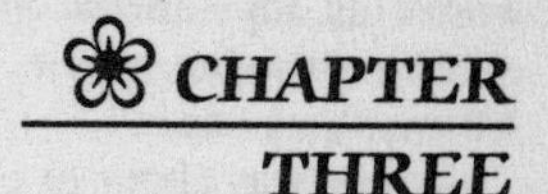

CHAPTER THREE

Eleanore secured the harness and scratched the base of her horse's ear. Poor old Ned, she thought, he's showing his twenty years. "I'm not planning any more long trips."

Jordon came upon Eleanore and overheard her talking to the horse. "Do you do that often?"

She started but didn't face him. She shrugged. "Papa bought him when I was twelve. Ned's about my best friend, aren't you, boy?"

"I was referring to your remark about trips. Do you travel about the country by yourself very often?"

"This was the first time."

She patted Ned's shoulder and faced Mr. Stone—and stared at him. Gone was his fine city suit. He now wore sturdy tan pants and a green shirt a few shades darker than his eyes. He only distantly resembled the rigid man she'd met yesterday. "Excuse me," she mumbled, sidestepping him. He's the same man. What's wrong with me? she thought.

Jordon grinned at her retreating back. She should smile more. It wouldn't put people off like her usual stern expression, or was that only for his benefit? "Miss Merrill . . ."

She hesitated near the rear wheel of the wagon. ". . . Yes, Mr. Stone?"

"I packed the supplies in the wagon and refilled the water jugs." Why wouldn't she turn around? She hid within that limp bonnet almost the way Amelia hid her gaze.

"We should get started, then."

Eleanore continued on around the back of the wagon, searching for Amelia. She was several yards up the creek staring into the water. "Amelia . . . we have to leave. Come along, dear."

Jordon was about to climb up to the driver's side of the wagon when Miss Merrill stepped in front of him. "I'll drive. You can be a passenger this morning," he said, and raised one brow. That usually intimidated the boys at the lodge, but it wasn't having the same effect on her.

"I'll drive, Mr. Stone. This morning, afternoon and evening. No one but me drives my wagon."

"You're joking."

"No, Mr. Stone. I am not." She climbed up to the hard seat and waited for him to do the same.

Fine, he thought, drive the damn wagon, and if it breaks down, she'll probably push it. All he'd wanted to do was share the work, do his part. The moment Amelia was settled and his pants touched the wooden bench, the wagon started forward at a good clip.

He steadied Amelia and felt her tremble. He kept his arm around her narrow shoulders, thankful she had returned quickly. In Miss Merrill's haste, she easily could have left the girl behind. After all, the child was his responsibility, no different from the others, or so he tried to believe. He released her and stared ahead.

Usually, in his experience, women didn't insist on handling the reins or take overnight trips alone. This woman did. Of course, he was learning that this woman did a lot of things most women did not.

After three hours on the road, Eleanore wasn't about to admit she wasn't sure how much farther it was to Abbyville. It had to be just ahead, she reasoned. She recalled this stretch of the road, mainly because of the numerous deep furrows.

She hadn't spoken to Mr. Stone since early morning.

She wasn't angry, but since he had remained silent, she assumed he must be rankled. The incident was so foolish. Why should she apologize for handling her own horse and wagon? However, the tension was tedious, more than tedious. It was driving her to distraction.

"Mr. Stone, the James farm *is* west of Abbyville, isn't it?"

"It is." He watched her. There it was again, that same throaty huskiness as when she'd introduced herself.

"It shouldn't take too much longer."

"If you would be kind enough to stop in town, I'll ask."

"Of course."

Jordon glanced at her and grinned. He reached into his shirt pocket and took out the last two peppermint sticks. "One more, Amelia, before we get to the farm." He held out the last one to Eleanore.

He had a dimple. She accepted his offering, entranced by the small dent in his right cheek. At the same time, one of the rear wheels slid down a deep rut. A brittle cracking sound rent the air. Forgotten, the candy dropped from her fingers. She immediately brought the horse to a stop and jumped down to check the damage. Damn, this was just what they needed, and it was her fault. If she hadn't been staring at Mr. Stone, it wouldn't have happened.

Jordon hit the ground at the same time. He found her on her knees in the dirt, pulling on the wheel, her bonnet dangling on the back of her head. He squatted beside her.

"Let me do this. You're getting your skirt dirty, not to mention what will happen to your hands if you persist."

"But I've—" He had a strange look in his eyes.

He took her hands in his and stood up. "Can't you let me do *one* thing for you?"

He glared at her as if he wanted to throttle her, his voice as harsh as his grip was gentle. He held her hands as if they were soft, unaccustomed to hard work, and when she gazed into his green eyes, she didn't want to offend him. "You're right. Thank you."

He started rolling up his sleeves as he spoke. "That bush," he said, pointing to the side of the road, "will offer some shade." She gazed at him as if he'd flattered her. He dropped to his knees and looked under the wagon.

Amelia joined Miss Eleanore. She was watching Mr. Jordon with a peculiar expression on her pretty face. Men and woman surely acted strange sometimes.

As she watched Mr. Stone, Eleanore sat absently stroking her hands. Countless pans of steaming water, lye soap and cleaning compounds had toughened her skin. But she had felt his feather-light touch. And she had liked it.

She noticed Amelia's gaze and self-consciously rubbed her hands on her skirt. "Are you thirsty, dear?"

Amelia shrugged.

Eleanore went over to the side of the wagon. Mr. Stone was still working on the wheel. "Is it all right if I climb into the back of the wagon to get the water jug?"

"Of course." He didn't look up until her skirt passed by him in a soft swish. He rubbed his forehead on his upper arm. He heard her footsteps return and stop in front of him.

"I think it's still cool." She handed him the tin cup of water.

He gulped down the liquid. "Thanks."

Eleanore refilled the cup for Amelia, then herself. A restlessness spread through Eleanore, and she started pacing. Mr. Stone's attitude left her unsettled, and the ride she'd offered him was taking much longer than she had bargained for. Usually she was making dinner about this time of day, not sitting or standing around. When she realized Amelia's gaze had followed her agitated steps, she paused.

"Would you like to take a walk with me?" Maybe she could use this time to become better acquainted with Amelia, what she'd wanted to do from the beginning.

Amelia stood up, brushed off the back of her skirt and fell into step beside Miss Eleanore.

Wandering away from the road, Eleanore glanced down at the solemn little girl, then out at the field of grass. "Do you miss the city?"

Amelia kept pace. She didn't know what was expected of her, so she remained silent.

"It must be very different here from what you're used to." Eleanore came to a halt and listened. "Do you hear that?"

Amelia stopped and frowned. "I don't hear anything."

Eleanore grinned. "That's what I mean. It's so quiet out here." She moved on again, slowly. "Tell me about New York. I've never been there."

Glancing sideways, Amelia thought for a moment. "The buildings are crowded together, and it's smelly."

"What did you like to do there?" Eleanore noticed Amelia gazing down at her skirt and smoothed the material.

Amelia concentrated on her path.

Trying another tack, Eleanore said, "When I was about your age, I liked to catch tadpoles. Have you ever seen one?"

Amelia shook her head.

Eleanore paused and plucked a strand of dried grass. "What is your favorite flower?"

The child shrugged.

"I like buttercups. Yellow's such a happy color." She looked back at the wagon and saw Mr. Stone wave to her. "I think the wagon's repaired. We'd better get back."

I've learned nothing, Eleanore thought. She wanted to take the little girl home and show her how different life could be. Not that Eleanore's home was fancy, the food exceptional or their life easy, but the children were happy. When they reached the wagon, she followed Amelia and sat at her side.

Miss Merrill isn't going to insist on driving, Jordon realized. He hid his smile and took up the reins. "Enjoy your walk?"

Eleanore waited for Amelia to respond, but she remained silent. "Stretching my legs felt good. I'm not sure Amelia enjoys walking through fields, though." Eleanore watched and waited for a response, a shrug, something, but the child sat still as if she were deaf to their conversation.

So Miss Merrill had tried to talk with Amelia—that made Jordon feel good. A few words from Amelia would have been better, but he was beginning to realize that it would take more than a little kindness to break through to her. He could only hope, now, that the Jameses were good, kind, understanding people.

Jordon pulled up in front of a building with a sign proclaiming, "Abbyville's Only Diner." "We can ask directions here and have dinner," he said.

"Mr. Stone, I can't . . . I haven't the funds to—" The only other time she had eaten in a diner was on her eighteenth birthday.

He held up his hand. "It will be my pleasure to escort two lovely ladies." He winked at Amelia. She blushed, and he grinned.

Eleanore glanced down at the old skirt and cringed. Her shoes were scuffed, her shirtwaist less than fresh, and her face felt as if it were covered with road dust. She wasn't vain, but she did have her pride.

"It really isn't necessary. We have enough food left over from last night."

"Then you'll have a hearty supper this evening." He climbed down and lowered Amelia.

Eleanore pushed the loose strands of hair back beneath her bonnet. She stood erect, chin up, as dignified as if she were properly dressed for the occasion. She looked down at Amelia.

"Your dress is very pretty. The blue almost matches your eyes. I'll just dust off the back of your skirt."

Eleanore straightened the child's attire and used a rag from the wagon to buff her new button shoes.

Jordon watched with amused interest, then ran his fingers through his hair. When Miss Merrill had finished, he held out an arm to each and ushered them inside, to a table near one of the two windows facing the street.

Amelia clasped her hands on her lap and gazed out through the window, at the storefronts across the way. A boy chased a dog down the hard-packed street, but there were no children sitting in the shade, or standing near doorways to beg a few pennies or pick a gent's pocket. The other two families she had stayed with lived in cities much larger than this but smaller than New York. With each move she had become more removed from all that was familiar.

Jordon noticed Amelia's bleak expression and met Eleanore's gaze. She blinked several times. He cleared his throat and was relieved to see the young waitress approaching.

The woman straightened the salt and pepper shakers and smiled at Jordon. "Haven't seen you folks before. Travelin' through?"

Jordon smiled at the young woman. "We are and we're hungry. What smells so good?"

"Fried chicken or chicken fried steak. They smell about the same to me." The waitress shrugged. "Each comes with corn, biscuits, a heap of potatoes and sour milk cake for dessert."

"Chicken sound all right?" Jordon glanced around the table. Amelia and Miss Merrill nodded their agreement. "Three chicken dinners, milk for the young lady, coffee for me and . . . Miss Merrill?"

"Water, please." Eleanore smoothed the soft woven tablecloth. The dining room felt like a parlor, with dried flowers, framed pictures and lace curtains. Eleanore glanced at Mr. Stone. It's easier to quibble with him, she reflected, than to feel this new unease.

The waitress returned a few minutes later, her tray laddened with three heaping plates, a cup and two glasses. "Call when you're ready for cake."

Eleanore placed her napkin on her lap and picked up her fork, watching Amelia through her lashes. The little girl copied her. Eleanore cut a bite of chicken and ate it. It did taste good.

Amelia carefully cut a piece of meat and put it in her mouth. It was delicious. She ate another, sampled the biscuit and corn. She washed it down with a gulp of milk, cold milk.

Jordon didn't waste any time on pleasantries; he was too hungry. He simply ate. When he had finished his meal, he noticed that Amelia and Miss Merrill were almost done eating, too. He drank some of his coffee and signaled to the waitress.

Eleanore folded her napkin. "I couldn't possibly eat any cake."

Jordon grinned at Amelia. "Want your cake now?"

Amelia glanced from Miss Eleanore to Mr. Jordon. "I think I'm too full, too, sir."

He chuckled. "I think I am also. We'll take it with us. Would you get the plate from the wagon, Amelia?"

Eleanore waited until Amelia stepped outside. "You're not serious, Mr. Stone?"

"Very, Miss Merrill."

"But . . ." Eleanore glanced around. "You and Amelia will be at the James farm tonight. You can't bring your own dessert!" She was beginning to wonder if he had a problem, one that might have caused him to leave the Society.

"Don't you ever have any fun? Amelia's so serious, I thought a little silliness wouldn't harm her."

"I'll wait for you outside, Mr. Stone."

He watched her march out as if he'd made an indecent proposal. He didn't know why he'd behaved so, except that it had been a long time since he had acted impulsively. Maybe he'd acted foolishly, but it had brought a light he hadn't seen before to Amelia's lovely blue eyes.

"That must be the James place ahead." Jordon observed the fields leading to the dugout. They didn't appear that fertile to him, but what did he know?

Amelia clamped her lips together and clasped her fingers so tightly her knuckles turned white. She was so afraid. She had to make this work. If she didn't, what would happen to her?

Eleanore felt Amelia shiver and put her arm around the little girl. "You won't be alone. I'll go in with you and Mr. Stone will stay the night." Eleanore hugged the child to her.

Jordon studied the front of the dugout as Eleanore pulled up to it. By the time he climbed down, a man had approached from the field. "I'm Jordon Stone from the Children's Aid Society. Are you Mr. James?"

"That's me." Mr. James craned his neck to see the front of the wagon. "You bring our little girl?"

"Amelia is here with me." Jordon glanced at the wagon and added, "I will have to stay the night, Mr. James. You realize the rules of the Society state there will be a second-day visit. Since that won't be convenient, I'll have to remain here." He wasn't usually so overbearing, but he felt it prudent to speak plainly to this man.

Mr. James ambled forward and saw Eleanore on the seat by Amelia. "I s'pose she'll be stayin', too?"

Eleanore answered. "No, Mr. James, I won't be in need of your hospitality." She climbed down while Mr. Stone handed Amelia down. Mr. James was shorter than Mr. Stone and wiry, with a farmer's weathered skin.

With his hands resting on Amelia's narrow shoulders, Jordon introduced her. "Mr. James, this is Amelia Howe."

Mr. James grinned down at Amelia. "Mighty happy to have you here, gal." He looked up at Jordon. "The missus's inside." Mr. James went to the open door.

Jordon stared at the dugout carved into a low knoll. The front wall was sod, with only the door and one small window for light. A tin smokestack jutted from the roof. He motioned for Miss Merrill to enter and followed Amelia inside.

Mr. James trudged over to the bed. "Mrs. James, this here's Mr. Stone and our little 'Melia."

Jordon glanced around in horror. The dugout was not only dusty, as expected, it reeked of unwashed clothes and untended slop jars. The woman abed in the far corner grasped the cover to her chest. "Ma'am." He removed his hat. "This is Miss Merrill. She was kind enough to give Amelia and me a ride."

Eleanore forced a smile. "A pleasure, Mrs. James." She knew the woman was in need of help, more assistance than a nine year old should have been asked to give. And there was Mr. James. She'd noticed a peculiar flash in his pale eyes when the man looked at Amelia that made her feel decidedly uncomfortable.

Mrs. James simpered, "Mr. Stone, Miss Merrill. Thank you for bringing the girl to us." She held out her hand to Amelia. "Come here, dear."

Amelia stepped over to the bed. It was worse than Eleanor'd thought possible. There was only one room and it was so dirty. Mrs. James looked nice enough but very sick. Some dirt drifted down from the sod roof onto Eleanore's face. She brushed it off and noticed the fine layer of soil covering the bed.

"You're such a pretty little thing. Isn't she, Mr. James?"

He grinned. "That she is."

Mrs. James glanced at her husband. "Get them some water, Mr. James. They must be parched."

Eleanore stepped aside to make way for him. He brushed past Amelia, eyeing her as a starving man would a morsel of food. Eleanore glanced at Mrs. James, but she was moving back against the head of the bed, not watching her husband. Eleanore offered to help Mr. James serve. He had filled four chipped cups.

She picked up two and carried them to Amelia and Mrs. James. She turned around, expecting Mr. James to hand her a cup. Instead, she observed Mr. James standing close behind Amelia, his hand stroking her bottom! His bony fingers had traced the curve hidden beneath her skirt.

Amelia winced and bit her lips. Not again, please God. She didn't dare move. Barely breathing, she stared at the bed and waited, sure that no one had seen what she felt. No one ever did.

Instantly outraged, Eleanore grabbed Amelia by the shoulders, pulled her back and wrapped her arms around the little girl. Breathing hard and not knowing if Mr. Stone had witnessed the incident or how he would react, Eleanore lifted Amelia up and ran from the dugout.

She kept going until she reached the far side of the wagon. Amelia shivered violently, her face as pale as snow. "I'm so sorry, honey." Eleanore held the girl against her breast and stroked her back. "*I promise,* you won't stay here."

His reflexes taking over, Jordon quickly blocked the doorway. He couldn't believe what had happened. Right in front of them! Mr. James started after Miss Merrill, but Jordon grabbed the man's grimy shirtfront. Mrs. James screamed, but Jordon ignored her.

"You'd better get back to your wife's side. If she'll have you." Jordon released his hold and stood his ground, glaring at the miserable excuse for a man.

"Git outa my way!" Mr. James shoved his hands at Jordon. "Why'd that woman run the girl outa here like that?"

Jordon grabbed James's wrist, spun him around and pulled the arm up his back. "You *touched* that child. You know it. Miss Merrill saw you. I saw you. And Amelia was humiliated by you."

James struggled a moment, then gasped when his arm was wrenched even higher. "You got no call—"

Jordon gave a twist to the man's wrist. "I have every right. I'm going to notify the Society and any group placing children about your interest in little girls." He took a deep breath. "Now, are you going to walk over there by your wife so we can leave in peace?"

"Git the hell outa here!"

"With pleasure."

Jordon pulled the door closed after him and joined Miss Merrill and Amelia. "Is she all right?"

Eleanore sat with Amelia on her lap, still cradled to her breast. "Please, get us away from here."

Jordon sat by the fire near Eleanore. After the day's events, he'd come to think of her as a colleague. "Do you think she's asleep?" he whispered.

Answering in an equally soft voice, Eleanore said, "I'll see. She should be." Amelia had been tucked in an hour earlier. Eleanore peered into the back of the wagon and saw the little girl curled up, eyes closed, hugging a wadded-up blanket.

Eleanore returned to the fire and motioned for Mr. Stone to follow her. Several yards away, she paused. "She's gone through enough. I don't want to chance her overhearing us." She stared back at the wagon. "What are you going to do?"

"I'm not sure. I'll have to send word to Brice." He stretched, feeling the tension still in his muscles. "I should take her back to New York."

"Not so soon. Give her a chance to recover."

"I can't just 'keep' her. The Society has rules. Besides, technically, I don't work for them any longer." Damn, this was a mess, but thank God Eleanore had been there and they had both witnessed the atrocity. He shuddered to think what Amelia's life would have been like if he hadn't seen what had happened.

"I'll take her back with me. She can share Beth Anne's bed. You can continue on as you'd planned." She wouldn't allow Amelia to be sent back to New York, not now.

Jordon grabbed Eleanore's arm and whirled her around to face him. "I'm not abandoning Amelia! You think I'm no better than James?"

"No. I just had the impression you were anxious to be on your way." His gaze bore into Eleanore and she met it full force.

"*After* Amelia is settled. That poor child has been through two other placements. I'm making damn sure she finds a good home the next time." He released his hold on her. Though it was dark, he knew she was glaring at him. "What have I done to make you think otherwise?"

That question caught her by surprise. "Just a feeling. You didn't strike me as a man who enjoyed working with children." She sensed, rather than observed, his body tensing up. "I was wrong. I apologize, Mr. Stone."

"Jordon."

"I beg your pardon?"

"I'd prefer you call me Jordon." It was a forward statement, one he might regret, but their formality seemed out of place under the circumstances.

She would prefer it, too, she realized, though such familiarity was strange to her. "I'm Eleanore." That was witless. He knew her name. So did everybody in Myles Creek, but only Harriet dared call her by her given name.

If they hadn't been standing almost chest to breast, he wouldn't have heard her. He grinned, then remembered their reason for standing out in the field. "I'd appreciate your taking in Amelia. I'll stay at a boardinghouse." He sighed and motioned for them to start back. "It won't be easy finding a suitable place for Amelia. Would you help me screen the families?"

"When the time comes. Since the Society wants the children to earn their keep, you can inform Mr. Brice that Amelia will be working for me." He stopped walking and so did she. "She isn't ready to face another family, Jordon. Not yet, anyway."

He chuckled. "And you came to see how the Society found homes and jobs for their children. Thank you, Eleanore."

She started strolling back to the wagon. "Oh, don't thank me yet. You can help me with repairs around my place in your spare time."

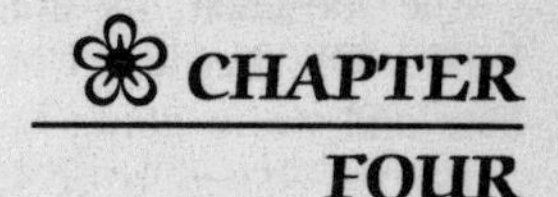

CHAPTER FOUR

Eleanore drove the wagon the next day. It was close to noon when she followed the familiar track east to Myles Creek. Except along the creek bank, the summer heat was drying the grass; earlier blooms and the sunflowers were going to seed. She slowed the horse.

Jordon looked around with interest. "We must be near the Missouri River."

"It's just east of here."

Jordon nodded. They passed three houses and pulled up in front of a fair-size wood-frame home. The fenced yard was full of children. Ahead was the center of Myles Creek, a town much like the others they had seen on the trip north. "Is this your house?"

"This is Mr. and Mrs. Blake's home. I have to pick up the children."

Eleanore climbed down from the wagon. The children gathered at the fence, screeching and whooping. She made her way between the eight of them, laughing and inquiring about their activities. Poor Harriet, she thought. Only three of the youngsters were hers. The other five were Eleanore's. When she glanced up, the front door opened and Harriet Blake stepped out, her cinnamon-colored hair in disarray and her two-year-old tangled in her skirt.

"Sorry I am so late, Harriet. There were complications." Two small arms went around Eleanore's legs. She ruffled seven-year-old Patrick's hair.

He looked up at her. "I was afraid you weren't comin' back, Miss Eleanore."

She loosened his hold and dropped down to his eye level. "Oh, Patrick, I'm sorry you were scared, but I'm here and we're going home."

Patrick stared over Eleanore's shoulder. "Who's that man? Is that his girl?"

Harriet came down the steps, smiling. "I would like to know who he is and how you came to bring him back with you."

Eleanore stood up. "I'll introduce you. He was with the Children's Aid Society."

Harriet left her youngest boy with his brother in the yard and followed Eleanore to the wagon. "Was?"

"Can we talk about that later?" Eleanore stopped near the front wheel. "Mr. Stone and Miss Amelia Howe, this is Mrs. Blake. Amelia will be staying with me."

Jordon removed his hat. "A pleasure, Mrs. Blake."

"Welcome to Myles Creek, Mr. Stone." Harriet grinned at Amelia. "Hello."

Amelia nodded. It was too bad Mrs. James hadn't been like Mrs. Blake. The boys and girls looked happy.

"I should get the children home, and Mr. Stone needs to find a room." Eleanore turned back to the yard. "I don't know how to repay your kindness, Harriet."

"You needed some time to yourself. You've had a house full of other people's children for the last two years and not even a man to keep you company." Harriet glanced back at Mr. Stone.

"You know how I feel about men."

"I thought I did." Harriet peered at Mr. Stone again. "Have you changed your mind?"

Eleanore grinned at her friend's expression. "You mean Mr. Stone?"

"Do you have another man in the back of your wagon?"

Eleanore shook her head. "Honestly, Harriet. He's here to find a good home for Amelia."

She picked up Beth Anne, who was sitting on the step, and gathered the rest of her children. "Let's get your things bundled up." She followed them, carrying Beth Anne and helped gather each of the children's clothes and favorite toy.

Jordon watched Mrs. Blake and Eleanore disappear into the house. With a friend like Mrs. Blake, whose eyes sparkled with laughter, how did Eleanore remain so straitlaced? Even from what little he'd observed of the two, he was sure they were close friends. Possibly there was another side to Eleanore. A movement caught his attention, and he blinked.

Eleanore hustled the five boisterous youngsters out to the wagon, laughing and talking. He could easily have pictured Mrs. Blake doing the same. He glanced at Amelia and knew she was nervous. His misgivings returned. He hadn't left the Society to end up in a similar situation.

Eleanore paused by the wagon. "Children, this is Mr. Stone." She smiled at Beth Anne. "Mr. Stone, this is Beth Anne Eddy. She's five years old and had an accident a few weeks ago."

Jordon smiled; he couldn't resist the girl's big brown eyes. "Beth Anne. What happened?"

She stared up at him. "I was climbing an old tree like Patrick. I fell 'n' broke my leg."

"My, you're very brave." That got a big grin and sent her blond curls bouncing. Jordon smiled back.

"And this is Patrick Turner. He just turned seven."

"Hello, Patrick." With his carrot hair and freckles, Jordon thought the boy could have passed as one of Mrs. Blake's brood.

"Walter Clayton. He's a year older than Patrick."

"Walter." The boy was trying to stand still, but Jordon had the feeling Walter was anxious to dash off. Even his light brown hair was in motion.

"Lottie Gordon is ten."

"Lottie." She resembled a smaller version of Eleanore,

from her brown hair knotted at the back of her head to the proud, frank look on her young face.

"And this is Martin Linder, he's the oldest, thirteen."

"Martin." He stood tall, with dark hair and light blue eyes, and looked as if he were attempting to be the man of the group. Jordon met Eleanore's gaze, then smiled at the children. "I'm happy to meet all of you."

Eleanore looked at each of the children. "I want you to thank Mrs. Blake before you get into the back of the wagon."

She nodded to each one as they said thank you. Beth Anne clutched her rag doll to her chest as Martin lifted her up to the back of the wagon and then made sure the others followed with their bundles of clothes before he climbed up himself.

Eleanore checked to make sure everyone was seated. "We'll be home in a few minutes, so please sit quietly." She returned to her seat and waved to Harriet.

Harriet stood with her youngsters, waved and called out, "I'll be by in a few days."

Eleanore turned the wagon around, drove up her street and stopped at the end, in front of her house. The once white paint was chipped and faded, and the place needed repairs, she thought. Shutters on the front window would look nice, too. But she was having trouble making her mortgage payments, let alone fixing up the place.

"I wanted to show you where I live so you won't have to worry about where Amelia will be staying. I'll take you to Renton's Boardinghouse now."

Jordon liked the unassuming single-story clapboard house. As Eleanore pulled away and headed back to the main road, he noticed an elm tree behind the house, a corral and a weathered barn off to the side. The house and yard looked suited to children. A porch across the front would have been nice, but it wasn't his house and he wouldn't spend much time there, he figured.

She brought the wagon to a halt in front of a yellow house near the dry goods store. "This is the boarding-house. Please give Mrs. Renton my regards."

Jordon stepped down and retrieved his canvas valise from under the seat. "I will. And thank you, Eleanore. I'll see you in the morning, Amelia."

Jordon stood about where Eleanore had left him a few minutes earlier. Mrs. Renton had been nice, but she had no available rooms right now. Maybe next week—she wasn't sure how long her three boarders would be staying, and she didn't know of another rooming house in town. He glanced back toward Eleanore's street. No, first he had to send a message to Brice.

He walked to the general store—and learned that they didn't have a telegraph. Heading back down the main road, he turned onto Eleanore's street. There was one small house next to hers and a field of wildflowers past their bloom across the way. From the green bushes on the other side of her place, he assumed the creek lay just beyond.

As he approached her door, he heard the children. It sounded as if everyone were talking at once. The high-pitched voices reminded him of the Children's Aid Society lodge in New York City. He had to find a good family for Amelia—soon.

He raised his hand, hesitated, and knocked on the front door. It flew open, and the redheaded boy grinned. "Hello, Patrick. Is Miss Merrill here?"

"You can wait in here. I'll get her."

Patrick ran off, and Jordon stepped inside and into the parlor. It was almost completely decorated with children's drawings, on the walls, the tabletop, and one was pinned to a green drape. An old piano sat in one corner, a wood stove across the room. There was a worn sofa and a wing chair, and a large braided rug helped muffle the noise made by the approaching children.

He removed his hat. "Hello." Amelia wasn't with them.

Lottie stepped forward. "I'll take your hat, Mr. Stone. You can put your bag down by the door."

He did as she suggested and realized she was staring at him with a rather suspicious expression. What did she expect him to do? "Mind if I look around?"

"Miss Merrill will be here directly." Lottie frowned at Walter and marched over to the sofa. "Get down! Miss Eleanore's told you not to jump over the back. Go play with Tubby."

"*Toby!* And he's the best dog in the world!"

Lottie pointed toward the kitchen.

Walter got off of the sofa and glared at her. "You're so bossy. You're just tryin' t'look good in front of him." He punctuated his statement by pointing to Jordon, then ran out of the room.

Jordon hid his amusement as the boy and dog ran out. The mutt was light brown with floppy ears, big amber eyes and puppy enthusiasm. They were well matched.

"Boys," Lottie mumbled.

Eleanore entered the parlor and heard Lottie's disparaging tone. "Wouldn't life be boring without them?"

Lottie glanced up and clamped her lips together before she answered. "It would be quieter . . . and cleaner."

After Lottie departed with her head high and walking with the confidence of the righteous, Jordon chuckled softly. "Quite the housemother, isn't she?"

"Please, sit down." Eleanore motioned to the sofa and sat on the wing chair nearby. "Her mother died when she was six. She was the woman of the house for four years, until three months ago. It isn't easy for her to learn to be a little girl again, if she ever was one." She glanced out the side window and back to Jordon. "What happened at Mrs. Renton's."

"No rooms." It was different talking to her in her parlor. Jordon started to cross his legs and changed his mind.

"Can I bed down in your barn? I'll start riding around to the farms tomorrow."

Eleanore brushed at her skirt. The idea of Jordon staying almost in her house was definitely unsettling. She peered at him through her eyelashes. If only he were older, it might have been easier. She closed her eyes when she recalled Harriet's reaction to Mr. Stone, how she had seemed to find him fascinating. Or was it because he was with her? Eleanore wondered.

He noticed a clock on one of the tables. Its ticking seemed to grow louder in the silence. She just sat there as if she were ready to take flight, so very prim, with a pensive expression.

"Just a corner in the barn, Eleanore, for a couple days. You have enough children to chaperon us, if that's what's bothering you." He waited several ticks of the clock and stood up. "I'd better leave."

He took two steps and paused. "How is Amelia?"

"She's in with Beth Anne." Eleanore heard Lottie issuing orders to the boys, probably in the kitchen, and watched Jordon. He picked up his hat. "Wait, Jordon. You may stay in the barn . . ."

He chuckled. "Thank you." He retrieved his valise, then remembered Brice. "I have another favor to ask. I need to write Charles Brice."

"Use that desk in the corner. The top drawer should have what you need." She went over to the open window and stared down into two surprised faces.

"Since you haven't anything to do, Patrick and Walter, you can help Mr. Stone in the barn."

"Yes, Miss Eleanore."

"Yes, Miss Eleanore."

"Okay, you two, go on." She was laughing when she ducked her head back inside. "They're good boys. I'll send Martin out, too. Follow me."

She didn't have a room to offer him, other than sharing the attic with the boys, and she didn't feel comfortable suggesting that. She led him down the hall, through the kitchen and outside. "It," she motioned to the barn, "needs work, too, but it should be cool at night."

Jordon followed her brisk pace across the dirt yard. He had seen many in worse condition. The corral was off to the side, and there was another field of wildflowers behind her house. "How long have you been running this place by yourself?"

"Since we moved here, about four years ago. Papa never was too interested in how fancy a place was."

"That must have been hard for you. Is he . . ."

"He passed away . . . two years ago last winter." Had it really been that long? That's when she had begun taking in orphaned children. She stopped in her tracks, momentarily lost in thought. The children had filled her days, her life, and she loved each of them dearly.

Jordon was in mid-stride and about to step to Eleanore's side when she suddenly stopped. He bumped into her and put his hand on her shoulder to steady both of them. "You all right?"

"Fine." Mr. Stone's large hand still held her arm—strong, warm, secure. She stepped out of his grasp and motioned to the barn. "It isn't much."

"It will do." Jordon heard Patrick and Walter laughing. "I think they've started without me." He looked up to the hayloft. Dirt and straw floated down from there. On the ground was the same dog joining in the fun that had been in the parlor. "I'll write the letter in a little while, if that's all right with you."

"Of course, anytime."

He was determined to put Amelia in another home in the next two days, and the child wasn't ready. Two days, Eleanore thought, she must change his mind within that short time. She touched her fingers to her shoulder, where his hand had been, and returned to the house, her stride unwavering, her emotions in turmoil. He affected her in a way she refused to think about.

* * *

After exploring the interior of the barn, Jordon decided the corner to the left of the wide double doors would afford him the most privacy. He upended a barrel and set his valise on top.

"Patrick . . . Walter . . ." Jordon watched the loft until the boys' heads appeared. "Either of you know where to find a broom?" They both nodded. "Would you like to help me clean out that corner?"

Patrick followed Walter down the ladder. "I will. What do ya wanta do?"

Walter ran over to Jordon huffing and puffing. "I found a broom."

"Good. What I want to do is fix up that corner so I can sleep there."

Walter frowned. "Why do ya wanta sleep here? There ain't even a bed."

"No, there isn't. But a blanket or two will do." Jordon recalled the many nights during the war when his canteen and rifle were all he'd had to bed down with. A blanket was a luxury not every man had. He worked with the boys until the area was cleaned out.

After helping, Patrick climbed back up to the loft, then called to Mr. Stone. "There's enough straw up here to make a bed."

Jordon looked up and smiled. "Good idea."

Martin entered the barn and glanced around. "Miss Eleanore said you might need help. What are you doing out here?"

"He's goin' to sleep out here. Wish I could." Patrick hurried down the ladder, sliding over the last three rungs in his haste to face Jordon. "Can I stay out here with you, Mr. Stone? I'll make a place in the other corner. An' I won't even talk, if you don't want me to. Can I?"

"Whoa, just a minute, Patrick." The lad was likable, but Jordon didn't want the boy sleeping out there with him.

"You have a good room in the house. You'd better stay there."

"I'll ask Miss Eleanore." Patrick started to leave.

Martin grabbed Patrick's arm. "Walter, you better find Toby. Miss Eleanore'll get mad if he's pestering the hens again."

"Oh, gosh. I forgot." Walter ran out to the yard.

"Come on, Patrick, we have to go."

"I wanta stay 'n' help."

Martin looked at Jordon.

"Go along. We're finished up here," Jordon said.

"Now, Patrick. It's *important,"* Martin grated out, glaring at the younger boy.

"Oh, yeah."

Martin walked out with the boy in tow.

Jordon shook his head. He just couldn't get involved in these children's lives. He wouldn't. He started for the house. He had a letter to write.

Amelia sat on the side of the bed she would share with Beth Anne. She said she was five years old and her rag doll's name was Missie. She had nice brown eyes, curly blond hair and a ready smile. Amelia smoothed her skirt and stood up.

Beth Anne watched. "Your dress is real pretty. I wish Missie had a nice dress." She glanced down at her doll and tugged at its skirt.

"It's new. I must save it for . . . special times." Amelia opened a drawer where she had placed her other two dresses, folded neatly. She picked up the gray one on top. It was old, mended, a bit snug in the waist, a little short, but it was soft and felt good

After changing clothes, she self-consciously met Beth Anne's gaze. "Do you have any chores?"

Beth Anne scratched at the bandage on her leg. "Not till my leg gets better. I used to gather eggs and dust and set the table. Sometimes I got to help make a cake." She placed Missie on her pillow and looked back at Amelia.

"Maybe I should go collect the eggs," Amelia said.

"Lottie's been doing that."

"Oh." Amelia saw her roommate fussing with the wrapping on her leg again. "You really shouldn't do that. When will your leg be better?"

"Doc Os-ger-by, that's hard to say. He said next month, if I don't walk on it." Beth Anne fidgeted on her side of the bed. "When is that?"

Amelia remembered the date they were supposed to arrive in Kansas. "This is the end of July. He must've meant in a couple weeks."

"That sounds like a long time."

Amelia nodded. "Can I get you anything? Some water?"

Beth Anne stared at Amelia a moment. "Can you read?"

"Yes."

Beth Anne pulled a book from under her pillow. "Would you read to me?"

Amelia nodded. "Why do you keep it in bed? Aren't you allowed to have it?"

"My mama gave it to me, and I don't want to share it with the others." Beth Anne handed the book to Amelia.

"Andersen's Fairy Tales." Amelia smiled.

"Read 'The Ugly Duckling' one first, please."

"If you promise not to touch your leg."

Beth Anne grinned and nodded enthusiastically.

Was the man hoping for an easy sale? Or just relieved to unload the horse?

"Not bad at'all."

Jordon finally led the horse back to the stall. He checked the rails for teeth marks and didn't find any evidence of cribbing. "How much are you asking?" He didn't need a horse that was a chewer and colicky.

"He's worth a lot more, but I'll take sixty-five."

Jordon chuckled. "I would, too." He examined four other horses and checked the teeth of one, but none were as good as the sorrel. "I'll give you fifty-five, including the tack. I'll also need hay and a bag of oats." That should soften the deal, Jordon thought.

Tucker frowned, paced and, in the end, shrugged. "Deal. Where do you want the feed delivered?"

"Miss Merrill's place." Jordon just hoped she wouldn't be too upset, though he suspected she took to animals and children better than she took to him.

He paid Tucker and rode his mount back to Eleanore's house. The animal needed exercise and would get it beginning tomorrow. As he entered the yard, Walter screamed, "Miss Eleanore . . . Miss Eleanore, come out 'n' *see* what Mr. Stone's got . . ."

The children gathered around as Jordon dismounted.

"Is he yours? Where'd you get him?"

"Ya got him from Mr. Tucker, didn't ya?"

"Can I ride him?"

"Can I put him in the corral? Sometimes Mr. Tucker lets me." Walter raised his chin and glanced around.

"Whoa. Now, let me see. Yes, he's mine. I got him at the livery. I haven't named him yet, and *no*, you may not ride him. I don't want any of you getting too close to him. He seems gentle enough, but I don't want any accidents. I'll put him in the corral later, after I speak to Miss Merrill."

He was about to lead the horse into the barn when he noticed Eleanore coming toward him, her skirt swaying, her hair a little worse for the pace she evidently kept, and an unmistakable sparkle in her eyes.

Eleanore stopped in the midst of the children and met Jordon's gaze. "That's a handsome animal. Did you buy or rent him?" It was a beautiful horse, she thought, and watched the way Jordon calmed him with a gentle touch.

"Bought." She cocked her head and gave him a wry grin. He didn't want to read her expressions, didn't want to know her that well.

Odd, he didn't seem to want to get involved with the children but had purchased a horse that needed attention as much as they did, Eleanore mused. "I understood you to say you were going to take the train to the end of the line." With each passing day, he was looking much less forbidding, more threatening to her solitary way of life.

"You didn't misunderstand. I just got to thinking about what the prices would be like there and decided to save a few dollars." The sorrel sidestepped. Jordon calmed him and looked back at Eleanore. "Do you mind if I keep him in your corral?"

"Of course not."

"Thanks. I ordered some hay and oats. I don't want to use up your supplies. They should be delivered later this afternoon."

Eleanore glanced at the children. "Martin, I want you and Patrick to fill the water trough. Walter, please try to keep Toby away from Mr. Stone's horse, for a while anyway. We'll have supper in an hour and a half." She started back to the house.

Lottie rushed to catch up with Eleanore. "I peeled the potatoes you set out."

Jordon made a pallet using his blankets and the straw from the loft. After organizing his meager possessions, he washed up and went into the house. Enticing aromas filled the kitchen, where Lottie and Eleanore were working.

Eleanore's cheeks were flushed, and she'd tucked some of her hair behind her ears. "Isn't Amelia helping you?"

Eleanore heard the back door open and shut. Assuming it was one of the boys, she didn't look up. The sound of his deep, full voice struck her like a bass cord on the piano. She gasped and spun around. "Jordon . . ." How could he have slipped from her mind? "She's . . . in the dining room with Beth Anne setting the table." The room was suddenly silent, and his retreating footsteps sounded especially loud on the wood floor.

Jordon paused in the doorway to the dining room. The walls were light and the drapes were a gold color, darker than Beth Anne's blond hair. He watched Amelia. She looked like any other girl her age, until she noticed him and appeared to wilt. "Hello, Beth Anne, Amelia. Do you need any help?"

Beth Anne giggled as she handed Amelia the last folded napkin. "Men don't know how to set a table."

After straightening a knife and spoon, Amelia looked up at Mr. Jordon, then frantically at the table. "What did I do wrong?" She clasped her hands together.

"It looks very nice, Amelia. I was just offering to help you."

He wandered into the parlor and sat down at the piano. He was doing well. He'd managed to frighten two females in less than three minutes. His fingers struck a few cords. It had been years since he'd played, and he'd never done it very well, only for his own enjoyment. The bawdy ditty "Corydon and Phyllis" came to mind and lightened his mood. The piano needed tuning, but that suited the tune he hammered out.

He was trying to remember the notes to "Oh Susanna" when he heard Eleanore's soft footsteps. She'd taken off the apron, fixed her hair and had her usual no-nonsense expression in place. "Sorry, I should have asked."

"No. I enjoy music." She stared at his hands, large hands with long, broad fingers. She reached up and again touched her shoulder where his hand had rested. "Supper is ready." She didn't wait for him, just walked back to the dining room and wished her memory were not so clear.

Jordon followed her, wondering why she had acted so strange. He entered the dining room, where the boys scrambled for their seats. Walter's hair had been slicked back, Patrick's also, and there were damp spots on their trousers that looked as if they'd dried their hands on them. Eleanore motioned Jordon to the other end of the heavy plank table.

"Whoever is not seated in one minute can eat standing up."

Eleanore kept her lips pressed together, hiding her amusement over Patrick and Walter's vying for the chair to Jordon's left. The dispute was settled immediately. Walter quickly took the empty chair across from Amelia. Lottie recited her blessing, then Eleanore passed the biscuits and serving dish.

After helping Beth Anne, Amelia served herself. The creamy sliced potatoes and ham smelled good. While they cooled, she buttered a biscuit. She glanced around the table. When she saw everyone eating, she took a bite of ham. All afternoon she had listened for Miss Eleanore's voice raised in anger but hadn't heard one mad word, not even when the boys wanted the same chair.

Patrick gulped his bite of potato. "Mr. Stone, is your horse fast?"

"Fast enough. A good temperament's more important." He regarded Amelia. She sat quietly except for a whispered word in response to something Beth Anne said. It was a good beginning.

"Mr. Stone," Martin said and cleared his throat. "Did you fight in the war?"

Jordon met the boy's earnest stare. "With the Forty-fourth New York."

"Where?"

"Did you kill anyone?"

"*Boys,* this is hardly a subject to discuss at mealtime." Eleanore noticed Jordon's clenched jaw and eyed each boy. "Besides, Mr. Stone may not wish to talk about it. You will ask next time and not before tomorrow."

"Yes, ma'am" was said in unison by all three boys.

Lottie glanced from Miss Eleanore to Mr. Stone. "Amelia said you rode the train from New York City to Kansas. What was it like?"

He smiled, greatly relieved by the change of topic. "You should ask Amelia. I think it was her second ride."

"Was it, Amelia?"

She looked up, not quite meeting Lottie's gaze, and nodded.

Patrick stabbed a piece of potato. "What did you see?"

Amelia swallowed her bite and wiped her mouth. "I saw a man on a horse try to race the train." She took a sip of milk.

"Well?" Walter was almost out of his chair with excitement. "Did he win?"

"No. He gave up."

Walter dropped down on his chair. "He must've had a slow horse."

Jordon couldn't miss Eleanore's hard gaze. "Racing a train isn't the smartest thing to do, unless you have a very good reason. A horse is a responsibility, and you should take care of the animal." She nodded, and her reproving expression disappeared with the softening of her lips. She hadn't smiled, just relaxed a bit. It was enough. Jordon turned his attention to cleaning his plate.

"Patrick, please don't play with your biscuit." Eleanore found herself glancing at Jordon, again. It was disconcerting. She simply had to stop watching him. After all, she wasn't a schoolgirl; she was old enough to be Lottie's mother.

The next morning Jordon visited five farms in the area and had given up near suppertime. He had talked with the men. After the disaster with Mr. James, Jordon was being very cautious. Maybe he was overly suspicious, but he watched each man's expression, especially when the subject of girls came up—and he made sure it did. He didn't want to see Amelia in a situation without a father. She needed to learn there were good men in the world and not grow to adulthood fearing them. To clear his mind and exercise his mount, he took a long, hard ride.

The air was fresh, no gun smoke hung in the air as it had after a battle, no fumes as he'd hated in New York City. The only sounds he heard were the creaking of leather and his mount's heavy breathing. After a good run, he slowed the horse to cool him down on his return to Eleanore's.

He dismounted near the barn. The kitchen door was open, but he couldn't hear one high-pitched voice. Quiet, until the dog ran his way barking. He dismounted and stood by as the animal stopped a few feet away. One of the dog's ears flopped like a pup's; the other stood at attention.

"Toby, sit." The dog cocked his head and obeyed. "Good boy." Jordon held out his hand, and Toby inched forward.

"He doesn't bite," Eleanore called from the kitchen doorway. She wiped her hands on her apron as she went out to meet him. "I think he makes a row to feel important."

"He's not full grown yet." Jordon stooped down and scratched behind Toby's ear. "Where're the children? It's too quiet." Her cheeks were rosy, wisps of hair drooped over her ears and her eyes were bright, as if she were happy to see him. She sure was a sight—he didn't need.

"Beth Anne and Amelia are helping me in the kitchen. The others are doing chores." She felt a rare breeze brush against her hot neck and wished it could cool more of her skin. "I saved your dinner."

She didn't need to do that, he thought. "Thanks. I'll be

in directly." He left his hat in the barn and turned his horse loose in the corral. Before he entered the house, he smelled bread and what he thought was freshly baked cake.

Amelia saw Mr. Jordon at the door and reached for his plate. "I'll take it to the dining room."

Jordon glanced around. "Can't I eat in here?"

"It is cooler in the dining room, but if you'd rather eat in here, you can." Eleanore cleared a place at one corner of the worktable. "Sit here."

Amelia set the plate down, retrieved the utensils she had set out for him in the other room and returned to where she had been working. "The icing is creamy, Miss Eleanore," she said.

Beth Anne reached over, dipped her finger in the bowl and licked the sweet spread. "That's good." She stuck her finger toward the bowl a second time.

Amelia pulled the bowl out of reach. "Don't put that finger in the icing. You licked it."

Beth Anne's other hand was in motion. "Enough tasting, Beth Anne. There won't be any left." Eleanore set the cake near Amelia. "Have you iced a cake before?"

Amelia chewed on her lower lip before answering. "I tried once."

"Try again. Start by spooning the icing onto the top, then spread it around with the table knife."

Beth Anne wiped her finger on her skirt. "What can I do?"

Jordon dawdled over the last few bites. It was a pleasure watching Eleanore with the children. She had a way of encouraging and putting them at ease. He was sure Beth Anne was itching to dig her finger into the bowl again, but she didn't.

He carried his plate over to the dry sink. "Eleanore, you said there were some repairs you needed help with. Where do you want me to start?"

She had mentioned the repairs without thinking. Most

would require materials she couldn't afford to purchase. "The corral, I guess. Two of the posts are loose. I would appreciate it if you could just straighten them, and the gate's beginning to sag."

"I'll get started."

Eleanore asked Jordon to meet her in the parlor after supper. He followed her in and sat down in the wing chair. Beth Anne was watching Amelia and Lottie do the dishes; Martin was milking the cow; Patrick and Walter were checking the horses. "Thank you for mending the fence."

"I doubt Old Ned needs much restraint. It should hold, for a while."

"You left early this morning. Did you find any good prospects for Amelia?" He looked more relaxed, she realized, and she tried to feel the same.

"Not really. Most of the people had several children and weren't interested in taking in another." He rubbed his hand across his forehead. "I knew it wouldn't be easy, but I found myself looking for Mr. James in each man I spoke with." He watched her reaction. "You must have talked with most everyone around here who might take a child. Any suggestions?"

"I thought you would've had more experience than I have. I've placed a few children in this area. I also try to contact any relatives. I finally obtained Martin's aunt and uncle's address and wrote to them two weeks ago. It takes time. You should know that."

She realized he was struggling. She hadn't known he was a finger tapper, but she watched him drumming on the arm of the upholstered armchair. It was tempting to go over and cover his hand with hers, but she couldn't do that.

"I worked in the lodge with the boys." He shrugged. "Oh, I know flyers describing the children were sent out along with newspaper notices, but I never worked with the ones who decided on a particular area or why one was chosen."

She looked so maternal with the children, but he wouldn't add another child to her household so he could leave as scheduled. He noticed her hands resting so serenely on her lap. Then he glanced at her face. Her complexion had a slight ripe-peach cast to it and reminded him of silk.

"Have you talked to any families around Middleburg? I could ride down there tomorrow. Or up to Miles Ranch."

"Last year I spoke with a family in Middleburg, but no one else." His brows puckered, and she rushed to give him an alternative to think about.

"Amelia seems to be getting along with Beth Anne. I would like to keep her here . . . at least until she regains her confidence." She knew better than to insist, feeling gentle persuasion would work better on him. He had a stubborn jaw, and a streak to match, she was sure.

"You already have five children to find homes for. You don't need another." He absently started drumming his fingers again on the rounded arm of the chair. "Besides, I should take her back to New York."

"You must do what you feel is right, of course, but couldn't she spend a few more days here to get over the incident with Mr. James?" She hid her clenched fists in the folds of her skirt and silently prayed Jordon would agree. The metronome-like tapping of his fingers meant he was at least considering her proposal. Then the room was silent.

He nodded. "A few days. It will take me that long to make more calls. I'll leave early in the morning."

"Good night, Martin." Eleanore kissed him on his forehead and smoothed his dark hair back.

"Walter." She kissed him, too.

"Patrick." She kissed him also.

"Sleep well . . . and quietly, boys."

She went down to the girls' room last. "Amelia, you

don't have to read to Beth Anne all day long." She raised one brow and eyed the younger girl, then smiled.

"But *I* can't read, Miss Eleanore."

"I know. We'll resume your lessons tomorrow. Right now it is time to go to sleep." Eleanore closed the book and put it on the dresser Beth Anne shared with Amelia.

Eleanore kissed Lottie and turned down her lamp. Next was Beth Anne. "How does your leg feel?"

"A'most better."

"You haven't tried to stand on it, have you?"

"No. But I want to."

"Just wait until Dr. Osgerby says you can. If you try now, you may end up with a crooked leg and walk with a limp."

Beth Anne nodded and hugged Missie to her.

Eleanore walked around the bed and brushed a few strands of dark hair away from Amelia's eyes. "Tomorrow's a new day and will be much better than this one." Eleanore kissed her forehead and went to the door.

"Sleep well, girls."

With the children tucked in for the night, Eleanore entered the kitchen and put the kettle on. A cup of tea, a few solitary minutes and a good night's sleep in her own bed were in order. While she waited for the water to boil, she glanced out through the kitchen window. A light was on in the barn. Jordon. His shadow moved back and forth, paused facing the doorway a moment and resumed pacing again.

Should I take him a cup of tea? she wondered. No. He probably enjoys his seclusion. She stood at the window watching his shape, the breadth of his shoulders, his trim waist, his long stride. A shiver wove its way down her spine.

She abruptly turned her back to the window and reached for the tea. After brewing a single cup, she carried it to her bedroom and closed the door, as if closing her mind to

Jordon. She quickly changed clothes and slid between the cool sheets on her bed.

The night was quiet, except for the thumping of her heart. There were no flowers to scent the still-warm air, but the faint aroma of hay drifted through her open window. She reached for her old frayed copy of Joseph Ware's *The Emigrants' Guide to California* and opened it on her lap. Thirteen years ago, when she'd found the book, she had dreamed of joining a wagon train. Now it was a familiar tale of adventure and hardship.

CHAPTER SIX

Early the next morning, Jordon rode over to Middleburg. It was a larger town than Myles Creek, but after spending the day talking to many people, he returned to Eleanore's bone weary. The house was dark. Just as well, he thought. He unsaddled the horse and walked him back to the small corral.

Stretched out on his bedroll, he planned his next day's travel north to Miles Ranch and reminded himself to leave a note for Eleanore. He'd be gone two days and didn't want her to fret or think he'd ridden off and abandoned Amelia. The thought that Eleanore believed he wanted to leave so badly that he'd abandon the child still chafed at him.

The woman was baffling. Reserved to the point of indifference; laughing, loving and warm with the children, definitely standoffish with him. And why should that bother me? he wondered. Because he'd like to keep in touch with her? Maybe. Or perhaps because he had seen a glimmer of the softer side that she normally hid so well.

A light breeze stirred, and a piece of straw danced around in the dirt. He closed his eyes and inhaled the sweet smell of hay and listened to the crickets. As he dozed off, he recalled standing in the field with Eleanore, so close he heard her breathing and felt the heat of her body.

Snuggling farther under the light covers, Eleanore heard the soft tapping on her door. She had stayed up waiting for

Jordon's return, listening for the sound of his horse, and hadn't slept well after giving up the vigil. Peering over the edge of the covers at the bright window, she realized she had overslept.

"Come in."

Lottie opened the door a few inches and peeked in. "Do you want me to start breakfast, Miss Eleanore?"

"Please put a kettle of water on for me. I'll be right there." She dressed quickly and rushed to the kitchen.

Lottie held out a note to Eleanore. "This was on the table."

Eleanore took the message and stared at it. The folded paper resembled her own. As if expecting a prank or dreadful news, she unfolded the paper very slowly and looked down at the bottom of the page. Jordon. His penmanship was distinctive, handsome, and her heart skipped a beat. She quickly refolded the message and tucked it in her skirt pocket.

"I'd like some griddle cakes." She went to work and noticed Lottie watching. "Lottie, would you see if we have enough corncob syrup?"

As soon as Lottie went to the pantry, Eleanore slipped Jordon's note from her pocket and read it. "I didn't want to wake you. I'm riding up to Miles Ranch and may be gone for three days." She sighed, returned the message to her pocket and continued mixing the batter. Miles Ranch was a day's ride away. She understood why he felt he must search for a good position for Amelia but didn't agree with his determination to place her immediately.

By the time Eleanore had the first griddle cakes stacked on a plate, all of the children were dressed, helping serve and setting the table. She had a firm rule about meals. No one was allowed to eat until all of the food was served.

Everyone was seated at the table when Eleanore joined them with the third stack of griddle cakes. She sat down and nodded. Lottie picked up one serving plate. Martin stuck his fork through four cakes; Walter and Patrick followed before she could speak.

"Boys—" She waited until their forks were on their plates before continuing. "Did you behave this way at Mrs. Blake's house?"

Martin glanced down and over at the two younger boys. "No, ma'am."

"Thank goodness." Eleanore noticed Amelia holding a plate of cakes as if she were waiting for permission to serve herself. "Go ahead, Amelia." She glanced at the three solemn boys. "You may take what you can eat and pass the plate—and I do not want to see any of you grabbing food again."

Holding the plate while Beth Anne took her serving, Amelia glanced around the table. The boys were talking, plainly not too taken aback by Miss Eleanore's reprimand. The seat at the end of the table opposite Miss Eleanore was empty, and it had been last night, too, Amelia remembered. Had Mr. Stone left without saying good-bye?

Martin finished eating first. "May I be excused? Mr. Anders wants me to help him all summer. I have to be there by nine."

Eleanore sat back, studying the way his clear blue eyes watched her. "You're excused, but I don't want you in that saloon, Martin." When he fabricated a story, he couldn't face her as directly as he had.

He stood up and slid his chair forward. "I won't be, Miss Eleanore. Today I'm to clean out the storeroom." He picked up his plate and glass. "Don't we need the money?"

She nodded, though she wasn't completely resigned to the children working odd jobs. "Tell Mr. Anders you must come home for dinner and be home by five this afternoon." He got as far as the door before she added, "Remember, *do not* go into the saloon."

"Yes, ma'am."

Lottie used her napkin and stood up. "Old Mrs. Peterson is expecting me, too. We're working on a quilt."

"All right, Lottie." Lord, Eleanore thought, how can I sanction this? And what if they didn't raise enough money?

Patrick and Walter jumped to their feet next. "We—" Patrick started.

Walter bumped him and finished speaking. "He promised Mrs. Renton he'd weed her garden. Mr. Tucker said I could help him out."

"Thank you, boys. Be home for dinner at one." Eleanore listened to them run out through the kitchen and waited for the bang of the back door, then looked at the girls. "Take your time, Amelia. Beth Anne, do you want to stay with her until she finishes?"

"Uh-huh."

"I'll carry you out to the kitchen when she's done." Eleanore paused at the door. "Amelia, would you collect the eggs each morning? Lottie was doing it, but with her work—"

Amelia interrupted. "Yes, ma'am. I'd be happy to."

"Thank you."

The morning passed with the daily chores: washing dishes, starting the bread and picking up forgotten items around the house. Casually observing Amelia, Eleanore noticed how painstakingly the child completed each task. It was near dinnertime, and she heard the other children outside in the yard.

Amelia was pouring milk into each glass when one slipped and shattered on the hardwood floor. She covered her mouth mumbling, "Clumsy, clumsy, clumsy," then dropped down to the floor.

"Don't, Amelia, you'll cut yourself on that glass." Eleanore took hold of the girl's arms and moved her away from the splintered glass. She felt Amelia shaking and wrapped her arms around her. "It's okay, honey."

Amelia shook her head. "No, it isn't. I wasn't careful.

I . . . I'm so *sorry,* Miss Eleanore. I'll clean it up . . . and . . . I'll go without." She bit her lips, waiting for the slap on her face. Slowly, Miss Eleanore's warm hand rubbing her back penetrated through Amelia's fear.

"I will help you and you won't go without milk. Everyone has accidents once in a while." Eleanore tipped Amelia's chin up, wondering and at the same time fearing the trials she had suffered. "Would you bring me two rags from the basket in the pantry?"

Amelia nodded and rushed to do as asked. Miss Eleanore surely was different from the other women who controlled their homes with a heavy hand.

Beth Anne watched Amelia run out and whispered, "Did she think you'd wallop her?"

"I am afraid she did, but if she can stay with us, she will learn different, won't she?"

"Uh-huh. You never wallop anyone."

Eleanore hid her grin. "You shouldn't say, 'wallop,' Beth Anne; it doesn't sound very nice." She eyed the little girl, whose brown eyes were sparkling with merriment. "Where did you learn that word?" Of course, she realized, there wasn't a "nice" word for striking someone.

"Walter." Beth Anne giggled.

"Harriet, please sit down. I'll finish the dishes while we visit." Eleanore pointed to a chair at the worktable.

"Why don't we go into the parlor?" Harriet suggested. "Pour yourself a cup of tea and come along." She picked up her cup.

"We can talk in here." Eleanore put the last glass away. "Tell me, did the children drive you to distraction while I was away?"

"They were fine. Lottie helped with little Henry. Martin kept an eye on everyone, and Walter wore everyone out so they slept through the night." Harriet chuckled. "However will you manage when you find homes for Lottie and Martin?"

Eleanore shrugged. "As I did before they came."

"Where is Mr. Stone?" Harriet glanced out through the window. "I have not seen him around town."

"He rode up to Miles Ranch, hoping to find a suitable position for Amelia."

"Is he here very much? At least you do not have to feed him. Mrs. Renton is a good cook."

"The boardinghouse was full. He's staying in the barn." Eleanore picked up the stack of dry dishes and put them in the cupboard.

Harriet set her cup down and leaned forward. "Enough, Eleanore. You said he *was* with that society. Was he discharged?"

"He resigned. His last duty was to help place the children in Tuttle, Kansas. At the last minute he was asked to take Amelia out to the couple who was to take her."

"But how did *you* get involved? You hardly give a man the time of day."

Eleanore raised her chin a tad, looking her friend in the eye. "He had to take Amelia to a farm, as I said, but he didn't have a buggy. I had been watching Amelia and was concerned about her." She lifted one shoulder. "So I offered to give them a ride."

Harriet leaned forward. "So . . . tell me the rest."

After explaining the rest of the journey, Eleanore sighed and raised her cup. "I couldn't let him take Amelia back to New York. She needs time to heal."

"She will do fine here." A slight grin appeared on Harriet's face. "How are you getting along with Mr. Stone?"

"Just fine. Why wouldn't I?"

"Oh, botheration. You have ignored every man who ever glanced your way." Harriet brushed at her skirt. "Has he mentioned how long he will be here?"

"He's due back tonight. I hope I can convince him to leave Amelia with me." Eleanore heard Beth Anne giggle and looked forward to the day Amelia laughed.

"Do I detect a hint of interest in the handsome Mr. Stone?"

"Goodness, no. Why would you ever think that?"

Harriet laughed. "That deep blush across your cheeks, for one."

Her laughter was contagious. Once Eleanore calmed down, she shook her head. "You are a hopeless romantic. He's impatient, stubborn, and he doesn't particularly like children." That wasn't completely true, she realized, and knew her tone was overly harsh. He cared for Amelia, and he had treated her most civilly.

"Well, I think he is very handsome. His eyes resemble green glass." Harriet sighed dramatically. "And they followed you close enough . . . for a man who isn't interested."

Jordon awoke in the barn with a pounding head. The trip had only served to remind him of the difficult task the Society performed. He was one man trying to accomplish the same and knew he was a fool, but he always fulfilled his obligations. The problem this time was that this obligation was a little girl, and though he didn't want to, he did care about her.

"Mr. Stone . . . you up?" Patrick inched his way into the dark barn. "I saw your horse. Did ya name him yet?"

"Good morning, Patrick." Jordon stretched and sat up. "No, I haven't. Got any ideas?"

Patrick frowned. "I'll have ta think on it."

"Why don't you do that outside while I get up?" Jordon covered his eyes. He just couldn't ride around today interviewing more prospective employers for Amelia, not after the last four days. He quickly dressed and went over to the well to wash up.

"Mornin', Mr. Stone." Walter picked up the towel hanging over the side of the well. Toby grabbed one end and tugged. "No, Toby." Walter pulled the towel free and held it out to Jordon. "I knew you'd come back. I looked in the barn, to make sure you didn't take *everything*."

Bright lad, Jordon thought with a touch of sarcasm. He'd better get Amelia settled before he voiced his impatience aloud. "Did I miss breakfast?"

"Nah. Lottie'll be callin' anytime now." Walter glanced to the corral. "You gonna ride your horse t'day?"

"I planned on helping Miss Merrill out today."

Lottie opened the kitchen door and called out, "Breakfast is ready."

Jordon hung back and followed Patrick into the dining room. Patrick and Walter raced to see who could finish eating first. Lottie and Martin ate without distraction. Beth Anne said little but grinned a few times at Amelia. Jordon noticed Eleanore glance at him and concentrated on finishing his meal.

Walter stuffed the last three bites of mush into his mouth and beamed at Patrick.

"Patrick . . . do not copy Walter. Walter, don't do that again." Eleanore watched Walter struggle to swallow what he had shoveled into his mouth. They went through this about once a week. She didn't want to know what he would think up next.

Walter gulped hard, guzzled the remaining milk and sighed. "I can't. My food's all gone."

Eleanore stared at him and slowly counted to three. "You know what I mean. There will be no more competitions to see who finishes eating first. No one will put more than one bite into his mouth at a time."

"Yes, ma'am." He elbowed Patrick. "May we be excused?"

"You may all be excused when you're done eating." Each of the boys filed out with his dishes in hand. Their moods swing like a pendulum, Eleanore thought, from imps to angels.

Jordon covered his chuckle with an exaggerated cough, avoiding Eleanore's gaze. "When you mentioned repairs, you only talked about the corral. What would you like me to do today?"

Slowly wiping her mouth, then folding her napkin, Eleanore mentally went down the list of things that should be attended to around the house and wouldn't require a purchase. "Two of the windows stick, and another will not open."

He pushed his chair back and stood up. "Which rooms are they in?"

"I'll show him, Miss Merrill, on my way out." Lottie was on her feet with her dish in hand.

"Thank you." Eleanore watched him leave and hoped he wasn't particularly good at handyman work, though she had the feeling he was the kind of man who could do whatever he set out to do.

As soon as Lottie stood up, Amelia stacked Beth Anne's dishes on her own and took them to the kitchen. Amelia made several trips, clearing the table. She carefully scraped the bits of food into the bucket and put the dishes into the pot of warm water.

Eleanore carried Beth Anne into the kitchen and put her on one of the chairs. "You can dry the flatware." After handing her a dish towel, Eleanore took another and picked up a glass to dry.

"Miss Eleanore, make Lottie stop bossin' us round." Beth Anne set the dry spoon down and picked up a wet one.

"She is only trying to help." Beth Anne's so young, Eleanore thought, how could she understand Lottie's need to mother? "What is she doing that makes you mad?"

Beth Anne frowned. "She tells me I have ta put Missie away—when I'm playing with her! An' she told Amelia she had to make our bed. An' I can't help."

Eleanore inhaled to keep from chuckling. The child was so serious. "I'll speak to Lottie."

After the kitchen had been cleaned, Eleanore asked Amelia if she would play with Beth Anne while she attended to several tasks. Eleanore was once again following her daily routine. She served dinner on time. Everyone ate and returned to their activities, and she sat down to do the mending. One day soon, she would have to make a new shirt for Martin and a dress for Lottie. They were growing, and their outgrown clothes could be passed down.

Wouldn't it wonderful, she mused, to have all the children dressed in new clothes at the same time? Always wanting something just beyond my reach, she thought. I should be thankful for this house; Papa worked and traded until it was a real fine home. He also borrowed money against it, and she had been left to repay the loan.

"Ple-e-ease, Amelia, can't we play puppets?" Beth Anne scooted across the bed.

Amelia put her hand out and stopped the younger girl. "Do you have puppets?"

"Yes . . . well, kind of." Amelia helped Beth Anne to the floor, and she scooted over to the chest. She pulled the bottom drawer open, pulled out two socks and held them up. "See."

"They're just socks."

Beth Anne slipped her hand into one sock and held it up. "Now I see a face. Don't you, Amelia?"

Amelia looked away. She didn't see. She wanted to, but she didn't. She shook her head.

Beth Anne cocked her head, then reached into the drawer again. This time she brought out an old worn pair of socks. "We could draw faces on these . . . if that would help."

Amelia swallowed hard. She dreamed of being happy, loved, but she had never played make-believe. She gave Beth Anne a weak smile. "I'll do one if you do the other."

Jordon checked and made sure all of the windows were in working order. He found some nails and a hammer and tacked a few pieces of loose siding. After supper, all the children raced off, again. It was a puzzle, but he decided to take advantage of their absence.

He climbed up into the old elm tree behind the house and tied both ends of the rope he'd found in the barn to the stoutest branch. Before going back down, he glanced at the roof. Even from that distance, he could tell it needed repair. She tried, he thought, remembering how work-toughened Eleanore's hands had felt. He shimmied back down to the ground. She needed help around there—a man and, by the look of things, a few dollars.

Between the ropes he placed the small board he'd smoothed and notched for a seat. He pressed on it, then sat down to make sure it would hold. The cords creaked under his weight, but the knots were secure. Walking back to the barn, he reminded himself that he had plans. Plans that most certainly did not include getting stuck in another orphanage.

He washed up and went into the house to find Eleanore. The kitchen was empty, so he wandered down the hall and paused by the girls' room when he heard Beth Anne and Amelia's voice, though they sounded strange.

"I didn't mean to drop the glass. Honest, ma'am," one squeaky voice said.

"I know you didn't, dear. Why would you want to break your glass? It's okay. Want a piece of cake?" a softer, younger voice said.

Jordon carefully peered into the room. Beth Anne had a sock on her hand with a face drawn on it and was evidently playing the part of the mother. Amelia had a similar sock on her hand and was the child. He felt his stomach knot up and his throat go dry. He composed himself a moment, forgetting Eleanore, knocked on the door frame and stepped forward.

"May I come in?"

Beth Anne grinned and held up her sock. "See my puppet? She's a mama."

"That's a fine puppet, Beth Anne." Amelia hid her hands in the folds of her skirt. Jordon felt the knot above his belt tighten. "How would you girls like to go outside?

I put a swing up in the backyard, and someone should try it out."

"Can I, Mr. Stone?" Then Beth Anne looked at her leg and pouted.

"Sure. I'll carry you out." He gazed at Amelia. "How about you? Wouldn't you like to swing?"

Amelia struggled to take the sock off of her hand without being noticed. "Would it be all right with Miss Eleanore?"

He smiled and nodded. "I'm sure she'll approve."

Beth Anne slipped the sock off of her hand, dropped it on the bed and held her arms out.

Jordon lifted her up and motioned to Amelia. He walked out through the kitchen and into the backyard. He put Beth Anne on the seat. "Hold on." He gave her a gentle push.

"Ohhh!" As she floated above the ground, a wide grin spread across Beth Anne's face. "See me, Amelia! I'm flying . . . just like a bird." Toby ran up, barking at her. "Hush, you bad dog."

Jordon kept the dog away from Beth Anne's feet. "You can pet him, Amelia. He's excited and just a pup."

Amelia called Toby over and scratched his neck as she watched and couldn't resist returning her friend's smile. It looked like fun, but surely she was too big to try it. Mr. Jordon kept the swing going in a slow, easy motion, and she realized she was anxious to take her turn.

Beth Anne called to Jordon, "Let Amelia ride now. We can take turns."

Jordon lifted Beth Anne from the seat and set her down near the tree trunk by Toby. He motioned for Amelia to take her seat. "You may have to hold your feet up."

Amelia grabbed hold of the ropes and stretched her legs out in front of her. Mr. Jordon pulled her back and let go. She was floating above the ground like a leaf in the breeze! She closed her eyes and tipped her head back. She didn't want the ride to end.

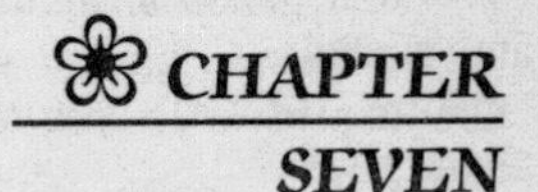

CHAPTER SEVEN

Walter ignored Toby's wagging tail and followed Jordon into the barn. "I gotta name for your horse. Golden Boy. How 'bout that?"

Patrick trailed along with Walter and his face lighted up. "How about Nugget? Now that he's clean an' eatin' good, he's as bright as gold."

Walter elbowed his friend. "That's dumb."

"No, it ain't." Patrick looked up at Mr. Stone. "That horse wasn't near as handsome when you bought him as he is now. I hear gold is like that. You gotta shine it up, like you did with Nugget."

Jordon chuckled. "Tell you what. I'll think about it." He wiped his damp brow and picked up the ladder. "Right now I'd better get up on the roof." As he carried the ladder over and leaned it against the wall of the house, the boys rushed to stay in step and Toby scampered at his heels. "Don't you boys have something to do?"

"*I* don't." Walter grabbed hold of the ladder.

Patrick yanked on Jordon's trousers. "I don't either."

Toby dashed around the three of them and the ladder twice before Jordon managed to grab his furry neck. He kneeled and patted the frisky dog. "You should take him for a run. Have you taught him to fetch?"

Walter shrugged. "He's not too good at it."

"It takes practice." Jordon picked up a one-inch-thick piece of branch and broke it to about twelve inches in length. "Make a game of it. He'll learn quick enough." He held the stick down for Toby to smell, then tossed it out into the yard.

Walter gaped at his dog. "He's goin' after it."

"He likes to play as much as you do. You'd better take him out back so you don't hit anything. You two take turns."

As the boys ran off with the dog, Jordon shook his shirt, trying to create a cooling breeze down his back and across his chest. There wasn't a cloud in the sky, and the heat shimmering over the ground didn't help. He climbed up to the sharply peaked roof to check on the needed repairs.

After checking front to back and side to side, he had found one damaged area. He stretched and pulled his shirt-tail from his pants. Damn, it was hot. He went to the barn, got the tools and supplies. By the time he climbed back up to the roof, his shirt was stuck to his back and chest.

"Hell." He quickly stripped the wet shirt off and wiped his neck, then hung it over the top of the ladder to dry. It didn't take him long to remove the broken shingles and replace them. He was positioning the last two when he noticed a movement out in the corral. Eleanore.

He sat back on his heels and watched her checking on the horses. She gave old Ned a treat and patted his neck. She hadn't forgotten his mount, and fed him next. In the sunlight, her hair looked bronzed, and he could imagine the tender expression on her face as she spoke to the animals.

He wiped his sweating brow and shook his head. The next moment he was sliding down the roof. He grabbed for the edge of the eave. Splinters from the sun-baked shingles knifed into his fingers as his body slid over the edge of the roof and plunged down to the ground.

Eleanore scratched Jordon's horse behind the ear. "You really need a name, don't you, boy?" She had avoided looking up at the roof after her first good view of him with his shirt off. She had never seen a man's bare torso before, not even her father's. She was entranced with the way his muscles flexed, and she didn't think she would ever forget the sight.

As she turned to leave, she heard a deep thudding sound and glanced at the house. Jordon lay on the ground a few feet from the kitchen door. She raised her skirt as she ran to him. He hasn't moved, she thought. It hadn't taken her long to reach him, but Toby was already licking Jordon's face.

"Toby, no!" She sent the dog running and turned back to Jordon. He lay on his side like a forgotten doll in the dirt. She wiped his face with the hem of her skirt and noticed a scar on his chest rise and fall with each breath. He was alive but unconscious. She traced the puckered ridge and closed her eyes a moment.

Dreading he might have broken his legs, she carefully traced each limb with her hands, all the while glancing back to see if he had awakened. The thighs beneath the trousers were hard, the knees a little knobby and the calves as solid as his thighs. She eased him onto his back. He'd been lying on his right arm, and she feared it was broken. He still had not roused.

She had to get him into the house. She couldn't leave him long enough to get help or wait for one of the children to find someone. Besides Patrick and Walter had wondered off. Her thoughts went to improvising. She found an old board in the barn, then raced to the house for an old blanket and long strips of cloth. Back outside, she found Toby stretched out on the ground by Jordon, almost nose to nose. After shooing the dog away, she rolled Jordon onto his side and positioned his legs to keep him steady while she spread out the blanket and placed the board on top.

Staring at his still body, she noticed a puckered scar on the left side of his back. She stretched her tense muscles and wondered if this would work. It had to, she told herself. She bent over Jordon and gently rolled him onto the board. Once she had him positioned, she bound him to the plank, with his injured arm on his chest. Looking at the back doorstep, she knew she would have to have help.

She found Amelia in the parlor with Beth Anne. "Amelia, would you help me a moment?"

Amelia followed Eleanore into the kitchen. "Mr. Stone fell off of the roof. I'll need your help getting him into the house."

Amelia bit her lips and glanced at the open door. "Is he . . . all right?"

"I'm sure he will be, after he gets some rest." Eleanore prayed that would be the case and led her outside. "I'm going to pull the blanket and hope the board slides over the steps. I want you to grab hold of the other end and let me know if he starts slipping toward you. Can you do that?"

"Yes, ma'am." Amelia watched his face. He almost looked as if he were asleep, and she said a silent prayer that he would wake up and ask what was going on.

Eleanore took a corner of the blanket with each hand. When Amelia had done the same, Eleanore tugged, easing Jordon across the dirt. She backed into the kitchen and paused to reposition her hands closer to Jordon's shoulders, then pulled with all of her strength. She knew he'd be heavy, and he didn't disappoint her.

Amelia raised the end of the blanket, moved nearer to Mr. Jordon's feet and pushed on the plank while Miss Eleanore pulled. The blanket and board skidded over the doorstep.

Eleanore dragged him all the way into the room and sighed and grinned at Amelia. "You're strong."

Amelia shrugged. "Where are we going to put him?"

"My room. He can't sleep in the barn like this. You won't have to push now. But I'd appreciate your keeping an eye on him."

It was easier drawing him across the smooth floor. Once Eleanore had moved him next to the bed, she worried over how to get him onto it. She wasn't a doctor and couldn't afford to send for one, unless he didn't wake up. Besides, Dr. Osgerby was hours away. He was still out, which she had considered a blessing until that moment.

Amelia whispered, "I'll take his feet. Can you lift him? He's awful big."

"I'll do my best." Eleanore turned the covers back on the bed.

After summoning her courage, she raised her skirt, stepped over Jordon—straddling him—squatted down and grabbed him in what probably appeared to be a very peculiar embrace, she thought without humor. She pulled him into a sitting position and scooted him to the edge of the bed.

With her arms firmly around him, she stood up. His head tilted forward and rested on her shoulder. Lord, he was heavy. And he was resting against her from knees to shoulder. She stood there a moment, breathing deeply, savoring the foreign nearness of his body. His weight was more than she could support, and they fell onto the bed.

She landed square on top of him with a deep "Oooh." They were face-to-face, and her arms were pinned beneath him.

"Was that him?" Amelia asked.

"Me." Eleanore managed to free her arms and quickly rolled off of him. She maneuvered his bottom onto the bed while Amelia carried his feet. "Thank you, dear. I don't know what I would have done without you." Or would rather not think about it, she reflected.

"Do you want me to get a towel and some hot water?"

"Please." Eleanore stared at his right arm. She didn't like setting broken bones but knew what to do. While he was still out, she placed her hands below his elbow and moved them downward until she felt something like a lump midway to his wrist on one of the bones. It was too soon to tell if the arm was swelling. If she did nothing, it would probably heal with a noticeable knot.

Amelia carried the pan of hot water carefully and set it

on the floor. "I'd better tell Beth Anne what happened. She might try to come see what we're doing."

"Tell her you'll be back in just a few minutes." Eleanore smoothed Jordon's hair away from his face and traced the two lines between his dark brows with her finger. He must recover, she thought, and moved her hand to her side. What if his lovely green eyes opened and he found her touching him so intimately?

When Amelia returned, Eleanore asked her to take a firm hold of Jordon's hand. "We are going to set his arm. I want you to pull on his hand—not jerk it, just a steady pull." She held his arm with her fingers over the break. "Okay, start now."

Amelia leaned back and tried to do as directed, but her hands slipped down his.

"This isn't easy, I know. Try locking your fingers just above his wrist. It may be easier."

Lacing her fingers and twining her thumbs around Mr. Jordon's wrist, Amelia gritted her teeth and pulled.

Pain knifed through the fog in Jordon's mind. "Ugh!" His eyes snapped open and focused on Eleanore. "What the hell are you doing to me?"

Ignoring him a moment, she smiled at Amelia. "Perfect. That was difficult, and you did a good job." Eleanore wiped her damp forehead with the back of her hand and sighed. "We were setting your broken arm."

Amelia backed away from the bed.

"Amelia, do you remember the sunflowers I pointed out?"

"Yes."

"Would you get me four green leaves?" Amelia nodded, as Eleanore had known she would. "From the front door, go to your right. There should be some plants down just a ways."

"I'll hurry."

Eleanore wrung out the washcloth soaking in the water and wiped Jordon's face.

He ground his teeth and continued glaring at her. "I can wash my own face." Eleanore's face became fuzzy and seemed to change shape. He closed his eyes and felt as if he were sinking into the soft bed.

"I'll wrap your arm and let you rest."

She kept a small collection of smooth pieces of wood for this kind of emergency. She returned with the needed supplies. He appeared to be asleep, so she eased the slat under his arm and bound it. His hands were covered with splinters, especially his fingers. She pulled the largest sliver from the middle finger on his right hand.

Jordon's eyes suddenly opened. "Don't you have anything else to do besides pester me?"

She reached over, grabbed his left hand and held it up in front of his face. "Can you take these out?"

"Not right now," he grumbled. Damn, his arm hurt. So did his fingers, now that she'd shown him how they looked. A measure of whiskey might help. He moved his hand, and a sliver that had been driven deep into his middle finger caught in his trousers. A flash of pain shot up his good arm. He gritted his teeth. Think about something, he thought, anything.

He glanced around for the first time. It had to be her room, not that it was all lacy and pink. The drapes were light blue, the walls a lighter shade; there was a framed mirror above the chest of drawers and a doily on the chest. A worn easy chair sat in one corner, near an old trunk. On the wall nearby were several children's drawings. The room had a comfortable feel to it. And he wanted out.

"I'll rest in the barn." He used his good arm for leverage and leaned forward, then sank back against the pillow. The room spun around and around and around. "Did I land on my head?"

"I don't know, but you must have hit it." She settled her fingers into his thick brown hair and gently probed until she felt an egg-size knot on the back of his head. "I think you'd better sleep on your back or left side." She moved down to the end of the bed. "I'm going to take your boots off and get those splinters out."

"Go ahead. I'm in no shape to stop you." He didn't actually mind the help. He felt as if he'd tangled with a huge pincushion. It bothered him that she was the one tending him, like one of her children. She'd better draw the line with exposing his feet, he thought. She won't get my pants off, and I won't spend the night in here.

She pulled the first boot off with little difficulty, but the second seemed permanently attached. She glanced back at him. His eyes were still closed, so she turned her back to him, straddled his ankle hanging over the end of the bed and grabbed the boot. The next moment his other foot landed on her backside and shoved. She stumbled forward with the boot in hand.

She gasped and whirled around. "Thanks for helping."

"My pleasure." He flexed his foot and grinned. Her bottom had felt soft and nicely rounded. Just the kind of memory he needed.

Amelia ran into the room and held out the leaves. "Are these okay? There weren't many real green ones left."

"These will be fine." Eleanore smiled and smoothed Amelia's hair from her eyes. "Get a drink of water and rest."

"What do you need those for?" He pointed at her hand.

"Your hands." She put the leaves on the chest. "Be right back." She went to the kitchen, refilled the bowl with warm water from the stove, mixed in a measure of Epsom salt and returned to her room.

He watched her approach the bed as if she were ready to do battle. He might have thought she looked charming if she hadn't been charging at him. "What now?"

"I'm going to remove the splinters." She set the bowl on the table by the bed. "Would you turn onto your side so I don't have to move your arm very much?" When he did, she kneeled on the floor at the side of the bed and began working on his right hand.

Jordon watched, her face within kissing distance of his.

As she bent over his hand and concentrated on her task, strands of her hair dropped down and framed her face. Her cheeks were rosy and her lips were pressed together. They were nice lips, neither too full nor too thin. Her dark lashes resembled little lace fans. He glanced down—her face would be forever in his memory.

She felt his gaze on her, and her fingers began to tremble. "Hold still, please." She was almost done. Just another couple minutes and she could soak his hand.

Her voice was husky, and he wanted to hear her say something else. It didn't matter what. She was silent. The back of his hand lay at a strange angle as she gently worked each sliver free. Her fingers felt cool on his reddened skin. He stopped counting after she'd pulled out twenty-five splinters. He closed his eyes and felt her fingers skimming over his hand. It felt better already.

She stared at his angry flesh. He wouldn't be handling any tools for a while, especially with that arm. She moved the bowl over to his side and lowered his hand into the water.

"Let it soak while I work on your other hand." She brought his left hand closer and started removing more slivers. She tried not to think about him, but the heat from his body invaded her senses. The aroma was subtle—spice mixed with sweat. She worked as quickly as she dared.

"Now scoot up and rest against the pillows." She moved the bowl and put his left hand in it. She picked up the sunflower leaves.

"What are you going to do with those?"

"Bind them to your hands. Grandma Tillie said they helped stay inflammation." She put two of the leaves over his palm and fingers and wrapped his right hand.

"Your grandma sounds interesting."

"She was a friend. I think she took pity on me because—" She shrugged. "She just did."

He wanted to know more. "Why? Were you such a runt everyone laughed at you?"

She pursed her lips and refused to look up while she wrapped his left hand. "Mama died when I was born. Papa raised me. She was the closest I came to having a grandmother." And no one ever thought of Tillie as a lady, but she was quite a woman, Eleanore fondly mused.

Jordon watched her long, dark lashes, waiting for a glimpse of her lovely brown eyes. The room was hot. Her shirtwaist was plastered to her chest and revealed each pleasing curve. Damnation, he shouldn't think like that about her. If she suspected, she'd break his other arm.

She tied off the end of the soft cloth. "Don't use your hands for anything, if you're tempted to try." She found a sash in a drawer and returned to the side of the bed. Taking care to avoid inflicting more pain, she slipped the scarf under his bound arm. "Can you lean forward just a little?"

He did. When she put her arm around his neck, he found his face almost between her well-rounded breasts. The woman did know how to torture a man—in a variety of ways.

She felt his breath through the fabric of her dress and realized that having him lean forward was a terrible mistake. She quickly tied the sash at the side of his neck and stepped back. "I can adjust the sling later, when you're able to get up, if it's too short." She gathered the odds and ends she had used.

Where were her brains? How was he supposed to unbutton his pants? With bloodied hands, he decided, but his were only sore; his fingers weren't broken. He rolled onto his left side and closed his eyes—and inhaled a faint lavender scent on the pillow.

"Can I get you anything?"

My own pillow, he thought. "Don't fuss, Eleanore. Just let me close my eyes for a few minutes."

Eleanore checked on Jordon throughout the afternoon. He slept like the . . . very tired. She served the children supper and took a tray into him. He hadn't moved. She set the tray on the chest and went over to the bed. He didn't look flushed. She laid her hand on his forehead.

"What?!" He jerked his head around and grimaced. He ached from his head down to his ankles.

She snatched her hand back to her side. "I was just checking your temperature." His skin wasn't hot. It was smooth, and she wondered if his back was as soft, how the curly dark hairs on his chest would feel.

"Is supper ready?" If she were anyone else, he'd have sworn she was blushing. Why?

She reached for the pillow. "If you lean forward, I'll stack these behind your back."

"What for? I'm going in to eat at the table." He slowly rolled into a sitting position without moving his arm and slid his legs off the side of the bed.

She braced her hands on his shoulders. "No. You are going to eat in here. Give yourself a chance to heal." She quickly fluffed the pillows and stacked them at the head of the bed.

He shook his head. He wasn't dizzy, but he definitely felt off his feed. "I'm not too hungry."

She carried the mug over to him. "This is chicken broth. Just sip it." She handed it to him and placed a napkin on his leg. "Is your stomach queasy?"

"Don't think so." He sipped the broth and glanced up at her. "This's good. Go on and eat before the food's cold. I'll be fine."

"I'll come for the tray later. You can set the mug here on the table." She walked to the door and turned back. "Call if you need anything."

She went into the dining room and took her seat at the table. The boys were talking softly. The girls were silent. She put a chicken leg and a spoon of green beans on her plate. She stabbed at the beans with her fork, knowing she should eat a few bites.

Patrick glanced around the table and cleared his throat.

"Miss Eleanore, did Mr. Stone really fall off the roof? Will he be all right?"

"Yes, he did. He has a broken arm, and I believe he will be fine." She smiled. "Thank you, boys."

Martin, Walter and Patrick looked at one another. Patrick spoke. "What for?"

"Being more quiet than usual.

Martin took another biscuit. "Can I help him?"

"Thank you, but I think he just needs rest now." She picked up the chicken leg and began nibbling on it.

Walter gulped down his bite. "Can we see him? I bet he wants to talk to someone."

"In a day or two." She fixed Walter and Patrick with a stern eye. "I don't want anyone sneaking in to see him. Do you understand?"

"Yes, ma'am." Walter slumped back in his chair.

Patrick glanced sideways at Walter. "Yes, ma'am."

Eleanor wiped her mouth. "Lottie, would you bring the cake in? Amelia, the small plates, please."

Soon the children had finished eating. While they cleared the table, Eleanore went to her bedroom door and listened a moment. She didn't hear a sound. She pushed the door open and peered around. Jordon was on his side facing away from the bedside table.

She tiptoed over and set the old chamber pot she kept for emergencies near the bed. After sending up a prayer that he wouldn't need her help with the buttons on his pants, she watched the dark curly hair on his broad chest rise and fall with each breath. She flexed her fingers and bolstered her courage. She heard her heart pounding, but his even breathing was almost mesmerizing. She extended her hand and paused, then grabbed the mug and fled from her room. No. She ran from him—her reaction to him.

Amelia entered the parlor and found Eleanore mending a pair of the boy's pants. "Can I sit in here awhile?"

"Of course, dear. You may read any of those books. We

share everything around here." Eleanore snipped the thread and tied it off. "Are you worried about Mr. Stone?"

"Mm-hm." Amelia sat down at the end of the sofa. "A girl at the lodge broke her arm and she didn't sleep like Mr. Jordon is." She curled her legs around her and tugged her nightshirt down over her knees.

Eleanore folded the trousers, set them aside and picked up a shirt with a torn sleeve. "He also hit his head. If he isn't better tomorrow, I'll have to send someone to Nebraska City for Dr. Osgerby. He's only here in town one day a week." She threaded the needle, wrapped the ends of the thread around her finger twice and formed a knot. "Has Mr. Stone been a good friend?"

"I saw him at mealtimes at the lodge sometimes." Amelia rubbed her knee. "At first I thought he didn't like us. He acted like he didn't care, but he does . . . like putting up that swing out back yesterday." She shrugged. "I don't think he wants anyone to know he cares."

How very wise, Eleanor thought. Amelia was far more mature than some adults.

"He's like that." Amelia glanced at Eleanore through her lashes. "Do you fancy him?"

Eleanore met the girl's gaze a moment and jabbed the needle through the material. "No, of course not. But I am concerned about his injuries."

"Oh." Amelia didn't believe her. She'd seen the way Miss Eleanore gazed at Mr. Jordon today when she washed his face, and that was no ordinary "concern." Amelia hoped he would get his senses back and some of his strength, but not too soon.

"Would you like a cup of warm milk? It'll help you sleep." Amelia looked so worried. She was a girl with the insight of a woman. Eleanore wanted to hold her close and tell her she was safe, but it was too soon.

Amelia yawned and shook her head. "Good night, Miss Eleanore."

Eleanore held out her hand, and when Amelia approached, Eleanore kissed her good night. "Pleasant dreams, dear."

After watching Amelia leave, Eleanore returned her attention to the mending. Why had the child gotten it into her head that she was attracted to Jordon? All she had done was tend the man's injuries. What choice did she have, anyway?

He was hurt, and it had happened while he was repairing her roof. She was responsible for his care. His image became sharp in her mind—his stubborn jaw, eyes that could flash cold or warm, hands with fingers that inspired thoughts she dared not explore.

She rarely thought about her looks. However she knew she wasn't attractive. She could be obstinate and outspoken on occasion. She was a woman who'd grown up without a mother to teach her how to be what the word "woman" implied. She wasn't delicate and ladylike like Harriet. Didn't know how to be like her. She was just Eleanore, plain of face and form.

Suddenly she felt very weary. She put the mending aside, removed her shoes and quietly went to her room. Jordon mumbled something. She stepped over to the side of the bed and leaned down, but his deep voice was more like a rumbling than words. She laid her hand on his forehead and sighed. He wasn't running a fever.

She collected her nightdress and wrapper and returned to the parlor. The day had felt forty hours long. She turned the lamp down, changed clothes and returned to her room. She moved the old chair—the stripes once scarlet and pale gray long faded into a brownish-gray—closer to the bed.

She checked him one last time and covered him. With a blanket around her shoulders, she settled down for the night, oddly comforted by the sound of his steady breathing.

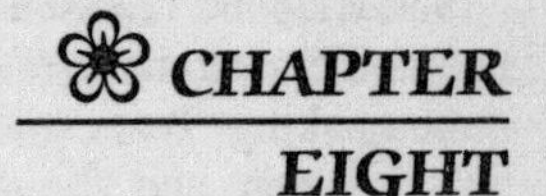

CHAPTER EIGHT

Eleanore balanced the tray with one hand while she eased the door open and peered into her bedroom. Jordon was still asleep. She approached the edge of the bed, wondering if she should wake him. He lay on his back, his feet at opposite corners of the mattress, and she was sure he was smiling.

"Good morning, Jordon."

He was watching his sister, Liza, searching under bushes in the yard for the birthday present he'd hidden. It was her tenth birthday, and she was already a beautiful young lady. The scene blended and ran together like a watercolor in the rain. The war was over and he was returning home. As he left the road and walked up the path to his house, Liza ran to meet him.

Eleanore watched his expression change and wondered what memory or thought made him so happy. "Jordon . . ."

He opened his eyes and stared up. She *was* there. He sprang up out of bed and threw his arm around her. God, she had grown. She was a woman now. He kissed her lips, then rested his head on hers. "Liza, I thought I'd lost you."

Eleanore heard the tray, on which was a cup of tea and a bowl of mush, clatter on the floor as if in the distance. Jordon held her in a fierce embrace. The next moment his lips descended on her, bold yet tender. If her chest hadn't been pressed into his, the kiss might have been chaste, except her heart beat like the wings of a hummingbird and the touch of his lips sent a peculiar feeling down her back.

Suddenly he released her, dropped back down onto the bed and closed his eyes. She covered her mouth and stood there quaking. Tears streamed down his cheeks, but he was sound asleep, and she didn't want to disturb him.

His words echoed in her mind: *Liza, I thought I'd lost you.* Who was Liza? Witless question. She had to be his sweetheart. Eleanore bit her lips and turned her back to him. What a fool she was. Hadn't she sworn never to wear her heart on her sleeve?

The toe of her shoe sent the cup spinning, and she realized the front of her skirt was dripping tea and that the mush had splattered on the floor. She dashed off and returned with rags. Once she'd put the dishes back on the tray, she worked on cleaning the drying mush from the braided rug. She added the rags to the tray, rolled up the rug and was leaving when she heard Jordon moan. She glanced back at him.

"Morning." He rubbed his eyes with his bandaged hand and frowned at her. "What's that?"

"A mess I cleaned up." She waited, expecting an apology for his earlier indiscretion.

"I must've slept like the dead. I didn't hear a thing." He rubbed his upper right arm. Damn, it hurt. Then he noticed the loosened strips of cloth on his left hand. "You might as well take this off."

"I'll be right back." She returned with a bowl of water with Epsom salt, a washcloth and a towel.

Jordon held out his hand and watched Eleanore unwrap it. He stared at the pink spots peppering his palm and the pads of his fingers. The warm water felt good. He pressed his thumb to his middle finger. They were a little tender but better than they looked. "Those leaves must've helped."

"I'm glad." Her gaze rested on his bare chest.

He glanced down to see what she was looking at. "Where's my shirt?"

She glanced around the room. "I don't know. I'll get one from your pack in the barn, and your breakfast, too." She placed the towel within his reach. "Keep your hand in the bowl until I get back."

"Yes, ma'am. But I can't lay around here all day." His gaze fell on the old chair a few feet from the bed, with a blanket folded on the seat. "Where did you sleep?"

She stopped in the doorway, ignoring the chair, shifted the weight of the tray to her hip and decided to ignore his question also. "Do you recall waking up a few minutes ago?"

"No. I remember seeing . . ." God, that dream was real. He closed his eyes. Liza had felt so very real, but that was impossible. He knew. He'd buried her one year ago. "I just woke up."

"You'd better stay in here another day." He'd been out of his head when he kissed her, she realized now, that or dreaming.

"I need to make a trip out back." He sat up and swung his legs down to the floor.

She pointed to the chamber pot and noticed he'd used it sometime earlier. Relief spread through her as she realized she had been spared unbuttoning his pants. No wonder his bandages had come loose. "You can use that again." She nodded at the porcelain pot. "I'll be right back with your breakfast."

Jordon took her suggestion. He felt rested, stronger, but Eleanore sure had acted strange. And where had that mess come from? He felt truly at ease, something he hadn't experienced in the last fourteen months. He didn't question it. Maybe that thump on his head had helped, begun healing his deepest wound—his memories.

The door opened and Eleanore entered with the promised food, but he stared at her skirt. "What happened to your dress?"

She involuntarily glanced down. "I . . . spilled some tea." She walked over to him.

He couldn't remember her spilling anything on herself before. "Did I eat last night?" The smell of food brought a loud rumble from his stomach.

She handed him one of his shirts she had found in the barn. "A little broth, but it stayed down." She stood by the bed and waited for him to sit. "As long as you don't feel sick, you can have a small meal."

"I'm hungry. *Starving*." He put his left hand in the sleeve and raised it. The shirt slid down partway.

She put the tray down and helped him into the shirt, draping the right side over his shoulder. "If you don't throw up, you can have a normal dinner."

"Thanks." Her cheeks were pink, but he suspected her dashing around had caused that. "You didn't get much rest, did you?"

She avoided looking at him. "As much as usual." She picked up the napkin and handed it to him.

He stared at the bowl. He expected to see mush. He didn't. He picked up the spoon and held it over the dish. "What *is* it?"

"Warm milk with buttered toast."

"Oh." *Ugh* was more like it.

"It'll be easy on your stomach." Her gaze wandered to his midsection.

He frowned. "What is your fascination with my stomach?"

"My?" She busied herself with straightening the bed covers. "Sometimes people with head injuries can't keep food down." She stood straight as a broom handle. "I won't ask again." If his stomach revolts, he can suffer, she decided. She would be as disinterested as he appeared to want her to be. She removed the bowl of water and dried his hand.

He stirred the bloated pieces of toast around. "You won't have to. You'll have your answer, one way or the other, in a few minutes." He glanced up and knew his lips were twitching.

His cockeyed grin caught her by surprise. The dimple was back. In spite of her resolve to stay impersonal, she returned his smile. "Enjoy your meal." She never had been one to hold a grudge for long.

As she left, he debated even tasting the browned things coated with butter and floating in the milk. He glanced at the chamber pot. If he dumped the concoction in there, she'd see it. He couldn't intentionally hurt her feelings. He scooped up one piece of toast with the spoon, held it to his mouth, then gulped the bite down. It tasted a little sweet and a tad salty, but it wasn't all that bad.

He came close to licking the bowl after the last spoonful. He was still hungry. He wanted half a dozen eggs, biscuits, ham and a pot of coffee. He settled for the tea she'd brought. There was nothing else to fill up on. Two swallows emptied the cup, and he returned it to the tray.

He couldn't lie around all day, so he stood up, intending to walk out to the barn. The muscles in his back were tight. His legs quivered and threatened to give out. He dropped down on the bed. Why was he so weak? One sharp rap on the door brought him to attention.

Eleanore stepped into the room and paused. Jordon was sitting on the side of the bed glowering at the floor, his face pale. "Are you—"

He glared at her. "Don't say it!" He reached around and rubbed his lower back. "I'm stiff as a board."

"That isn't surprising. You landed rather hard." She walked over to the side of the bed and examined his right hand. "How does it feel?"

"Fine. Don't fuss, Eleanore."

"I don't want your hands to get inflamed. I only wish I could do more for your arm. I feel responsible."

"You weren't, unless you pushed me." He came close to saying, *You were. If I hadn't been watching you, I wouldn't have fallen.* But she wouldn't have appreciated his humor.

She smiled and glanced at the bowl for the first time. "Would you like some more?" She pointed at the dish.

"If that's my only choice. And . . . I've got some coffee beans in my pack. Could I trouble you to make me a few cups?"

"The tea was for . . . I'll get the coffee."

When she started to close the bedroom door, he stopped her. "Leave it open. A little noise would be a pleasant distraction."

After helping Eleanore, Amelia walked down the hall and stopped at the open door. "Mr. Jordon?" He was sitting up in bed with an open book on his lap.

"Come in. How're you doing?"

She stepped into the room, and her gaze furtively darted around. "Okay." She moved closer to the bed. "How's your arm? Does it hurt a lot?"

"If I forget and move it." He grinned, hoping to put her at ease. "It'll soon be good as ever." She stood by the bed, her hands behind her back, and he wondered what was bothering her. "You can sit in that chair. How is Beth Anne doing?"

Amelia shrugged and sat down on the edge of the seat. "She wants to go out and play."

"I know how she feels. Maybe I can take her outside tomorrow and you can both swing."

She thought a moment. "If she put her arms around my neck, I bet I could get her out." She had had to tote heavy burlap bags and small kegs at her last place. Surely Beth Anne wouldn't weigh any more. "I'll ask Miss Eleanore."

He chuckled. "You might at that." He closed the book he'd found by Eleanore's bed and set it aside. "How do you like it here?"

"It's nice."

"Are you getting along with Miss Eleanore?"

"I think so. She never gets mad, even when I do something dumb. She's nice."

"Has she assigned you chores?"

Amelia frowned and shook her head. "She just asked me to gather the eggs and do things, mostly help around the house." She ran her hand down her skirt. "Miss Eleanore was real worried about you."

"My fall must have given her a start, but she took me in hand like she seems to do with everything." A memory flashed in his mind—Eleanore's startled eyes so close to his. She was disciplined and levelheaded most all of the time. He was intrigued with those few moments when she wasn't.

Amelia nodded.

"Where are the other children? It's awfully quiet."

"I don't know. Everyone leaves after breakfast. Lottie sews for a woman in town." Amelia wondered why she hadn't been given a task. If she had one, it might mean she wouldn't have to leave. "If I can find work, could I stay here, Mr. Jordon?"

"Do you want to?"

She watched her tightly clasped hands. "Yes. It's different here. The boys argue and laugh and play, and no one gets really mad." It's like a real home, she thought, at least while Mr. Jordon's here.

He sighed. He needed to fulfill his obligation to the Society and to Amelia. "I'm expected to place you with a family." Her eyes grew large and looked like they were about to spill tears. "Now, don't think the worst. Miss Merrill said you can remain here until I find a place for you. When I find a suitable family, we'll talk it over. It will be your decision. All right?"

She smiled, and a few tears slipped down her cheeks. "Thank you." She stood up. "I'd better find some work. Bye." She dashed out of the room, her mind spinning with ideas. She just had to prove she could take care of herself.

Her face had just lit up. He had never seen her so happy. Damn. How could he be expected to break a child's heart in order to do what was best for her? Well, he'd be there for a while longer. *Everything happens for the best.* He didn't believe that, but he hoped it would be true for Amelia.

After Jordon had finished his second helping of breakfast and relished a cup of coffee, Eleanore dragged the zinc tub into her bedroom. "A bath might make you feel better. Are you strong enough to manage?"

Before he could say a word, she left and returned with towels, washcloth and soap. "I could go over to the stream. It'd be a lot easier than you hauling water in and out of here."

"You are more fit than you were when you woke up—" She glanced at the floor, remembering the way his lips had felt on hers. "But not enough to take off on your own just yet."

He noticed her flushed cheeks before she turned away from him. She wasn't one to put on missish airs. "Eleanore . . ." He waited for her to face him.

"Yes?"

"Look at me." She fidgeted with the soap and towels, then met his gaze. "Tell me what happened this morning that's got you so flustered."

"Nothing to be concerned about. You were a little confused." She pushed the tub closer to the bed. She didn't want to think, remember.

"Did I cause that mess you were cleaning up?" He reached out and touched her cheek. It was soft, lightly tanned and growing pink again, but there was no sign that he'd hit her.

"I thought you were asleep. When you suddenly got up, you startled me and the tray fell." As his fingers trailed the line of her jaw as lightly as a feather, her stomach knotted up. She stared at his lips and began swaying forward. She quickly pulled back. Good Lord. She'd almost kissed him! "I'll get the water."

He felt sweat break out on his forehead. He had been

withdrawing his hand when she leaned forward for a fraction of a moment. He must have really cracked his head; he was imagining things. "Did I strike you?"

"No! Why would you think that?"

"If wakened suddenly, I might lash out." He'd learned that during the war, but something had definitely happened. She had been acting peculiar all morning. Well, he'd move back to the barn today. A little distance would make him feel better—her, too, he guessed.

"I'll remember that." As if she would need that bit of information.

She made several trips with heavy buckets to fill the tub. She tested it and decided more hot water was needed. When she was satisfied, she set the pails aside. "Do you need help . . . with anything?"

He grinned. "Wanta scrub my back?"

"Just keep your arm out of the water." It really was hard to resist his smile, she thought. "Call when you're finished."

"Can I have another cup of that good coffee? I might as well soak in that warm water."

She took his cup, filled it and returned. "I'll set it here so you can reach it." She put the cup down by the soap dish on the table. "I can wash you hair after you're done, if you like."

He thought a moment and knew he wouldn't be able to accomplish that with one hand. "You wouldn't use any fancy-smelling soap, would you?"

She smirked. "No. Unless you have a favorite scent." She clamped her quivering lips together. "I have a little vanilla, honey, pickling spices and, of course, molasses."

"Hm." He raised one brow. "I think I'll settle for smelling clean without drawing flies."

"As you wish," she responded as sincerely as she could without smiling.

She closed the door behind her. She didn't want to hear the splash of water or think about his virile body unclothed, and she sent up a silent prayer that he wouldn't call for help. She went to check on Amelia and Beth Anne and concentrated on the commonplace chores. She had cleaned, organized and gotten dinner almost ready when she heard his footsteps.

He walked through the kitchen to the back door. "Anyplace special you want me to dump this?"

"There are a few bushes out front that could use the water." She watched him leave, his sure stride, the way he shielded his injured arm. He had to be in pain. Men and their pride. She had struggled with her father once when he'd hurt his back and didn't want her to know how bad it was. She filled the other bucket and watered a rosebush in the backyard.

On her way to refill the pail, she and Jordon met in the kitchen doorway. She put her hand next to his on the bucket handle. "I'll take this if you check on Beth Anne and Amelia."

"Why don't you? I'm not incapacitated." He was fast becoming frustrated with her fussing.

She withdrew her hand. "Fine. You're the one who'll be sore."

He headed for the back door. "I already am," he grumbled on his way out.

If he wanted to empty the tub, he could, she decided. When she glanced up, she saw Amelia. "How are you doing with Beth Anne?"

"She wants to go out and swing. I can carry her out, if it's okay with you."

"Do you want to swing?"

"Mm-hm."

"I'd like to go outside, too," Eleanore said and carried Beth Anne to the outhouse, then set her on the swing. "Hold on."

Beth Anne grinned and leaned forward. "Push harder. I wanta go high." Toby ran up and sat by Amelia. Beth Anne pointed to the dog. "Can he ride, Miss Eleanore?"

"I think he'd rather watch. Hold tight." Eleanore pushed the swing a little harder and stood back. It felt somewhat cooler in the shade. She wiped her brow with the sleeve of her dress and noticed Jordon backing out of the kitchen door.

Amelia followed Eleanore's gaze and stared at Jordon as he tugged the tub through the doorway. "Miss Eleanore, is he all right? He shouldn't do that." Amelia got to her feet and started off. Toby tagged along.

"Amelia . . . no."

"Ma'am?"

"Stay here. He doesn't want any help."

"But, Miss Eleanore—" Amelia bit her lips and glanced from Eleanore to Jordon.

"Sometimes men do rather foolish things and it's best to leave them alone."

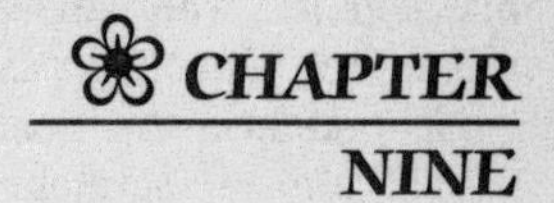

CHAPTER NINE

After dinner, Jordon pulled the covers up on Eleanore's bed, set her tattered book on the Oregon Trail back on the bedside table and removed any sign that he had occupied the room. He paused at the door and glanced around the room one last time. He'd come to know Eleanore better there. He eased the door shut and went out to the barn. This was where he belonged, not in her room or in her bed.

Toby evidently liked his bed, too. He was sprawled across the end of the blanket. "Later, we'll discuss the sleeping arrangements."

They hay smelled sweet and the earth familiar. Everything was just as he'd left it, except for the dog hair. Then he saw the pillow with a clean white case. He reached down and picked it up as if it might bite him. After staring at it a moment, he raised it near his nose and inhaled. It smelled of soap and sunshine. A part of him felt disappointed. He tossed the pillow back down to his bed and went out to the corral.

"Hi, Nugget. How you doin', boy?" The horse raised his ears and eyed him a moment. Jordon calmed him with soft words and a gentle touch. The horse needed to be ridden, but he wasn't up to that just yet.

On the way back to the barn, Eleanore waylaid him.

"I can wash your hair now." His face was pale. He had done too much that morning, but if she suggested he rest, she felt sure he would drive himself to exhaustion.

"Sorry I got your pillowcase dirty."

"I didn't say that." She met his bullheaded gaze and matched it. "You landed in the dirt. I just thought you might feel better with clean hair."

He watched the heat glimmering over the dirt and caught himself scratching his head. He smirked. "You win." He followed her into the kitchen and sat down on the appointed chair. "You'll be gentle, won't you?"

She rolled her eyes skyward and mixed the hot water with cool. "Bend over the bucket." She poured some of the warm water over his head and added soap. His hair was so soft. As she worked up a good lather, she thought about his bath. Was the hair on his chest as silky? Her hand trembled. She rubbed a little harder, thankful he was bent over and facing the floor.

He propped his forehead with his hand and closed his eyes. He thought he smelled a hint of lavender, but that had to be his imagination. At first, she was gentle, almost teasing, then she massaged his scalp with more energy.

He felt the tension drain from him and fancied her hands kneading his neck and shoulders and her fingers easing the stiffness from his back, working their way down to his waist, hips. A new tightness began growing below his belt. His imagination was too vivid. He opened his eyes and watched the hem of her skirt swaying.

She felt the large knot on the side of his head, as round as a coin, and avoided putting any pressure there. "Close your eyes." She rinsed out the soap and added more.

"Again?"

"To make sure I get all the dirt." She was only stretching the truth a might, she told herself, as her fingers worked the soap into his hair.

He didn't know how much longer he could stand the sweet torture. "You're good at this. Had much practice?"

"With the children."

"How long have you lived here?"

"About five years." She stopped a drip of soap from

running down his neck. "You said you fought with the New York Forty-fourth. Are you from there?"

"Outside of Albany. We had a small farm."

"Papa said he couldn't cotton to farming."

She became quiet, and he was curious to learn more. "I'm surprised your father didn't marry you to some hard-working man. My pa used to talk about what kind of man he wanted for . . . my sister."

"He needed me and said it was my choice."

She stilled her hands and withdrew them from his hair. "And you never met anyone that met your standards?" Damn, that wasn't exactly how he'd wanted to put it.

She stared at the back of his soapy head, remembering the few nights she had cried because she wasn't pretty or clever enough to attract a boy's attention. "After the years with Papa, I learned to take care of myself. What more could a man do for me?"

"You might be surprised."

She dumped the rest of the water over his head.

"Don't drown me." He grabbed the towel from the table and dried his face. "I thought most women wanted their own family."

"I'm not most women. I wouldn't know." She took the towel from him and rubbed his hair.

Suddenly Patrick burst into the quiet kitchen, tears streaming down his face. She knelt down in front of him. "What happened?"

He held out his hand. "I . . . I shut the door on it."

Eleanore cradled his hand in hers and stared at the angry red mark across his fingers. "We'll soak it in cool water." She dried his freckled cheeks and gave him an encouraging smile before she left to draw water from the well.

Jordon put his hand on Patrick's shoulder. He was trying to be brave. "You must've been in a hurry. Can you move your thumb?"

As he stared at his thumb, Patrick's lips quivered. "It'll hurt."

"It may not. See if it'll move—just a little."

Patrick gritted his teeth, wagged his thumb and grinned. "I did it!"

"Good. Now try one of your fingers."

With his mouth puckered, brows drawn together, Patrick concentrated and straightened his finger. He smiled up at Jordon.

"Good boy."

Eleanore dashed back into the kitchen. Jordon nodded at Patrick. "The cold water'll make your hand feel better."

Eleanore put the bowl of water on the table and lowered Patrick's hand into it. She smoothed his red hair back and smiled at him. "You can sit down, if you want."

Jordon stepped aside and hung the towel on the back of the chair. "Thanks, Eleanore." He watched her mothering the boy a moment and went outside. She should have been married with a brood of her own.

Jordon swallowed a piece of carrot. Suppertime, usually noisy, was boisterous that night. Beth Anne, Martin and Walter were more than a little curious about Patrick's accident and Jordon's fall. He took another bite.

"Mr. Jordon." Walter leaned over the table to see him. "What does it feel like t'break your arm?"

"It hurts like the devil."

"Oh." Walter slumped back on the chair.

Patrick looked across the table. "Amelia, did you really pull Mr. Jordon's arm straight?" He stared at her, his fork in midair.

Amelia's gaze darted around the table. "I only did what Miss Eleanore asked." She stabbed a piece of chicken, wishing everyone would not watch her.

"You're strong—for a girl."

"Did you hear the bone snap?"

"Were you scared?"

Eleanore raised her hand, momentarily bringing the rash of questions to a halt. "Amelia was very brave and did a wonderful job, but you've asked enough questions for now."

Lottie glanced sideways at Amelia and clamped her lips together. The boys were quiet, but they kept peering at Amelia. Lottie stood, picked up the pitcher of milk and went around the table refilling everyone's glass. When she came to Eleanore, Lottie smiled.

"Thank you," Eleanore said.

Lottie beamed.

Jordon watched Patrick a moment. "How's your hand feeling?"

Patrick wriggled his fingers. "See. It's better."

Walter glared at Patrick. "You just wanted a broken hand 'cause Mr. Jordon broke his arm."

"Did not."

"Did too."

Eleanore eyed Walter. "Enough. I'm sure Patrick would rather his hand didn't hurt, and I don't think Beth Anne enjoys watching you run around when she can't. Please, finish eating." She felt Jordon's gaze and tried to cover a smile. It was pleasant having him there to share unspoken thoughts. She would miss him, and that she didn't want to consider.

Walter frowned at Beth Anne and grumbled, "She doesn't have t'do nothin' round here anyhow."

Amelia stared at Walter. "She helps fold clothes and napkins and helps Miss Eleanore in the kitchen. She shouldn't have to . . ." She hesitated a moment and rushed on. ". . . to do much more than that at her age." She glanced through her lashes from Miss Eleanore to Mr. Jordon and wondered if she had said too much.

Jordon nodded at Amelia and was rewarded with a girlish blush. The boy probably felt left out. "Walter, are there any fish in the stream?"

Walter nodded. "Was last spring, but I haven't . . . been there for a while."

"I'd like some fish for supper. Would you show me the

best spot in the morning? We'll have to get up early." Jordon met Eleanore's approving gaze. Walter just needed a little attention.

Jordon must have been good with the children, Eleanore thought, and wondered why he wanted to give up his position. She was aware of his gaze several times during the meal. She felt a wave of disappointment when he finished eating and carried his dishes to the kitchen without returning.

Jordon let Walter lead the way back to the house. The other children were leaving. The boy proudly held up his catch, a catfish.

Patrick stared into one glassy fish eye and touched one of the whiskerlike feelers. "You really catch him?"

"Yep."

"He sure did. Knew just where the best place was to find him," Jordon said, motioning to the fish. He held his string back, hoping his four carps wouldn't be noticed.

Martin stepped over to see the fish. "You go to that spot I told you about?"

"Mm-hm." Walter scuffed his feet in the dirt. "Thanks for tellin' me 'bout it."

"Hurry up. You're late."

"I will." Walter looked up at Jordon. "We can have these for supper, can't we?"

"Here." Jordon handed his line to Walter. "Take them to Miss Eleanore and ask her."

"Yes, sir!" Walter ran to the kitchen door. As he passed Lottie, she jumped back from the swinging line of fish.

"Don't you have to go to—" Lottie glanced at Jordon and lowered her voice. "Work?"

Patrick snorted and ignored her. "Can I go with you next time, Mr. Jordon?"

"We'll see."

Walter glared at Lottie's back.

Jordon fixed Walter with a stare. "Go along."

"Okay."

Jordon watched the children leave. What were they up to? It wasn't as if they wanted to leave, more as if they felt they had an obligation. To Eleanore? Had to be. But why? Surely she wasn't forcing them to work. Not her. The children were happy, loyal. He'd have to be more alert.

Three days later Jordon saw Eleanore doing the wash. Beth Anne and Amelia were helping. After the clothes had been hung out to dry, he joined Eleanore in the kitchen. She was flushed, and strands of her hair looked bronze on her cheeks.

He watched her with an odd expression, almost a grin, that made her uneasy. "I haven't seen you since breakfast." She went to the cupboard and reached for a glass. "Thirsty?"

He nodded. "I walked to town." He watched the sunlight on her hair and wished she'd loosen that damn knot. He debated whether to ask about the children's work. Eleanore stood with the glasses in hand as if fearing his question. He changed his mind. "I've been wondering, why isn't Beth Anne using crutches?"

Eleanore poured two dippers of water into each glass and handed him one. "Dr. Osgerby didn't have any small enough. Besides, I feel better knowing she won't fall again."

He chuckled. "Glad I didn't break my leg." He raised his glass as if saluting her.

She grinned. "You, I'd tie down in bed."

He choked on the water and wiped his mouth. "That might prove interesting. I wouldn't have guessed you were that type of woman."

"Of all the . . . you . . ." She whirled around and brought her arm up, intending to slap his arrogant face. He laughed. A hearty, rich sound filled the room. She felt flushed and grimaced. "Your sense of humor is wicked."

With the slightest touch of his finger on her chin, he

tipped her head upward. He leaned forward and spoke, his lips nearly on hers. "Haven't you guessed? I like the way you blush. It's most becoming."

She stared into his misty-green eyes and was taken with his sincerity—for a long moment. His breath felt warm on her mouth. She wanted to lean forward and find out what his lips would feel like. Instead, she spoke, shifting the direction of her thoughts, and tried to ignore the reason for her heart pounding in her breast.

"I haven't been teased in years."

"I wouldn't have guessed." He should leave, but damn, she needed to be kissed and he couldn't resist. He slid his arm around her shoulder and lowered his lips to hers in one swift move.

She just stood there feeling, breathing in the scent of his warm body, tasting him. She wanted more. She put her arms around his waist, yielded to his light urging and opened her mouth. Tentatively, she touched her tongue to his. This wasn't like the first time, she realized somewhere in the back of her mind. A hot tingling sensation spiraled downward. She held onto him, not trusting her own strength.

Jordon heard footsteps approaching outside the door. Reluctantly, he ended the kiss and held her close a moment. "You okay?"

Eleanore closed her eyes and rested her cheek on his broad chest. "Mm-hm."

The kitchen door opened and Amelia walked in. "Miss Eleanore—" She saw them and covered her mouth.

Eleanore stepped back, steadied by Jordon's hand still on her back. "Yes, dear?" Ugh! She had completely forgotten that the girls were out back.

Amelia stared at the floor. "Can I bring Beth Anne in? I'll be careful and won't drop her." She wished she had stayed outside.

"I'll get her." Jordon released Eleanore and left the kitchen.

Amelia peered through her lashes. "I'm sorry, Miss Eleanore. I should have knocked." Miss Eleanore had looked so happy. Mr. Jordon, too. Hope welled up in Amelia, and she had to fight to hide her happiness.

"The only closed doors in the house you have to knock on are bedroom doors. You did nothing wrong." Neither did I, but I feel like I did, Eleanore thought.

Jordon returned with Beth Anne balanced on his good arm. "Ma'am, where would you like me to put you down?"

Beth Anne giggled, then put her head on his shoulder.

Jordon raised one brow at Eleanore. "Well?"

"Set her here on the chair." Eleanore drank some of the forgotten water and met his gaze. She felt warmer, as if he'd put his arm around her. She gulped down the rest of the liquid. She must have been out of her mind. After years of proving she didn't need a man, she had almost thrown herself into Jordon's arms.

She gave each of the girls a glass of water. "Amelia, I'm going over to the general store. Would you like to walk with me?"

"What about Beth Anne?"

"I'll carry her."

"No need." Jordon winked at Beth Anne. "I'm sure we can keep busy."

"Thank you." Eleanore avoided looking at him. "We shouldn't be too long." She set her empty glass in the dry sink. "I'll be ready in a few minutes."

She went to her room. As she brushed out her hair, she noticed her reflection in the small mirror. There was a slight upward tilt to her mouth, her cheeks were pinker than usual, and were her eyes brighter than normal? She was being foolish. She pulled her hair back, knotted it and wiped her face with a damp washcloth. Ignoring the mirror, she returned to the kitchen feeling like herself once again.

Jordon noticed the difference in Eleanore the moment

she entered the room. She was back in control. The strands of loose hair were now in place. Her back was stiff as a beam, and she had that no-nonsense expression in place. This Eleanore was easier to deal with. "You don't need to hurry. Beth Anne and I will be fine."

Eleanore kissed Beth Anne's cheek. "Be good."

Beth Anne nodded and peered around at Amelia. "Mr. Gunther's cat had babies. See if he'll let you pet them."

"When you can walk"—Amelia looked to Miss Eleanore—"maybe we can go see them."

"I'm sure Mr. Gunther wouldn't mind." Eleanore opened the door. "Come along, Amelia."

Jordon cleared his throat.

Eleanore paused and glanced at him. "Yes?"

"Do you usually go to town in your apron?"

She stared down and snatched it off. When she looked up, a flicker of a grin threatened to soften the corners of his mouth. She closed the door behind her, humming tunelessly. Amelia waited in the yard, watching the horses, and hurried to catch up with Miss Eleanore. "Can I see the cat . . . at the store?" The first family she had been placed with had had one, but she wasn't allowed to touch it. "It's a mouser, not a pet," she had been told.

"I'm sure it will be all right."

Eleanore waved to her neighbor, Mr. Kirton, old enough to be her grandfather and not happy about Eleanore taking in so many children. The sun was bright and the air hot, even when the breeze ruffled the grass. "I'm sorry you haven't had a chance to get out. I want you to have some time for yourself, to do what you'd like."

Amelia paused and stared at Miss Eleanore. "But—" Amelia followed in a rush. "Lottie and the boys all have jobs. I should, too."

Eleanore glanced at Amelia, so serious and trying to sound mature. "That isn't necessary. Besides, I really do appreciate your collecting the eggs, helping around the house and with Beth Anne. She enjoys your company. The others tend to treat her like the baby of the family, and you don't."

"But I'm not earning any money."

"That's my fault. If I could, I would pay you for your help." Guilt threatened to dampen Eleanore's spirit. The girl was supposed to be earning money of her own. Somehow, everything would work out. It must.

"But that's not what I meant." Oh, now I've done it, Amelia thought.

"I know, dear." Eleanore smiled at Amelia.

They passed Harriet's house, Mrs. Renton's, and a boarded-up storefront. The saloon and barbershop were across the street. The door to the general store stood open. In the heat, the aromas of coffee, cheese and kerosene were strong.

Eleanore stepped inside. "You can look around, Amelia." She went over to the counter. "Good day, Mr. Gunther."

"Miss Merrill. You're lookin' as bright as the day. What do ya need t'day?"

She felt the coins in her pocket. "Smoked beef. Not a large piece, though."

Mr. Gunther went to the back room and returned with the meat. He held it out for her inspection. "Will this do, Miss Merrill?" He looked around the store. "Isn't Lottie with you? Haven't seen much of her lately."

"She's been helping Mrs. Peterson . . ." Eleanore's voice faded as she gaped at the meat and envisioned the meals that slab of beef would provide. "It's a fine cut . . . but more than I had in mind." She spoke with more composure than she felt. "Don't you have a much smaller piece?"

Mr. Gunther shrugged. "You have enough credit to buy another fifteen or twenty of these, if you'd a mind to."

She stared at him openmouthed, then snapped it shut. "You must be mistaken."

"Not at'all. That Mr. Stone came by this mornin'. Said he owed you. Ya got a ten-dollar credit."

Eleanore raised her chin. "I'll take that beef." She glanced around. "And a pound of coffee beans, please." She would not allow her surprise to show more than it had. Jordon hadn't said anything, and a part of her was grateful he hadn't. Her pride wouldn't have allowed her to accept money—food was another thing, and he understood.

Amelia wandered around the store, peering into the corners and on lower shelves for the cat. She saw some pretty yard goods, a pair of shoes for Miss Eleanore and a basket of peaches. She joined Miss Eleanore at the counter. "I couldn't find the cat. It must be outside."

Mr. Gunther turned around and smiled. "She's in the back. I'll show ya."

"Go on, Amelia. Mr. Gunther's used to children coming in to visit his cat." Eleanore watched Amelia go through the side door.

A minute later Mr. Gunther returned. "She's sure a nice girl." He wrapped the meat and tied the bag of coffee with string. "Have you seen the kittens, Miss Merrill? Got five this time. Have to find homes for 'em before long."

Eleanore started to smile and caught herself. "I'll think about it, Mr. Gunther."

"Bet them young'uns'd like one. A cat don't eat much. Table scraps and mice'd be 'nough."

Eleanore nodded.

"You go on back. Your girl's prob'ly still there."

"Thank you." Eleanore picked up her package and stepped over to a short counter with a "Mail" sign above it. "Good day, Mrs. Gunther. Do you have anything for me?"

"Miss Merrill, why, I think I do." Mrs. Gunther thumbed through several envelopes. "Yes, here it is." She handed it to Eleanore.

Eleanore was expecting a response to the letter she'd

sent to Martin's aunt and uncle. This was from the bank down in Middleburg. She thanked Mrs. Gunther and stepped away from the window. She took a deep breath, opened the envelope and scanned the page. A foreclosure notice. She carefully refolded it and tucked it into her skirt pocket. Now was not the time to let her guard down. She found Amelia sitting by the deep basket of kittens.

"Look at this one, Miss Eleanore. It's trying so hard to climb out." Amelia ran one finger along the kitten's black silky back.

Eleanore scratched the mother cat's neck. "They are cute." The black one Ameila was taken with had three white paws and a matching spot on its belly, as if it had been drawn by a child. It was adorable.

"Can I bring Beth Anne to see them when her leg's better?"

"She would like that." Eleanore petted the mother once more. "We'd better let them rest now."

Amelia picked up the kitten and kissed the top of its head. "I'll be back, Smidgen."

Eleanore walked out with Amelia. "Smidgen?"

Amelia shrugged. "It's little, and Mrs. Charles, a woman I worked for, called small bits of things smidgens."

"Don't get too attached to that kitten, dear."

"I'd share my food with it and take care of it." Amelia walked along, oblivious to everything but the memory of Smidgen. Beth Anne would like it. Amelia wasn't sure if Lottie would. She always fussed about keeping their room so perfect.

Naming the cat was only the beginning, Eleanore thought. She didn't need to feel responsible for anything else, but maybe Amelia did. Eleanor stopped in front of Harriet's house. "I'd like to pay a call. We won't stay long."

Harriet greeted them and told Amelia the children were

out back. "How have you been, Eleanore? I heard about Mr. Stone's accident. How is he feeling?"

Following Harriet to the kitchen, Eleanore laughed, and it felt good. "Fine."

Harriet poured two glasses of lemonade. She handed one to Eleanore and set one on the worktable. "How did it happen?"

Eleanore's mood lightened with her friend's curiosity. "He was repairing the roof, slipped and fell." She shrugged. "What can I say?"

"Did you see him fall?"

"No, but I heard him land on the ground. I was in the corral." I'd watched him working, she recalled, fascinated with his bared torso, but she couldn't say that.

Harriet grinned. "He must have been distracted."

"You're ever the romantic. I should have known how you think." Eleanore felt the letter in her pocket and sobered.

"What is wrong?" Harriet frowned. "Do you feel ill?"

Eleanore shook her head and withdrew the letter. "I just got this." She unfolded the tape. "It's from the bank."

"Bad news?"

"They'll take the house if I can't make up the payments by next month. I thought I had more time."

"No! You've worked so hard." Harriet stared from her glass to Eleanore. "I wish I could help."

"I know, but this is my problem. If Papa had only told me about it." Eleanore bit her lips. Her father's only secret had been a mortgage on their house, and it was her heaviest burden.

Harriet reached out and took Eleanore's hand. "Will the bank take some on account?"

"I've tried and will again, but this letter says I must pay the regular payment plus the eleven dollars I was short in July."

"Do you have part of it?"

"Yes, but I don't know how I can come up with all of

it." Eleanore had a moment of absurdity. "Not even if I went to work at the saloon."

"You wouldn't!?"

Eleanore met Harriet's shaken expression with a somber gaze. "I don't think so."

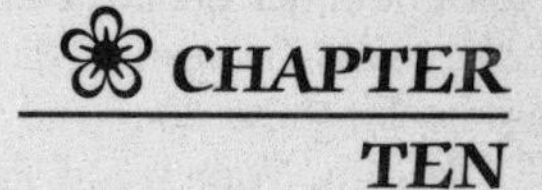

CHAPTER TEN

After supper, Eleanore waited until Jordon went out to the barn before she counted the money she had managed to save. Fourteen dollars and sixty cents. Oh, Papa, why? She had never seen one extra dollar and probably would never know where their money had gone. She wouldn't cry. Several families, some business owners, had moved away, but no one had opened a new shop. There was no hope of employment. A soft knock on her bedroom door interrupted her thoughts.

"Come in."

Lottie entered quietly and closed the door. "I got paid today." She walked over to Eleanore and held out her hand. "Three dollars and thirty-five cents. A payment's due, isn't it? Will this help?"

"That's wonderful. You've been working very hard."

Lottie dropped the money into Eleanore's hand. "Half this is yours, you know." She counted out a dollar and a half and returned the rest to Lottie. "That's the agreement."

Lottie pocketed her share. "I'll tell the boys to count their money. Maybe it will be enough." She left and closed the door behind her.

"Not unless they've found a gold mine," Eleanore said after Lottie's footsteps had faded down the hall.

When the children had discovered she was having trouble making the loan payments, they insisted on helping pay their way. Eleanore knew she shouldn't have agreed, but she was so desperate and felt sure she could find work and end the arrangement. She hadn't. She failed—the children and her dream. Damnation, it wasn't fair. How could she raise the rest of the money? She heard the boys approaching the door and told them to enter.

Martin, Walter and Patrick filed into the room. Martin stepped over to Eleanore and put their wages on her lap. "Seven dollars and I got one for a tip. Mr. Anders said he wants me to stay on."

"You boys have worked so hard for this. Remember our deal. Half and half, and the tips are yours, Martin."

"But—"

She held up her hand, ending the discussion.

"Night, Miss Eleanore." Martin led the other two boys out.

"Sleep well."

She closed her eyes and thanked God for the children. They had worked so hard all summer. Tomorrow she would visit the bank, see if Mr. Cullen would accept the eleven dollars she was short on the last payment and give her more time to raise the one due in September. She put the money back in her bottom drawer.

Jordon was checking the horses and enjoying the suggestion of an evening breeze when he noticed all three boys over near the outhouse. They were busy talking and making gestures as if arguing. Curious, he wandered over, listening to their whispered words.

"We gotta do somethin'."

"We know *that*. What?"

"Mr. Anders will pay me more if I work in the saloon. But you *can't* tell Miss Eleanore. She'd skin me alive!" Martin glanced over his shoulder and elbowed Walter. "Evenin', Mr. Jordon."

"Boys. It's kind of late for you to be meeting out here, isn't it?"

Martin glanced sideways at Walter and Patrick. "We had to visit the joe. We're going in now."

"See you in the morning."

What kind of mischief were they planning? Why would they need money? A gift or possibly to repair some damage done were Jordon's first ideas. He returned to the barn and stretched out on his bedding. He'd wondered about the children rushing off each morning. The fastest way to get an answer was to ask Eleanore, but he doubted she would be any more openmouthed than the boys. It was worth a try.

He woke not long after sunup the following morning and went to the kitchen. He wanted a cup of coffee. He opened and closed the door quietly and turned to see Eleanore setting the coffeepot on the stove.

"Morning. I didn't think you'd be up." He'd caught her with her hair down. It spilled in light brown waves over her shoulders almost to the belt holding her robe tight about her. He grinned at her back, glad he'd gotten up early.

"The coffee won't take long." She put a pot of water on the stove. "Thank you for the beef and coffee"—she glanced over her shoulder at him—"and more. You didn't have to do that." His hair was wet, slicked back, and his eyes were bright.

"What is the 'more'?"

"The credit." She felt him behind her, not touching but close enough to feel as if he were.

"Feeding two extra mouths has to be a hardship." He leaned forward and peered over her shoulder. A few strands of her hair caught on the stubble of his jaw. She trembled, and he put one hand on her waist, his other hand resting a little higher, to steady her.

The coffee began boiling. Her hand shook as she moved the pot to the side so the coffee wouldn't bubble over. Standing at the stove was always warm, but never so much as now with his large hands on her midsection. His breath fanned her cheek, and she quivered.

"Is that better?" he whispered near her ear.

As he slipped his arms around her, she rested her head back against his chest. "Yes . . . I'm not so sure."

He nuzzled her neck and kissed her soft cheek. "This is a nice way to begin the day."

"Mm." It was. It was heaven. It was dangerous. He would be leaving, but she would always remember him. She felt his lips on the corner of her jaw, and his hand cupped one breast, then the other. Her mind spun like a whirligig. She wanted it to go on and on, to turn around and hold him tight against her, but she dared not. It might lead to more unbridled feelings and desires.

"Jordon, I have to take the water into the children."

"Now?"

"Now." She lifted her head and stood erect.

He slowly slid his hand down to her waist and over the curve of her hip. "I'll check on the horses and bring the milk in."

She nodded. She had to regain her composure before she faced the children. She had never experienced such exciting, wonderful sensations. However, she had to keep these feelings hidden. Her resolve back in place, she went about her usual early morning chores.

After the children had left for work, Toby followed Eleanore when she brought old Ned to the barn. The dog ran ahead, tail wagging in every direction, then Jordon stepped into view. Her body reacted instantly at the sight of him—she felt breathless; her heart beat as if she had been running, and she couldn't resist staring at him.

"You want me to hitch the horse to the wagon?" She'd done her hair before breakfast, but her face was rosy and her sparkling eyes told him she hadn't forgotten that morning.

"I will." She walked toward the wall where the harness hung.

He reached the harness first and took it down. "No need. I can manage." He walked to the open double doors. "Where're you off to?"

"Middleburg."

"I'll drive. Making a call or shopping?" She dropped down and scratched Toby's neck, avoiding his gaze, or so he thought.

"The bank, but I'll be all right."

"It'll be a nice trip. I imagine the girls'd like the outing." It wasn't as easy one-handed, but Ned was patient and Jordon maneuvered the harness into place.

"I'll drive." Eleanore dashed back to the house. Lord, what a pickle. It was bad enough having to go to the bank, but he didn't have to know. Well, at least she hadn't told him the reason.

She put her brown calico dress on and the straw bonnet. Mrs. Moran, a dear neighbor and friend when Eleanore and her father lived near Peoria, Illinois, had given her the bonnet on her fifteenth birthday. It wasn't as elegant as it once was. The straw was now faded and the sheer peach silk was snagged in several places, but it was nicer than the slat bonnet. She went through the house looking for the girls and found them already out in the wagon.

"Miss Eleanore." Jordon cocked his head to the side, more than a little surprised by the hat.

She paused, confounded, several feet in front of him. "Mr. Stone . . . Jordon."

"Well, let's get going." He took her arm and handed her up to the bench seat.

On the outskirts of Myles Creek, Jordon noticed Eleanore's hands fussing with the reins. He glanced back at the girls. "I've got an idea. Why don't we play a game?"

Beth Anne puckered her forehead. "What can you play, Mr. Jordon? You're not supposed to use your arm."

"A counting game. Beth Anne, you look for rabbits. Amelia, crows." He grinned at Eleanore. "Bears?"

He was watching her with a devilish leer. "But I've—"

He winked at her and glanced at the girls. "Then you better keep a sharp lookout for the beasts."

Beth Anne giggled.

Amelia smiled.

Eleanore saw the girls scanning the landscape before she met Jordon's gaze. "What will you be counting?" The first two buttons of his blue shirt were open, exposing part of his chest, and his hat was tipped down, shading his eyes. He smiled, teased, and was beginning to make her think she wasn't as plain as dishwater.

"Flies."

She laughed in spite of her worry over the meeting. He really was foolish at times. "That should keep you busy."

"Not all flies. Just the ones that land on Ned." He smirked. "Oh . . . one. There . . . on the rump." He shook his head. "It's gone."

Eleanore gave him a mock scowl. "All right, girls, start looking. He's one ahead."

The ride passed quickly. Amelia laughed at Beth Anne and Jordon's silliness, and Eleanore felt her worries ease. Before she had time to mentally rehearse her plea for an extension, she pulled up in front of the Middleburg Bank. She stared at it and moistened her dry lips.

Jordon noticed Eleanore set the brake out of habit. She stared at the bank as if it were the jail and she were under arrest. "Want us to go in with you?"

"No." She tried to act as if she visited the bank routinely, as if it were the general store, but she didn't fool herself. "I won't be long."

He nodded, jumped down to the ground and walked around the wagon. She clutched the little bag with a death grip. He held out his hand to her. "I'll take the girls for a walk and leave the wagon here."

She stepped down, shook her skirt and looked at the girls. "Be good."

Eleanore paused at the heavy door to the bank, straightened her hat, raised her chin and opened the door. She withdrew the letter from the reticule and reread the signature. Mr. Cullen. There were two desks to her right, one with his nameplate. The man behind the desk wore wire-rim glasses and had a thin mustache and a clipped beard, and when he noticed her looking at him, she wondered if he really saw her.

As she stepped over to the desk, she silently asked for strength. "Excuse me, Mr. Cullen."

He glanced up. "Yes?" Mr. Cullen motioned to a wooden chair at Eleanore's side.

She sat down, hands folded on her lap. "I am Eleanore Merrill." His lips thinned, and she felt herself becoming angry. "I—"

He cut her off. "Can you make up your back payment?" He reached into a file and withdrew a sheet of paper. "You owe thirty-nine dollars and eighty cents as of today."

"That includes the quarterly payment due next month." Eleanore loosened the strings on her reticule. "I have eleven dollars with me. I'll try to pay what's due next month."

"I'll take that on account. But if you don't come up with twenty-eight dollars and eighty cents by the twentieth of next month, you will lose the house. This is the third time you weren't able to make the full payment." He held out his hand. "Why did you take out a loan you couldn't repay?"

Ignoring his question for the moment, she asked one of her own. "I don't believe I've seen you before. Have you been with the bank long?" The man was insufferable, and she wasn't about to be humiliated by him.

He pushed his glasses up to the bridge of his nose and stared at her. "Almost six weeks, and this is the first time I've seen you in here."

"In answer to your question, I think if you read that paper my father signed, you'll see that it was his loan." She met his stern gaze with her own. "I am trying my best to repay it." She jerked on the reticule drawstrings. She resented his attitude and realized she didn't trust him. If she couldn't make the next payment, she would lose her funds and her home. One would have been bad enough.

"The money, Miss Merrill."

She stood up, their gazes still clashing. "I'll pay the full amount next month on the twentieth, when it's due. Good day, Mr. Cullen."

She snapped her skirt aside, spun on her heel and marched out of the bank. Pausing on the boardwalk, she took a deep breath and felt more like herself, in control again. Why she had ever allowed the threat of losing her house to rob her of her one strength, she didn't know. She had been in a fog, but the air was now clear.

"Miss Eleanore?" Amelia watched Miss Eleanore's face and wondered at her changing expression.

Eleanore smiled. "I'm finished here." She marched over to the wagon and climbed up to her seat before Jordon had a chance to help her. When she realized he was staring at her, she turned and faced him. "Is something wrong?"

He tipped his hat back and gave her a you-tell-me look but she sat there on the hard bench seat as cool and remote as he'd ever seen her. He glanced at Amelia and Beth Anne, then back at Eleanore. "Want me to take the reins?"

Amelia hooked the last button on Beth Anne's shoe. "Are you scared about getting the bandages off?"

"Mm-hm." Beth Anne picked at a loose thread near her knee. "What if I can't walk?"

"You will. I'll help." Amelia straightened Beth Anne's skirt. "I'll tell Miss Eleanore you're ready."

"Amelia, will you go with us?"

Amelia paused at the door and gave Beth Anne a reassuring smile. "If I can." Amelia returned a minute later, grinning. "She said we'll leave soon."

Beth Anne nodded. "Tell me about the kittens again."

Amelia described each one and had answered most of

the younger girl's questions when the door opened. She let out a deep sigh.

Eleanore smiled at Beth Anne. She was pale and quiet. "This is the day you've been waiting for. Dr. Osgerby is expecting you." With Beth Anne on her hip and Amelia by her side, Eleanore left the house and walked at a brisk pace until they reached the barbershop. She led the way around back and knocked on the door.

Dr. Osgerby opened it and stepped aside. "Eleanore. Beth Anne. And who is this?"

"Amelia Howe."

Beth Anne tugged on Dr. Osgerby's lapel. "She's teaching me to read, and she helped Miss Eleanore set Mr. Jordon's arm."

"Amelia." He shook hands with her. "I hope you and Miss Eleanore don't open up shop and take my patients away." He lifted Beth Anne from Eleanore's arms and set the child on the table.

Amelia ducked behind Miss Eleanore but was gently moved closer to the table. The room wasn't very large, but there were two windows and a second door Amelia guessed opened to the barbershop. She stared at the black bag on the table, wondering what strange things the doctor kept in it.

Dr. Osgerby unwound the strips of cloth binding Beth Anne's leg. "There." He gently checked the pale limb. "Good as new." He stood up and lowered her down to the floor.

Beth Anne stared up at Eleanore.

"See if you can walk over to Amelia."

Eleanore stepped behind Amelia. "We can see the kittens on the way home."

Amelia inched forward and held out her hands to shorten the distance. "You can do it."

Jordon had been to the general store, talked with Mr. Gunther, and asked if there was any mail for him. He was handed a letter from Brice, which he stuck in his trouser pocket, then he stopped at the livery and decided to visit the barbershop. It wasn't easy to learn about people, to try to find out if a family might be open to taking in Amelia, without raising suspicions. It was near to dinnertime, but he figured there was time enough for one more call.

He entered the shop, the aroma familiar. A barefaced man with a shock of dark hair got up from a chair. Jordon hung his hat on the coatrack.

The barber motioned to the chair he had just vacated. "What d'ya need t'day, sir?"

"Haircut and shave. I haven't managed too well with this." He motioned to his sling and sat down.

"That would make some things a bit tricky." The barber draped a towel around the front of Jordon's neck and started mixing up a good lather. He applied it liberally to Jordon's face. "You just passing through town?"

Jordon sat with his head back against the headrest, eyes closed. "Thought I was." He clamped his lips together for a moment as the brush threatened to lather his mouth. "Now I'm not sure."

The barber stropped the straight razor. "It's kinda quiet round here these days. Didn't used to be—is now."

"I haven't seen a schoolhouse."

The barber drew the blade down one cheek and wiped the lather on a towel. "Almost built one couple years back. Never got built. Folks has been movin' 'way ever since. "Thinkin' of movin' north m'self."

"Omaha?"

"Nah. Mebbe Grand Island. Gotta friend there. Where'll you be headin'?"

"Not sure. My plans got as far as seeing what's at the end of the rail."

"Seen others doin' the same."

As the barber finished and dried Jordon's face, Jordon heard a back door open and close. He opened his eyes and saw a smiling, weathered face and hunched shoulders.

The man pointed at Jordon's arm. "I heard Miss Eleanore and one of her girls . . ." he rubbed his jaw, "Amelia, I think, set a man's arm. Would you be that man?"

Jordon held out his hand. "Jordon Stone." The barber drew a comb through Jordon's hair and picked up the shears.

"Doc Osgerby."

Jordon shook Doc's hand. "I've heard a little about you, too. Beth Anne's looking forward to getting around on her leg again."

Doc chuckled. "Took the bandage off an hour ago. Her leg'll be fine now." He motioned to Jordon's arm. "How'd that happen?"

"Fell off Miss Merrill's roof."

"May I take a look?" Doc pointed to Jordon's arm.

"Sure." He held his injured limb out.

Doc moved the sling aside and felt the arm. "I'm here one day a week—only reason Eleanore let me set the child's leg's because she was scared she'd make her a cripple." He put the sling back in place. "Nice work. Understand the new girl, Amelia, helped. Haven't seen her before."

"She was being placed by the Children's Aid Society in New York City. It didn't work out. I've been interviewing families in the area. If I can't place her, she should go back to the lodge in New York." Jordon shrugged, momentarily forgetting the shears in the barber's hand.

Doc rubbed his chin. "How old is she?"

"Nine."

"Looked older."

The barber brushed hair from Jordon's shoulders and handed him a tin-backed mirror. "Short 'nough?"

Glancing at his image, Jordon wanted to wince but said, "Easy to comb one-handed." He settled with the barber and slapped his hat on.

Doc opened the front door. "Mind if I walk a piece with you?"

Eleanore took her childhood journal out of the drawer. She kept important names there and found the paper she needed. Reverend James, Boulder, Colorado, and Pastor Wilkins, Frankford, Iowa. They might have moved, she realized. After all, she'd tucked the scrap of paper in the journal before her father's death over two years ago.

Next to burying her father, this was the most difficult thing she had ever had to do. She didn't want to hand the children over to someone else who would try to find homes for them. However, she must think of them, not her pride.

Summoning her courage, she wrote to the two preachers. After explaining her situation, she described each of the children and asked if good families could be found for some of them. By the time she addressed the letters, tears were streaming down her cheeks and spilling on the desk. She dashed to her room, closed the door and fell across the bed. All her work and promises to settle the children in homes she approved tormented her. A wave of hopelessness threatened to overwhelm her, but she became determined to keep her dignity. That was the least she could do. She was wiping her face with a damp cloth when she heard a horse enter the yard.

She quickly combed her hair back and pinched her cheeks. She dropped a few coins into her skirt pocket, picked up the letters and went out to the yard, where she met Jordon. "I'll return shortly," she said.

He watched her march away. She hadn't faced him, he realized. Her voice sounded raspy, and now he saw that her hands were balled into fists. As he unsaddled and rubbed down Nugget, he went over little things that had been nagging him. Tonight, Eleanore Merrill, he thought, I'll find out what the hell's going on.

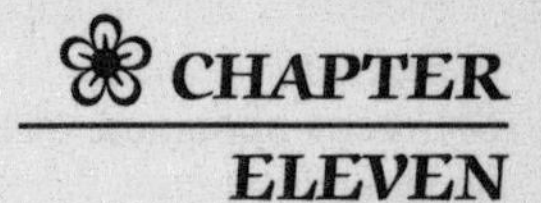

CHAPTER ELEVEN

Eleanore posted the two letters, then bumped into Mrs. Peterson, the woman who employed Lottie. "Excuse me."

Mrs. Peterson puffed herself up. "You have a nerve sending those poor children out to work while you spend your days with that man!"

"Mrs. Peterson, what—" The woman darted out of the store before Eleanore could finish. She glanced up and saw Mrs. Gunther shake her head, as if embarrassed for her. Two other women nearby did the same. Someone tapped her shoulder. She whirled around, ready to defend herself.

Harriet took Eleanore's arm. "If you are ready to leave, we can walk out together."

Eleanore nodded, thankful for a friendly face. She kept silent until they were on the boardwalk. "Did you hear what she said?"

"No, but from the look on your face, it must have been terrible."

They were passing a vacant store when Eleanore replied. "She accused me of . . . making the children work so I'd be alone with Jo— Mr. Stone." She heard the tremor in her voice and increased her pace, as if she could outrun her anger and embarrassment.

"Everyone knows she is a little strange. I think her barbs have been aimed at most of us at one time or another." Harriet hesitated, then added, "She asked me why little Jimmy didn't look like Mr. Blake or me. Can you imagine?"

Eleanor's gaze snapped to Harriet. "You never said anything."

Harriet shrugged. "Mr. Blake convinced me to pay her no mind."

"You've got a good man."

"That I do." Harriet glanced sideways as they came to her house. "You know, Eleanore, I understand why you are truly opposed to searching for a man to marry, but why discourage a man who might be interested?"

"I'm used to doing things my way. Besides, a man would be someone else to take care of."

Harriet smirked. "Our little ones were not all accidents. There are certain . . . benefits to marriage."

"Thank you, Harriet." Eleanore walked with measured steps back to her house. Before kissing Jordon and sharing an intimate glance with him, she would have told her friend there couldn't be any reason for her to marry. But recalling the way her body had responded to Jordon, she realized there definitely could be an advantage.

That evening, Eleanore served beef soup, made from the last of the meat, and fresh bread, with Amelia and Beth Anne's help. Eleanore had kept busy, hoping to put the unpleasantness with Mrs. Peterson behind her.

Walter looked under the table. "Beth Anne, how does it feel to walk on it?"

Beth Anne shrugged.

"Walter, please sit up." Eleanore became aware of Jordon's gaze on her. When she looked down the length of the table at him, a warm sense of closeness spread through her. Self-conscious, she felt a smile tug at the corners of her mouth before she glanced away. She didn't want to think about how empty that end of the table would be after he left.

"Mr. Jordon," Beth Anne peered around Amelia, "have you seen Mr. Gunther's kittens?"

"No, I haven't. Have you?"

She nodded. "Miss Eleanore took me and Amelia. They're so cute and soft." Beth Anne pushed her spoon around the edge of her bowl. "Did you have a cat when you were little?"

Eleanore was drawn to the downcast smile that softened the lines around Jordon's mouth for an instant. She doubted he was aware of the tilt of his lips. She suddenly, belatedly realized she knew so little about him and wanted to know him better.

He had given one to Liza on her fifth birthday, he remembered. "Tilly. She was gray with a white nose and tail." He continued eating his soup, determined to banish the image of his sister, not the smiling happy girl he knew so well but the one who had died in his arms.

Patrick smirked at Beth Anne. "Do you know what cats eat?" His face was aglow with a rascally grin.

"Leftover food and milk."

"Mice and rats . . . and baby birds," Walter eagerly volunteered in a rush.

"No! Mine wouldn't have to, wouldn't it?"

Beth Anne stared at Eleanore, tears beginning to drip down from her sad brown eyes. Eleanore glared at the two boys before turning to Beth Anne. How could she explain survival to a tenderhearted little girl? "If you had a cat, I'm sure you would keep it well fed." Eleanore gave the young girl a reassuring smile.

Lottie glared at Beth Anne. "Don't be such a dunce. There's hardly enough money now for our . . . food . . ." Lottie gasped. As she covered her mouth, her attention darted to Eleanore.

She snatched up the serving bowl and blurted out, "More soup, Jordon?"

He glanced down the table at her. "I'm fine." He bit into the slice of bread, casually observing her. Her hand trembled; she appeared unusually interested in her food, and the only sound was that of eight people breathing. "I've changed my mind. I think I will have more of that good soup."

After passing the bowl to Amelia, Eleanore dropped her hands to her lap and clasped them together to keep them from shaking. The silence was deafening. Her gaze shot to Jordon's left. "Patrick—"

"Yes, ma'am?"

"How's your hand?"

He held it up over his bowl, holding a spoon. "See."

"I'm glad it's better." The subtle sounds of eating, spoons scraping bowls and a couple feet scuffing the floor resumed, to Eleanore's relief. She, however, had lost her appetite. Surely Jordon would have questions—or maybe not. She didn't know which would be worse.

As Eleanore reread the same line of an old letter that usually brought her peace, the evening felt as if it would never end. Jordon had played the piano, sang songs with the children and told them a story before he finally went out to the barn. She kissed the children good night, changed into her nightgown and wrapper and went to the kitchen. A cup of tea would settle her stomach, she hoped.

She poured the heated water over the tea. While it steeped, she kept her back to the window, as if that would keep her thoughts away from Jordon. A noise outside startled her. She glanced at the window. The glow of lantern light in the barn was all she could see, and she decided that the noise must have been Toby. A moment later the kitchen door opened.

Jordon stepped in and closed the door. "I'm glad you're still up."

She stared at him. Why hadn't she just gone to bed? "Not for long. I'm on my way to . . . retire." She picked up her cup and held it with both hands.

"I heard from Brice today. He's glad Amelia has been placed where she feels safe."

"I'm happy, too."

He watched her a moment, but he couldn't be deterred by her soft voice. "We need to talk. Bring your cup."

"I'm tired, Jordon. Tomorrow would be better." She started to pass him, but his hand clamped onto her arm.

"Now. Outside."

She gaped at him, dumbfounded. "But I'm not dressed."

"Then we won't dance." He started to open the door, with his hand poking out from the sling, but she wouldn't move. "You don't want the children listening, do you?" he asked and slid her a couple feet closer to the door.

She grabbed the doorjamb with one hand. "To what!?" She stood on tiptoe and sniffed his breath.

He smirked and touched noses with her. "Satisfied?"

"Let go of me!" She jerked and pulled, but it did no good. In fact her struggling made it worse. He had maneuvered his arm around and held her against him with the cup pressed into her breast and his stomach. She forced herself to go limp and asked, "Have you lost your senses?"

He felt her heart pounding, saw the way her eyes flashed and watched the way her lips quivered. He was tempted. Oh, he was tempted, but he wasn't about to be distracted. "Maybe I have." The heat from her body smelled of flowers. He had lost his mind.

His hard grip became an embrace. For one moment she almost leaned into him, but when he stepped back, the hot tea spilled down his shirt and pants.

He jumped back, muttering, "Damn, damn, oh damn!"

"Oh, Lord. I'm sorry, Jordon." She grabbed the flour-sack towel and handed it to him. "I didn't mean—"

As he sopped some of the tea from his trousers with the towel, he said, "We still have to talk." He tossed the wet cloth in the dry sink, took her hand and marched her out into the yard.

She tore her gaze from the damp area on the front of his pants and didn't fight him. She was like a lamb, though no one would ever have thought her so docile, being led to the slaughter. Toby ran over to join in, but Jordon sent the dog scurrying away.

As soon as she entered the barn, he released her and closed the large doors behind them. She backed away from him. His bed was in one corner, the lantern nearby. She turned away from that area and faced him. "What is so important at this time of night?"

"Privacy. Sit down."

She glanced around. "The parlor's more comfortable." The smell of hay and leather calmed her a bit, until her attention returned to his determined presence.

He watched her every move and understood her immediate fear. "I'll keep my distance." He paced the depth of the barn. He'd rehearsed his gentle questions since leaving the house, and now he couldn't recall even one.

She wasn't sure how to take that softly spoken assurance. "Is something wrong?"

He came to a stop two paces in front of her. "You tell me."

She shrugged and moved back.

"All right." He resumed pacing. "Start with Lottie's comment. It must be hard for you, alone and responsible for five, now six, children, if you count Amelia."

"It is, sometimes." She didn't look at him, didn't want to see his pity.

He stared at her rigid back. "Are the children working to pay room and board?"

She spun around. His expression wasn't accusing. His voice had been gentle, and she nearly sagged in relief against the post behind her. "They've been helping this summer," she said.

He lifted his hand, wanting to comfort her, but she flinched. "They're learning responsibility."

"Responsibility? For what? My debts?" She began

winding the sash to her wrapper around two fingers. "I promised to take care of them, not the other way around." She yanked on the end of the belt, then pulled her fingers free.

"Charles Brice believes children should be proud of their efforts, that one cannot expect to receive what hasn't been earned. Isn't that what you're doing?"

She shook her head, disgusted with herself.

Jordon picked a piece of straw off his shirt. "Did the bank refuse you a loan?"

His question struck her as funny, a jest, and she started laughing. She couldn't help it. She collapsed on his bed holding her stomach.

He stared at her and wondered how her laughter could hit him like an embrace. Two minutes later her hysteria alarmed him. "Eleanore, stop it! You're overwrought." He dropped down to his knees in front of her and put his hand on her shoulder. "Eleanore . . ." She raised her head, her cheeks awash with tears. She hiccuped. "Are you all right, now?"

"Y-es." She brushed the back of her hand over her cheek, grateful for his support.

"Now—back to the bank . . ."

She stiffened within his hold. "That is my business."

"If it affects you, it'll affect the children. Tell me."

She sniffed. "I promised to care for them, do what's best for them, and I will." She pulled a handkerchief from her pocket and blew her nose. "We'll be fine."

She started to rise, but he easily held her down with one arm. "Your pride may endanger the children. For God's sake, let me help you." He smoothed the hair from her damp face and kissed her cheek. As important as her pride was to her, he *needed* to help her.

"I've managed so far." Her chin came up a fraction; she hoped to reinforce her statement and bolster her courage.

He made a disparaging sound. "Have you? Lottie was almost in tears tonight because she said more than she thought she should have in front of me. Your secret is hurting them. Can't you see that?"

"My life is none of your concern! Why don't you leave? I'll see to Amelia with my last breath." She jumped to her feet and almost fell over him.

He grabbed onto her waist and pulled her back down to the bed. "I think you care more about your stubborn pride than those boys and girls!" Understanding hadn't worked. He'd try anger. Something had to crack her granite-hard shell.

"Damn you!" She shoved him backward and ran to the door. She pushed it open and was halfway across the yard when he caught her around her midsection.

He hauled her, kicking and struggling, back to the barn. "You didn't ask for a loan, did you? You already have one and can't make the payments. Right?" He released her. They both gasped for air, then he took hold of her wrist. "What's going to happen to them if you can't pay off the loan?"

She balled up her fist, sorely tempted to punch him, but that wouldn't erase his accusations or her guilt. She met his gaze and felt her strength drain away. "I've written to two ministers who may be able to take the children in or find them homes."

He turned and wrapped his arm around her. "God, Eleanore, please tell me what is going on. Everyone needs help sometime."

She clung to his strength as if she could draw from it. For a moment, her problems and the world receded. She rested her head on his chest and listened to his strong, steady heartbeat. "After my father died, I discovered he had taken out a loan on land we didn't own. Until last May, I baked bread, cakes and pies for a restaurant to keep up with the payments and buy food. Families moved away, there weren't enough customers, so Mrs. Witty closed up and left."

He felt her ragged breath brush his chest. "And?"

"If I don't make up what I owe, I'll lose the house in September."

"How much do you owe?"

"Forty-seven dollars and eighty cents, due September twentieth."

"How much to pay it off?"

She closed her eyes for a moment. "Almost two hundred dollars."

He kissed the top of her head and held her trembling body close in his embrace. "We'll work something out."

She nestled her head over his heart, "*we*" echoing through her mind. She felt tears pool beneath her closed eyelids. Other than her father, no man had ever included her in "we." Did that mean . . . ? "But what about your plans?"

He chuckled. "Can wait."

Amelia looked around the yard. There were so many places for Beth Anne to hide. When she was found, she had promised to practice reading. Amelia peered around the tree, the corner of the house, then behind the outhouse. Beth Anne was on her knees peeking around the other side. Amelia tiptoed up and called "Boo!"

"Oh!" Beth Anne plopped down on her bottom. "You gonna make me read now?"

"Mm-hm. Soon you'll be able to read the stories you like me to read." Amelia helped Beth Anne to her feet and pulled a leaf from her blond hair. "Have you made a sampler?"

"No. Have you?"

They started walking back to the house. "Yes. If Miss Eleanore has thread to spare, I'll help you start one after your lesson." Amelia sent Beth Anne to get her book and stopped in the kitchen.

"Miss Eleanore, after Beth Anne finishes her lesson, can I teach her a few stitches?"

Eleanore nodded. "I'll find thread and a piece of muslin." She eased her arm around Amelia and hugged her. "Thank you."

Amelia stiffened. It was a long moment before she relaxed a bit, put her arms around Miss Eleanore and felt warm, safe.

"Miss Eleanore, Beth Anne wants to see the kittens again. Can we?" Amelia saw the apples on the table. "Or do you want me to peel these?"

"No. You may go. And would you see if there's any mail for me?"

Eleanore wrote a missive giving Mrs. Gunther permission to turn her mail over to Amelia, in case there was a problem. She handed Amelia the note and peeled an apple as she watched the girls leave. Making the pie kept her hands busy. The last four days, Jordon's grin or understanding gaze had caused her to blush.

At times she almost convinced herself that she had only dreamed he had said "we," but he was still there and showed no sign of leaving soon. As she tended her daily chores, she couldn't imagine life without any children—or, she feared, without Jordon. That thought set off a mingling of anger and resentment directed at herself.

She wasn't a weak-kneed miss, didn't *need* a man to prop her up. What had happened to her? she wondered. She pinched the edges of the pie crust with such vigor she almost mangled it. After putting the pie in to bake, she made quick work of cleaning up the kitchen.

As she hung the towel over a peg, Toby barked three times. In the quiet, she heard someone at the front door and went to answer it. "Harriet, come in. Hello, Henry."

Harriet eyed Eleanore's apron. "Don't you ever leave the kitchen?"

"I know I should bake in the morning." As she untied and took off the apron, Eleanore led Harriet to the parlor. "But time gets away from me. You're the orderly one."

Harriet chuckled. "I had time to plan for our new additions to the family." She sat on the sofa and put Henry on the floor at her feet with his wooden toy wagon.

Eleanore grinned at the little boy. "He's adorable." He reminded her of a dark-haired cherub.

With Henry settled, Harriet sat back. "I have been worried about you. Did you go to the bank?"

Eleanore nodded.

"Well . . . did they accept part of the money?"

"Mr. Cullen would have gladly taken every cent I have without extending the due date on the balance. If I can't make up the payments by next month, then I'll lose both the house and my money. I decided to wait until I had all the money."

Harriet stared at her and slowly shook her head. "That sounds unlawful. Can he really do that?"

"He seems to believe he can." Eleanore sighed. "I still have some time to work it out, but I am tired of thinking about it."

Harriet nodded. "What do you think about Mr. Kirton moving?"

"It's the first I've heard. We aren't on the best of terms, you know. The only time he talks to me is when the children throw something near his house."

"I hear he is moving to Omaha. In fact I believe he is there now." Henry crawled away and Harriet went after him. "I also heard Mr. Tucker was thinking about moving away. Mr. Blake says we have to stay. The soil is good and he has worked so hard."

"Have you thought about leaving?"

Harriet shook her head. "I just hate to think we will be the only ones left here."

"The land's good, you said so. More farmers will come."

"Mr. Blake is counting on that. Have you thought about what you will do if . . . you cannot stay in the house?"

Eleanore clasped her hands together on her lap and glanced around the parlor at the children's drawings. "I never intended to raise them, just put them with good families." She rubbed her thumbs together. "I used to dream of going to California or Oregon. But I'd never try such a hard trip with them."

Harriet checked the doorway and whispered, "Even Amelia?"

Eleanore pressed her lips together and nodded. "I have to do what's best for her."

"Does Mr. Stone know?"

"Mm-hm." Eleanore didn't trust her voice to say more. Her feelings about Jordon were so muddled.

"You do know he has spoken to everyone in town about Amelia?"

Eleanore heard Amelia and Beth Anne before they darted past the window, and she lowered her voice. "He was responsible for her. I agreed to keep her. He had doubts before. Now I fear he may send her back." The two girls came in the front door. At the sound of Amelia's voice, Eleanore's head snapped up.

Beth Anne came to a sudden stop in the parlor. "Sorry, Miss Eleanore. Hello, Mrs. Blake."

Amelia stood behind the younger girl. "Mrs. Blake."

Beth Anne dropped down by Henry. "Can we play with him?"

"I am sorry, dear. We have to leave." Harriet grinned at the girl. "It is good to see you up and about again." She gathered up her son and his toy.

"Miss Eleanore, Mr. Jordon said we"—Beth Anne looked over her shoulder at Amelia—"could ride the horse round the corral—if it's okay with you."

Harriet started walking to the front door with Henry in her arms. "We will see you later."

"Beth Anne, please wait outside." Eleanore walked Harriet out front and circled back to the corral. Amelia and Beth Anne were already there with Jordon.

Jordon watched Eleanore rush toward him, skirts fluttering in her wake. She did have nice ankles—legs too, he'd bet, but he hadn't had the pleasure of actually seeing them, yet. "They told you."

She came to a halt and planted her hands on her waist. "Why? Beth Anne's leg just healed, and you don't know if Amelia—"

He cut her rebuke short with a hand on her shoulder. "She'll be fine, and I'll be right there."

"Ple-e-ease, Miss Eleanore." Beth Anne pulled Amelia closer.

Jordon slid his hand down Eleanore's arm and took hold of her hand. "You ride, don't you?"

His touch was warm, and when she gazed at him, his grin sparkled in his eyes. "I used to."

"Good." He gave her hand a reassuring squeeze. "All right. Miss Eleanore's going to ride Ned. Watch her. You'll be next."

Eleanore faced away from the girls and whispered, "I don't want to ride!"

Still holding her hand, he rubbed his thumb along the length of hers. "It would give Amelia confidence . . ."

She peered over at the girls and sighed. "Oh, all right."

Together they saddled Ned. On her second attempt, with the girls and Jordon watching, she sprang up and swung her leg over the saddle. Once she'd anchored her skirt with her calves, she sat back and smiled at her audience. Mounting a horse had been easier when she was eighteen.

"You all right?" If his arm hadn't been so weak, he would have enjoyed boosting her up, his hands on her waist, her hair brushing his jaw.

"The stirrups are a bit low."

He adjusted one. "See if that's better." When she agreed it was, he shortened the other one, taking a moment's pleasure from touching her slim leg.

She gripped the reins with a stranglehold as he put her foot in the stirrup. His movements were thrifty, his touch distracting. The sun added a richness to a wave of his brown hair that had fallen over his forehead. The horse stirred, reminding her they weren't alone.

He stepped back. "Your knuckles are white. Ease up."

She started Ned out at a walk and noticed that Amelia kept Beth Anne from tumbling over the top of the fence. As Eleanore's confidence grew, she urged Ned to a faster gait. Jordon eyed her with a thoughtful expression, but when he said nothing, she assumed she was in no danger.

Beth Anne teetered on the top rail. "Mr. Jordon'd go faster."

"Maybe, but not with his arm." Amelia glanced from Miss Eleanore to Mr. Jordon and saw a strange look on his face, like when Beth Anne stared at the kittens.

Jordon overheard the girls. He flashed them a quick grin, his attention barely wavering from Eleanore. She brought Ned to a halt near him. Her face was glowing.

Eleanore patted Ned's neck. "He hasn't been saddled in years." She swung her leg over the horse's rump and dismounted, her legs a little shaky and tangled in her skirts.

Beth Anne ducked through the fence and ran to Jordon. "Me next!"

Eleanore took Beth Anne's hand. "Let Amelia take her turn."

"But I want to."

"So does Amelia, and she always lets you go first."

"Oh, okay."

Eleanore met Jordon's gaze. She felt his respect and something more. Dressed in pants that hugged his hips and a loose shirt, he resembled the kind of man young girls dreamed about. Instead of dwelling on that, she recalled how his lips had felt on hers, the musky scent of his damp skin and the steady beat of his heart.

"Come on, Amelia."

After a glance at Beth Anne, Amelia stepped through the fence and cautiously approached Mr. Jordon. The closer she got, the bigger Ned looked. They lifted Amelia up to the saddle and gave her a few basic instructions. She stared down at the ground while Mr. Jordon made some adjustments.

"I'll lead Ned around once so you can get used to the feel of the horse." After walking the perimeter of the corral, Jordon climbed up behind Amelia. "Now you can relax and let me do the work."

Ned seemed to shoot forward. Amelia sucked in warm, dry air, clung to the saddle horn and tried not to bounce too much.

Jordon bent his head down to Amelia's. "Lean back against me. I've got you. You can't fall." Several strides later, he felt her slight weight and took her around again.

When he brought Ned to a halt, Amelia wished the ride had lasted longer. She got down with Miss Eleanore's help and patted Ned's shoulder.

Eleanore lifted Beth Anne up to take Amelia's place. "You mind Mr. Jordon."

"Oh, yes." Beth Anne turned her head around and grinned up at him. "Can't I ride alone like Amelia did?"

"This saddle's too big for you." Jordon put his sling-covered arm around Beth Anne. "Keep one hand on the horn and lean against me."

Amelia and Eleanore stood outside of the corral fence and watched. Eleanore felt better about Jordon's riding lessons. She should have known he'd be careful. He always was with the children. She leaned against the top rail and studied the way he seemed to control the horse with no effort while he talked to Beth Anne. Eleanore couldn't resist smiling.

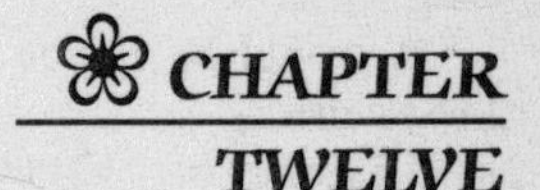

CHAPTER TWELVE

Lottie carried the clean plate back to the kitchen. "Miss Eleanore, should I serve up Martin's food and set it on the side of the stove for him?"

"I'm sure he'll appreciate it." Eleanore looked out into the yard again and frowned. "I expected him before now."

When Amelia left the kitchen, Lottie went over to Eleanore. "Walter said Martin's trying to work more hours."

"Did Martin say how late he'd be?"

"Walter didn't know."

Leaving the girls to finish cleaning up after supper, Eleanore went outside and strolled around the yard, debating whether or not she should go to the saloon and bring Martin home. She really would have to talk to Mr. Anders about Martin's hours. The sun was dropping below the horizon, and the sky was a watery blue. It would be dark soon. He'd never been this late.

"Miss Eleanore . . ."

She turned around and shaded her eyes against the last brilliant rays of the sun. "Lottie? What's wrong?" She had wandered farther than she realized and ran back to Lottie.

"Walter let Toby in the house, and he won't listen to me."

"Oh." Eleanore sighed and started back to the house with Lottie. "I was afraid— Never mind."

Lottie pouted. "I thought I was in charge when you were out," she whined.

Eleanore slowed her pace and put her arm around Lottie's narrow shoulders. "Being in charge isn't always easy, is it?"

"It would be if you would let me swat him when he sasses me."

"That may be." Eleanore opened the door to the kitchen.

Lottie followed Eleanore into the house and picked up the towel. "A switch on his backside's what he needs."

Eleanore shook her head. Sometimes she didn't know which was worse—Lottie's prudishness or the boys heckling her.

"Look, Miss Eleanore, I'm washin' dishes." Beth Anne was kneeling on a chair happily scrubbing a plate.

"Be careful."

Eleanore crossed the kitchen and went up to the boys' room. Toby was sprawled on the floor chewing on . . . something. "Patrick, Walter, what is Toby eating?"

Walter crawled out from under the bed and glanced at his dog. "Looks like"—he peered over at the dog's paws—"part of a tree branch."

"Make sure he takes it outside with him before you go to bed."

Martin still hadn't returned by the time she checked on the girls. She stepped outside and went over to the corral. Jordon was exercising his horse. She rested her arms on the fence and watched him. His deep, soothing voice as he spoke to Nugget was momentarily spellbinding.

Jordon glanced over at her. He released the lead and joined her at the fence. "Want to take a ride?" he asked. She stared at him as if puzzling something out. When she didn't answer, he traced her jaw with his knuckles and tipped her chin up.

"Hm? Oh." She blinked and saw his lips, near enough to kiss if she relaxed. His gaze was unwavering, as if . . . She quickly raised her hand to the buttons on the bodice of her dress. "Have you seen Martin?"

He shook his head. "Want me to check on him?"

"Please." She stared off in the direction of the saloon.

She had spoken softly, as if to herself. He covered her hand with his. "I'll have a talk with Anders, if you want me to."

"Just find Martin, for now."

When she turned toward the house, Jordon shook his head. One minute she gazed at him with a sweet curve of her lips, then her mouth straightened and she pulled back behind her icy reserve. Hell! He took off, cutting across the back lot. It was almost dark, but he made his way to the road.

The brightest, noisiest place in town was the saloon. Inside, it took a moment for his eyes to adjust to the light and smoky haze. Four men were seated at a table in one corner playing poker. Anders stood behind the plank bar drying a glass. It wasn't a showplace but served its purpose. Jordon sauntered over to the bar and nodded at Anders.

"What'll ya have?"

Jordon glanced around the room, again. "Thought it was about time Martin called it a day." He met Anders's blank stare and was struck with a dubious twinge.

"Martin, the boy that cleans up?"

Jordon nodded.

"He left— No, wait. He was hangin' round later than usual. Long gone now, though." Anders wiped the bar with a towel.

"Mind if I check the back room?"

Anders pointed to a door at the far end of the bar.

Jordon searched the storeroom. It was clean and organized, except for a toppled mug in one corner. He left by the back door. It was so dark he could barely see the outhouse. He followed the back wall and turned the corner. One moment he was walking toward the soft light up ahead, then he landed in the dirt, facedown on his good arm. Someone nearby groaned and retched.

Jordon rolled to his knees and bumped what felt like a

leg. "You okay?" The responding moan and strong stench of whiskey brought a few choice words from Jordon. He stared at the shadowy figure slumped against the side of the saloon. The fellow didn't look too tall. In fact . . . Jordon leaned forward. Oh, hell. "Martin?"

"Ugh."

Jordon sat up. This might put a kink in Eleanore's spine. "Come on, boy. Miss Eleanore's waiting for you." With his arm around Martin's shoulders, Jordon led the way back home. As they neared the house, he saw her pacing between the barn and the corral.

Eleanore heard a noise in the field beyond and spun around. It was dark, and the light from the kitchen didn't help. "Jordon, is that you?" She held her breath and listened. Even the crickets were silent.

"And Martin." Jordon glanced at the boy. His shirttail was barely tucked in his trousers, and his dark hair hung down over his eyes. "Feel up to facing her?"

"I-wanna-sleep-for-a-week."

Eleanore saw Jordon and rushed to meet him. When she realized that he was almost dragging Martin, she covered her mouth to muffle her anguished cry. Martin was safe. She watched the way Jordon supported the boy and felt an odd sense of pride in how he brought Martin home like an old friend or his own son.

Jordon stopped a few paces from her, hoping she wouldn't smell the whiskey on the boy.

Martin's head wobbled as he struggled to look at Eleanore. "Sorr . . . ree, Miz El'nore."

She stared as he weaved from side to side and attempted to stand tall. Did she smell liquor? She leaned forward and sniffed, then balled her hands into fists as she fought to restrain her rising temper. "I hope you are sorry. I *know* you will be tomorrow."

"Yes, 'um."

Jordon had to admire her control. There'd been a flash

of anger, but she hadn't lashed out at the boy. "It might be best if he spent the night in the barn," he suggested.

She wanted to drag Martin back to the saloon and confront Mr. Anders, but she couldn't lay the blame on him. "That would be best. I'll get a blanket."

After Martin was bedded down on the hay, Jordon walked out to the yard beyond the corral with Eleanore. She glanced back at the barn every few steps. "He's out cold and will be for some time," Jordon said. "Do the others know yet?"

"No. They're in bed."

"Good."

She stopped at the corner post and looked up at Jordon. "Thank you for bringing him back. Did you scold him?"

He stood toe to toe with her. The top two buttons at the neck of her dress were unbuttoned, her slender white throat exposed to him. "It wouldn't have done any good. I doubt he'll even remember how he got back here." She drew her lips in and nodded, apparently resigned to his opinion.

If he hadn't been here, she thought, I would've made a scene and embarrassed Martin in front of half the town. "Do you think he's learned his lesson about spirits?"

"That's hard to say now. If he gets no sympathy, he may."

She watched his gaze slide down from hers and trembled with anticipation. She leaned against the fence post. Her palms were moist, and her heart pounded loud enough to be heard in the silence.

The moment he noticed her tongue moisten her lips, he focused on her mouth and the invitation she mutely sent him. He stuffed his hands in his pants pockets. He wanted to take her in his arms, taste her sweet mouth and make love to her as his body urged him to do. At least it was dark, and his desire for her would go unnoticed. He couldn't make love to her, then leave.

"It's late. You'd better get some rest. There'll be questions about Martin tomorrow." He took her hand and started back to the house.

She said nothing, just walked beside him and wished he weren't holding her clammy hand. What was he thinking? She'd been so sure he was going to kiss her. As they neared the pool of light spilling into the yard from the kitchen, she slipped her hand from his and went in alone.

He veered toward the barn. A moment later, the light was extinguished. He knew she was confused and hurt. So was he. He shed his boots, pants and shirt and stretched out on his bed. When had she become so important to him? He knew he had to leave soon, because he was beginning to wonder why he had to leave.

Eleanore wiped down the last shelf in the pantry. In the last few days, she had cleaned every room in the house, spent extra time preparing dishes one or another especially liked and, in the evenings, sung songs with the children or read to them. She felt driven by some strange force. At the end of each day, there was still an unsettling, restless energy pulsing through her. Worst of all were the sniping remarks that came to mind when Jordon happened to be nearby.

After three days, the house was spotless, the children wordlessly watched her and shook their heads when they thought she wasn't looking, and she only saw Jordon at mealtimes.

The kitchen door opened and closed.

"Miss Eleanore . . . where are you?"

"In here, Walter." She found him peeking at the fresh bread. "That's for supper."

"I know." He waved his hand at the loaf. "Sure smells good."

"Thank you." He looked so serious. She clamped her front teeth down on her tongue for a moment to keep from smiling. When he didn't say anything, she asked, "Do you need something?"

He shrugged.

She eyed him. This wasn't like Walter. He was never at a loss for words. "Don't you want to tell me?"

"I was just wonderin'," he peered up at her, "if I can sleep in the barn tonight."

"I haven't changed my mind, Walter."

"But Martin got to. It's not fair. Patrick an' I'd be real quiet. An we won't bother Mr. Jordon. Honest."

This had to be the fifth time she had gone through this with either Patrick or Walter. Jordon had taken Martin to the creek the morning after his bout with the whiskey. None of the children had learned what happened, and she preferred it that way. "Martin didn't have much fun out there. The answer is still no. Go on, now."

She went back to the pantry. While she was putting the dry goods back on the shelf, she heard the door open and close again. She stood up, arched her back and sighed. Without turning around, she called out, "I'm not changing my mind."

Jordon grinned, the image of the way she looked the other night fresh in his mind. "That's nice to know." He was still smiling when she spun on her heel and saw him.

"Oh. Sorry. I thought you were Patrick." This was the first time he had sought her out since that night. His attention went to the small basket she picked up as if it were fine china.

"Patrick and Walter still hounding you?" Her hair was a little mussed, her cheeks pink, and she glowed with a warmth he hadn't seen the last few days. He liked her much better like that, rather than the schoolmarm look.

"They don't give up easily." She brushed wisps of hair back from her eyes with the back of her hand, feeling rather self-conscious under his scrutiny. "Did you need something?"

Ah, Ellie, I need so much, he thought, but he said, "I saw Dr. Osgerby—"

"Did you hurt your arm again?" She reached for the sling, but he shook his head. "We just talked."

She sighed and nodded. For a moment she'd thought . . . She realized he was watching her. "How is he?" Before he could answer, Amelia ran into the room.

"Miss Eleanore." Amelia skidded to a stop and stared at her. "Beth Anne's trying to climb up onto Ned's back."

"I'll take care of Beth Anne." Jordon met Eleanore's gaze. "We can talk after supper."

Jordon occupied himself until the children were asleep, then found Eleanore in the parlor reading. "It's quiet."

"Now. Sit down. I believe you wanted to finish our conversation." He glanced around uneasily, and her stomach did flip-flops. "Jordon . . ."

"Let's take a short walk." Creases appeared between her brows, and she stiffened. Damn. He hadn't meant to sound so impatient. "It's a bit cooler outside."

"All right." His responding smile appeared strained, his green eyes almost pleading, or was that just her imagination? She set her book aside, took his hand and stood up. "I wish you'd tell me what's happened. You're scaring me."

He released her hand. "I didn't mean to. It's really good news."

His expression softened. She sighed and welcomed the reassurance he offered. The restlessness that had driven her these last days changed to a deep, aching coil of anticipation.

As they left the house and strolled toward the creek, the crickets quieted. He smiled at her, took her hand in his and rubbed his thumb over the back of her hand. "Dr. Osgerby said he and his wife want to take Amelia." He felt her shoulders tense up immediately.

She pulled free of him. "You think Amelia should be placed with Doc?" She started slowly backing away from him.

"I thought you liked him."

"I do. But he must be over sixty!" She gaped at him, stunned. "Amelia's only nine. He may not . . . Well, I thought you were looking for a family, where she'd be more like a daughter than a granddaughter."

"She would be safe, well cared for, and he'll see that she's well educated. It's the best situation I've been able to find." He had known Eleanore would be disappointed. He reached out, wanting to comfort her. "What more can I do?"

She faced him. "Let her stay with me. I *love* her. You must know I'd do anything for her. I thought you . . ." She clenched her jaw. She had never felt so betrayed.

"Eleanore—" He approached her slowly. "Have you forgotten the bank loan? You've asked for help with placing the other children." He paused, close enough to see her pale face, her mouth tight and grim. "We have to do what's best for her."

She raised her chin and challenged his judgment. "Is it in her best interest to remove her from where she's happy?"

He paced the width of the path, crushing the dried leaves on the ground. "Eleanore, you're not being reasonable. I'm responsible for her. This placement has to be the last one or she may never trust anyone again."

She stared at him, almost shaking with anger and disappointment. She drew in a ragged breath. "That's why you can't take her away from me, Jordon. Surely you must see that." She gazed at him, pleading, praying he would understand.

He clenched and unclenched his fists in frustration. "How is she different from Beth Anne? Or Lottie?"

She shrugged and stripped a leaf off a nearby chokecherry bush. "It was something in her eyes . . . almost like she had given up." She glanced over her shoulder at him, then at the leaf twirling between her fingers. "She reminded me . . . Never mind. She's beginning to gain confidence in herself. Do you know she wanted to get a job so she could earn enough to pay for her room and board? That's how badly she wants to stay . . . with us." She meandered to the edge of the creek. As he approached, she listened to the sound of crunching leaves, dreading his response.

Jordon came to stand at Eleanore's back. The hand exposed beyond the sling moved to cradle her arm; his other encircled her waist and drew her back against him. He lowered his head near hers, softly stroking his jaw on her silky hair. "You're right. She does belong with you." He kissed her behind the ear and felt her soften.

A cry of relief shattered the silence. She whirled about within his embrace and wrapped her arms around his waist. "Thank you," she managed to say with a shaky voice against his chest.

He held her quaking body and suffered responses to her he could not restrain. Her unique scent magnified his longing for her, and her soft, pliant body pressed so intimately into his nearly drove him past reason. His hand moved from her arm to her chin and tipped it upward. "Better?"

"Oh, yes." She knew her eyes were brimming with tears, but they were joyous tears. She'd heard his heart pounding in her ear. He wasn't immune to her feelings, but would he leave now that she was keeping Amelia? She stood on tiptoes and kissed him. He was the only man she'd ever been interested in, and she knew this might be her last opportunity to explore the passions he awakened in her.

God help me, I'm not made of stone. She stirred against him as if trying to get closer. He knew she couldn't be aware of the danger she was putting herself into, alone with him, beyond anyone's hearing. He groaned and delved into her sweet mouth. He allowed himself one frustrating, searing kiss.

When his lips left hers swollen and wanting more, she stepped back on weakened legs and took his hand. Never in her life had she been so bold, but feeling this was her last chance to be with him gave her the courage. They strolled to the house, but she passed by it and continued toward the barn, until he pulled her up short.

"We'd better say good night here."

Something, the resonance or warmth of his voice, or the tilt of his head, brought back the first time he'd kissed her. The time he called her . . . "Who is Liza?" If the woman was his sweetheart, she would do as he suggested and try to remember what her life had been like before she met him, when her heart had only been touched by children. She forgot to breathe while she watched his jaw stiffen.

"Why do you ask?" It was his turn to feel the icy fingers of fear.

"The first morning after your fall . . . you kissed me . . . and called her name." She hugged herself with a sudden chill. "Was she your—"

"Sister," he finished for her. "She was my sister."

Eleanore reached up and trailed her fingers along his jaw, her heart pounding. "I'm sorry."

He nodded. "Get some sleep. It's late."

She shook her head and tugged him on. "I started something I want to finish." They were in the barn when she stopped and faced him.

"You don't know what you're doing." He moved to sidestep her, but she put her hands on his shoulders and brushed her lips across his. He groaned and braced his hands on her waist.

"Then show me how." She slid her hands around the back of his neck, lowered his head and covered his lips with hers. He didn't move or kiss her back. With her mouth still pressed to his, she smiled and opened her eyes.

He'd managed to control his response to her bold taunting but only by the thinnest thread. When she stared at him, he saw desire in her luminous eyes. Her look implored him to accept her open invitation.

"Oh, Ellie, are you sure?" He lightly traced the pale column of her throat up to her stubborn chin.

A delicious shiver of wanting spread through her. "Yes," she sighed and kissed the palm of his hand.

He reached around and loosened the knot of hair at the back of her head. "That's better." He lightly massaged the nape of her neck as he feathered kisses over her eyes and temples and drew her lower lip between his.

No one had ever touched her the way he was. She had never thought anyone's lips or mouth particularly exciting, but his were. She clung to him. His fingers played on her neck and his tongue teased her lip. She felt weak and yet hungry for more.

He drew back and steadied her, forcing himself to go slowly. He wanted to make love, not ravish her. "You can change your mind, leave anytime." She had a dreamy look on her face, and her breasts rose with each deep breath.

She met his heated gaze. "I'm where I want to be." She rested her hand over his pounding heart. "Are you?" His smile sent her blood rushing.

He slid her hand from his chest down to the evidence of his desire. Her hand trembled and curved to mold him. He gasped. A moment of that sweet torture was all he could allow, and he pulled her close.

Slowly, they undressed each other, and she lay on his pallet chest to breast, thigh to thigh with him. There was no embarrassment, only a growing sense of need and trust on her part. As he explored the curves of her body, she grew brave and her fingers mapped the hard muscles she'd only imagined caressing until then.

He rolled over onto her, and the heat of his smooth skin mingled with hers. She welcomed his weight, amazed at how well they fit together. His breath cooled her neck, and a new restlessness stirred within her, each move causing its own wave of pleasure.

As he roused her inexperienced passion, a desire, stronger than any she could have imagined, swirled and grew and spread. Her body began to throb with uncontrollable bursts of sensations. As if he might be torn from her, she held onto him, wanting never to let go.

He cradled her head with his hands and joined their bodies together. She stiffened for only an instant, then moved to his rhythm. They were perfect, as if their coupling was meant to be.

He rested his head by hers, her body still pulsing, reluctant to release him. He was shaken. He had wanted to make love to her but hadn't expected to feel so fulfilled, satiated, complete. It was frightening, shocking. He'd been so sure his destiny lay far beyond Nebraska. Now he wasn't. The pleasure of her warm, yielding body jolted him to his core.

As her breathing slowed, she lay exhausted and exhilarated, his weight a pulsing comfort. She kissed his shoulder. "Is it always like that?"

Her voice was deep, soft, caressing, but he wasn't sure how she felt. He nuzzled her neck, then rested his weight on his arms so he could see her eyes. "No. Were you disappointed?"

"Oh, no. It was wonderful. I just never thought . . ." She grinned. "Harriet said there were certain advantages . . . and she was smiling, but how could I know why?"

"I'm glad you didn't." He kissed her and got to his feet. "I'll be right back." Later he'd ponder why the subject had been discussed.

She was too replete to think. He returned with a damp, warm cloth and gently bathed her. It seemed as natural as their lovemaking.

He set the cloth aside, put out the lamp and stretched beside her, too spent to do more than hold her in his embrace.

Sometime later, she awakened, still in the circle of his arms, his body pressed firmly to hers. All of a sudden she wondered how long they had slept. Her eyes snapped open and her gaze darted to the door. There was no light showing through the spaces between the boards. She sighed, knowing she had to leave him, return to her room before any of the children woke up.

She stroked his arm beneath her breasts, but he only murmured and snuggled closer. She whispered, "Jordon . . ." and waited for him to stir. She tried to roll over and face him, but his hand closed around one breast.

He blew on her back. She shivered, and he felt himself grow hard. He traced the curve of her belly downward.

She moaned and rolled over to face him. "I should get back to the house."

"In a little while."

She parted her legs in invitation and smiled as he moved over her. Now she knew what that coiling pressure building inside was and where it would lead. She refused to think. She'd have the rest of her life with only the memory of this night to keep her company.

The second time Eleanore woke up, she was in her own bed. She had never felt so completely at peace. The sunlight gave her room a warm glow. She stretched beneath the sheet and smiled. The sound of footsteps in the hall struck her like a bucket of cold water. The room's too bright. She scrambled off the bed and reached for her wrapper.

Lottie had put water on to heat by the time Eleanore arrived in the kitchen. She smiled. "Thank you, dear." She put on a pot of coffee and started fixing breakfast. She was hungry and cooked accordingly.

Lottie watched a minute, set the table, watched Eleanore a little longer and frowned. "Are you expecting company?"

Eleanore flashed a quick smile and shook her head. "Why would you think so?"

"You're humming and making enough food for two meals."

"It's a lovely morning. I'm hungry. Aren't you?"

"Yes, ma'am."

After Lottie left to get dressed, Eleanore continued cooking and humming. The outside door opened. It was too early for Jordon, but she couldn't resist glancing over. He grinned at her and pushed the door closed. Her heart fluttered and she smiled. "Good morning."

"It definitely is." She hadn't put her hair up, her cheeks were rosy, and her lips were poised for a kiss. He took advantage of the private moment and tenderly pressed his mouth to hers.

She leaned into him, her arms encircled him, her body savored his touch. After a long moment, she drew back before they were discovered by one of the children. "They'll be in any minute to get their plates." She quickly heaped large portions of bacon, eggs and griddle cakes onto a plate and handed it to him.

He sniffed appreciatively at the steam rising from the plate. "You're a mind reader."

"Today, my appetite matches yours." She shrugged and continued dishing food onto the plates.

"I'm not surprised." He heard the children and headed for the dining room.

Amelia, Beth Anne, Patrick and Walter converged on the kitchen. Each picked up a plate and left for the dining room.

"Smells good."

"Oh, boy."

Eleanore chuckled and followed them in to eat. No one else questioned the special meal, but she noticed Amelia and Lottie giving her and Jordon pondering glances. The morning passed as any other, except that Eleanore caught herself humming and smiling at no one in particular.

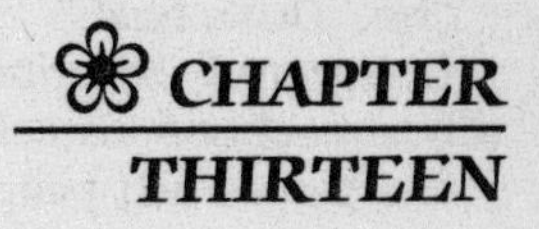

CHAPTER THIRTEEN

It wasn't until after dinner that Eleanore and Jordon had the opportunity to speak privately in the parlor. She stared at him, the wonder of the night before still fresh in her mind. Now she saw concern in his expression.

He watched her hands fidget and her glance slide away from him. "Second thoughts?"

She quickly looked at him. "No. Have you?" She held her breath until the straight line of his mouth softened and he shook his head. She sighed and held her hand out toward the sofa.

He sat down facing her; his knee brushed her skirt. "What's wrong?"

"I . . ." She gazed into his eyes. "I don't know what you expect . . . now. You look worried."

"Just be yourself." He took her hand and traced her thumb with his. "I've been thinking about that bank loan."

"This is the first day I haven't." She really hadn't, and that surprised her.

"I have some money set aside. I'll send for it tomorrow."

"No! You can't." Oh, she didn't like the niggling thoughts trying to form in her mind. "If I can't repay the bank, how could I pay you back? Thank you, but I cannot allow you to do that."

"Why not let me help? The money's just sitting in the bank." He raised her hand and kissed her palm.

"It's my responsibility, not yours."

"Don't be stubborn, Eleanore. Take it—for the children."

"No. That's final."

Exasperated, he gritted his teeth, trying to figure out why she refused his help. "What's gotten into you?"

She gasped and pulled her hand free. "You don't owe me anything for last night."

"What's that supposed to mean?" Damn, he couldn't follow her thoughts. Why would she . . . "You couldn't believe I'm trying to compensate you for last night?"

She glared at him. "You said it."

He drew in a long breath and exhaled slowly. "You can't mean that. A man doesn't make *love* to a soiled dove."

"I wouldn't know about that." She sprang to her feet.

"If you did, you'd know most of them will . . . keep you company for a dollar." He gazed at her, waiting for her to realize the ridiculousness of her suggestion. Her cheeks turned pink, her eyes were the size of dimes, and her mouth opened as if she were about to speak, but no sound came out.

She gulped and stepped over near the piano. That was definitely more information than she wanted or needed. "Why offer to lend me money now? Why didn't you say something last week?" She watched him, heart pounding as she silently pleaded with him to convince her. She reminded herself that last night had been her decision, not his, and she wouldn't allow that memory to be soiled.

He rubbed the palm of his hand down his thigh. "I didn't think you'd accept it then." He gazed at her. "After last night, I hoped you'd understand. I just want to help you." He knew he'd send for the money. Whether or not she rejected it was her decision.

He had never expected her reaction. Embarrassment wouldn't have been unusual, but for her to think he was attempting to *pay* her was a laughable insult. But he wasn't laughing. He stood up. "Think about my offer. If you still think so little of yourself and of me, it would be better for both of us if I left."

She listened to his receding footsteps and heard the back door close before she dropped down on the piano stool. She'd had no choice but to ask that painful question, however that didn't ease the anguish. She glanced around the parlor. It was a homey room, with its books, pictures, wood stove and piano, but she had never felt so lonely as she did at that moment.

During the rest of the afternoon, Eleanore kept thinking about what he'd said. By suppertime, she had come to terms with Jordon's offer. Having settled their disagreement in her own mind, she was anxious to speak to him.

She found him in the corral with Nugget. His back was to her, his movements stiff, not his usual catlike agility, and he didn't look up from what he was doing. He must have heard her approach. She ducked between the rails of the fence. "Is he having trouble?"

"Just checking."

She clasped her hands behind her back and took a deep breath. "I'm sorry, Jordon. When I asked you about the loan, I didn't really think of the implications. I hope you can forgive me." She waited. He didn't move, not even his hand, and she feared she had unthinkingly gone too far.

He finally let go of his horse's leg and faced her. "Apology accepted." He patted Nugget's rump, his gaze fixed on her. "Something else?"

"I hope we can be friends."

She really didn't understand, he realized. "I don't hold grudges. I couldn't believe you thought so little of yourself."

"And I know you were only trying to help me." He leaned forward and kissed her so tenderly she was afraid she'd cry. "Supper's ready. I'd better get back."

Beth Anne gaped with outstretched arms at the black-and-white kitten. "Is it really ours, Mr. Jordon?"

"Yes, ma'am." He placed the kitten in her hands.

"Thank you, oh, thank you." She cradled it against her chest. "Amelia! Come see what we've got."

"Remember, you two have to take care of it, not Miss Eleanore." He was still grinning when Amelia came down the hall.

"What . . ." She couldn't see Beth Anne until Mr. Jordon stepped aside. "Smidgen! What is she doing here?"

"Mr. Jordon gave her to us. She belongs to both of us. Right?" Beth Anne stared up at Jordon.

"That's the deal." He heard a noise and glanced down the hall and saw Eleanore. He hadn't discussed giving the cat to the girls with her. He winked and motioned her forward.

Eleanore stopped by his side and peered over Amelia's shoulder. "Smidgen?"

"Yes. Isn't she sweet?" Beth Anne rubbed her cheek down the kitten's silky back.

"Adorable." Eleanore glanced at Jordon and motioned for him to follow her. She stopped in the kitchen and eyed him, then shook her head. "Do think that was a good idea?"

"They'll care for it, and they both want something to love." He reached out and took her hand.

She watched their joined hands and felt her pulse quicken. "What if we find a home for Beth Anne? That will be hard on both of them." She stroked her thumb across the back of his hand.

"If you spend all day worrying about tomorrow, you may miss what's happening today. It'll work out." He pressed his lips to hers and leaned back. "Trust me?"

"Mm-hm." She heard the girls and tried to free her hand from his. He held on. "Jordon . . ."

He gave her a devilish grin. "What?"

"The girls'll see us."

He shrugged. "I didn't know it was wrong to hold hands."

"Honestly, what's gotten into you?"

Amelia entered the kitchen with Smidgen asleep in the crook of her arm. "Can she sleep with us? We'll be real careful."

"She's so small. I think you'd better make her a little bed with a couple rags from the box." Jordon was right. The girls did need something to love. Eleanore glanced at him. We all do, she realized.

Amelia glanced at Beth Anne. "Would you get the rags? I don't want to wake her up."

The girls had just left to make the cat's bed when Lottie burst into the room.

"Look at this, Miss Eleanore." Lottie held up a pieced-together dress. "Mrs. Peterson said I'm to make this for *me*." She ran her hand down the front of the dress. "Isn't it beautiful?"

Eleanore looked at the cloth, fine muslin the shade of buttery cream. "It certainly is. Did she say why?"

"Just that I need a good dress. She said it was a reward."

"That was very generous of Mrs. Peterson. She must be pleased with your work." Eleanore shared a smile with Jordon. She refused to feel guilty because she couldn't afford to give the children better clothes. "I hope you thanked her properly."

"Oh, I did." Lottie hugged the basted-together dress to her chest, twirled around once and skipped out of the kitchen.

Jordon chuckled. "I've never seen her so happy and acting her age."

"Beth Anne couldn't even charm Lottie out of her self-appointed mother role. She needs to be a child, but she's resisted every attempt I've made."

"She needs a couple older brothers and sisters."

Lottie marched back into the room. "Do you know Beth Anne and Amelia have a cat in our bedroom? Surely you didn't give them permission to keep it."

Eleanore met the girl's frank stare. "I did. They will care for its needs, and I doubt the kitten will bother you."

Jordon cleared his throat. "I gave the cat to the girls. I'm sure they'd be happy to let you play with it." Lottie glanced up at him and backed off, physically and verbally.

"I just thought they had sneaked it in." Lottie clamped her lips together, turned on her heel and left.

Jordon shook his head. "Has she ever had a pet?"

"I'm not sure." Eleanore glanced at the empty doorway. "Sometimes I think she's afraid to care too much for anyone or thing since her father died."

Jordon nodded. "She's not the only one."

The next week proved hectic. More than once Eleanore wanted to throttle Jordon for bringing the kitten home. Walter teased the cat and Beth Anne, and Lottie threatened daily to give "the little beast" away or move out herself.

Eleanore had just found the kitten hiding in a corner of the kitchen. She didn't blame her. Sometimes Eleanore wished for a cool, quiet place where she could escape her worries. There were only nineteen days left until she had to make the payment on the mortgage, and she was no closer to an answer than before. The thought of turning the house over to the bank wasn't as frightening as it had been at first, but that didn't solve her obligation to the children, and she couldn't drag them cross-country with few provisions.

Lord, it was hot and muggy. She dampened a cloth and wiped her forehead, neck and wrists. A cool dinner was already planned and prepared. She looked outside. The children weren't running around; even Toby was stretched out in the shade. It was Saturday, and all of the children were home. She decided they would have a picnic by the creek. After packing what they'd need, she went out to the yard.

The air seemed heavy, still. Odors she took for granted—hay, horse dung, soil as if it were freshly turned—were sharper, and even the flies were lazy. There'd be a change of weather; she felt it even though the sky was clear. She found Amelia, Beth Anne, Patrick and Walter gathered around the elm tree, taking turns on the swing.

"How would you like to have a picnic by the creek?"

The idea was welcomed with listless enthusiasm until Eleanore said they could cool off in the water. She asked them to tell Martin and Lottie and meet at the kitchen door in a few minutes. Jordon met her in the yard. Rivulets of sweat dripped down his neck and dampened his shirt.

"What's the excitement all about?" He wiped his forehead with a kerchief.

She grinned. "Picnic dinner by the creek. It'll be shady, and the children can cool off in the water." She fanned her hand to cool her face.

"Good idea. When do we leave?" Her cheeks were rosy, her eyes sparkled, and her lips were pursed as if for a kiss. He jammed his hands in his pockets to keep from reaching out to her in front of the children.

"Now. All I have to do is get a couple old blankets."

"Miss Eleanore—" Beth Anne stopped just short of bumping into her. "We can take Smidgen with us, can't we?"

"Not this time. She's still little and needs her rest to grow."

Beth Anne pouted and looked to Amelia, who had followed at a slower pace.

Amelia glanced from Beth Anne to Miss Eleanore. "Could she bring Missie?"

Eleanore smiled. "That's a wonderful idea. Do you want to do that, Beth Anne?"

"Oh, good!" Beth Anne ran off with Amelia to get her rag doll.

Jordon returned to the house with Eleanore and helped organize. Everyone pitched in. The adults led the way to a clearing by the creek. The first three buttons at the neck of Eleanore's dress were open, and wisps of hair clung to her cheeks. She looked more like Lottie's older sister than her foster mother.

Lottie spread one blanket out and set a basket down. "Miss Eleanore, do you want me to start serving dinner?"

At the sound of her voice, the other children stopped in their tracks and stared at Eleanore. "I think we can wait awhile." She grinned at them. "Go on. And take your shoes off before you get your feet wet." Patrick and Walter giggled. "Boys, do not push anyone down. If your clothes get wet, you'll have to wear them till they dry."

She shook her head. Those two barely had their shoes off when they ran into the water and plopped down. "So much for discipline."

"On a hot day, what could be better? Wouldn't you like to sink down in a pool of water?" Jordon took one side of the blanket and helped her spread it out.

She nodded. She envisioned the two of them in a secluded pond, the water cool, their bodies— She forced her wandering thoughts to there and then and sat down to watch the children's antics.

Jordon sprawled out on his side, resting his head on the palm of his hand. While she observed the children, he regarded her. She sat with her arms around her bent legs, her chin resting on her knees. He was struck with the idea that she was accustomed to overseeing other people rather than partaking in activities herself.

He rolled to his knees and held out his hand. "Why shouldn't we have some fun, too?"

She glanced around. "Don't be foolish. I'm too old to play in the water."

"Let's see." He picked up her right foot.

"What are you doing?" She struggled, trying to free her foot from his grasp.

"Wouldn't you rather go barefoot?"

She stared at his boots. "How about you?"

"I'd rather remove your shoes than my boots." The heel of her shoe still rested in his hand.

He leered at the hem of her skirt, and she laughed. "I'll take my own off, and you do the same." With a gallant shrug, he gave in and sat back down. She managed to take her shoes off, then her cotton stockings beneath her skirt.

The moment she set the second shoe aside, he pulled her to her feet. "Do you know how to skip pebbles on the water?"

She gazed up at him. "No, but I'll stand in the water while you show me." She hobbled over to the water's edge, each rock and twig poking into the tender soles of her feet.

Jordon continued walking into the water and stopped when he realized she hadn't followed him. "Come on." He held out his hand.

She ignored his hand, raised her skirt with both hands and stepped into the creek. The stones were smooth, and the water actually felt cold, amazingly so.

Her slow, deep sigh sounded inviting, seductive, but he doubted it was intentional. He put his hand on the back of her waist and urged her forward. "We should have done this weeks ago."

Weeks ago it didn't occur to me, she thought. He had made a difference in her life, and she wondered if anyone else would notice. She glanced downstream.

Amelia and Beth Anne had their skirts bunched up at their knees picking something out of the shallow water. Martin, Patrick and Walter were playing leapfrog, getting soaked, and Lottie was sitting on a rock with her feet in the water.

"What about my lesson?"

He reached down and picked out four flat, round stones and handed her three. "You have to keep your wrist loose and toss it like this." The stone hopped twice before sinking. "Now you try it."

She flipped her skirt over her arm, held the flat rock between her thumb and finger and did her best to imitate his throw. The pebble flew in a perfect arc and sank. "It looked easy."

He slipped another rock into place. "A lot of things do." He sent the stone skipping across the surface of the water.

She studied his technique, bent over and sent the last stone flying. It bounced once before it dropped beneath the surface. She forgot about her skirt and raised her arms over her head. "I did it." She didn't even care about her skirt floating on the water.

He laughed and put his arm around her. "You're a good pupil." They waded back to where the children were playing.

"You're a good teacher," she replied without looking at him. She didn't need to see him. She easily imagined the wicked grin that had a way of unsettling her.

It was Walter's turn to be the frog. He made it over Martin and Patrick, landing with a big splash at Jordon and Eleanore's feet. He peered up at them. "Sorry."

Jordon laughed. "Good jump."

Eleanore shook her head. There were times when she felt that the only difference between boys and men was a few years. "Dinner will be ready shortly. You'd better dry off a bit before you can sit on the blankets."

Belatedly, she realized her skirt was dragging in the water. She flashed Jordon a cross between a smirk and a don't-you-say-a-word look and stepped onto the bank. After wringing most of the water from her skirt, she began unpacking the baskets.

Amelia grinned at Beth Anne and went to help. Miss Eleanore always acted so proper. It was nice seeing her having fun with Mr. Jordon.

The food was dished out and the children settled down to eat. Eleanore served herself last and sat down by Jordon. As they ate, the boys calmed down. Amelia and Lottie were quiet, while Beth Anne pretended to feed Missie. Eleanore nibbled at her food, growing uneasy. If asked, she'd have sworn there was a storm coming. The sky above was clear, but there was a breeze now.

Jordon felt the tension in her. "What's wrong?"

"Don't you feel it?"

He sat motionless. "The breeze? Feels good."

The leaves began to rustle, and the creek water was lightly rippled. "The wind's picking up." She glanced around at the children. "If you're finished eating, bring your plates over."

Jordon leaned closer to her. "What are you worried about?"

"A thunderstorm. We'd better get back to the house." She took the plates as they were handed to her and scraped the scraps of food onto her plate.

"We aren't far from the house. If the wind gets worse, we'll have time to get back." He rested his hand over hers. "Are you afraid of storms?"

She shook her head. "It's the air. It feels heavier, not like the usual storm." She gazed at him and finally managed a weak smile. "You don't smell it, do you?"

"Sorry. Why don't we take a walk?"

She thought a moment and agreed. Maybe she just needed to stretch her legs a bit. She spoke to the girls, and Jordon to the boys. Whatever he said to them they appeared to like, and they started scratching pictures in the dirt with twigs.

Jordon met her and they wandered upstream. "What are the boys doing?"

"Drawing pictures. I suggested a raft, something they could weave with vines and float downstream."

She chuckled. "We shouldn't be gone for long. Patrick and Walter may try to send Beth Anne's doll downstream on it."

"I didn't think of that, but I'm sure they will." The brush became thicker, so he veered her away from the creek.

He didn't feel the need to keep talking. He was enjoying

the solitude with her. He realized that he'd grown accustomed to her strength, even relied on it. He chuckled. He'd changed. Her independence was what had riled him most when they met, and now he relied on it, too.

She glanced sideways. He was smiling, so at ease, and that helped calm her, until she noticed her skirt billowing out in front of her. "The wind's getting worse. We better get back."

They turned around, still hand in hand. She stopped in her tracks and stared ahead. "My God . . . look!" The western sky was dark and moving in their direction rapidly. Then they felt the first drops of rain.

"You were right." Jordon stared up at the dark clouds. "That's one hell of a storm. Come on." With each step they took, the wind and rain increased. They charged into the clearing and found the children playing in the same spot.

Martin looked up from the raft he was working on and frowned. "What happened?"

Eleanore gasped for breath, relieved all the children were together. "We have to get back to the house."

Jordon grabbed one basket and handed the other to Martin. Lottie and Walter each took a blanket. Jordon leaned over to Eleanore. "Can you carry Beth Anne?"

"Yes, but—" She stared at the dark sky again, almost entranced.

"Hurry!"

She lead the children, and Jordon took up the rear. She was very grateful that for once, there was no discussion. As if sensing danger, the children silently obeyed. When she dashed to the kitchen door, Toby perked up and ran in with them. She set Beth Anne down and made sure everyone was present.

Jordon dropped the basket on the worktable on his way to the front door. When he turned the doorknob, the wind nearly knocked him down, but he managed to get the door closed and latched.

Eleanore quieted the children's questions and herded them along to the parlor, where she met Jordon. "It's getting worse, isn't it?"

"Yes. That storm's bearing down on us. I don't know if the house'll be safe. Do you have a root cellar?"

"Papa didn't get around to it."

"Do you know of any ditches or trenches near here?"

"I do." Martin stepped around the corner. "Sorry, I overheard. There's a ditch over there, in the field." He pointed at the front window.

Jordon glanced out and saw the funnel. "God Almighty! A tornado!"

Eleanore grabbed for the children. "I've heard stories about twisters tearing houses apart, picking up wagons and uprooting trees. Will we be safe?"

He looked out again. "It's headed straight for us!"

CHAPTER FOURTEEN

Jordon leaned over and spoke near Eleanore's ear. "There isn't time to get rope. I'll carry Beth Anne and hold Amelia's hand. You take Patrick and Walter." He turned to Martin. "You lead the way and hold onto Lottie's hand. Don't run so fast that Amelia and Patrick can't keep up."

Jordon picked up Beth Anne. "Put your arms around my neck and don't let go."

"Okay." Beth Anne did as she was told and snuggled her face near his neck.

He grasped Amelia's hand. Martin and Lottie were at the door, Eleanore with the boys behind them. "All right, let's go!"

As Eleanore stepped outside, she was horrified at the sight of dirt and rubble whirling skyward. Patrick and Walter ran at her side, each with his head down against the gale and covering his mouth with his free hands. Martin appeared to know where he was going. They ran at an angle that would lead to the creek. She couldn't see a ditch, but she'd never explored the field. Martin waved and led them down to a waist-high trench.

As soon as Eleanore reached the ditch, Jordon handed Beth Anne to her. "Keep them down."

She nodded. Her hair came loose from its bun and was carried on the wind behind her like a banner. Jordon moved up the line near where Martin was squatting. "Sit down. Everyone's got to keep down below ground level."

Eleanore crouched down in the muddy ditch, trying to hold onto both girls and the boys, praying they all would be safe. She motioned to Lottie and Martin. They crowded around like a litter of puppies and huddled together. The sky above was as dark as night, and the rain beat down on them. Feeling they were secure for the moment, Eleanore prayed Harriet and her family were in their root cellar.

Jordon ran down the length of the ditch. There was room for each of them to lie down, but he decided they'd feel more assured bunched together, touching. He peered over the edge. All he could see was the upper part of the funnel—moving their way. He returned to the mass of bodies.

Walter was doubled up behind Lottie when Toby pushed his wet nose up to his. "Toby, boy." Walter hugged the dog to him.

Beth Anne squirmed and frantically looked around. "Where's Smidgen? I want Smidgen! Miss Eleanore, we can't leave her in the house!"

Amelia tugged on Beth Anne's arm, pulling her back down. "I'll get her."

"No! You can't go back." The horrendous, thundering wind made it impossible for Eleanore to hear what Beth Anne had said, but Amelia was on the other side. Eleanore changed places with Amelia and tried to scramble out of the ditch without kicking anyone. Just as she swung her leg up, Jordon's hand latched onto her ankle and pulled her back.

He bent over her and yelled, "What'n the hell are you doing!?" She was soaking wet, trembling, and he could little more than hold her a moment.

"The kitten's in the house," she cried.

"It's too late to go back." His lips were nearly on her ear. He just hoped she heard him.

Patrick quickly worked free of the bodies pressing on him, slipped out and started back the way they'd come.

Walter kept Toby at his side when Patrick ran off, then waved his arm. "Mr. Jor-r-rdon!"

The storm was closing in on them. Jordon didn't hear anything but the rain and the gale-force wind. However, he did see the boy motioning to him and quickly scrambled to his side.

Walter put his mouth near Jordon's ear. "Patrick left. Looked like 'e went back ta t'house."

Jordon nodded, leaned over Lottie and Martin's backs to Eleanore and shouted, "I'm going after Patrick."

She grabbed his wrist with both hands. "Where is he?"

Jordon frowned. "Went after the damn cat."

She started to stand up, but he broke free of her grasp and held her down.

"Stay put! I won't be long."

She pressed her lips to his hand and mouthed, "Be careful."

He nodded and moved away. Before leaving the safety of the trench, he stared into the wind. The dark funnel didn't look too wide above the ground, but it reached upward farther than he could estimate. The gale carried him to the house and nearly slammed him into the front wall. The front door was closed, so he figured the boy must have gone around the side.

Eleanore stared after him, praying for their safety. Boards and brush and a wagon wheel flew through the air several yards away. It was worse than a nightmare. She felt Amelia begin to rise and held onto her. "All of you, cover your heads." Eleanore couldn't stop watching for Patrick and Jordon.

At least with her back to the wind she could breath a bit easier. A moment later, a section of fence came out of nowhere and shot into the side of the barn. She thought she saw something move at the side of the house, but there was so much debris being tossed around, she couldn't be sure.

Without warning, shards of glass seemed to pop out and

up; planks, shingles and timber were pulled from the house and carried up into the whirling mass above. The wind was so loud she didn't know if she had screamed or not. Dear Lord, keep him safe, she prayed, he's been through too much to die here. She balled her hands into fists, as if ready to do battle with the terror coursing through her.

Something caused her to look down the street. The twister suddenly veered south of town, then east again, as if following a road. As quickly as the tornado had come, it moved on. Eleanore ducked down and stretched her arms out over the children. "Don't get up yet. It still isn't safe." She inched upward, willing Jordon to show himself.

She stood up. Odds and ends of people's lives littered the ground. The wind and rain lashed at her back. She wanted to run across the field and search for Patrick and Jordon, but she knew it was too soon for the children to leave the protection of the trench. It felt as if she'd been waiting hours to see his face when he finally appeared at the corner of the house.

He ran across the field, stopped where Eleanore stood and sat on his heels. "Patrick's fine." He grinned at Beth Anne and Amelia. "Smidgen's okay."

He met Eleanore's gaze and put his hand on her shoulder. "The house was hit pretty bad. There's glass and wood everywhere. Make sure everyone has shoes on before they leave here." He felt her determination take hold—her back stiffened, and there was resolution in her lovely brown eyes.

She nodded, fear and loss swirling in her mind. She had worried that the bank would take her home. Instead, a tornado had all but destroyed the house her father had worked so hard to build. The wind was easing up. At least she wouldn't have to yell to be heard by the children.

"Do all of you have your shoes on?" She watched each in turn to be sure. "We can go back now, but I want us to stay together until I see what's happened."

Martin glanced around and stepped over to Jordon. "Where's Patrick?"

"Behind the barn with the kitten and horses."

"Are they hurt?"

"No. Just scared." Martin sighed, and Jordon ruffled the boy's hair. Everyone was quiet. They had matured a few years in the last hour.

Eleanore smiled at the children. "Be careful. And don't go into the house." She led the way out of the trench and across the field.

Walking with Martin and Walter, a pace behind Eleanore, Jordon saw the survivor in her, the one who knew what had to be done and did it. The woman who was used to being alone, who didn't need help—or a man. Maybe that was why he felt secure in caring for her. She wasn't a simpering female who'd demand more than he could offer.

The muddy ground was strewn with various objects—an axe handle, a barrel and a butter churn both undamaged, broken chairs, an iron kettle, a harness—so many bits and pieces of other people's lives lying about as if discarded or forgotten. The front door stood open. Eleanore continued on around to the side yard. The back half of the house resembled a framework more than a finished building, and two large branches of the elm tree had been torn off but not the one with the swing. She clamped her jaw shut and surveyed the damage. A loud creaking sound made them all flinch. The barn looked as if it were swaying.

"Patrick!" She left the others behind and ran toward the barn, screaming for him.

"Here, Miss Eleanore." Patrick came around the corner carrying a pillowcase.

His red hair was plastered to his head, but his grin was as bright as ever. As if he had tried to get away from her, she ran over and held him. "Thank goodness. Are you okay?" She stepped back and smiled at him. "I should throttle you for running off like that."

He held up the pillowcase. "I had to find Smidgen. She coulda been smashed or blowed away."

Her smile was replaced with a chiding glare. "So could you."

"Oh, no. Mr. Jordon and me took the horses and hid behind the barn. He's sure strong."

"Yes . . . he is." She put her arm around Patrick and rejoined the others. "Why don't you give Smidgen to Beth Anne?"

Eleanore told the children to wait behind the house and tentatively stepped through the open kitchen doorway. The ceiling and roof were gone; only a few beams remained. The attic no longer existed, and the rain had soaked everything. She gritted her teeth against the tremors threatening to undo her.

It was a consolation that the coffeepot, the dry sink and the table hadn't moved, but the rest lay on the floor or was missing. She stepped over books, papers and clothing on her way to the bedrooms. The girls' and her own room were messy, and the windows were missing, but there was no major damage. The parlor was the same, except her father's upholstered chair was now backed against the sofa and faced the open door. She closed the door and gazed unseeingly at the room.

"Eleanore?"

She spun around and saw Jordon watching her. His clothes were muddy, his dark hair carelessly brushed back from his face, and there were deep lines between his brows. She glanced around. "It's such a mess . . ."

He eased his arm around her waist and kissed her temple. "I'll help you clean up. At least two of the bedrooms are livable."

She stared at the children's drawings, untouched by the wind or rain. "Is the barn still standing?"

"So far."

"You'd better get your things out and put them in here." She stepped away from his side and pushed the chair back around where it had been before the storm. "I'd better get the children." She dashed past Jordon on her way out.

He followed at a slower pace. Everyone reacted to disaster differently. He'd seen it during the war. She wasn't hysterical; she just needed to keep busy until she calmed down.

She found the children huddled in the driest section of the kitchen. "Lottie, Amelia, I want you to collect all the dry bedding you can find and put it in the parlor. Beth Anne, take Smidgen to your room and quiet her down. Martin, see if you can find a couple boards and nail them over the window in the girls' room." She wiped her brow, trying to focus her thoughts.

"Walter, Patrick, I'm afraid the wind blew everything from your room. Please look through the mess in back and see if you can find anything that was in your room—bedding, books, clothes . . ." She shrugged. "Do what you can."

Jordon observed Eleanore while he worked alongside the children the rest of the afternoon. The storm moved on, and the sun had never been so appreciated. By the time the supper dishes had been put away, she still hadn't slowed down and he was beginning to worry about her.

Eleanore stooped down between Patrick and Walter. "What have you got there?"

Patrick held up a knife. "I found it in back. Can I keep it?"

She pretended to ponder the problem. "Did you find all of your things? Your whistle?" She saw Jordon walk away and actually felt a whisper of relief from his careful scrutiny.

Patrick stared at the knife. "Nah."

"If someone found your whistle, wouldn't you want him to give it back to you?"

"Course I would." Patrick glanced at Walter, who nodded as if in agreement.

She gave him a think-about-it look.

He frowned and hemmed and hawed a bit, then shrugged. "But who do I give it to?"

"Leave it on the table for now. Tomorrow we'll have to sift through the things that were left here. If everyone in town works together, we may find some of our belongings." She ruffled his hair and went over to Amelia and Beth Anne.

Amelia held up the cloth Beth Anne was working on. "This is her sampler. Aren't her stitches nice?"

Eleanore looked at the sampler. "Very good." She noticed Martin sitting at the piano staring at the keys and went over to him. "Why not try playing it?"

"Oh!" Martin glanced up and shrugged. "I don't know how to play. I was just sitting here."

"That's all right." Eleanore wiped a spot off the side of the piano with her skirt. "I'm grateful you knew about that trench."

He pressed one of the black keys.

"It's been a long day, hasn't it?"

He dragged his first finger across several ivory keys. "I've never seen anything like it."

"Me either. Maybe once in a while we need to remember how fortunate we are."

"I've been thinking about that, too."

"At least we're all safe. That's important to remember. Maybe tomorrow we'll find more of our things." His woebegone smile nearly brought tears to her eyes, but she'd vowed not to weep. It would serve no purpose.

"Yeah. Maybe we'll wake up tomorrow and the house will be whole again."

"I don't think so, but more than likely we'll find a lot of things that belong to others." She glanced around and wondered why Lottie had been gone so long. She started for the kitchen but met Jordon in the hall. He signaled for her to be quiet and pointed at the girls' room.

Eleanore peeked in and saw Lottie smiling at Smidgen

while the cat lapped at a saucer of milk. Eleanore clamped her lips together as she fought back the tears. Then she felt Jordon's hand take hers, and she went to the kitchen with him.

"I watched her leave here carrying something." He shrugged. "I didn't guess it was milk for the kitten."

"She's beginning to learn what it's like to be a girl." Eleanore grinned at him. "That's why I love the children so." She slipped her hand from his and stared up at the clear night sky.

"You're good with them . . . for them." He joined her and put his arm across her shoulders. "Lumber's going to be scarce for a while."

Suddenly, she felt her energy fade. She turned and embraced him, drinking in his presence, his strength, the comfort he offered. The heat of his body stirred memories and a response from her that she'd been evading since the storm. She raised her mouth to his.

He kissed her forehead, stepped back and avoided her questioning gaze. "Shouldn't we get back to the parlor before someone comes looking for us?" He'd waited all evening to hold her in arms, then when he did, he suddenly felt wary. It didn't make sense, but he'd learned long ago to follow his instincts.

He was right, of course. For a moment she'd allowed his comforting her to kindle her newly discovered desire for him. Fortunately he hadn't. "It is getting late."

She followed him as far as the girls' room and went in to see Lottie. She was smiling and petting the kitten.

Lottie glanced up and pulled her hand back from the cat.

Eleanore knelt down and ran her finger along the kitten's back. "She's cute, isn't she?"

"Mm-hm."

"It's been quite a long day. Do you want to sleep in your bed or in the parlor with the others?"

"Aren't Amelia and Beth Anne going to bed in here?"

"Beth Anne wants to stay out there."

Lottie stared at the little black cat. "Smidgen might be afraid. I'll stay here."

"All right." Eleanore leaned forward and kissed Lottie. "Good night. If you change your mind, bring your blanket and pillow out and sleep with us."

Lottie smiled. "We'll be fine. Night, Miss Eleanore."

Feeling more uncertain than ever, Eleanore went to her room for her bedding. She had promised to sleep in the parlor with the others and hoped there wouldn't be any nightmares to deal with. She was tired to the bone and didn't want to think about Jordon, or anything else for that matter.

She placed her pallet so Beth Anne was between Amelia and herself. Martin, Walter and Patrick were stretched out together. Jordon spread his bedding at the end of hers. She leaned over and whispered, "You'd have more privacy in the dining room." He was so close. What if she moved about in her sleep? What if he did? What if . . . ?

He muttered softly, "I'll be fine right here, Eleanore. G'night."

Nestled together, the children had slept soundly through the night. After breakfast, Eleanore organized their activities. "Today we'll sift through the things left by the storm and set them—neatly—in front of the house."

"*Everything?*" Walter scowled. "Even the rubbish?"

Eleanore eyed him. "No. That will be piled up in the back and burned."

"Oh, no!" Walter looked around in panic.

Patrick jabbed Walter in the side with his elbow. "What's wrong now?"

"Our money! All our money's gone!" Walter raced out with Patrick on his heels.

Eleanore glanced at the rest of the children. "All right, let's get started." She went out to help Patrick and Walter.

It was so unfair for them to lose the wages they'd worked so hard for.

Jordon threw himself into the project. He helped Martin clear the front yard, then went around back to help search through the clutter. As if by consent, he and Eleanore spoke to each other only in brief exchanges, but he watched her. She directed the children and settled differences with a firm but just hand. She frequently laughed and smiled, and he feared she had worked herself into his heart.

The following two days were spent as the first. The fourth morning Eleanore saw Jordon assess the skeletal back wall. He appeared to be deep in thought. She gazed at him for a moment—the way he drew his brows together in concentration, the firm line of his jaw, the pleasing sight of him totally unaware of her. She stepped closer. "Why are you taking measurements?"

He glanced over and smiled at her. "Trying to figure what the repairs would cost."

"I couldn't possibly afford to rebuild."

"You can't leave the house open. You'll freeze this winter." She didn't look upset or worried, and that concerned him. "What will you do? The barn's not safe. I could brace it up temporarily, but it should be leveled."

She stared at the barn. "How would you brace it?"

"Nail boards at the corners, maybe a few in the rafters. But another strong wind could blow it over. I'd feel better if it were torn down."

"You're right." She glanced at his sling. "How's your arm? You aren't using it, are you?"

She met his gaze, and the raw emotion she felt made her tremble. She wanted to take three paces forward and put her arms around him, press her lips to his, feel his warm strength, but she sensed that he was as reluctant as she was to take that first step. Of course, she realized, he'd be leaving soon. She took a deep breath to slow her pulse and moistened her dry lips.

His attention focused on the tip of her tongue as it darted between her lips. He could almost taste her. He was about to step forward when something wet brushed over the back of his hand and he looked down. "Toby." He kneeled down and rubbed the dog's neck, grateful for the intrusion but frustrated.

He suddenly recalled her question and glanced up at her. "Not very much. Besides, it's almost healed." Strong enough to put around you, he thought.

She bent over and petted the dog. "Thank you for helping clean up the mess the storm dumped." Their hands brushed and stilled. She buried her fingers in Toby's thick fur, then stood up. "I'd better get back to work."

He took her hand and rose at the same time. He didn't want her to leave and didn't know how to say what he was feeling. "I'll see you later."

She nodded and walked away, smiling to herself.

After dinner, Martin went to help Mr. Anders, Lottie to Mrs. Peterson's, while Amelia, Beth Anne, Patrick and Walter went in search of some of the boys' missing clothes. Eleanore took the opportunity to call on Harriet. She paused a few feet away before approaching her door. The neat fence that had marked the front yard was gone, but the front of the house appeared the same. Fortunately, Harriet did, too.

"Eleanore, I have been so worried about you, but there has been so much to do." Harriet led the way to the kitchen.

"This was the first I was able to leave." Eleanore glanced around at the empty window frames. "Did all of you get to the root cellar?"

"Yes. Mr. Blake saw it in time for all of us to get down there safely. I wanted you to join us, but he said there was no time."

Eleanore smiled and linked hands with Harriet for a moment. After explaining how they had survived the twister and the damage to the house, Eleanore glanced outside. "Did the storm leave any clothes or tools in your yard?"

"It still is a real mess."

"I had the children put everything in the front yard. If others do the same, then we may be able to find some of our own goods. What do you think?"

"Oh, yes. That is a wonderful idea." Harriet went over to the window. "Have you talked to anyone else about it?"

"You're the first."

Harriet smoothed back her hair. "Together we can speak to everyone here in town. I will get Henry and be right with you."

Eleanore sipped on a glass of water and watched the children through the kitchen window. Evidently Harriet had told the children to move the mound of things left by the storm to the front. A few minutes later, she returned to the kitchen with Henry on her hip.

Eleanore set her glass down and left the house with Harriet. "I'll go by the barbershop, saloon and livery."

"That leaves me Mrs. Renton, Mrs. Peterson and the general store."

"I'll meet you at the store."

Eleanore walked across the road. She spoke with the barber, and Mr. Anders at the saloon, then stopped at the livery. The front of the building looked the same. However, when she entered, she saw that the back wall was gone. Mr. Tucker rushed up to her. "How are you faring, Mr. Tucker?"

"Miss Merrill." Mr. Tucker shook his head. "I can't 'member seein' such a jumble of things. Least my horses're still here."

"That's a blessing." She glanced around. "Mrs. Blake and I are asking everyone to place the things left by the storm near the road so people might find their belongings. Would you help us, Mr. Tucker?"

"Sure 'nough. I know the missus'll like the idea." He

scratched his head. "Do you think Walter could help us out? When he ain't foolin' round, he's a real help."

She smiled and nodded. "I'll tell him as soon as I return home. Will you rebuild?"

"Just don't know yet. Heard some folks talkin' 'bout leavin'."

"I understand. It is a difficult decision. Take care, Mr. Tucker."

She left wondering how the town would survive without a livery and arrived at the general store before Harriet. She stopped at the post office counter. "Hello, Mrs. Gunther. Is there any mail for me today?"

"I think there is." Mrs. Gunther checked. "I hope the children weren't injured during the storm." She handed Eleanore one letter.

"They're doing well. The store appears to have weathered the storm, too." Eleanore glanced at the back of the envelope and saw Charles Brice's name.

"We were lucky. We've had a lot of folks in asking for window glass and had to order most of it." Mrs. Gunther shook her head. "A few'll have to rebuild. That sure was a bad twister."

"Indeed it was. Mrs. Blake and I are asking everyone to set anything left on their property out front so people can find what they've lost."

Harriet rushed in and nodded at Mrs. Gunther.

"Hello, Mrs. Blake. I was just about to tell Miss Merrill that I think putting misplaced items out front is a sensible idea. We'll spread the word, too."

CHAPTER FIFTEEN

Eleanore sat down on the front step of her house to read the letter before going inside. As she read, she smiled. Mr. Brice was only inquiring about Amelia. Eleanore looked for her and found her out back.

"Amelia, this came to me, but I thought you might like to read it." Eleanore hoped Amelia would realize people did care about her, but it was something she had to figure out for herself.

After handing the letter to Amelia, Eleanore studied the slightly slanted barn. It was a danger. The problem was that she couldn't imagine how to tear it down without damaging the corral or possibly Mr. Kirton's house, though that wasn't all that close.

"Miss Eleanore—" Amelia handed the paper back to her. "Do you want me to write him?"

"Only if you want to. I'll send a reply and would be happy to enclose yours. It's up to you." Eleanore saw Walter and caught up with him. "Mr. Tucker would like you to help him out. The livery was hit hard."

Walter ran a few steps and stopped. "Were the horses hurt?"

"No. They're all right. Don't forget to tell Mr. Tucker you have to be home for supper."

"I'll tell him." Walter took off running across the field.

Eleanore met Jordon on the way back to the house and paused. "Were you looking for me?"

"Yep." He gave her a lopsided grin. "Where's Walter off to like a house afire?"

She continued on at a brisk pace. "To help Mr. Tucker." His sunny disposition was a comfort, his smirk infectious. "Why did you need me?"

He stopped and stared after her, sure she didn't hear how that sounded to him. He ran to catch up. "I've been thinking about the barn. If I help some of the others around town, they'll probably help me level the barn. What do you think?"

She slowed down and smiled at him. "I'm sure they would appreciate an extra hand, and one is all you have to offer."

He grinned. "Good." He stopped and put his hand on her shoulder. "I'll get started now." He impulsively kissed her and then started across the field toward town, feeling better than he had in days.

Amelia finished the note to Mr. Brice and handed it to Miss Eleanore before meeting Beth Anne outside. "Why don't we go around and see if we can find some of the boys' clothes? Maybe Patrick would like to go with us."

"Okay. I'll tell Smidgen we're going." Amelia ran off.

Amelia found Patrick out back collecting boards. "Hi."

"Hi."

"What do you want with those?"

Patrick shrugged. "Something."

"Beth Anne and I are going to look for some of the things from your room. Want to go with us?" Amelia watched him kick at the pile of rubble.

"Yeah. You wouldn't even know what you're lookin' for."

"Come on." Amelia returned to the house with Patrick, wondering why boys were so crabby.

Beth Anne joined them in the yard. "Miss Eleanore said we can go."

"Are you two gonna stand here all day?" Patrick walked ahead, muttering, "Girls."

The house was so quiet with all the children gone. Eleanore wrote to Mr. Brice, telling him the changes she had noticed in Amelia and assuring him that she seemed happy and was adjusting very well. After adding Amelia's note, Eleanore addressed the letter and set it aside.

The sleeping arrangements bothered her. The parlor should be a gathering place, not a bedroom. The only time she remembered sharing a room since she was ten years old was one night when her father was sick. If she put the boys in with the girls, no one would get any sleep. The only answer was to move the girls in with her and the boys into the girls' room. And, like it or not, Jordon's bed would be in the dining room unless he wanted to sleep outside.

By the time Amelia, Beth Anne and Patrick returned, Eleanore had moved Smidgen and the two pine beds to her room and the boys' bedding to the girls' room. She found the three children in the parlor. "How did you do?"

Patrick held up two shirts and a wooden wagon. "One's Martin's and these are mine."

"Good. What is all this?" Eleanore pointed to the small mound of odds and ends.

Beth Anne giggled.

Amelia glanced sideways at Patrick before answering. "He said some of this might belong to Martin or Walter. Most of this was in the field on the other side of the saloon."

"I see. Patrick, do these things really look familiar?"

"I know I've seen these." He held up a pair of trousers, then a belt. "Doesn't this look like Walter's?"

Eleanore noticed his freckles become more prominent. "Yes, it does. But he only has one, and I believe he's wearing it."

Amelia frowned at Patrick. "We'll take them back if

they don't belong here," She glared at him. "Won't we, Patrick?"

"Yeah, right after supper."

Eleanore put her arm around his shoulders. "If these things aren't Martin's or Walter's, you can put them out front so they'll be found."

He smiled up at her and nodded.

"Go wash up. We'll have supper as soon as the others return." Eleanore gave his shoulder a reassuring pat before he dashed off.

"Did he fib, Miss Eleanore?"

"No, Beth Anne. He was trying to help. Go wash your hands now. The table needs to be set."

Amelia glanced around. "What happened to the boys' bedding?"

"You girls will be sleeping with me, and the boys will have your room."

"Where's Mr. Jordon's bedroll? He didn't leave, did he?"

"No. He wouldn't leave without saying good-bye to you. His things are in the dining room."

Amelia grinned. "He'll be the first one in to breakfast."

Eleanore laughed. "You're right. I hadn't thought of that."

Amelia started to leave and turned back. "Where's Smidgen?"

"She was asleep on your bed." Amelia dashed down the hall to see the cat.

In the next half hour, Lottie, Martin and Walter came home followed by Jordon. After Eleanore explained the change in sleeping arrangements two more times, the children accepted it.

Jordon didn't object, only shook his head. After all, when Eleanore made up her mind, there was little he could do to alter it, especially with the children there.

"You couldn't sleep in the parlor indefinitely. At least you'll have some privacy."

Her voice was low, suggestive, and she had a soft, hold-me look about her that made him want to do just that. As luck would have it, Toby darted between them, with Martin closing in on the dog. The moment passed, and Jordon saw the change in her.

"I'll serve supper."

"Wait. I have a message for you. I was talking to Tucker, at the livery. He and his wife have been thinking about taking Walter in. Said he'd like to see you in the morning, if that's all right with you." He noticed a momentary flicker of surprise, and he thought her eyes were filling with tears. As if he'd imagined those signs of dread, they were gone. She kept her feelings well hidden.

"Does Walter know?" She had to be happy for the boy. This was what she'd been hoping for for each of the children, wasn't it?

"Tucker talked to me, but I don't think he said anything to Walter. They appear to get on well."

"Walter likes helping him out. I won't say anything to him until I speak with the Tuckers."

With Amelia and Lottie's help, Eleanore soon had the meal on the table. She'd been hungry earlier, but now she only picked at her food. The conversations between the children sparked her interest, but when she glanced up, Jordon was watching her with what seemed like, or maybe she only hoped was, tender concern.

As much as she wanted to believe she didn't need him, she enjoyed his quiet presence, his heartening strength, a shared gaze. She smiled and finished eating. The dishes were washed, put away and the commonplace chores completed without any squabbling.

Jordon gathered everyone in the parlor. "It's almost bedtime, but I bet I could talk Miss Eleanore into a story, if you're interested."

Beth Anne grinned sleepily. "Tell one about a prince." Just then the kitten came into the room meowing. Patrick reached for it, but Beth Anne picked Smidgen up first.

Walter made a face. "No. That's dumb. Tell one about Indians."

Jordon chuckled. "This is going to be a 'round' story. I'll start it, and each of you will add part of it." He eyed Eleanore. "You can tell the end."

Eleanore pulled Beth Anne, who was holding the kitten, onto her lap and whispered, "The prince will ride away with the pretty princess."

Jordon turned the two lamps down, settled back in the armchair and glanced around at the expectant faces of the children, all except Beth Anne. She and Smidgen were half-asleep in Eleanore's arms. He started the story.

"Once a very long time ago there were six children, three boys and three girls. They were taking a long journey across the country—"

Walter interrupted. "What country?"

"Hmm." Jordon raised one brow. "You tell me."

"England."

"No. Mexico."

"Why not this country?" Eleanore gently rocked Beth Anne.

"Yeah. They're goin' to Californy." Walter grinned at Patrick and they laughed.

"All right," Jordon continued, "the children were going to California. Each rode a fine chestnut horse. They—"

Walter puckered his brows. "They were all alone?"

Jordon nodded. "Why don't you tell us what happens next?"

"Okay." Walter thought a moment. "The boys had rifles . . . 'n' shovels. They were goin' to find all that gold in Californy. One night they were camped by a river . . . and a bear came after their food." He stood up and postured like the animal. "He scared the girls, but the boys grabbed their guns and shot him dead!" He dropped back down next to Patrick, grinning.

"Very good." Jordon glanced around. "Lottie, what happened next?"

Lottie looked sideways at Amelia then sat up. "The girls were only pretending to be frightened because they wanted the boys to feel brave. The girls skinned the bear, tanned the hide and smoked the meat. There was enough to last for most of the journey."

"They were clever. Patrick, what happens next?"

"There was so much meat they couldn't carry all of it" —Patrick paused to make a face at Lottie— "and the wolves ate what they left behind. They were chased by wild Indians, but the boys shot them and saved the girls and they cried and the boys couldn't make them stop, so the boys told them to stop or they'd give 'em to the Indians. The girls went to bed." He elbowed Walter, and they both rolled over laughing.

Jordon cleared his throat and met Eleanore's gaze. It wasn't easy to still the laughter, but he managed. "Amelia, it's your turn."

Beth Anne was asleep, but Amelia noticed Lottie and was surprised by her silent encouragement. "During the night, the Indians stole the bear meat. The next morning the boys were mad because they hadn't heard the Indians. The girls found berries and dandelion greens to eat. They took some of the food with them and rode all day. They followed a river, sure they would come to a town, but the river curved south, so they had to cross it. The girls started a fire, and all of them fished until dark. The girls fried the fish for supper, and the boys weren't mad anymore." Amelia looked to Lottie and smiled shyly.

Jordon leaned forward. "This is getting interesting. Martin."

Martin cleared his throat. "They rode hard for the next few weeks. The boys snared some rabbits and caught fish when they were near streams. Finally, they arrived at a gold camp. But it wasn't what they had expected. Some of the people looked hungry, and some of the men weren't very friendly. They went higher up into the hills and found a bend in the stream where there weren't any other miners.

The boys found a gold nugget and the girls began looking in the water, too. That night they hid their gold so no one could steal it."

"Ah, will they strike it rich?" Jordon peered around at their anxious faces. He smiled at Eleanore and gave her a nod.

She spoke with a hushed voice. "The children worked very hard and soon learned that it wasn't as easy as they had thought it would be to find the gold. And they weren't all that sure that their hidden treasure was gold. They woke up one morning and saw a dusting of snow on the ground. They were living outside and knew they had to leave. Each child put an equal share of the gold in their saddle pack before they left. After two hard, long days on the trail, they came to a town and located the assayer's office."

Eleanore shook her head. "The children were told they'd only found a few small nuggets of gold. Most of the shiny pebbles were fool's gold. They were very disappointed. Their nuggets were worth more money than they had ever seen, but it wasn't the fortune they had hoped for. That night they all shared a room in a boardinghouse. After talking most of the evening, they realized that the gold wouldn't get them what they wanted. Each of them wanted to feel safe, cared for, part of a family, but in a way, they were a family. They set out together, a little older, a lot wiser, and soon found a farmer who was happy to take them in to help him work the land." She leaned down to Beth Anne and whispered, "They were very happy."

Jordon added, "And very sleepy." He got up and lifted Beth Anne from Eleanore's lap. "I'll carry her in to bed for you."

The children left quietly, and Eleanore kissed each one good night. She returned to the parlor and found Jordon sitting on the sofa. She felt anticipation surge through her in spite of common sense.

He held out his hand. "I'm glad you didn't go to bed.

Are the children asleep?" She sat down by him, and he casually draped his arm across her shoulders.

She smiled and yawned. "Almost. You look tired, too. I wanted to give the girls a chance to get to sleep before I go in. You don't have to wait up with me."

"No, but I like your company." He pulled a couple pins from her hair and watched it cascade down her back. He couldn't resist combing his fingers through the rich, silky strands.

She almost purred. The simple act of letting her hair down was so arousing, when he did it. She rested her head against his chest and listened to the pounding of his heart. She closed her eyes and snuggled up to him, as if she did it every night, too tired to think about the difference between needing and wanting.

Lowering his arm, he tipped her face up and covered her lips with his. She responded to his gentle probing, and her soft murmuring sparked a desire he'd fought to control. He broke the kiss and rested his lips on her temple for a moment. "Are you sure about this? You know where it will surely lead?"

"Mm-hm. Very sure." She rolled onto his lap and put her arms around his neck before she began nibbling on his neck. She had never felt so free to express herself as with him.

"What if one of the children comes looking for you?"

She grinned and rested her cheek on his shoulder. "I had each of them make a trip outside before they went to bed."

He chuckled. "So you planned this. What would you have done if I'd gone to bed?"

She sat up and glared at him. "I did not plan this. I thought you had."

"Nope. I was just waiting to say good night." He kissed the tip of her nose. "You made it plain enough to me the last few days that you . . . had changed your mind." He felt her tense up, then soften.

"I guess I did." She sank back down onto him. "I never

wanted you to feel obligated to me, but I wasn't sure what I wanted either."

"Are you certain now?" His breathing slowed and he sat perfectly still. He couldn't promise her marriage and had no right to ask. All the same, he waited, hoping she wouldn't turn away from him again, though he had been guilty of that himself.

She snuggled into the curve of his healing arm and unbuttoned his shirt. She kissed his chest and breathed in his musky scent. Her fingers drifted through the dark curly hair covering his chest and felt his nipples harden at her touch. She traced the growth of hair down to the waistband of his trousers and loosened those buttons also.

He gently held her roaming hand at bay. "Now it's my turn." Before his lips found hers, her mouth opened for him. Slowly, with measured patience, he opened her dress and skimmed his knuckles across her creamy skin while his kiss deepened. Her breathing became harsh, but he was as relentless in his attack on her senses as she had been with hers on his.

Her dress fell away and she removed his trousers. She wanted to feel him without any barriers and soon savored the weight of his body covering hers. She clung to him as they moved together and that delicious burst of sensation mounted and overflowed in intense waves.

He rested his head by hers, still reeling from their heated union. No woman had ever filled his senses, become part of him, the way she did. He'd thought the second time would be less intense. It wasn't. If anything, her effect on him had increased. He felt her move and started to get up.

"No, don't move, please." Dear Lord, she wouldn't have believed she was capable of repeating their lovemaking so soon. But the weight of him felt so very good.

At breakfast the next morning, Amelia noticed that Miss Eleanore and Mr. Jordon were both happy and smiling, and she crossed her fingers that they liked each other enough to marry. Amelia felt a little guilty, but if they would be happy, she hoped it wasn't too wrong to want them to be her mama and papa.

Beth Anne dried the spoons and put them away. "Can we play with Smidgen now?"

Amelia put the glasses in the cupboard. "I'd better ask Miss Eleanore if she wants us to do anything else." She hung up the towel and found Miss Eleanore in the parlor. "Can we do anything else to help?"

Eleanore looked at Amelia. "You've cleaned the bedrooms, the kitchen, fed the chickens and gathered the eggs." She smiled. "There's nothing left to be done. Go outside for a while."

"Beth Anne wants to play with the kitten. Can we take her out?"

"Of course. She'll have fun chasing bugs."

Eleanore looked around the parlor. Jordon had told her that Mr. and Mrs. Tucker would come by this morning, and Eleanore didn't want the room to be a shambles. She usually went to the prospective family's home. In this case, she knew them. Mr. Tucker was a good, hardworking man, and his wife was a good woman. A knock on the door sounded like a gunshot. She quickly recovered and answered the door.

"Miss Merrill. Mr. Stone said you were expecting us." Mr. Tucker nodded at his wife.

"Please, come in." Eleanore showed them into the parlor and offered them refreshments. Once the amenities were over, she asked them if they had told Walter they wanted to adopt him.

Mrs. Tucker glanced at her husband. "We thought we should talk to you first. Walter's such a lively boy. Our Tom Junior would have been about his age. I sure like having Walter around. Mr. Tucker does, too, don't you?"

Mr. Tucker nodded. "He's a good boy. Likes to play around a bit, but most boys his age do."

"Do you know he has a dog?"

Mr. Tucker smiled. "Sure do. That boy talks about Toby half the time."

Eleanore grinned. "Are you still thinking about moving away?"

They looked at each other. Mr. Tucker answered. "We'll be leaving next week. That's why we thought it might be easier for the boy if he moved in with us now, to see if it'll work out."

"I think that is a wonderful idea. I'll talk to Walter after dinner." Eleanore smiled at Mrs. Tucker. "You will see that he goes to school?"

"Oh, yes, ma'am. That he will." Mr. Tucker stood up, then Mrs. Tucker. "Thank you, Miss Merrill. We'll do right by the boy."

"I'm sure you will."

After the Tuckers left, Eleanore went through Walter's clothes to be certain all tears were mended. She kept her hands busy while telling herself he deserved a good family, but that didn't lessen her sadness and feeling of loss. She went through that each time she kissed a child good-bye.

By the time everyone returned for dinner, she'd managed a smile, of sorts, and served the meal. Walter and Patrick joked and laughed, Beth Anne told everyone how Smidgen had hopped like a bunny through the grass, while Martin, Lottie and Amelia were relatively quiet. Finally, the meal ended.

As Walter picked up his plate to take it to the kitchen, Eleanore spoke up. "Walter, please meet me in the parlor."

He glanced at Patrick, shrugged and said, "Yes, ma'am."

Walter was fidgeting with the end of his belt when Eleanore entered the parlor. "I didn't ask you in here because you're in trouble."

He sighed.

"Please sit down." She sat on the sofa, Walter on the

edge of the armchair. "Do you like working with Mr. Tucker?"

He cocked his head as if figuring something out. "Yeah. Doesn't he want me to work there anymore?"

"He likes your work. In fact, he and his wife like you so much they want to adopt you." She gave him a moment to understand. "Would you like that?"

"Really?" His voice was soft.

"Yes. Has Mr. Tucker said anything to you about their moving?" Walter looked genuinely surprised and happy.

He shook his head. "He did say it wasn't worth re-building . . . I didn't figure . . ."

"They would like you to move in with them today. They won't be leaving until next week, so you can still come over to see us, if you want to."

"Well . . ." He frowned, his gazed darting around the room.

"You may think about it if you wish. It is an important decision."

"Yeah . . . but . . ." He swiped at his nose with the back of his hand. "I don't want you to feel bad." He sniffed and stared at his shoes.

Eleanore moved closer to him. "I want you to be happy. I didn't take you or the others in to live with me until you were grown. My job is to find good homes for all of you."

He grinned. "Mr. Tucker's got horses. I bet he'd let me ride sometimes, if I'm good."

"He just might."

He bounced to his feet and threw his arms around her. "Thank you, Miss Eleanore."

"I'm happy for you, Walter." She clamped her teeth down on her lip to keep from crying. I am happy for him, she thought, I really am.

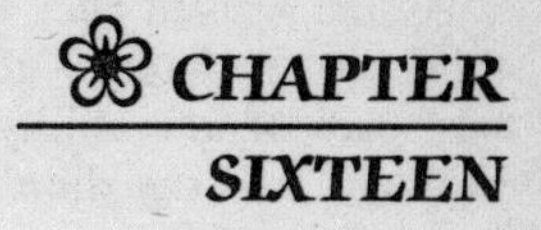

CHAPTER SIXTEEN

After supper, Patrick followed Eleanore into the kitchen. "Can I go see Walter? It isn't dark yet."

She set her dishes on the worktable and dropped down to his eye level. "You miss him, don't you?"

"Mm-hm. Martin's always busy and the girls do dumb things."

She took the plate he was holding and set it on the table. "I think Amelia and Beth Anne might enjoy some of the things you do. And you like Smidgen."

"Yeah, but *when* can I see Walter?" His puckered mouth trembled.

"Tomorrow you can ask Mr. Tucker." She put her arms around him a moment.

"Okay, Miss Eleanore." He smiled. "Tomorrow." He dashed outside.

She shook her head. It would take both the boys time to adjust. She scraped the plates into the pail and realized that Toby wouldn't be there to eat them. The most painful part was that this was just the beginning. Each of the children would be leaving. She nearly dropped the plate in her rush to get outside.

She ran straight to the creek and dropped down to her knees crying. Mrs. Moran had once told her that the Lord never gave a person more than he could bear. If that was true, Eleanore thought, then she was meant to go on. Maybe there were other children who needed her help. She moved over to the creek and splashed cool water on her face before drying it with her skirt.

As she walked back to the house, she forced herself to think of the future—no responsibilities, only herself to take care of, the ability to do anything she wanted. The problem was she didn't know what she wanted, except for Amelia. Eleanore vowed she would keep her. Beth Anne and Patrick were adaptable, would thrive anywhere they were loved. Lottie and Martin would do well given responsibility. But Amelia, she needed a special understanding love to overcome her past, and Eleanore was determined to be the one to shower her with it.

Jordon followed Eleanore into the dining room. She was checking the table for the third time. "That's enough. Everything looks fine." He put his hand on her shoulder, but she continued on around the table.

"It's . . . unbalanced. Two chairs on one side, three on the other. I don't know what to do about it." She moved Patrick's chair to the right a few inches.

"There's nothing you can do unless you get a round table or find a home for another one of the children."

She spun around and faced him, torn between crying and screaming at him. "How can you suggest such a thing!?"

With his arm around her shoulders, he pulled her to his chest and held her while she cried. "I was attempting to make you smile. I didn't mean to cause you more pain."

She hiccuped and sniffed. "I . . . don't know if I can do this."

He held her tighter and rested his chin on her head, wishing there were some way he could absorb her pain. "You will because you love them and want what's best for each of them." He felt rather than heard her deep, wrenching sigh.

She mumbled into his shirt, "I feel like I'm losing everything." She hiccuped again. "Damn, I hate this."

"What? My shirt?"

His chest rumbled under her cheek. She leaned back, and his chin dropped to his chest. She grinned. "Thank you."

He slid his hand down her back and gently swatted her bottom. "I hear little feet in the hall."

"Oh, dear." As she fled to the kitchen, his laughter followed her.

With her spirits lighter, she dished out supper and sat opposite Jordon. The children knew where Walter was and avoided mentioning his name. Martin ate, saying little as usual. "Martin, was there much damage to the saloon?"

He glanced up and gulped his food down. "The back wall's gone, and some bottles and a lot of glasses were broken. It took me a whole day to mop up the floor."

Jordon winked at Eleanore. "Is Anders open for business?"

"Yeah. The regulars don't care what shape that place's in, long as they can buy a drink." Martin shrugged and continued eating.

Eleanore was determined to get them talking. "Lottie, how is Mrs. Peterson?"

Lottie looked at Eleanore. "She's scared. She says she's too old for twisters. Part of her roof was carried off by the wind. I was going to tell you . . . she's leaving tomorrow." Lottie stared at her plate and then glanced up. "She told me to . . . finish my dress. Wasn't that kind of her? She said she *knows* I can do it all myself." She pressed her lips together.

"Indeed that was very generous of her." Eleanore understood how Lottie felt and attempted to give her a reassuring smile.

As if hoping to reassure herself, Lottie inhaled and nodded.

"I told her I'd see her off. Is that all right?"

"Of course, dear. Would you like me to go with you?"

"No! I mean, that won't be necessary. I'll be fine."

So Lottie knew how Mrs. Peterson felt about her, Eleanore realized. She grinned at Beth Anne. "How's Smidgen?"

Beth Anne beamed. "She's just fine. You were right. She bounced through the grass after a fly. She was so funny."

"She's smart, too." Patrick shared a look with Amelia. "We tried to trick Smidgen, didn't we, Amelia?"

Amelia nodded. "Patrick didn't think she would know the difference between tiny pebbles and flies. But she did."

Eleanore's gaze met Jordon's, and she feared she might start crying all over again, but when the children weren't looking, he screwed up his eyes and mouth and made her smile. She felt better. "Lottie, after you say good-bye to Mrs. Peterson tomorrow, would you stop by the general store for me on your way home?"

Jordon saddled Nugget and was about to mount him when Patrick ran up to the corral fence.

"Mr. Jordon, can I go visit Walter now?"

Jordon mounted his horse. "I don't know. Have you asked Miss Eleanore?"

Patrick shook his head. "I just thought I'd ask you an' I wouldn't have t' go all the way to the house."

Jordon cleared his throat. "That is a fair piece. How would you like to ride behind me while I circle the corral?"

"Really?!"

"Climb up on the fence. It'll be easier for you to mount from there." Jordon turned Nugget and stopped by the fence.

Patrick put his leg out and slid onto the horse's rump.

"Wrap your arms around me and hold on." Nugget sidestepped, then started at a walk. Jordon kept a tight rein. After the weeks of riderless exercise, he wasn't sure what to expect from the horse. They made one circle. "You okay, Patrick?"

"Yessiree!"

Jordon chuckled and let Nugget pick up speed, then turned him in figure eights before bringing him to a halt by the fence. "Slide off and try not to kick him."

Patrick did as he was told and sat on the fence.

Jordon dismounted, feeling a little stiff but more like himself. Patrick followed him around the rest of the morning. Jordon answered his questions and praised his knowledge. When Amelia called them for dinner, they went into the house together.

Eleanore saw Patrick and Jordon walking along like father and son. No, she mustn't think that way. "Did you two wash up?"

Jordon winked at Patrick. "Yes, ma'am."

Patrick mimicked Jordon, drawling, "Yes, ma'am," and giggled.

She held out two plates. "You can take these in with you. Amelia's pouring the milk."

"Where're Martin and Lottie?"

"Martin's waiting to eat. Lottie should be here soon."

Eleanore watched Patrick take off almost at a run while trying not to tip his plate. "He's in high spirits. Did he see Walter?"

Jordon glanced at the doorway. "He asked me if he could, but he got sidetracked."

"Thank you." She put a slice of beef on her plate and a spoon of peas. "I'll let him visit Walter this afternoon. Patrick'll have to learn that Walter has work to do."

Jordon chuckled and followed her into the dining room. "They'll end up sharing the chores." As they entered, Patrick was telling Martin, Amelia and Beth Anne about riding Nugget.

Beth Anne stared up at Jordon. "Did he really ride with you?"

"Sure did." Jordon sat down. When he reached for the bread, he noticed Beth Anne pouting. "It's only fair. You and Amelia took turns riding, too."

Beth Anne persisted. "But we rode Old Ned, not Nugget."

Amelia nudged Beth Anne. "I enjoyed it, so did you. Don't be selfish. Be glad you got a turn."

Beth Anne nodded and picked up her fork.

Eleanore hid her smile by taking a bite. She heard the kitchen door close and went to see if Lottie had returned. Eleanore saw the coffee on the worktable and Lottie at the stove. "I'm glad you remembered."

Lottie handed a letter to Eleanore. "Mrs. Gunther asked me to bring it to you."

"Thank you." Eleanore didn't recognize the handwriting, but the paper was of good quality. She carefully broke the sealed envelope and withdrew two pages folded separately. One had her name on it, the other Martin's.

Lottie started out of the room and paused. "It isn't bad news, is it?"

Eleanore put Martin's letter back in the envelope. "I don't know yet." She unfolded the page. "Go on in and eat. I'll be there soon."

She read the neatly penned message and smiled. Martin's aunt and uncle had just received her letter and said they were looking forward to having Martin with them. Eleanore saw the date of the missive and realized they could arrive any day. She quickly refolded the page and tucked it in her pocket as she returned to the dining room.

Jordon glanced at her as she sat down. She appeared calm and smiled at Martin, though the boy didn't notice. He'd been asking Jordon about life in the army. "It can be rough. Some men take to it easily, some don't. But you've got a few more years before they'll let you sign up."

Eleanore handed Martin the envelope. "Lottie just brought this. Your aunt and uncle wrote to both of us. That's your letter."

Martin stared at it. "What does it say?"

"I don't know. I didn't read yours. Your aunt signed mine and sounded very nice." Eleanore put her hand on his arm. "You may be excused now if you'd rather be alone."

"No . . . I don't think so." He slid the paper out slowly.

He looked to Eleanore and unfolded the page. She watched him read as if taking in each word, then his face lit up. She beamed at Jordon, instinctively sharing the moment with him.

Jordon instantly responded to her flush of happiness, then spoke to Martin. "Must be good news."

"It is. At least, I think it is." Martin flashed a wide grin. "Uncle Clayton is Papa's brother. He hadn't learned about the fire or Mama and Papa's death until they got your letter, Miss Eleanore."

"That makes sense."

"I wonder if he looks like Papa."

"Your Aunt Mary said they would be here around the ninth. That's tomorrow."

Martin sat back in the chair, staring at the letter he still held. "I didn't think they . . . would answer."

"Don't you remember, we weren't sure where to write. I'm thankful they received my letter." Eleanore reached over and gave his hand an encouraging clasp.

"He even seems to want me to live with 'em." Martin glanced up. "I never met him."

"They are family, your family now. That's what you should keep in mind." Eleanore hastily ate a few bites of her cold dinner and noticed that she was the last to finish. "Oh, Martin, maybe it would be best if you quit working for Mr. Anders."

"Gee whillikens! I forgot." He saw Eleanore's face and quickly added, "Sorry. I won't be long."

Patrick picked up his plate and stacked it on Martin's forgotten dish. "Is Martin leavin', too?"

Eleanore nodded. "We aren't sure just when, though."

Amelia watched Patrick and Lottie's reaction to the news. One by one they were finding homes—leaving.

Amelia stood up and spread her hands out on the table. "Mr. Jordon, you're not going away . . . are you?"

He allowed the barest hint of a smile to show. "No, Amelia, I'm not, and I wouldn't without telling you." She'd lost her color and her voice almost broke. He should've known she'd be frightened. He felt Eleanore watching him and met her gaze. She was becoming second nature to him, and he vaguely wondered if he'd told Amelia more than he realized.

Lottie stood up with her plate. "Mrs. Gunther asked if I could help out at the store. Is it all right?"

"Yes, of course."

Patrick darted back into the dining room. "Miss Eleanore, now can I go see Walter?"

That day and the next would have been agony for Eleanore if not for Jordon's easy smile and gentle teasing. Her prayers were being answered, but why all at once? She carried on as usual, or tried to for the children's sake—nevertheless, they felt the loss, too.

Patrick shadowed Jordon or went to the livery. Lottie spent her days at the general store and talked of having her own store where she'd sell the dresses she made. Amelia continued tutoring Beth Anne in reading and seemed to be happiest when everyone was together.

As Eleanore hung the last of the laundry up, Beth Anne ran up to her.

"Mr. and Mrs. Linder are here! Amelia's in the parlor with them. Where's Martin?"

"He was helping Jordon—in the corral. See if you can find him. I'll go in and talk to the Linders." Beth Anne ran off and Eleanore dashed to the house. She paused in the kitchen for a gulp of water to moisten her dry mouth and went to the parlor.

Amelia jumped to her feet. "Miss Eleanore."

Mr. Linder stood up. "We're both very happy to meet you and grateful for your letter."

"Thank you. Please, sit down." Eleanore perched on the edge of the armchair. "Would you like something to drink? Coffee? Tea? Lemonade?" They both declined. She smiled and clasped her hands together on her lap. "Martin and I were so relieved when your letter arrived. Yours was the only name I could find, and I had no idea if you had moved or . . ."

Mrs. Linder clutched her reticule. "That's why it took us so long. You see, we did move—about four years ago." She looked around. "Is Martin here?"

"He was out near the barn just a while ago. Beth Anne went after him." Eleanore saw the barn through the empty window frame and suddenly realized that the Linders must be wondering about it. "I apologize for the condition of the house. There was a tornado last week."

Mrs. Linder gasped and covered her mouth.

Mr. Linder passed the brim of his hat through his hands. "All of you survived, I presume."

"Yes. In fact Martin led us to the trench we hid in during the storm. He's a very good young man. I'm so glad you want to share your home with him." A movement caught her attention outside. "I think he's coming now."

Mr. and Mrs. Linder looked at each other and then stared at the doorway. She pulled a lace-edged hanky from her sleeve and twisted it with her hands.

Eleanore smiled, wishing Martin had come straight to the parlor, though she understood his wanting to make a good first impression. The seconds stretched to a couple minutes. Hearing his approaching footsteps increased the tension. She turned to the doorway. Martin had slicked his hair back and put a clean shirt and trousers on. She held her hand out to him.

"Mr. and Mrs. Linder, this is your nephew, Martin." She urged him forward as his relatives stood up.

Martin rubbed his hand on his pants and shook his uncle's hand. "It's good to meet you, sir."

"And you, boy." Mr. Linder grinned at his wife.

Mrs. Linder tucked the rumpled hanky back up her sleeve. She hesitated a moment, then stepped forward and embraced Martin. "I'm so sorry. If we'd known, we would have been here within the week."

Martin was almost a head taller than his aunt, but he slowly responded to her. Eleanore blinked several times to clear her vision. The Linders greeted him like a long lost son.

Mr. Linder cleared his throat and gently prompted his wife to release the boy. "You've your father's dark hair and light eyes. Look just like him at your age."

Martin grinned.

Eleanore stepped away from the chair so Martin could sit there. "Wouldn't you like some refreshments now?"

Mr. Linder took his wife's hand. "I must apologize. We've made arrangements to take the train back Thursday night. I thought you were closer to Omaha. We should start back as soon as possible." He looked at Martin. "Will it take you long to pack your things?"

"No, sir. No longer than five minutes." Martin dashed out of the room.

Eleanore waited until she was sure he was in the bedroom. "He started packing the day we received your letters. I'm afraid the tornado blew away most of his belongings, even the money he'd saved. The boys' room was completely demolished."

"I understand, Miss Merrill." Mr. Linder took his wife's hand. "We'll see that he has everything he'll need. I have already enrolled him in school." He reached into his pocket. "I . . . we would like you to have this."

Eleanore hid her hands in the folds of her skirt. "I can't possibly accept that for taking Martin in and helping him contact you."

"You had expenses. I know. We have two almost grown boys of our own."

Eleanore gave him a tight-lipped smile and shook her head.

Mrs. Linder peered up at her husband before speaking. "I would like to keep in touch with you, let you know how Martin is doing. Would you mind, Miss Merrill?"

"Thank you. I'd appreciate that, however I will have to let you know where I'll be."

Mr. Linder glanced up. "You are moving?"

Eleanore looked around. "It's a good possibility. The back of the house was badly damaged."

Mr. Linder patted his wife's hand. "How many children are you caring for here?"

"Five, with Martin. Walter recently moved in with a family here in town."

"That is admirable, Miss Merrill. Mrs. Linder and I are very grateful you were here for Martin."

"You're very kind to say so."

"Please, do keep in touch. I shudder to think what might have happened to him if . . ." Mrs. Linder dabbed her eyes with her wrinkled hanky.

Martin returned carrying a bundle and his coat. He stood awkwardly, shifting his weight from side to side.

Eleanore smiled at him. "Be happy." She hugged him a moment and quickly stepped back. "Don't forget to write."

He gulped. "I won't. You either."

Beth Anne ran into the room and skidded to a stop near Martin. "Smidgen got away and I had to find her."

Martin grinned. "Take good care of her."

"Oh, I will." Beth Anne glanced at Mr. and Mrs. Linder. "You going to live with them?"

Martin nodded.

"They look nice." She reached up to him. "You'll have to bend down. I'm not tall enough." When he bent down, she gave him a kiss and a hug, then she stood at Eleanore's side.

Martin smiled at Amelia.

She met his gaze and spoke softly. "I'm happy for you."

"You'll be fine." His voice cracked and he stared at his coat.

Mr. Linder ushered his wife out the door and to the rented carriage. After handing her up to the seat, he motioned for Martin to climb up.

Martin looked around. "Where's Mr. Jordon?"

"Out back."

"Thanks, Amelia." Martin went over to Mr. Linder. "I'll be right back," he said, and ran around the corner of the house.

Jordon watched the boy slide to a stop and smiled. Martin wouldn't be a boy for long. "Ready to go?"

"Yes." Martin rested his arms on the fence and shuffled his feet. "The Linders are waiting, but I had to . . . wanted to thank you for helping me."

Jordon nodded. "I trust you won't make that mistake again, at least for a few years."

"No, sir. That whiskey didn't even taste good."

Jordon held his hand out to the boy. "Good luck, Martin."

"Thank you, sir. And take good care of Miss Eleanore." Martin ran back to the front yard and stopped in front of Eleanore.

He's afraid, she thought, for all of his enthusiasm, he's still unsure. She reached out and embraced him one last time. "We'll miss you."

He hugged her tight and stepped back saying, "Me, too," and climbed into the buggy.

Eleanore watched them until they were out of sight. "Come on, girls. I don't know about you, but I'm thirsty."

Amelia followed after the dust on the road had cleared. Martin was one of the lucky ones. As she entered the house and closed the door behind her, She decided she would not leave her fate to chance; she would do what she could to help.

Jordon saw the carriage leave and went in the house to see how Eleanore was dealing with Martin's departure. He found her standing in the hall staring into the boys' room. "You okay?"

"Fine." She motioned to the room. "I'm trying to decide what to do. Patrick's always shared a room. I don't think he'll be too happy in there alone, especially now."

He leaned around the door frame and surveyed the room. "What are you planning?"

"If I could make room for Patrick in mine, you could take this one. But there's no bed. You'd still be sleeping on a pallet."

"That's no problem. But why not move the girls back in here with Patrick? You'd have your own room to yourself."

"I don't mind sharing, and you must be tired of eating and sleeping in the same room." When she glanced at him, his mouth was puckered and he was frowning as if in deep thought.

"Well, there's one other alternative. Move the girls back in here and I'll move in with you."

"Oh, I . . ." She faced him and was struck by his distinct dimple. Then he broke out laughing. She clamped her lips together and shrugged. "It might work out, as long as you don't snore."

He slid his arm around her waist and kissed her neck. "I'll help you move the beds back in here." He was being foolhardy and counted on her good sense to bring it to an end.

She turned around and lightly kissed him. "I accept."

"What?"

"You can help me move the beds back." She grinned and ducked under his arm. "Come on. They're in here." She opened the door to her room and quickly pulled the mattress off the smaller bed.

"You win." He followed her into her room. "I'll bring my things in after we get these beds out of the way." He waited for her rebuke and was about to worry when he noticed her shoulders quaking with laughter.

CHAPTER SEVENTEEN

Eleanore stared at the boiling pot. Jordon had said he was tired of beef and gone hunting. He'd brought three rabbits home, more than enough for the eight of them, only now there were six. She wasn't alone in having to adjust to the changes. When the meat was tender, she removed the pieces from the simmering water, dried them and dredged them in flour. As she placed the meat in a pan with some bacon grease to brown, Lottie came into the kitchen.

"Is it true? Martin's gone?" Lottie stood by the worktable.

Eleanore put a portion of rabbit in the pan and turned around to face her. "His aunt and uncle arrived this morning. They were happy about taking him home with them."

Lottie nodded and stuck her finger in a tiny mound of flour on the table. "He must be pleased." She dragged her finger through the flour, making a zigzag design.

"I believe he is. He's also relieved to find out his relatives wanted him." Eleanore set the last piece of meat in the pan and wiped her hands on a towel. "I wish we'd been able to locate your family."

Lottie shrugged. "Papa always said we were alone in the world." She stared at the sharp marks she had made in the flour and quickly rubbed them out. "I'll set the table."

Eleanore put her arm around Lottie's shoulders. "It's already set. I would like you to go out back for a while. See what Amelia and Beth Anne are doing. I'm sure they'd let you join them."

"I . . ." Lottie gazed at the doorway.

"I think they're playing with Smidgen." Eleanore watched her a moment. "Go on, dear. You've spent the day in the store. I'll call you for supper."

With a mournful sigh, Lottie went outside. Eleanore watched her leave as if being punished. For all of her haughty behavior, the girl wanted to feel needed, just like every child. While the meat browned, Eleanore stepped outside and wondered what Jordon was doing.

He came up behind her and tapped her shoulder. "Looking for me?"

She spun around and shook her head at him. "How do you manage to sneak up on me so often?" His teeth and eyes appeared to have grown brighter, then she noticed how tan he had become in the last few weeks. Harriet's comment flashed through her mind. There was no denying it. Jordon was an uncommonly handsome man. Beth Anne's laughter brought her back to her senses.

"Luck, I guess."

If the boys had grinned at her the way he was, she'd have been sure they were up to mischief. "What have you been doing?"

"Some people came by looking for their butter churn and plow." For a long moment, she had stared at him with the sweetest expression. He was tempted to kiss her, but the instant passed.

"Have you seen Patrick?"

"Not recently. He's probably still helping Walter. Want me to get him?"

"Would you mind? Supper's almost ready . . . Oh, I almost forgot the meat."

She dashed back and turned the pieces of rabbit over before the golden brown color turned black. When everything was done, she moved the skillet away from the fire and went to get the girls. She rounded the back corner of the house and saw the three of them sitting together.

Amelia noticed Miss Eleanore and picked up the cat. "We better take Smidgen back inside."

Beth Anne grabbed Missie and the two sock puppets and stood up.

Eleanore waited for them. "Supper's ready."

"I'll get the milk." Lottie ran ahead.

"And I'll set the glasses out." Amelia put the kitten in Beth Anne's arms and dashed to the house.

Beth Anne put her cheek on Smidgen's black head. "What can I do?"

"Your arms are rather full. Why don't you take your doll and kitty inside before you wash up?" Eleanore followed Beth Anne into the kitchen.

As Eleanore dished the food onto the plates, Jordon returned with Patrick. Everyone carried their own dishes to the dining room. Lottie was the first to notice the change in the seating arrangements.

"Where do I sit?"

"You can take Martin's seat." Eleanore motioned to the seat on her right. She could almost feel the tension drain from Lottie and smiled.

Patrick took his seat and looked around the table. "Me an' Mr. Jordon are the only boys."

Eleanore smirked and met Jordon's gaze.

"That we are. But we're also in the company of four lovely ladies. That makes us very fortunate." Jordon winked at Eleanore.

Patrick glanced around again. "Why? They're always here." He puckered his brows. "Do I have to sleep alone now?"

Eleanore watched his face pale slightly, then light up. Before she could answer, he continued speaking.

"Can I share my room with Mr. Jordon?"

Jordon quickly took a bite of rabbit.

"This afternoon we moved the girls back into their

room." Eleanore met each of the girls' concerned gazes. "And you'll be sharing their room." Amelia and Lottie said nothing, though Eleanore was sure she'd seen a flicker of a grimace cross Lottie's face.

Patrick slumped back on his chair. "How come I can't sleep in here? Me an' Mr. Jordon oughta stick together."

Jordon cleared his throat and avoided looking at the spark lighting Eleanore's eyes. "I snore something fierce, Patrick. You'll be more comfortable in the bedroom. Besides, the kitten sleeps in there, too. Doesn't she?" He nodded at Amelia.

She glanced across the table at Patrick. "Every night."

Eleanore lowered her glass. "I guess you could sleep on the sofa, if you really don't want to share the girls' room," she said and continued eating.

Patrick snorted and jabbed his fork into a bite of meat. "All right."

Eleanore felt the cat brush her leg and noticed Beth Anne lower her hand toward the floor. "Beth Anne, don't give Smidgen any bites of food while we're at the table."

"But she's hungry and we're eating." Beth Anne dropped the bit of meat.

"If you don't stop, I'll put her out and close the door. Is that what you want?"

"No." Beth Anne ate a few kernels of corn. "Can I save some for her to eat later?"

"Just two bites." Eleanore didn't say anything when Beth Anne pushed two large pieces aside.

"This rabbit sure is good." Jordon eyed Patrick.

"Yes, ma'am. It's real tasty." He looked from Eleanore to Jordon.

Jordon gave him a nod of approval, but he didn't want the boy to think there was a contest—the boys against the girls, so to speak. Jordon glanced at Amelia. "How is Beth Anne doing with her reading lessons?"

"Fine." Amelia smiled at the younger girl. "She can read and almost write her name and Smidgen's."

"Very good. You girls have been working hard." As if they had touched, Jordon shared the moment silently with Eleanore.

Amelia noticed the way Mr. Jordon and Miss Eleanore gazed at each other. "Miss Eleanore's bread is real good, too."

Jordon hid his smile with his hand. "It sure is."

"Do you know how to cook, Mr. Jordon?"

"Not as good as Eleanore, but I can roast meat over a fire." He feared a verbal trap coming from Amelia and decided he'd better eat more and talk less.

Eleanore picked up the plate of biscuits, set one on her plate and passed them to Lottie. "Do you still like working at the general store?"

"Oh, yes." Lottie handed the dish to Patrick. "Mrs. Gunther's teaching me the prices, when she's not busy with the mail, and Mr. Gunther let me help Mrs. Blake today."

Eleanore smiled at her. "That's wonderful."

"And since I worked with Mrs. Peterson, I'm allowed to cut the yard goods, lace and ribbons, too." Lottie took a drink of milk. "I do like working there. Mr. and Mrs. Gunther are nice."

"Yes, they are." Eleanore knew Lottie enjoyed and needed responsibility. "They must be happy with your work."

"They said they are." Lottie pushed the last bite of meat around her plate with her fork. "Mrs. Gunther invited me to have dinner with her tomorrow." She looked at Eleanore. "Is it all right?"

"Of course, dear."

Patrick watched Lottie. "Are going to live with them? Like Walter lives with the Tuckers?"

Lottie stared at her plate. "I don't know. They haven't asked me."

"Well, would you if they ask?"

She shrugged and glanced sideways at him. "Maybe."

Patrick chewed on a piece of meat. "How come nobody wants me?"

"Oh, Patrick, I love you and want you here. I want all of you here." Eleanore stared at him, Lottie, Beth Anne and Amelia. "But when one of you has a chance to be part of a real family, I'm happy for you."

Amelia waited for someone to speak, but no one did. "Why can't we be a real family? We look like one."

There was immediate silence. Jordon gulped the bite he'd been chewing and was sure everyone heard him. He wiped his mouth and looked at Eleanore. Her cheeks were turning bright pink. "It isn't as easy as that, Amelia. There's more to being a family than resembling one."

Lottie caught Amelia's attention and wordlessly encouraged her.

"Don't you like Miss Eleanore?"

Jordon didn't want to dampen Amelia's spirit, but damn, she was cornering him. "Yes, of course I do, but—"

Amelia interrupted him and turned to Eleanore. "And you like Mr. Jordon, don't you?"

Eleanore couldn't face Jordon. She focused solely on Amelia. "You know I do, but—"

Again, Amelia interfered as soon as Miss Eleanore had agreed. "If you like each other *a lot*, and we," as if gathering support, Amelia glanced around, "like you both, isn't that enough?"

Lottie stared at Jordon. "I know Mr. and Mrs. Gunther like each other."

Beth Anne saw Lottie mouth the name "Blake" and grinned. "Mr. and Mrs. Blake *really* like each other." Beth Anne giggled. "I saw him kiss her. Then he patted her bottom and she didn't even get mad."

Eleanore gave Jordon an imploring gaze for help, but he was extremely interested in his fingernails. "The Blakes are very fond of each other." She pushed her chair back and stood up. "Besides, I think we've discussed this subject enough."

Jordon met Eleanore in the kitchen. "Are you all right?"

She nodded. "I can't believe Amelia did that. She's usually so considerate and mannerly." She gazed at him. He was grinning. "You think that was amusing?"

"You have to admit, she was persistent and logical, too."

"Then why didn't you speak up, answer her questions?" She grabbed her plate from the worktable and dumped the scraps into the bucket. "You just examined your fingers."

He dropped the only thing left on his plate, part of a biscuit, into the pail. "Would you have me propose marriage to you instead?" He watched her closely. They had never discussed marriage, and he wondered what her reaction would be.

Her response was instantaneous. "No! What would make you think that?" She noticed that the thin scar along the right side of his jaw was more pronounced. She'd forgotten about it. Was he as uncomfortable with the idea of marriage as she was?

"Just asking. We never talked about it. Haven't you thought . . . about it?" For some reason, he couldn't bring himself to say marriage again. I must be out of my mind, he thought, why else would I be pursuing the subject? I should be grateful she isn't insisting I do right by her.

"I told you once I don't need a man to take care of me. That hasn't changed." She busied herself at the stove until she heard him walk out into the yard.

Amelia watched Miss Eleanore say good night to Lottie and Beth Anne. Then it was her turn. "I'm sorry if I bothered you at supper. I . . . we were hoping you and Mr. Jordon would keep us all together."

"Oh, dearest, we don't always get what we want. I've been trying to find good homes for the others. I'm in no position to raise all of you." Eleanore kissed Amelia and smoothed back her long hair before stepping over to Patrick's pallet. "Sleep well." She kissed him and closed the door behind her.

She walked by the parlor and opened the front door. The air had cooled a bit, the crickets were chirping, the stars were clear in the night sky. She left the door ajar and sat on the front step, the children's questions tormenting her. Questions she had avoided or refused to acknowledge echoed as if on the wind.

What she'd said to Jordon was the truth, but she hadn't told him all of the truth. Some part of her seemed to liken wanting to need and need to loss. Her father only settled in one place long enough for her to begin to believe they wouldn't move, then off they'd go. Suddenly, it all seemed too much.

She dropped her forehead to her knees and released the tears. Sometimes it helped to cry. Maybe tomorrow she would think of a clever plan to keep them together.

"Eleanore . . ." Jordon sat down on the step by her. "What are you doing out here?"

She quickly dried her wet cheeks with her skirt and stared across the road at the field. "I just wanted to sit here awhile before going to bed. What about you?"

Even though she spoke softly, her voice sounded different, but he didn't want to question her, not after what had happened at supper. "I got sidetracked earlier. Anders and Gunther offered to help tear down the barn. We'll do it Thursday morning. Is that all right with you?" He leaned forward, rested his arms on his thighs and glanced sideways at her.

"Fine. The sooner the better." She felt the heat of his body next to hers. She wanted to rest her head on his shoulder, but she had already grown too used to his being there, too dependent on him, and she knew that that was dangerous.

She stood up. "See you in the morning."

He reached out and grasped her hand. "Sleep well."

She forced her feet forward. She'd learned two things

from her father: rely on yourself and don't cry about what might have been. She entered her bedroom and whispered, "I'm doing my best, Papa."

Jordon worked with Anders replacing the back wall of the saloon. The next day he helped Tucker remove his storm-damaged wall. Each morning he took off the sling and put it in his trouser pocket so it would be in place when he returned to the house. By his calculation it had been six weeks and his arm was fine, though a little weak. He spent Wednesday evening in the parlor with Eleanore and the children.

Lottie worked on her dress, while Amelia took turns reading with Beth Anne and Patrick. Eleanore had let out a dress for Beth Anne. Jordon sat down at the piano and picked out the notes to "Jeannie with the Light Brown Hair." He sang to the music the next time, and the children joined him.

"Play it again, Mr. Jordon." Patrick moved closer to the piano. "Miss Eleanore, you sing this time."

She nodded and watched Amelia close the book and Beth Anne scoot over by Patrick. They did look like a family, their setting perfect for a portrait. Eleanore blinked rapidly and jabbed the needle through the hem of Beth Anne's skirt. She should be enjoying this time with them.

Jordon started playing "Mr. Froggie Went A-Courting." Amelia and Lottie sang along. When he sang the lines "He went down to Missy Mousy's door/ Where he had been many times before, mm-mm," he glanced over his shoulder at Eleanore. She noticed and blushed prettily.

She put the sewing aside and endured the verse about "I wouldn't marry the President, mm-mm," before he took a breath, which gave her the opportunity she wanted. "I hate to break this up, but it's time for bed."

"Oh, can't we sing a little longer?" Patrick was on his knees at her feet. "It's half-over."

Jordon didn't turn around. He was sure he couldn't keep a straight face. "I could sing until they get into bed."

Eleanore wanted to scream at him. He was as bad as Patrick and Walter when they acted up. "If you wish." She led the children out while he sang, "Where will the wedding breakfast be, mm-mm . . ."

By the time the children had gone outside and dressed for bed, Jordon was playing a softer tune, for which Eleanore was very grateful. After saying good night, she paused in the hall. She wasn't ready to sleep. She got her *Emigrant's Guide to California* from her room and returned to the parlor.

Jordon stopped playing and glanced at her, then went over to the shelf of books. What he'd have really liked to study was the book she was reading. He went over and sat on the sofa near her. "If you moved that a tad closer to me, we could both read it."

She did as he asked but soon found she'd gone over the same line three times and still wasn't sure what it said. He was too close. The sound of his breathing was louder than usual. He must have washed up, because he smelled of soap, and she even imagined hearing his heart beat.

"You don't look comfortable. Here." He put his arm across the back of the sofa. "Maybe this'll be better." He slid the book so that it rested on both their legs.

It wasn't, not as far as she was concerned. Her right arm didn't fit anywhere, not at her side, or behind or in front, and she wasn't about to put it around him. "You can read it tonight. I'd better get to bed. The men will be here early."

He held onto the book but didn't move otherwise. "See you in the morning."

"Good night."

His gaze followed her to the doorway. He had no right to reach out and ask her to linger. He didn't know what the hell he wanted. Neither did she.

* * *

Eleanore sat on the edge of her bed trying to understand why she felt so edgy. She closed her eyes and quickly opened them. She had wanted Jordon to put his arm around her, but she didn't trust her feelings or his. There was a soft knock on her door.

"Miss Eleanore, can I come in?"

She opened the door. "Lottie, is something wrong?"

Lottie shook her head. "Can I talk to you?"

"Of course." Eleanore sat on the bed and invited Lottie to do the same. "What's bothering you?"

Lottie stared at her hands. "Mrs. Gunther said she and Mr. Gunther want me to work in their store and . . . live with them." She looked up at Eleanore with tears in her eyes.

Eleanore moved over and put her arm around Lottie's shoulders. "What do *you* want?" She was trembling and Eleanore held her close.

"I . . . I want to . . . to live with them." Lottie sniffed and rested her head on Eleanore's breast. "It will be easier for you if I go . . . and I really do like working in the store."

"Oh, sweetie." Eleanore kissed the top of Lottie's head. "I want what's best for you. If you *truly* want to live with them, then I'm happy for you. If you're doing this because you think it'll help me, don't. We'll make out okay." With tears building up in her own eyes, Eleanore put her other arm around her and gently rocked.

Lottie clamped her lips together and breathed deeply before she sat up and looked into Eleanore's eyes. "I really do want to live with the Gunthers . . . as long as it's all right with you."

"Would you like me to speak with them?"

Lottie nodded.

Eleanore dried Lottie's cheeks and smiled. "I'll talk to them tomorrow." It seemed the good Lord was working overtime to answer her prayers. Eleanore decided she'd better ask for strength, too.

CHAPTER EIGHTEEN

Eleanore started the second pot of coffee and stared out the window at the men in the yard. Jordon pointed inside the barn. Mr. Anders said something and Mr. Gunther nodded. She had given each man a cup of coffee. Jordon had said not to worry about making breakfast until later. She blinked. He'd taken the sling off! She couldn't embarrass him in front of the other men, but she would definitely ask him about it the first chance she had.

She served the children their meal earlier than usual. The girls were less excited about the activity in the yard than Patrick. Eleanore refilled his glass.

He gulped down half of his milk and sat back. "I can't eat all that. Walter might be out there already."

"I've told you. You are not to go out to the yard by yourself. The men have enough to do without worrying about you getting in the way."

Patrick frowned. "Gosh, I never seen a barn come down. Can't I even watch?"

Beth Anne looked at Eleanore. "I want to, too."

Eleanore mentally shrugged. "I'll go with you. We can sit out back . . . after we finished cleaning up the kitchen."

"What about Walter?" Patrick squirmed around on his chair.

"If he comes to watch, he'll have to stay out back with us." Eleanore sipped her coffee.

Lottie glared at Patrick. "Sit still."

"Oh . . . mind yer own business."

"Patrick!" Eleanore eyed him. "That was rude. Apologize to Lottie now, and don't speak that way again."

He looked in her direction. "Sorry."

Eleanore glanced around. "If you are finished eating, take your dishes to the kitchen." For the umpteenth time, she hoped Lottie had made the right decision and would be happy.

Lottie washed, Amelia and Patrick dried, and Beth Anne put the flatware and pots away. Eleanore set the dishes in the cupboard. "Who wants to go outside and watch, besides Patrick?"

Lottie dried her hands. "I have to go to work."

"Go on, dear. Your help will be needed this morning." Eleanore gave her a smile and hoped she wasn't making it more difficult for Lottie.

Patrick held onto the doorjamb and swung in and out. "Can't we go now? We're gonna miss *everything*."

Eleanore came up behind him and rested her hands on his shoulders. "You have a better view from here." Three sections of the barn walls had been stripped of boards. Jordon had taken off his shirt, and she couldn't tear her gaze from him. The sun glinted on his back and arms. She took a deep breath. He looked improperly attractive for such an early hour.

She glanced at Amelia and Beth Anne. "Do you want to go out and watch the men level the barn?" The kitten scampered from the stove and hid under Eleanore's skirt.

Amelia looked at Beth Anne and smiled. "Can we?"

"Where's Walter? I don't see 'im." Patrick craned his neck, searching for his friend.

"Mr. Tucker must need him at the livery." Eleanore was more concerned about the children's safety. "Come on. It doesn't look like they've truly started to bring it down. Walk next to the house."

"Smidgen?" Beth Anne dropped to her knees. "I have t' get Smidgen."

"She'll be safer in your room." Eleanore raised her

skirt, exposing the cat. "Amelia, please put her in your room and close the door."

As soon as Amelia returned, Eleanore walked the children outside, beyond the elm tree. Amelia and Beth Anne took turns on the swing. Eleanore sat down and tried to figure out what Jordon was doing.

There were axes, picks and shovels laid out on the ground, and ropes leading into the barn. She glanced at the corral. Ned was harnessed and Nugget was saddled. She saw Jordon wave—at her or the children, she couldn't be sure. He wiped his brow and turned to Mr. Anders.

Mr. Gunther ran out of the barn, then there was a deep, rumbling creek, as if the twister had blown against the far wall. She rose to her knees.

Jordon shouted, "Everyone back! Anders, help me bring the horses over here."

Each time he entered that rickety pile of lumber, he feared it might fall down on his head. He led Nugget to the front of the barn, tied the rope to the saddle and mounted him. Anders fastened the other rope to Ned's harness and handed the horse's lead to Jordon. The moment he kicked his mount, Anders cracked Ned on the hindquarters and both horses bolted forward.

Eleanore stood by the tree with Amelia, Beth Anne and Patrick in front of her and within her outstretched arms. When the horses bounded forward, there was an almost painful shriek as the barn collapsed in a heap of rubble.

"Golly!" Patrick ducked under Eleanore's arm and ran over to Jordon. "I've never seen anything like that."

Jordon dismounted and ruffled the boy's hair. "We're lucky it didn't come down on us during the storm."

"Yeah."

"Patrick—do not go near that pile of boards yet." Jordon gazed at Eleanore. "How're you doing?"

She released the girls and stepped forward. "I thought there'd be more of a mess." Like my life, she thought, bits and pieces scattered all over.

"We'll start clearing it up." He rested his arm on her shoulder and grinned. "Still want to make us a meal?"

She returned his smile and nodded. He made everything seem so easy. If only there were a simple solution to her problems. He moved his right arm, and she remembered. "What happened to your sling?"

He held up his hand and wagged his fingers, the way Patrick had. "See, it's fine."

Patrick ate dinner in spurts. Eleanore was pleased with his behavior, though. He didn't interrupt or pester the men with questions; he listened to every word Jordon, Mr. Anders and Mr. Gunther said during the meal. She took pity on Amelia and Beth Anne and allowed them to leave the table when they were finished eating. The men soon thanked Eleanore and left.

Jordon returned to the kitchen after walking the men out. Eleanore was doing the dishes by herself. "Where're your helpers?"

She glanced over her shoulder. "Out back."

"You were quiet." He watched the way her skirt swayed as she scrubbed a plate. "Was it hard for you . . . seeing the barn come down?"

"No, more a relief." She dipped the dish in the rinse water and set it on a towel. "How did you level it without damaging the corral fence?"

"The whole structure was weak. We pulled the main supports loose. Without those, the walls caved in." He picked up the drying towel and a plate. "Why didn't Lottie come home for dinner?"

She met his gaze. "She ate with Mrs. Gunther." After a moment, she added, "Lottie was asked if she wanted to live with the Gunthers. She told me last night and said she does. I'm going over to talk with them when I'm finished here."

He set the dry plate on the worktable and rested both

hands on her shoulders. "Did she decide for the right reasons?" He massaged her stiff neck and shoulders.

She dropped her chin to her chest and closed her eyes. His strong fingers felt heavenly. The tiredness became a hunger, a longing for him. She wavered and raised her head. "That feels . . . wonderful."

"Mm-hm." He kissed the nape of her neck and grinned at her quivering response.

She turned around, put her hands on his waist and pressed her parted lips to his. He enfolded her in his arms and, for a moment, shared his tenderness and warmth. She clung to him, adrift in a host of emotions she shared with no one but him.

He slid one hand down her back and held her firmly against the evidence of his desire. He didn't dare do more, not then, and ended the kiss, though he continued to hold her close. He wanted to feel her body melting into his for a while longer.

"Mr. Jorr-don, where are you?"

He stepped back and stared into her passion-glazed eyes. "I'd better see what Patrick wants." He framed her face with his rough hands and gave her a tender kiss.

"Yes . . . and I'd better get busy, too."

He stepped over to the doorway and paused. "I'll keep an eye on the girls."

She nodded and watched his long, confident stride as he crossed the yard. She touched her fingers to her lips and smiled. When she saw him and Patrick picking up scattered boards, she realized she'd been woolgathering. She quickly discarded her apron, checked her appearance and left the house. By the time she entered the general store, she'd regained her composure. Mrs. Gunther was sorting mail.

Eleanore stepped up to the counter. "Do you have any letters for me today?"

Mrs. Gunther glanced up and smiled. "Matter of fact, I

do." She handed Eleanore two envelopes. "Did Lottie tell you what I spoke to her about?"

"Yes. I wasn't able to get away this morning. Can we talk now?" Eleanore folded the envelopes and tucked them in her pocket without looking at them.

"We can go in back." Mrs. Gunther stepped from behind the counter and led the way. "Mr. Gunther said it went real well this morning."

Eleanore saw Lottie and smiled at her. "Yes, very well."

Mrs. Gunther stopped in the parlor. "Please, have a seat."

Eleanore sat down on the gold brocade settee. Before it there was a round table covered with a needlepoint-decorated cloth and a lovely dry flower arrangement. The room was comfortable and filled with mementos.

Mrs. Gunther sat on a nearby chair. "I hope you are not upset with me for asking Lottie about living with us. I didn't want to speak to you until I knew how she felt."

"She seems to enjoy working here with you. Last night she told me she wants to live with you and Mr. Gunther."

"We like her very much. She's a good girl and a hard worker."

"That she is. Several families are thinking about moving. Are you and Mr. Gunther?"

"We have talked about it. Couldn't we take her with us?"

"Of course. My concern is for Lottie's education. I would like her to attend a real school, if possible. She reads very well and is good with sums."

"Oh, I will see to that. Until we move, I will work with her in the evening. She is very bright. Did she tell you she wants to open a shop and sell dresses she will make?"

Eleanore smiled. "She is determined and responsible. Sometimes I wish she would enjoy being a girl while she has the opportunity."

"Don't worry about our working her too hard. I will enjoy having a young daughter again. Ours are grown with their own children." Mrs. Gunther smoothed her skirt. "I hope you'll give us your approval, Miss Merrill."

Eleanore nodded. "I want to see Lottie happy, and I believe she will be with you and your husband."

Mrs. Gunther suddenly reached out and clasped Eleanore's hand. "Oh, bless you. May I tell her and Mr. Gunther?"

"Yes. I do have to get back home. I'll make sure her clothes are clean." Eleanore stood up.

Mrs. Gunther was on her feet in a flash and walked Eleanore out. "Please don't bother. I'll be happy to tend to her things. Thank you."

"You're welcome, Mrs. Gunther." Eleanore hugged Lottie before leaving. She would be happy and well provided for. What more could Eleanore ask?

The Gunthers came for Lottie's things that evening. Eleanore had her clothes folded in a bundle and ready. Lottie held her tears back as she hugged Amelia and kissed Beth Anne, Smidgen and Patrick good-bye.

When Jordon gave Lottie a bear hug, her tears spilled down her cheeks. He held her until her sobs slowed, then whispered, "Are you sure about this?"

She nodded. "It's just hard to say . . . g-good-bye."

He kissed her forehead and smiled. "Take care, little one."

She whispered, "I will," and quickly turned to Eleanore. "Thank you for . . ."

Eleanore quickly embraced Lottie. "Don't be afraid to cry, sweetie." Eleanore held her a moment longer, tipped Lottie's chin up and dried her face with her hanky. "Don't grow up too fast."

Lottie bit her lips and hurried out the front door.

Mrs. Gunther dabbed her eyes with a handkerchief and smiled at Eleanore. "Thank you. We'll take good care of her."

"I know you will."

Beth Anne ran up to Mrs. Gunther and held out her sock puppet. "Will you give this to Lottie? She doesn't have one."

Mrs. Gunther accepted the sock. "I'm sure she will treasure this."

Mr. Gunther cleared his throat. "We'd better get home. Thank you, Miss Merrill."

Eleanore stood at the door with Jordon and the children and watched Lottie and the Gunthers leave. "Good-byes aren't always easy. At least Lottie and Walter are still nearby."

Jordon clasped Eleanore's hand. "Come on, Patrick," he said. "We can move the rest of the boards before sundown."

As Jordon and Patrick left, Eleanore crouched down in front of Beth Anne. "That was very nice of you. I know Lottie will like your puppet."

"I didn't want her to forget us."

Eleanore smiled. "She won't."

Amelia took Beth Anne's hand. "Come on, we'll make another puppet."

Eleanore finished cleaning up the supper dishes alone. She needed to keep busy. After the kitchen, she picked up and dusted the parlor. She checked on Amelia and Beth Anne, who were busy in their room. Eleanore still felt restless and went out to help Jordon.

He tried to discourage her, then gave up. "Be careful or it'll be my turn to pick splinters out of *your* fingers."

"You'd think I'd never done a lick of work in my life." She picked up two boards and carried them over to the large pile. This was what she needed—something to wear her out.

By the time the stars were beginning to show in the fading sky, the rubble had been moved aside. She saw Patrick yawn and told him to wash up. She and Jordon cleaned up afterward.

Jordon took her right hand and turned it palm up, searching for splinters.

"What are you doing?"

"Checking. I'd hate to miss an opportunity to return your kindness."

He was smirking. She laughed and snatched her hand away. Patrick had gone inside. She realized they were standing there in the middle of the yard almost toe to toe. Jordon had pushed his hair back, but a wayward wave had slid down on his forehead. She put her hand on his chest, intending to kiss him, then thought better of that idea. "I'd better tuck the children in bed."

He covered her hand with his. "Don't forget to kiss me good night." He watched a slow grin light her face before she dashed to the house.

Eleanore kissed Patrick.

"Night." He looked around. "Can't Mr. Jordon sleep in here with us now? There's room for him."

"He's used to sleeping by himself."

"I'll share my bed with him. He don't even have one now."

Eleanore smoothed Patrick's red hair back from his eyes. "I'll tell him."

She stepped over to Beth Anne's side of the bed and kissed her.

Beth Anne sat up and whispered near Eleanore's ear, "I won't go live anywhere unless Amelia goes with me."

Eleanore hugged her tight. "I'll do my best." She walked around the bed and kissed Amelia.

"Good night, Miss Eleanore." Having overheard Beth Anne, Amelia held tight to her own dream. She didn't think it was likely that one family would take both of them, but she wasn't about to tell Beth Anne and hurt her feelings.

Eleanore stepped into the hall and closed their bedroom door. Lord, it had been a long day. She glanced up the hall and noticed light coming from the parlor. Jordon must have lit it, she thought, and went in to see him. The room was empty, but her book was on the sofa, leaning against the back with a piece of paper sticking out.

She pulled the paper out. It was a note from him. "I'm going to cool off in the creek." She grinned. She couldn't leave the children for long, but she liked the thought. After grabbing a towel to dry off her feet, she hurried to the creek and saw him standing in the water. He was bathed in wisps of moonlight—all of his backside bared for her to see.

He heard her approach and stood perfectly still, waiting for her to speak. When she didn't, he turned around and gazed at her. "The water feels wonderful. Come in and cool off."

There wasn't a sound, not a cricket or barking dog or rustling leaf, only the pounding of her heart. "I didn't know you were bathing." She thought he was handsome, but seeing him in the creek resembling a statue, she was stunned by his beauty—broad shoulders, trim waist, small buttocks and lean thighs. "I'll just wade. I didn't bring soap."

"I did." He held out the bar. "Come on. I'll scrub your back . . ."

As she stepped out of her dress and removed her camisole, she wondered if she'd lost her mind. She hesitated on the bank. Never in her life had she been so daring. She stepped into the water and shivered, then rushed to join him. "It is cold, isn't it?"

He dunked the soap in the water, lathered his hand and stroked her neck and shoulders. Her skin looked as light as the moonlight and felt like satin.

She closed her eyes and decided that everyone should have someone special to wash their back, at least once in their life. His hands kneaded and rubbed and dipped down to the base of her spine. "What are you doing?"

"I'm going to have the pleasure of washing all of you."

His voice was deep, soothing, seductive. She leaned back against his warm chest as his wonderful hands slipped around her waist and upward to cup her breasts. She tried to turn and face him, but he held her captive with one hand teasing her breasts. When his other hand drifted down from her belly and his hard member pressed against her bottom, she put her hand on his wrist to stop him. "No . . . That's—"

"Part of your body." He bent and kissed her ear.

"Ohh . . . we don't . . . have time for this." She selfishly cherished another minute of his heavenly attention before she pulled away. "I—" She took a deep breath. Lord, her heart was pounding. "I can't leave the children for more than a few minutes. They're uneasy . . . and I—"

He put his hands on her shoulders, closed his eyes and filled his lungs, then exhaled slowly. "I understand." He turned her around and kissed her forehead. "I'll rinse you off."

She pressed her lips to his damp chest. "I think I'd better do that." She quickly dashed the soap from her heated body and walked over to the towel. She dried off and dressed. As she fastened her dress, she heard the crinkling of paper and remembered the letters. At least they should divert her thoughts from what she would rather be doing.

Jordon was ready to walk back to the house with her by the time she was dressed. He put his arm around her shoulder and felt her tremble. If the children were okay, he'd sit with her until she calmed down.

Eleanore peeked in the children's room. All three were sound asleep. She closed the door and returned to the parlor, where Jordon was waiting for her. "They're fine." She sat down on the sofa next to him. "I'm sorry."

He dropped his arm from the back of the sofa to her shoulders. "I can't soap you up here, but we can pretend."

She grinned up at him. "Can I read my letters first? I put them in my pocket and forgot about them until I was dressing."

"You can read while I play with your hair."

She forced her thoughts from the way his fingers teased the nape of her neck, pulled the envelopes out and opened the first one. She read the few lines and dropped the note.

He felt her stiffen. "What's wrong?"

"Mr. Cullen . . . I have until the twentieth to make the payment or move out by the end of the month." She shook her head. "Even if I could make up the payments, we couldn't stay here with half the roof gone."

He absently traced the back of her neck with his thumb. "If you had all the money you'd ever need, what would you like to do?" A dreamy but bleak smile spread across her face.

"Buy yard goods and make some new clothes for the children. Get a sturdy wagon and go west." She shrugged. "But that can't be." She tore the second envelope open and slipped the single page out.

He ran his fingers through her shiny hair and massaged her scalp. He couldn't keep from touching her, and didn't want to try.

"Oh, no . . ." Her hands started shaking, and the letter drifted to her lap.

He picked up the paper and read it. "Reverend James has located three good homes for three of your children. Are you supposed to draw straws as to who goes? You told him about each of them, didn't you?"

She nodded, not trusting her voice.

"He didn't even use their names! How well do you know him?"

"He was passing through and gave a sermon here."

He refolded the letter, put it back in the envelope and jammed it in his trousers pocket. Later, he'd burn it. "Write him and tell him the children have a home. Or don't."

She burst into tears. It was too much. She covered her face and curled into Jordon's side. He was warm and she needed his strength.

He held her tight. "It's been a hell of a week, hasn't it?"

She sniffed and hiccuped. "I tried so hard. I shouldn't cry about Lottie and Martin and Walter. They're with people who love them." She hiccuped again. "But I'll miss them."

"That's only natural. You were like a mother to them." He kissed the top of her head. "Amelia, Beth Anne and Patrick still need you."

"I need them, too. God, help me, I can't give them up." She sat up. "I won't give them up!"

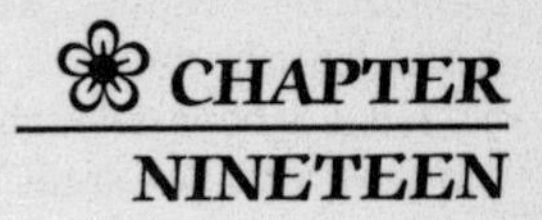

CHAPTER NINETEEN

Jordon stared at her, feeling as if he'd missed part of the conversation. "Who said you have to?"

She grabbed the letter from Mr. Cullen. "He can have the house." She dried her eyes with the back of her hand. "It was Papa's debt, not mine. I tried to pay it." She crumpled the paper into a ball. "How could he do such a thing to me?"

Jordon rested his hand on the back of her neck. "He must've had his reasons. And he didn't know he'd die and leave you with the debt. He probably figured he had many more years left."

"But why did he need the money? I didn't see any of it."

"You may never know." He paused, staring sightlessly at his right hand. "My pa had two bad spells before his heart gave out. I still don't know why he didn't get word to me or send my sister to our aunt's, except he never liked our mother's sister. Liza would've been safe there. Still alive." He gazed at Eleanore.

She reached up and placed her hand along his jaw. "I'm so sorry." As her thumb stroked his cheek, she felt closer to him than when they'd made love. "I've done all I can here. After the tornado, others are moving away, too." She grinned at him. "I'm going to take the children with me and head west. We'll be a family."

He covered her hand and slid hers over to his mouth and kissed her palm. "I know how you feel, but you can't pile them in the back of that old wagon and ride out. You'll need more than your copy of *Emigrants' Guide to California*—supplies, warm clothes, a better wagon, mules at the least, a guide or a man to ride shotgun."

"I don't have enough money to hire a guide. Maybe I can join a wagon train."

He raised one brow. "If you've read that book, you should know it's the wrong time of year to start out."

"You're planning on going. What's the difference? I can drive a team, shoot a rifle and make camp. The wagon is slower than riding horseback. Other than that . . ." She shrugged.

He knew that self-confident shield of hers was back in place the moment she sat very straight. "You don't have to hire anyone. You have me." It was as if she were moving away from him. He rested his hand on her knee, hoping to reach beyond the cool shell she was attempting to hide behind.

Her gaze snapped from his hand to his face. "People were already wondering about us . . . when you were staying in the barn. What would they say if we move out together?"

"What difference does it make?"

"To you, probably none, but I don't want people thinking I'm a harlot—"

"Enough!" He glared at her, shocked by the commanding edge to his voice, but God, he couldn't take her belittling herself.

She continued as if he hadn't spoken. "The children and I will not only look like a family but be one. I appreciate your offer, but you don't have to be responsible for us." She stood up. "I've got plans to make. I'll see you tomorrow."

He watched Miss Eleanore Merrill walk out of the room, chin up and with a definite purpose. He shook his head. If there was ever a time when he needed a drink, this came close enough. He left the house with less dignity than Miss Merrill but with an equal amount of determination, which carried him directly to Anders's saloon.

Jordon stepped up to the bar and signaled Anders.

"What're you doin' here?"

"I'd like a beer."

"Sure." Anders drew the lager and set it in front of Jordon. "You didn't strike me as a drinkin' man."

Jordon took a gulp of his drink. "There're times in a man's life when he needs to get primed to think straight."

"Thank the good Lord." Anders moved away to wait on another customer.

"Amen." Jordon took another deep swig and wiped his mouth. Two more gulps emptied the glass. He signaled for another.

Anders refilled the glass and set it back in front of Jordon. "How's Miss Merrill? She change her mind about rebuilding?"

"Nah." Jordon decided to take it easy with this drink and took a sip. The first one had calmed him down. The second wouldn't be finished until he'd made a decision.

Eleanore. So proud, so stubborn . . . so desirable.

How did she see him? She cared about him or she'd never have made love to him. But he couldn't help wondering why she seemed to think he would still ride out of her life and not care. Or did she? Hell, did he? That was the real problem.

How did *he* feel about her? Since his sister died in his arms, he had kept his distance from everyone. Even himself. Damnation! He cared about Eleanore. He took another sip of beer. They even got along . . . most of the time. Amelia was right. They did look like a family, even acted like one, with one exception. Didn't he eventually want one?

Another swig. Even when Eleanore was miffed, they still shared intimate gazes. She was a good woman with a head on her shoulders and was easy to look at. What more could a man want? What more could he expect to have . . . ?

He drained the glass and took the long way back to the house.

After a restless night, Eleanore woke shortly after sunup. She tended to her morning ablutions before going through every piece of clothing she possessed. She found two dresses she'd outgrown years earlier which could be used to make smaller ones with matching petticoats for the girls. Anything she couldn't use, she'd remake for them.

There was enough to increase the girls' wardrobe but nothing for Patrick. She glanced around the room and noticed her father's old trunk. She had packed it after his death, hadn't opened it since and couldn't even remember what she had saved. She pulled the trunk out a few inches from the wall, far enough to tip the lid back, and opened it. The aroma of lavender and tobacco drifted up.

On top was an old, rough sketch of her father, younger than she could recall seeing him. With a clenched jaw, she set it aside and methodically removed every item from the scarred trunk. There was a heavy wool coat, much too large for Patrick, even though her father hadn't been that big, but which would provide warmth, nonetheless, as would the shirts and woolen socks, and the trousers after she cut them down.

Anything that couldn't be used, she set on the seat of the chair. She stared at the empty trunk. Would it hold all their clothes? She hoped it would. The one treasure she refused to leave behind was the patchwork quilt given to her by old Mrs. Tully, a neighbor when she was twelve years old. She put that on the bottom of the trunk. One of the children opened their door. It was time to heat water and make breakfast. She stood up, her mind listing all she hoped to do that day.

She found Patrick returning to the kitchen from the yard. "You're up early."

"I had t'go. Where's Mr. Jordon?" Patrick yawned and rubbed his eye.

"He must be asleep. Don't wake him."

She stirred the fire in the stove, added kindling and put the water on. Soon Amelia made a trip outside, followed by Beth Anne. By the time breakfast was almost ready, the children were dressed and Jordon still hadn't opened the dining room door.

She stopped at the door, knocked and went inside. "You've overslept, Jordon. It's time to rise." She heard him grumble from the far end of the table. She walked around and saw him sprawled out on his pallet, hair mussed, his right arm across his eyes, reminding her of how Martin slept.

She crouched down, bent over and shook his shoulder. "Time to get up, sleepyhead." The arm covering his eyes lashed out, caught her on the forehead and toppled her backward. Her feet went up, and she landed unceremoniously on her bottom. "Ugh."

He came full awake a moment after and rolled over. "What were you doing?"

She immediately lowered her legs and glared at him. "Trying to wake you! Breakfast is ready and we're hungry, if you aren't."

"Sorry. Never wake a man like that." He rubbed his face and sat up.

"I'll try to remember that . . . if there's a next time." As if there'd be a next time, she thought. She got to her feet and left as he rolled up his bed.

Ten minutes later, Amelia, Beth Anne, Patrick and Eleanore sat at the table eating. Eleanore glanced up at Jordon when he joined them. After a sip of coffee, she looked at each of the children. "I have some news for all of you. We're going to move . . . take a long trip."

Patrick grinned. "When? When're we leavin'?"

Amelia dropped her hands to her lap. "Are *all* of us going?"

Eleanore smiled. "Yes, Amelia, all of us. We'll leave as

soon as I can get us ready . . . ten days, maybe two weeks."

"Can I go tell Walter? He'll be movin' before us, but I gotta tell him."

"After you finish eating, Patrick."

Amelia chewed her bite. "What about Lottie? Can we tell her? She might want to go with us."

Eleanore gave Amelia what she hoped was an encouraging smile. "I'll walk over to the general store with you, but don't get your hopes up. She'll be welcome, but she already has a new home."

Beth Anne leaned over to Amelia and whispered, "We'll ask her. Maybe she will."

Amelia grinned at Beth Anne and glanced at Mr. Jordon. He was awfully quiet, but Miss Eleanore seemed so happy, Amelia didn't want to say anything that might upset her again.

The excitement in Eleanore's voice sent a shiver down Jordon's spine. Did she really think she and the children were going to make the trek across country alone in her old wagon? He kept quiet. The more he watched her, the more convinced he was that he'd made the right decision last night.

Patrick pushed his chair back and looked at Eleanore. "Can I go now?"

"You may be excused, but don't you want to wait and walk over with us?"

Jordon saw the hesitation in the boy's face. "I'll go with you, Patrick. I need to talk to Mr. Tucker."

Patrick stared at Jordon's dish. "You aren't done eating."

"Yes, I am." Jordon picked up his dish and cup. With a nod to Eleanore, he left with Patrick.

She smiled at the girls. "It won't take long to do the dishes, then we can visit Lottie."

Beth Anne fed the cat and told her about the big adventure, but Amelia said little unless Eleanore prodded her.

By the time they arrived at the store, she was troubled. They had been excited at first. She must have said something to dampen their enthusiasm.

They entered the store together. Beth Anne dashed over to Lottie, and Amelia followed at a slower pace. Giving the girls a chance to talk, Eleanore stopped at the mail counter. She learned that Mrs. Gunther was very happy and still didn't know if they would move or not.

Eleanore heard Beth Anne's loud giggle and glanced at the girls.

"Oh, they're fine." Mrs. Gunther smiled. "I know Lottie must miss them."

"They miss her, too. They wanted to tell her that we'll be leaving before long."

"Oh, no. What'll you do?"

"I've wanted to see California or Oregon for years. Papa didn't want to go, but now I have the chance. I'll be selling everything I can't take with us—the piano, furniture, the kitchen and wood stoves—if I can."

"I'll talk to Mr. Gunther. Have you told anyone else?"

"Not yet."

"Mr. Anders may take the piano, though Lord knows they make enough noise without it." Mrs. Gunther laughed. "That's it. What do you want for it?"

"The piano?" When Mrs. Gunther nodded, Eleanore thought a second. "Ten dollars?"

"Wait right here." Mrs. Gunther hurried over to her husband, had a spirited conversation and returned. "We'll buy it for Lottie. A young lady should learn to play and sing."

Eleanore stared at Mrs. Gunther. "Are you certain? It's seen better days."

Mrs. Gunther glanced at her husband. "I am. When can we pick it up?"

"Tonight?"

"We'll be there after supper." Mrs. Gunther leaned forward. "Mr. Stone is such a nice gentleman. Will he be going with you?"

Eleanore stared at her, dumbfounded. "No, no he won't."

"Oh, I'm sorry. I heard that he'd been on his way west when he stopped here. I figured you would be traveling together."

"He was only here to find a home for Amelia. Since I'm going to keep her, he's free to continue on as he planned." Eleanore peered at the girls. "I must be going. I hope you won't be disappointed in the piano."

"Don't you worry. It will do just fine."

Eleanore stepped away from the counter and paused. If Mrs. Gunther thought Jordon would be traveling with them, others probably would also. As the horror of it struck her, Eleanore gawked at the floor, and her face grew warm. Lord help me, she thought and realized that once she left Myles Creek, she would be starting over. Just her and the girl and Patrick.

She joined them at the far counter. "Hello, Lottie." Her hair was held back with a pretty yellow silk ribbon, and she wore a new dress that brought the roses to her cheeks. Eleanore couldn't have been happier for her.

"Miss Eleanore. Are you really moving out west?"

"We are. Your new dress is very nice."

Lottie grinned. "They even let me keep one of the kittens. I named her Stitches."

Amelia peered at Beth Anne before speaking. "Do you really like it here?"

Lottie nodded. "They treat me like their own."

"We'd better let Lottie get back to work." Eleanore smiled at her. "Come by and see us when you can."

She walked out with Amelia and Beth Anne. They were more talkative after seeing Lottie, and Eleanore sighed in relief. When she saw Harriet leaving the house with Henry in her arms, Eleanore realized she still hadn't told her friend all that had happened in the last week.

Harriet stopped at the street. "We were on our way to call on you." She pulled Henry's thumb out of his mouth.

"I wanted to see you, too."

"We will walk with you, then." Harriet fell into step with Eleanore. "Have you decided what you're going to do about the house?"

Even though Amelia and Beth Anne were a few paces ahead, Eleanore spoke softly. "The bank can have it. I'm moving and taking Patrick, Amelia and Beth Anne with me. We'll be a real family."

"What about Lottie and Martin?"

"Martin's aunt and uncle have taken him home with them, and Lottie moved in with the Gunthers. Both children are happy."

"What about Mr. Stone? He's leaving with you, isn't he?"

Eleanore clenched her jaw. "I imagine he'll go on as he planned." They arrived at her house. She walked up the step and opened the front door. "I didn't think to ask. Have you replaced your windows yet?"

Harriet went into the parlor. "We managed to do two windows. The others have to wait a couple months."

"Please sit down. I'll be right back." Eleanore continued through the house to the kitchen. She filled two glasses with water and glanced outside for Jordon. The girls were out by the swing, but there was no sign of him, and she hoped he wouldn't return until after Harriet left.

Eleanore put one glass near Harriet and sat down in the wing chair. "I'm sorry, but I was thirsty."

"You look different."

"It must be the move." Eleanore sipped the water. "Once I made up my mind, I felt . . . free."

"My goodness, you do not mean that you intend to ride across the wilderness with only the children? You could be . . . hurt . . . or killed." Harriet fanned her face with her hand. "I cannot believe Mr. Stone would not offer his protection."

Some protection, Eleanore thought. Quite unwanted, the image of him standing in the creek was fresh in her mind. "I am planning very carefully. I only wish I had a better wagon." She shrugged. "I already sold the piano. If I can sell a few more things we can't take, there'll be enough money for supplies and new wheels. We'll be fine."

Henry stood at the piano, reached up and banged on the keys. Harriet sprang to her feet. "Sorry. He gets into everything." She picked him up and sat back on the sofa with Henry on her lap. "Will you join a wagon train?"

"If we meet up with one."

"But, Eleanore, fall is almost here. You cannot travel in the snow. Why not wait until next spring?"

Eleanore gazed at her dear friend. "Please don't worry yourself. I've wanted to do this for some years now. Be happy for me."

She explained her plans and how she felt it was meant to be, because the bank demanded more than she could give, the twister had damaged the house and, finally, three of the children had been settled in good homes. They talked about others who were leaving, about starting anew and the opportunity the move gave her.

Harriet put Henry up to her shoulder. "I will be sorry to see you leave, but you know I wish only the best for you." She sighed and patted the young boy. "I must be going. You will call before you go?"

"Of course." Eleanore came to her feet at the same time as Harriet. "I'm going to miss you, too."

Jordon spent all morning talking to some of the men in town. Tucker told him who and where the most reliable dealer was for wagons, Mr. Gunther promised to give him a good price on the supplies, and Anders urged Jordon to take some spirits along, reminding him that they were useful for injuries and warming one's self on a cold night. Jordon sarcastically wondered if he shouldn't give Eleanore a strong dose before telling her about his plans.

He walked into the kitchen and found her at the stove. "What smells so good?" He peered over her shoulder.

"Chicken soup. I think there's coffee left over from

breakfast if you want to heat it up." The side of his face brushed her hair. He smelled clean, familiar. She gripped the long-handled spoon tighter than necessary, forcing the metal edges to dig into her hand. She wouldn't lean to the side or turn her head to him.

Without moving from her side, he picked up the coffeepot, shook it and set it over the heat. "Has Patrick come back yet?" He raised his hand near her waist, then dropped it to his side. She had to make the first move.

His breath cooled her cheek and distracted her. "I haven't seen him. The girls are out back. Maybe he's with them."

"I'll go wash up and call them in."

She didn't *need* his help. Her hand shook so badly the spoon rattled against the side of the pot. Damn! Why did she have to care so much for him? Care enough to be . . . in love? She couldn't possibly. But when she closed her eyes, she felt him, saw him, even tasted him. When had she fallen in love with him? She'd been so sure she would never love anyone again other than a child. That was safer.

He returned with Amelia, Beth Anne and Patrick, all laughing. "We're volunteering to help serve."

Beth Anne and Patrick giggled, and Eleanore attempted to frown. She pointed to the bowls. "Bring your dish over and I'll fill it."

Each filed by. Amelia came back and carried the glasses into the dining room, and Eleanore brought the pitcher of milk. She sat down and caught a glimpse of Jordon. There was a spark in his eyes and an upward tilt to his lips, lips she realized were perfect.

"Miss Eleanore—" Amelia waited until she met her gaze. "Can we help you pack?"

Eleanore blinked, brought back from her musing. "That would be nice. We'll have to go through all of the clothes and linens." She filled Patrick's glass, then each of the girls' and her own.

Jordon remembered the coffee and went to get a cup.

Now Eleanore was nearly smiling. What had happened in the two minutes it had taken him to call the children? Why question it? Given the next fifty years, he still probably wouldn't completely know her mind.

While he ate, he listened to Eleanore telling the children about the move—what had to be done, some of what they'd need and how exciting it would be to see what most children only learned about in school. He finished the soup and his coffee. "Do you mind if I use your wagon for a couple days?"

Eleanore glanced up. "Are you leaving today?"

"Can I go with you?"

"I don't know, Patrick. I'll think about it." Jordon met Eleanore's gaze. "I'd like to leave Sunday."

"That's fine with me. I hadn't planned on using it. Oh, Mr. Gunther's coming by tonight for the piano."

He eyed her. "You sold it?"

"I can't take it with us, and I'll give Harriet the girls' beds. She could use them." Eleanore drank the last of her milk. Was he getting ready to leave, too? He should be, and she thought she'd better keep her hands busy and her mind on her own plans.

"I'll help him move it." He knew she was right, but he hated to see her selling off all her possessions. She was losing all her father had left her. That hurt. He'd been through the same and hoped to make it a bit easier on her.

Beth Anne swallowed the last of her milk. "Mr. Jordon, can all of us go with you?"

"Beth Anne, you shouldn't ask." Eleanore glanced at him as if to say, *I'm sorry.*

"Not this time. But you'll be going on a big trip soon."

She brightened up. "That's right. We'll all go then."

He said nothing and noticed that Eleanore had suddenly decided to finish the last drop of her soup. The children believed he was going with them, and even if he were not, they weren't old enough to fear traveling alone with

Eleanore. "Oh, Patrick, remind me to take the swing down. That won't take up much space in the wagon."

"What about Smidgen? We can take her, can't we?" Amelia glanced from one end of the table to the other.

Eleanore smiled. "Yes, she's going with us. We couldn't leave her here."

Amelia sighed and squeezed Beth Anne's hand.

"I have some work to do." Jordon stood up. "Want to help me, Patrick?"

"Yes, sir!" Patrick grabbed his dish and glass and walked out with Jordon.

Eleanore wondered how she was ever going to make Amelia, Beth Anne and Patrick understand why Jordon wasn't going with them.

CHAPTER TWENTY

Eleanore sat on the sofa with Mrs. Gunther and Patrick was in the wing chair, while the men moved the piano. "I'm glad you and Lottie came along. I know the girls will enjoy the visit."

"She was anxious to see them. She's still working on that fancy dress Mrs. Peterson gave her the yard goods for. Spends every evening on it. It'll be lovely."

"Indeed. She'll enjoy it all the more for her labor of love." Eleanore glanced at Jordon. He and Mr. Gunther were pushing the piano to the front door.

Patrick jumped up, ran around the men and opened the door.

"Thank you, son." Mr. Gunther turned back to Jordon. "I think I can supply—"

Jordon frowned and shook his head, cutting Mr. Gunther off. If Eleanore overheard him, she'd start in asking more questions than he was ready to answer just yet. "I'll take that end."

"The wagon's directly out front."

"Good." They lifted the instrument, then Jordon backed out the door and down the steps.

Mrs. Gunther averted her eyes from the doorway. "I hate to see his face get all red like that. I keep telling him not to lift heavy things." She shivered.

Eleanore saw Patrick by the door. "Patrick, stay right there."

"Aw, I wanta help'm."

"You can do that by standing right there at the door." Eleanore smiled at Mrs. Gunther. "Would you like a cup of tea?"

"No, thank you, Miss Merrill. Mr. Gunther still has to unload it when we get home."

Jordon and Mr. Gunther came back inside. "He'll need help getting it off the wagon. I'll be back later."

"Oh, thank you, Mr. Stone." Mrs. Gunther sighed. "I'll get Lottie."

Patrick latched onto Jordon's hand. "Can I go with you?"

Jordon grinned. "It's okay with me, but you better ask Miss Eleanore."

Eleanore went with Mrs. Gunther. They found the girls playing with Smidgen and the puppets. "I'm afraid Lottie has to leave now."

Beth Anne dropped her puppet and hugged Lottie. "I still want you to come with us."

"I know." Lottie glanced at Eleanore. "But my place is here, with the Gunthers." Lottie hugged Beth Anne, then Amelia. "I'll see you before you leave."

When Patrick turned from Jordon, Eleanore had gone down the hall with Mrs. Gunther. He fidgeted by the door until she came back, then stepped in front of her. "Mr. Jordon says it's okay if I go with him. Can I?"

She gazed from him to Jordon. "I guess it's all right, but I want you to mind Jordon."

"Oh, I will!" He ran out to the wagon and climbed into the back.

Eleanore and the girls watched the wagon pull away.

"Why couldn't we ride with them?"

Eleanore ruffled Beth Anne's hair. "Because it's about time for you to go to bed."

Beth Anne whined, "But Patrick got to go."

Eleanore closed the front door. "If you put your nightgown on, I'll read a story."

Amelia took Beth Anne's hand. "Come on."

Eleanore savored a dipper of cool water and wished she, too, could change into her nightgown and wrapper, but Jordon would be back soon. She did the next best thing. She let her hair down and brushed it out before going into the girls' bedroom. Both girls were sitting up in bed.

Beth Anne held out her book. "Please read from this."

Eleanore accepted the volume of Hans Christian Andersen's tales. "Scoot down and put your heads on the pillows." She sat at the end of the bed and leafed through the pages until she came to the story of the "The Shirt Collar."

"Once upon a time there was an elegant gentleman whose whole outfit consisted of a bootjack and a comb, but he also had the most wonderful shirt collar in the world . . ." She read softly, enjoying the story herself. ". . . 'I quite realize that you're useful as well as ornamental, my pretty one,' said the collar. 'I forbid you to speak to me,' said the garter."

Beth Anne giggled and so did Amelia. By the time Eleanore came to the end of the tale, both girls had dozed off. She set the book on the chest, turned the lamp wick down and quietly left the room. She had just entered the parlor when Jordon returned with a drowsy Patrick on his shoulders.

"The girls are asleep." Eleanore reached up for Patrick. "I'll walk him outside and put him down."

Jordon smiled. She had a cuddly, sleepy look about her. "I'll do it." He took her hand before she could pull back and kissed it. "I like your hair that way."

As he sauntered down the hall, she glared at his back and shook her head. He was impossible. His smiles appeared as fast as lightning and just as bright. And just as dangerous. She put the light out and retired to her room. She would have liked the chance to get a glass of water, but it wasn't worth the risk of being alone with him.

She undressed in the dark, hoping he wouldn't disturb her. With her old wrapper securely belted, she sat on the side of her bed listening while he put Patrick to bed and closed the door. His footsteps passed by her room without hesitating. She waited but didn't hear his door close.

Time seemed to stretch out. She started pacing the length of her room. The more she thought about having to wait for him to retire, the more she felt the need to make a trip outside and the more irritated she became. She lighted her lamp, stepped into her old shoes and turned the wick down so only the softest possible glow lit her room.

She eased the door open, stepped out, pulled the door to and tiptoed out through the kitchen. Before she returned to her room, she paused by the corral fence. The night was clear, the air was cooler, and the crickets chirped in the distance.

She stared up at the stars and wondered if they would look different out west. Suddenly an arm dropped around her shoulders. She jumped and felt a hand lightly cover her mouth.

"It's only me. I didn't want you to scream and wake the children." She sagged and glared up at him. "Should I have stifled your cries with my mouth? I didn't think you'd appreciate that, but if you like . . ."

She yanked his hand from her mouth. "You can be impossible." She gazed at him. Was there a time when he wasn't so handsome? If so, she hadn't seen it. "What are you doing out here?"

"Same as you—unwinding. Peaceful, isn't it?" He stood close at her side, with his arm still around her. She probably thinks I'm going to kiss her, he realized, but he wasn't about to give her cause to slap him.

"I thought you had . . . turned in."

"Not yet."

"I should. It . . . is . . . late." She stared straight ahead at his chest and could have sworn she saw his heart pounding. She knew hers was. She rubbed her moist palms on the arms of her wrapper. She glanced up at him. "I'll see you in the morning."

He endured her nearness, knowing she was suffering as much as he was. "Sweet dreams, Ellie."

He heard her sudden gasp but didn't smile. She reminded him of a skittish mount. Both needed to learn to trust. He was a patient man and she was worth the effort. He ambled back to the house, whistling until he entered the kitchen.

Jordon kept busy the next day and the following morning, until the mail arrived. He went to the general store. A response was due anytime from his bank. He'd expected it last week. "Morning, Mrs. Gunther. Anything for me?"

She smiled at him. "You must be expecting something to be here so early. The mail usually isn't sorted until noon."

He stepped over to the yard goods, where Lottie was working. "Hello. How're you doing?"

"Oh, Mr. Jordon. I'm fine." Lottie put a bolt of material back on the shelf. "How's Miss Eleanore? And the others?"

"They all miss you." He glanced over his shoulder at Mrs. Gunther. She was still looking for his letter, and Mr. Gunther was waiting on a customer. "It isn't too late to change your mind, if you want to."

She smiled and shook her head. "I do like it here with them, and they said they want to adopt me." She ran her hand across the smooth wooden tabletop. "It was hard saying good-bye. I hope Miss Eleanore won't be disappointed if I don't come back. She'll see it's for the best."

"You're a brave young woman, Lottie."

She lifted one shoulder. "Mrs. Gunther is waving a letter."

"I'll see you again." He returned to Mrs. Gunther.

"I hope this is what you're waiting for." She handed the item to him.

"Thank you." He stepped outside and ripped the envelope open. Inside there was a letter and a bank draft. He glanced at the letter and put both into his pocket. He walked back down the road whistling.

Jordon stashed his bedroll under the seat of the wagon, by the crate containing the coffeepot and enough food for two meals, at Eleanore's insistence. She'd even put her shotgun and knife by the crate. Suddenly Patrick was hanging over the side grinning at him.

"You 'bout ready t'leave, Mr. Jordon?"

"As soon as I fill the canteen."

Patrick trotted at Jordon's side over to the well, eager to help. "Miss Eleanore said you'd be home tomorrow. That right?"

Jordon grinned and filled the canteen. "That's my plan. Are the Tuckers still leaving Wednesday?"

"Yeah. How come we can't leave then, too?"

"They've been planning their trip longer than Miss Eleanore has. A lot of things have to be packed." He put the canteen in the crate and went down on one knee in front of Patrick. "I know you want to spend all your time with Walter, but I'd like it if you would find some time to help Miss Eleanore, too."

Patrick nodded. "I will." He saw Eleanore and the girls walking over to the wagon. "Hey, I'm the man of the house now, for a day anyway."

"That you are." Jordon ruffled the boy's hair. Eleanore approached, with Amelia on one side and Beth Anne on the other, her smile uncertain as if she weren't sure of his reaction, he thought. He grinned at her and tipped his hat. "Afternoon, ma'am."

Amelia smiled and Beth Anne giggled.

Eleanore rolled her eyes at this silliness.

Beth Anne went over to Jordon. "You're coming back, aren't you?"

"Yes, sugar, I am." He kissed her cheek, and she hugged him. "Be good while I'm gone."

"I will."

Jordon noticed Amelia watching him. He held out his arms to her. She took a hesitant step, then dashed over and threw her arms around him. He held her tight and realized she was frightened. "I'm coming back," he whispered. "Want to know a secret?"

Amelia nodded.

"Promise not to tell *anyone*?"

She put her mouth near his ear. "I promise."

He confided, "I'm going to see about getting a better wagon for Miss Eleanore."

Amelia stood back and nodded. She wouldn't tell, but she couldn't wait until he came back. Miss Eleanore was going to be *so* happy.

He winked at her and stood up. Eleanore didn't move, just stood there with a light breeze billowing her skirt and loosening her hair. "I should be back by tomorrow evening unless I have to cross the river."

"Good luck. I hope you find what you're looking for."

"I'll try." He flashed her a grin, climbed up to the bench seat and rode out of the yard.

As he followed the road going east, he thought about Amelia. She had seemed so happy he was surprised by her fear of his leaving. He hoped sharing the secret with her and his return would strengthen her ability to trust. Eleanore shared some of the same doubts, but he believed he knew how to convince her.

Not far out of town the road met another one that roughly traced the course of the Missouri River. He turned north and followed the trail with its lazy bends all that afternoon, until he was within sight of Nebraska City. He camped near the river. He ate the supper Eleanore had packed and turned in early. The next morning, he woke up to the chattering of a squirrel on a branch overhead.

He made coffee, broke camp and rode into town. By the time he located the livery Tucker had told him about, it was open. He stopped the wagon and went over to the only man there.

"Good morning. Are you Thompson?"

"I am. Can I help you?"

"Hope so. I'm interested in trading that wagon for a sturdier one." Jordon glanced at the back of the lot, where several large wagons were lined up.

"Are you lookin' fer one like that or a prairie wagon?"

"Prairie."

"Planned on strikin' it rich in Californy?"

Jordon chuckled. "Not rich." He followed Thompson back to get a closer look at what he had.

Thompson paused and scratched his beard. "How much you wanta spend?"

"That all depends. I don't have any money to waste." Jordon walked along, scrutinizing several wagons nearby. He stopped in front of one. It didn't look as new as a couple others, but it appeared to be in good condition. "What about this one?"

Thompson nodded. "Got a good eye. That one's well caulked, with new canvas, tongue and wheels. Fitted the iron tires meself."

Jordon nodded and strolled down the line to a new wagon. "What about this one? Looks new."

"Yep. That's a fine rig."

After peering in at the bed, Jordon stepped back. "What do you want for it?"

"Ninety dollars. Best I got."

"That's too high." Jordon wandered down to the other end of the line. The end wagon wasn't much better than Eleanore's. He returned to his first choice. "What'll you take for this?"

Thompson shrugged. "I kin let'er go fer fifty-five."

"I'll give you fifty, less my wagon on trade. Say forty?" Jordon checked the joints, axle and wheels while Thompson did the same to Eleanore's wagon.

"Yers needs some work. I'll give ya five fer it."

"Ten."

Thompson hitched up his trousers. "Shouldn't oughta

do't." He stared at Jordon and shook his head. "Aw, hell. Deal."

"Good. Now for the oxen."

Thompson led Jordon over to a large pen where there were twelve large oxen. "What do you want for four yolk?"

Jordon dickered for the animals and other gear. He also learned about the Fort Kearny cutoff and departed well before noon, with the oxen pulling the wagon. Nugget was tethered to the back. The team was fresh and the wagon light. He held them at a steady, plodding pace, faster than they'd take to the trail with a loaded wagon, determined to reach Myles Creek by suppertime.

His resolve paid off. He pulled into the yard and saw Eleanore in the kitchen. He waved and climbed down to the ground the same time she ran out to meet him.

She stared at the wagon, twice the size of hers, then at Jordon. "What's this? And where's my wagon?"

He went around to the back and unfastened Nugget. "I traded yours in on this prairie schooner." He walked his horse to the corral and unsaddled him.

"Who gave you the right to barter my property for your trip?"

"What gave you that cockeyed idea? It's *yours*."

She was poking around when the children came racing out.

Patrick slid to a stop near the back wheel. "Gee whillikens!"

"Patrick!" Eleanore dropped down from the rear of the wagon and glared at him.

"I'm sorry . . . but look at it! Is it ours?"

"That's what Jordon said." She couldn't believe it. She stepped around to the other side and met Jordon. His tan had grown darker, which made his green eyes even more startling. She jabbed her fingernails into her palms. "Tell me you didn't trade my wagon in for this one."

He covered her clenched fists with his hands. "I can't

because it's true." His thumbs stroked the backs of her hands. "Don't you like it?"

"How can I not? What worries me is how much money this put you back. Not even a dimwit would exchange one for the other. And the oxen . . . what do I owe you?"

He released her hands. "I could say a kiss, but that might be too high a price. Damn it! Can't you get your mind off of money?" He lowered the end gate and climbed in the back to unload his things.

Her lips quivered a moment before she glared at him. "This was costly. You can't expect me to accept it as a gift. It's not right." Oh, Lord, she thought, I don't want to hear what the townspeople will say about this.

She hurried to her room, found her savings and went back outside. Patrick was on the bench pretending to drive the team, and the girls were in back looking around. Jordon was looking at an axe. She held out her money.

He glanced at it. "What's that?"

She raised her chin and met his gaze. "All the cash I have."

He gave her a look he hoped expressed his disgust. "What'll you buy supplies with?"

"How I'll manage is no concern of yours." She locked her jaw, determined to stand her ground.

The pain, so obvious with the tears glistening in her eyes, was almost enough to break his resolve. Almost. "Thank you." He took the money and stuck it in his trousers pocket without counting it.

She licked her parched lips. "You're welcome." As she rushed back to the house, an old saying droned in her mind like a warning—"Pride goeth before destruction . . ." It was surely happening to her. She came to an abrupt halt at her bedroom door. All of her money . . . She marched back out to Jordon. "I must ask for my cash."

He smirked and handed it to her.

"Thank you, and you may keep that wagon." She spun on her heel, refusing to cry until she was alone. Now she had her nineteen dollars and her pride back and no wagon to cross the country with. Even if he paid her what her old wagon was worth, it wouldn't be enough. She closed the bedroom door behind her and tossed the money in the top drawer.

She paced the width of the room, her tears now forgotten. She was angry. Why had he swapped her wagon for the new one? She would've sworn he was honest. Had she allowed herself to be hoodwinked because of his good looks, his easy way with the children and her feelings for him?

There was a soft knock on her door. "Yes?"

"Miss Eleanore, are you all right?"

Eleanore frowned once to help relieve the tension. "Come in, Amelia."

Amelia opened the door and peeked inside.

"I'm okay, and you can come in." Eleanore smiled and held out her hand. "Mr. Jordon and I had . . . words. I didn't mean to upset you."

Amelia closed the door and took Miss Eleanore's hand. "You're mad about the wagon, aren't you?"

There was no use lying. Amelia was more aware than Eleanore had believed. "Yes."

"Maybe he just wanted to do something nice for you." Amelia glanced at her. "I know he likes you. I thought you liked him, too."

Eleanore gave her a lopsided grin. "I do, but it isn't proper to accept such an expensive gift." Or to allow a man to think you're the kind of woman to be kept, she added in her mind.

Amelia watched Eleanore carefully. "Then you aren't real mad at him?"

Eleanore shook her head. "Not really." Disappointed and insulted were more like it, but she didn't want to explain that to Amelia.

Jordon knew Eleanore needed time to think. He'd given her quite a jolt. He set the crate, in which was the coffeepot and the food he hadn't eaten, in the kitchen. He started to carry his bedroll back into the house but decided it would be better to sleep in the wagon.

Patrick noticed Jordon making his bed. "Can I sleep here with you?"

"You'd better sleep in your bed while you can." Jordon finished and jumped down to the ground. "Let's see if Miss Eleanore needs help." He swung Patrick down and followed him into the house.

Patrick ran up to Eleanore while she dished out the food. "Mr. Jordon's goin' t'sleep in the wagon!"

"Here's your supper. Your milk's on the table." She handed Patrick a plate, and as she reached for another, she met Jordon's gaze. He no longer seemed perturbed, and thanks to Amelia, neither was she. After serving up his meal, she handed it to him.

He gave a hint of a smile. "Thank you."

On her way to the kitchen, Amelia met Jordon in the hall and whispered, "I didn't tell her."

He grinned. "I knew I could trust you." She beamed like a beacon and dashed into the kitchen. He joined Patrick at the table feeling more encouraged.

Eleanore handed Beth Anne and Amelia their plates and carried her own into the dining room. She sat at her place at the head of the table. It felt so empty with only the three children and Jordon, after having become accustomed to seven places. At least he still occupied his chair. One day soon he wouldn't be there. She gritted her teeth, then forced a deceptively calm expression to her face.

While buttering a slice of bread, Jordon spoke to Beth Anne. "What did you do today?"

"Looked at *all* our clothes. Miss Eleanore said we'd need more." Beth Anne picked up her glass and took a drink of milk.

Patrick gulped down a bite of meat. "I went through my clothes, too, but I don't have many. And I saw Walter. He said they're leavin' Wednesday."

Jordon gazed at Eleanore. "We should go by tomorrow and say good-bye," he said.

Patrick slumped back on his chair. "Yeah. I won't see him ever again."

"You can't be sure of that." Eleanore gave him an encouraging smile. "You're both young. Who knows where you'll go when you grow up? And you could write to him."

"Can I?" Then Patrick frowned. "I don't write so good."

Amelia looked at him. "I'll help you."

Patrick grabbed his fork and scooped some corn into his mouth.

After the supper dishes had been washed and put away, Jordon moved the rest of his gear out to the wagon. In one of the used wagons, he had noticed that someone had sewn pockets onto the canvas, and he thought it was worth mentioning to Eleanore. When he returned to the house, she was in the bedroom reading a story to the children. He went into the parlor to wait for her.

Eleanore kissed Beth Anne, Amelia and Patrick good night. She closed their door and went to the kitchen for a drink of water. She'd seen Jordon pass the children's door. She wasn't sleepy. What she wanted to do was talk with Jordon. Not argue, talk.

She carried two glasses of water into the parlor and handed one to Jordon. He was sitting on the sofa. She could sit there, too, or on the wing chair. She chose the sofa. "Your wagon is very nice."

He refused to start a debate. "Thanks."

"Where are you headed for?" He appeared more relaxed than he had on Sunday before he left. She attempted to calm the flittery feelings coursing through her.

"I'm not sure. I might spend the winter at Fort Laramie, if I can get that far. A friend was working out of there last time he wrote." He shifted on the seat to face her. "It's too late to go much farther than that. What are your plans?"

She stared at her hand as her fingers drew circles on her

skirt. "I'm not sure. There doesn't seem to be enough time to think."

"You're set on keeping Amelia, Beth Anne and Patrick?" He wanted to hold her in his arms and tell her everything would be all right, but he knew she would balk if she thought she was losing control of her life.

She gazed at him unblinkingly. "They're mine. We need each other."

"Are you still hell-bent on living in the West?"

"If we can get there."

"I have an idea." He stretched his left arm out along the back of the sofa. "Since you lost your father and I lost my family, both of us have avoided taking a chance on caring for someone too much." He smiled, hoping she truly understood what he was saying, how much he was risking. "We even get along . . . most of the time, and we do look like a family, even act like one. When you're miffed at me, you get over it. You're a good woman with a head on your shoulders and easy to look at."

He took a deep breath. "I think I know how much you want to keep those children. I do, too. If we get married, you'll be able to care for the children without having to bear the burden by yourself. We can travel cross-country together safely, and I promise to do my best to protect and provide for you.

"What do you say?"

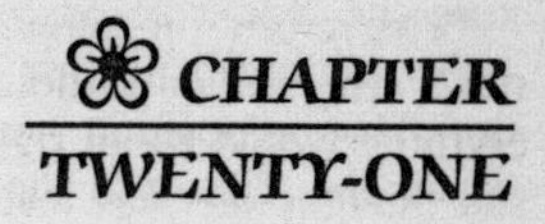

Eleanore stared at him dumbfounded, completely perplexed. "*What* are you asking?"

She looked confused, which didn't make any sense. He'd stated all the reasons very plainly. He cleared his throat. "Will you marry me?"

Her fingers stilled. Dear Lord . . . He was waiting, as if he'd asked her the time of day! "You've been out in the sun too long." She scooted forward, intending to stand up.

He reached out and put his hand on her knee. "Don't you see? We work well together. I thought you liked me, and I'm sure the children do. This way you can share the responsibility of raising them. You'll be safe. Have the home you wanted."

When she didn't answer, he continued. "Do you really think I'd trade your wagon in on a newer one if it weren't for you? Yours wouldn't have made it out of the territory. I'm trying to make the journey a little more comfortable and safer for you."

He said nothing about affection, not to mention love. "How can you barter with the children?! You know how much I love them." She glared at him with her lips pressed together to keep from crying. She'd never thought he could be so heartless.

"How about me? Don't you like me?"

She stared at him, astonished. *"Like?"* She massaged her forehead.

He felt as frustrated as she appeared to be. "I thought I

was offering you what you wanted. We'll raise our family together." The silence was a blow to his ego. He was so sure she would be happy. "Don't you trust me?"

She slumped against the back of the sofa. "I guess I do." His proposition was an answer to her problems. He was right. That was the problem. Except his offer didn't include love. She'd thought she would do *anything* for the children. But she hadn't expected this. Could she go that far for them?

"I accept . . . with one condition. My only wifely duty for you will be to cook your meals and wash your clothes." Since he hadn't said he loved her, that shouldn't pose a problem for him.

He watched her piercing gaze. In some respects he knew her better than she did. She couldn't deny her passions any more than he could. "I agree." He smiled at her and leaned forward. "A kiss to seal the bargain.

She gave him a slight nod and sat there as frigidly as he had proposed marriage. She could endure a kiss. After all, he had yielded to her condition, hadn't he? He moved closer, slid his arm around her shoulder and pressed his mouth to hers. He didn't try to part her lips. He gave her the sweetest of kisses.

This might be more difficult than she'd first thought. He apparently didn't share her need for love. Marriage, to her, required a deep emotional commitment, love. Otherwise it was no more than two people banding together for their mutual interest. Before she could be his wife in every respect, she would have to be sure of his affection. Until that time, she would work with him and deny the passion that seemed to spark between them.

Eleanore woke up early and went about her usual morning duties. She'd spent the night tossing and turning and doubting the seriousness of Jordon's proposal. As she stood in front of the stove, her gaze repeatedly veered to the wagon out in the yard.

She should be deliciously happy. And she would have been, if he loved her. Damnation! She whipped the mush, driven by her pent-up frustrations. When she was a little girl, she had wondered what hell was like. She had the awful feeling she would soon find out. How else could she describe what it would be like having him within reach, like candy behind glass was to a child?

The children came in and carried their bowls to the dining room. Jordon still wasn't up. Eleanore marched out to the back end of the wagon and called him.

He walked around from the front. "Good morning."

"Breakfast is ready." She should have scolded him for having to look for him, but she seemed to have forgotten that at the sight of him. He was shirtless, his hair damp, and the lines of his well-muscled chest and arms fascinated her, for a moment.

He put his shirt on, joined her and held his arm out. "Shall we?"

"You're impossible." She quickly turned around so he wouldn't see the smile she couldn't resist and walked back to the house without his assistance. She realized that if she didn't dampen his spirit, turn him sour on her, his silliness just might keep her from snapping at him, if it didn't drive her mad first.

As soon as everyone was seated in the dining room, Jordon gazed at her. He'd have sworn she was happy. "Has Miss Eleanore told you our good news?"

Amelia glanced through her lashes at Mr. Jordon and Miss Eleanore. He was grinning. She looked happy but not as much as he was.

Patrick stared at Jordon. "Aren't you gonna tell us?"

Eleanore waited as expectantly as the children, but Jordon only continued to grin at her. "Mr. Jordon and I are going to be . . . married."

Amelia hugged Beth Anne.

Patrick dropped his spoon in the bowl. "Wow. Really?"

Jordon chuckled. "Really."

"When?"

"I'm not sure, Beth Anne." Eleanore cast a frustrated look at Jordon. "We haven't picked a day yet."

"We truly are all going west together?"

"Just like any other family, Amelia." Jordon winked at her. He'd never seen her so pleased.

Beth Anne cocked her head and stared at Eleanore. "Are you going to have a baby?"

Eleanore choked on a bite of bread.

Jordon eyed Beth Anne in disbelief.

Amelia glared at her friend. "Why would you ask such a thing?" Miss Eleanore hadn't been as happy as Mr. Jordon. Now she had a funny look on her face.

Beth Anne frowned. "When ladies marry, don't they have babies?"

"That happens *after* they're married." Amelia grimaced at the younger girl.

"What'd I do?"

"Nothing's wrong, Beth Anne." Eleanore put another bite of mush into her mouth and hoped she could swallow it. She also sent up a prayer that the children wouldn't repeat that question to anyone else. Then a horrifying idea came to mind, and the mush lodged itself in her throat as securely as a dry chunk of meat. Would others think she *had* to get married?

Jordon saw the strange expression on her face and noticed that her eyes were watering. "Are you all right?" When she didn't answer, he jumped to his feet, ran to her side and thumped her on her back.

The lump in her throat passed, and she gasped for breath. "I couldn't breathe." While she dried her eyes, he rubbed her back. It felt wonderful, soothing. "I'm okay now." She met his concerned gaze. "Thank you."

He rested his hand on her shoulder as he studied her coloring. "Did you swallow the wrong way?"

He appeared genuinely concerned. It was difficult to believe he didn't feel something more than friendship for her. "I must have." She couldn't possibly tell him what had really caused her to choke.

After Mr. Jordon returned to his seat, Amelia set her spoon down. "Can we go to your wedding?"

Patrick perked up. "I've never seen a wedding. Can we?"

Eleanore glanced at Jordon and smiled. "We want you there with us."

"You'll be our ma and pa . . ."

"Yes, we will." Jordon liked the sound of that.

Patrick frowned as if worrying over a problem. "Will that make me Patrick Stone? All of us'll be Stones?"

Jordon nodded. "If that's what you want."

"Hey, you won't have t'sleep on the floor now. You can sleep in her bed." As if that solved a weighty problem, Patrick took a drink of milk.

Eleanore finished her breakfast. Why couldn't Patrick simply eat and quit thinking? Even she hadn't faced that predicament yet. When she peered through her lashes at Jordon, he looked very satisfied. She'd set him straight later—when they were alone.

Amelia tried out the new name very softly. "Amelia Stone." She liked it. "And we'll all be sisters and brother?"

Beth Anne grinned. "I'm glad you're my sister, Amelia. And that makes Patrick out brother."

"Wait'll I tell Walter! Gee, he's gonna be surprised." Patrick dug into his food.

Amelia and Beth Anne said, "And Lottie!" at the same time.

Eleanore's face was a delightful peach color. Jordon chuckled. Had she thought their marriage plans would remain a secret? As far as he was concerned, the more people who knew, the better. No one would think the worst of her. Hadn't she thought of that? "I'll walk over to the livery with you, Patrick."

Eleanore's glance slid from the girls to Jordon. "We'll go with you."

During the next hour, Eleanore felt as if her head were spinning. While she and the girls did the dishes, they asked questions such as, "What'll you wear when you get married?" "Don't you wanta baby?" "Do we call you Mrs. Eleanore or Mama?" "What kinda baby do you want, boy or girl?" She did her best without committing to anything. When she and the girls joined Patrick and Jordon, the children walked ahead, leaving her to walk beside Jordon.

He glanced at her out of the corner of his eye. She licked her lips, couldn't seem to find a convenient place to put her hands, and her gaze darted all over. "Are you okay?"

"Why wouldn't I be?" Her arms hadn't used to get in the way, why now?

He held his arm out. "Why don't you put your hand through here."

She stared at his elbow. Did she have to announce their intentions to the whole world? She tried to smile but knew she hadn't succeeded.

"I understand couples have been seen strolling arm in arm without raising too many brows." He heard her sigh and felt her hand brush his. He hooked his thumb over hers and smiled.

As they passed by Harriet's house, Eleanore saw her in the window staring with her hand up, as if she were about to wave. Eleanore smiled and kept walking right by Mrs. Renton's boardinghouse. They paused at the door to the general store and heard the children's excited chatter. She peered inside to see how many people were listening.

Jordon released her hand. "After you."

The moment she stepped over the threshold, seven faces turned their way. She smiled and dreaded what might happen next.

Mrs. Gunther beamed. "Congratulations, Miss Eleanore, Mr. Stone."

Mr. Gunther nodded. "Oh, Stone, I'll have those supplies for you Friday morning."

Jordon thanked him and followed Eleanore over to where the children stood with Lottie. "Morning, Miss Lottie."

Lottie came around the table and hugged Eleanore. "I'm so happy for you."

"That's nice of you, dear. Are you still certain you want to remain here?"

"I haven't changed my mind." Lottie peeked at the other counters. "I don't think we'll be moving. Anyway, not for a while."

Jordon leaned forward. "Remember what I said. It goes until we ride out of town."

Lottie nodded and stepped back.

After glancing around, Jordon casually put his hand on Eleanore's shoulder. "Get whatever you need. Gunther knows what supplies I ordered. He'll tell you if it's on my list."

Her gaze snapped to him. "Where're you going?"

"To the livery. I need to speak with Tucker and wish him luck."

He was going to leave her to answer the questions by herself? "But I thought we were going together?"

What was wrong with her? He gave her shoulder a gentle, hopefully reassuring squeeze. "You and the girls can meet me there when you're finished here." He looked at them. "See you later."

"Wait for me . . ." Patrick caught up with Jordon at the door.

Eleanore took Jordon's advice and began studying the items on the shelves and walls. She'd been so concerned about their clothing she hadn't thought about provisions. She had cooking utensils but needed beans, cornmeal, matches . . . thread, pants and a couple shirts for Patrick. She chose things she could carry and asked that the others be put aside with Jordon's goods. Mr. Gunther said she was to put everything on her account. She accepted graciously. She had no choice—she hadn't brought any money with her.

Amelia and Beth Anne came out from the back room. Beth Anne tugged on Eleanore's skirt. "Lottie showed us her kitten, Stitches."

"That was very nice of her. Are you ready to go see Walter?"

They both nodded. Eleanore said good-bye to Mrs. Gunther on their way out.

"Wait . . . Miss Eleanore. When's the happy day? You didn't tell us."

Mrs. Gunther looked at her with anticipation written across her face, and Eleanore realized there were several things she and Jordon hadn't addressed. "We haven't decided yet."

"Don't you let him get away." Mrs. Gunther laughed.

Eleanore smiled until she stepped onto the boardwalk.

Beth Anne stepped to Eleanore's side. "Why'd she say that? Does Mr. Jordon want to leave us?"

"She was just teasing. Don't give it another thought, sweetie."

Eleanore trailed behind the girls as they skipped into the livery and were greeted by Toby. She heard the boys' laughter coming from the front loft. "I think they're up there."

"Walter . . . Patrick . . . come on down here." Beth Anne planted her hands on her waist and stared up at the top of the ladder.

Amelia went down on her knee and petted the dog.

Eleanore rubbed near Toby's ear the way he liked it. When she stood up, she saw Jordon out back and joined him and Mr. Tucker.

"Congratulations, Miss Merrill. That's sure good news."

Eleanore thanked him and glanced around the yard. "Are you ready to leave tomorrow?"

"As much as possible. I'll have to make a few trips."

"Here, I'll take those." Jordon lifted the three bundles from her arms. "Mr. Tucker knows where we can buy a few head of cattle."

She gaped at him in complete confusion. "What do we need with them?"

Tucker chuckled. "They'll come in handy when you get hungry on your trek west."

"I'm only planning to buy five cows."

Eleanore stared at him. He'd already bought a wagon, oxen, ordered most of their provisions, and now he wanted cows? He hadn't declared his love, but he evidently was serious about taking care of them. She smiled. Maybe friendship was enough to bond them together.

The rest of that day and the next were spent sorting, folding and packing. Jordon told Eleanore about the pockets attached to the canvas. While he secured the larger tools and water casks to the wagon, she cut various size pouches, stitched them to the canvas and filled them. In the evenings, she cut down some of the clothes for the children. Amelia labored over a nightgown and helped Beth Anne with hers. Jordon let Patrick watch him build a storage box for the outside of the wagon between the wheels.

Jordon sat on the sofa near Eleanore, watching her nimble fingers put together a small dress. "Do the children have warm winter clothes?"

"They've grown since the last snowfall. They can put on layers of clothes." She held up the dress for Amelia. It was finished except for the hem.

"That's pretty. Do they have enough socks and . . . undergarments? What about Patrick? His shoes are about worn out."

"All could use some socks. I washed three shirts I found in Papa's trunk. The children can put them over their nightclothes if it gets too cold." She worked on the hem, wanting to complete the dress before she retired for the night. "What about you? Do you have winter clothes? A heavy coat?"

"We'll make an extra stop in Nebraska City." He yawned. "Did you ever find your things the storm carried away?"

She glanced over at him. "A couple blankets and the boys' chest of drawers, but it was broken up."

"Maybe you better make a list of what clothes or bedding's needed. It's going to get mighty cold without a wood stove for heat." He resisted touching her. Since the day before, when she'd been so reluctant to announce their upcoming wedding, he'd known he'd better tread lightly until they were legally man and wife. "If you have an idea what you want, I'll write it down now."

She stuck the needle through the cloth. "There's paper in the desk. I still have to pack it."

He found everything he needed in one drawer and sat down. "Socks, hats," he listed as he spoke, "yard goods . . ."

"Gloves or mittens."

He put those on the list, too. "What else?"

"I think that's it." She gave him a weary smile. "Are you sure you can afford all this?"

"I'm not a rich man, but I can see that we start out with the necessary supplies." He added a cloak for Eleanore, replaced the pen and top to the inkstand and left the paper on top of the desk. "Don't worry."

She tied off the end of the thread and set her sewing box on the table. "I'm tired. I'll see you in the morning."

"Pleasant dreams." He watched her leave the room. She didn't know it yet, but she would only spend two more nights alone. He grinned. After turning down the lamp wick, he sauntered down the hall to his room. He was looking forward to their Saturday afternoon wedding and the night that would follow.

* * *

Thursday morning, Eleanore was in the wagon deciding how she would pack all their belongings in there. She had no idea how much space Jordon's provisions would take up. She set aside room for the mattress that could also serve as a sofa during the long ride. She realized that she needed to bring the packed crates out and move them around.

On her way back to the house, she saw Harriet coming toward her. "What are you doing out so early?"

Harriet planted her hands on her hips. "I came to help you pack! It was bad enough that I had to hear about your forthcoming marriage at the general store, but I won't even be able to see you wed, since we have no preacher." She hugged Eleanore. "I am *so* thrilled for you!"

"Thank you. I wish you could be there."

"Well, I am here now. What needs to be done?"

"I was about to start packing the wagon." Eleanore went into the kitchen, where she'd stacked the crates. "I'll take one side, you the other."

Jordon saw Harriet and Eleanore struggling with the box. He met them at the wagon. "Let me take that." He took the container and swung it up to the seat. "Good morning, Mrs. Blake."

Harriet smiled. "Congratulations, Mr. Stone."

"I am a fortunate man, Mrs. Blake." He glanced at Eleanore. "Why didn't you ask me for help?"

Eleanore gazed at him. "I thought we could manage."

He climbed up, set the crate in the bed of the wagon and let the back end down. "Are the others that heavy?"

"Only one, but we can handle it."

He eyed her with good humor and stowed the second one for her. "Call if you need me." He went back to the corral.

Harriet grinned. "I would say you are very lucky, too, not to mention the sly one, Eleanore. You kept denying you had feelings for him."

After they stepped into the kitchen, Eleanore looked at

her friend. "I do . . . care for him." Harriet's eyes lit up like twin lamps. Eleanore shook her head.

"I knew it! And the way he gazes at you . . . It is enough to make me blush." Harriet hugged Eleanore. "You deserve it."

"Maybe I do. Thank you." Did she *deserve* to be locked in a loveless marriage? Of course Harriet didn't know it wasn't a love match, but Eleanore wondered what she'd done to earn such a fate. They carried two more boxes out and experimented with their placement. "There's so much I have to leave behind. I want you to take anything you want. Jordon said we could bring the beds by early Saturday morning, if that's all right with you."

"You mean you can't take them?" She crossed the yard and entered the kitchen with Eleanore.

"There's no room for more than the bare necessities and mattresses." Eleanore patted Harriet's hand. "I thought we'd be traveling in my old wagon. It was half the size of the prairie schooner, so I'm delighted to have the extra room."

Harriet picked up the emergency supplies. "I can keep some of your things if you want and send them after you are settled."

Eleanore shook her head. "I'd rather you take what you want and tell others to do the same. The bank is only interested in the land." She carried a stack of linen out to the wagon.

Harriet walked out with her. "Well, I think it is a sin, the way that man Cullen has treated you."

"He doesn't strike me as the kind of man who fears God or anyone else."

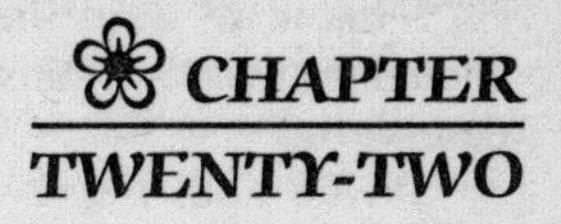

CHAPTER TWENTY-TWO

That night, after the children were asleep, Jordon found Eleanore in the wagon. She was perched on a crate, staring into space. "You spent most of the day hauling things out here. What are you doing now?" She was pale, her shoulders slumped, and fatigue showed in her lifeless expression.

Her gaze drifted up to him. "It's all coming true. We're really going to cross the country, like I'd always dreamed of doing."

He stepped over the bench and sat across from her. "You do know this trip will be much more difficult than your ride to Kansas? We'll have to winter at one of the forts, if we're lucky. And we won't reach the West until next summer." A dreamy smile softened the weariness in her eyes.

"But we *will* be on our way."

He shook his head and wondered if she were even awake. "Come with me. You're going to bed." He clasped her hands and stood, drawing her up with him. She had never seemed so fragile. "You've got to rest."

She glanced from one end of the wagon to the other. "There's so much to do."

"If we aren't ready to leave until Monday, that's okay." He helped her down to the ground. "I'll get the supplies tomorrow. You spend the day resting or sewing if you're not finished with that." He tipped her chin up with his knuckle. "Understand?"

She nodded. "I'm too sleepy to argue."

Before she returned from the necessary, he drew her bedroom drapes closed, hoping she would sleep in. He turned in himself. She was right. There didn't seem to be enough hours in the day. But everything was stored in the schooner except for last-minute items.

The next morning, Eleanore stirred under the light covers and resisted the urge to open her eyes. It couldn't be morning already. She burrowed under the pillow. Sometime later, whether a minute or thirty she didn't know, the smell of bacon frying and hot coffee roused her.

As she poured the water from the pitcher into the basin, she noticed the room was darker than it should be. She set the pitcher down and opened the drapes. The sun was far above the horizon. After quickly dashing the cold water over her face, she dressed and rushed to the kitchen.

Jordon was turning the bacon over when she dashed into the room. "Good morning. I hope you slept soundly." He glanced over at her. She was fully awake, with the color back in her cheeks.

He was at the stove with his back to her, as if he cooked breakfast every day. "Did you close my drapes?"

"You needed the rest." He poured her a cup of coffee and handed it to her.

"Thanks." She stared around the room. The bacon sizzled in an old skillet they weren't taking with them. Five table settings had been left out, to be packed last. It seemed impossible they'd be gone from there in twenty-four hours. "Where are the children?"

"In their room. I told them to be quiet and make sure they'd packed everything." He picked up a plate and dished out a generous helping of bacon, eggs and flapjacks. "Start eating while it's hot."

She took the plate, and he reached for another one. She shook her head. She felt as if she had stepped into someone else's shoes. He was acting strange. As if . . . "Jordon, we will be married tomorrow, won't we?"

He looked over his shoulder at her. "We'll find a preacher tomorrow in Nebraska City."

"Good." She set her plate on the dining room table and went to see the children. "Hello."

"Thanks, Miss Eleanore." Patrick hugged her legs. "I like these store-bought clothes."

"I'm glad, but you should thank Jordon." She motioned him back a pace. "You look very handsome."

Beth Anne giggled.

"I'm gonna show Mr. Jordon." Patrick ran out of the room.

Eleanore went over to the girls, who were sitting on their bed. "You're already sewing?"

Amelia held up her nightgown. "See. It's almost finished."

"That is very nice, Amelia. You've done a wonderful job."

Amelia smiled and elbowed Beth Anne. "Show her yours."

Beth Anne held her gown up. "I'm slower than Amelia."

Eleanore took the sleeveless garment and looked at the stitches. "You are doing very well. I'm proud of you." She smiled. "Breakfast is ready. Come on."

The girls went to the kitchen, and Eleanore the dining room. Patrick sat at the table smoothing the front of his new shirt with his hand. As Eleanore sat down, the girls and Jordon came in and took their seats.

Beth Anne tapped Eleanore's hand. "Can we really go to your wedding?"

"Of course."

"We wouldn't get married without you. We're all one family." Jordon smiled at each of them.

Patrick's eyes brightened. "You mean *we're all getting married*?"

Eleanore and Jordon shared the amusement silently before she answered. "After Jordon and I are married, you'll be our children."

"Gee, I thought we all were gettin' married."

Amelia spoke up without thinking. "We can't marry. Don't you know that?" She realized how that sounded and clamped her hand over her mouth.

"You're right, Amelia." Eleanore gave her an encouraging look. "Children cannot marry, but you can witness our marriage, and you will be *our* children."

Jordon held his cup up, saluting her tact, and drank a toast. "Now that that's settled, I'd better hitch up the oxen and pick up the supplies I ordered."

"Can I help you?"

"Sure. I'll need another pair of hands, Patrick."

Amelia drank the last of her milk and motioned to Beth Anne. "May we be excused? We have to finish our gowns."

"Why don't you bring your sewing into the parlor? I have a little more work to do on Beth Anne's dress." Eleanore came to her feet, too, and followed the girls to the kitchen with her plate. After the breakfast dishes were put away, she joined the girls in the parlor.

Beth Anne's dress and petticoat had been hemmed, and Jordon still hadn't returned. Eleanore was helping Beth Anne attach the sleeves to her nightgown when she heard the wagon pull into the yard. The three of them went out to meet him. Patrick was sitting on Jordon's lap, waving.

Beth Anne turned to Eleanore. "Can we take turns like Patrick?"

"We'll see." Jordon handed Patrick down to Eleanore. "What took you so long?"

"Wait'll you see!" Patrick grabbed her hand and pulled her to the back of the wagon. "Look!"

Eleanore glanced up at the end of the prairie schooner.

Jordon came up behind her. "I'll help you." He put his hands on her waist and lifted her up.

"Hey, look at Miss Eleanore!" Patrick did a jig behind Jordon.

Amelia grabbed his hand. "Patrick, what is he showing her?"

"All the food 'n' stuff."

Eleanore couldn't believe her eyes—or that Jordon was holding her up in the air like one of the children. "Put me down."

He chuckled. "Did you see everything?"

"Yes." She swung her legs, hoping he wouldn't be able to hold her much longer.

"Are you sure?"

"Please, put me down." She braced her hands over his, so he wouldn't drop her.

He pulled her to him and slid her down his body to the ground. With his mouth near her ear, he whispered, "Better?"

Her insides instantly reacted. She groaned and dropped her hands to her sides. She didn't need to be reminded how his body felt. "I will be," she said, taking a deep, calming breath.

The children had climbed up to the bench seat. "Then I'd better organize all that." He gave her bottom a pat and stepped away.

She whirled around with a not-so-quick reply, but he had walked away. She started to frown and ended up laughing. That was the only way to deal with him. Besides, who wanted to be coiled in a knot all the time? She certainly didn't.

Twenty hours later, Eleanore settled Amelia, Beth Anne, Patrick and Smidgen in the back of the wagon. "I'll be right back. Please, stay right there." Eleanore was glad Jordon had decided to take the bed frames to the Blakes the night before. It had been difficult enough saying goodbye to her dearest friend then, let alone seeing the last of her home.

She entered her house for the last time.

Jordon followed her inside. "Do you really want to do this?"

She nodded. "Besides, I need to make sure we haven't forgotten anything."

"You did pack that saucy straw bonnet with the silk scarf, didn't you?"

"No. I'd never wear . . ." She gazed at him. Saucy? "It's in my room."

He gave her a lighthearted wink. "I'll wait for you outside. Bring it with you."

"If you want me to."

She stepped into the hall, glancing at the walls and the scarred plank floor, recalling her father, then the children who'd walked down the corridor. She shook her head and blinked to clear her vision. This was no time to get teary. After checking each room and grabbing the hat, she went outside.

Jordon smiled. "Good. You found it." He took the hat and handed it to Amelia, then lifted Eleanore up to the bench. He made certain the back of the wagon was secure and that the horses were firmly fastened at each corner before he climbed up near her. "Ready?"

She nodded and attempted a smile.

He looked back at Amelia, Beth Anne and Patrick. After they answered with a resounding "Yes!" he started the oxen moving. It was barely sunup.

As they rode through town, the noise of the oxen and wagon seemed to bounce off the buildings. Eleanore stared straight ahead, her heart pounding in her breast. Several minutes later, she glanced at him and realized she hadn't even questioned his driving. They were leaving together. He appeared undisturbed, content, with his hat tipped down to shade his eyes from the rising sunlight.

She lifted the slat bonnet from where it rested on the back of her neck and set it on her head. The children were settled on the two stacked mattresses, playing with Smidgen. The four yolk of oxen kicked up dust. It drifted on the air.

"How long will it take us to reach Nebraska City?"

"We should be there by early afternoon." After he turned onto the road north, he met her gaze. "You can rest in back if you want."

"I'd rather stay here." She smiled and felt excitement bubbling within. He was giving her a precious gift—the realization of her dream. The jostling motion of the wagon and having slept for only a few hours the night before finally made her drowsy.

He settled back, feeling a subtle change in her. He'd heard that a woman could be a little strange before her wedding, that she usually cried or made peculiar demands. Nerves, a friend's father had said. Eleanore had been a little cool with him. He sighed. Maybe she had just been anxious and was now over it.

It was midday when he saw the city up ahead. "It won't be long now," he said.

The sound of his voice startled her. She blinked. "Nebraska City? Already?" His deep chuckle sent a strange sensation down her spine. She shifted on the hard bench.

"You dozed off. Feel better?"

"Much." She turned her head aside and brushed the fine coat of dust off of her face.

"We'll stop at the general store first."

She looked back at the children. All three were asleep. When Jordon pulled up in front of the store, she went back and roused them. The kitten was curled up on one of the blankets between two crates. They were careful not to awaken the cat.

Beth Anne stood by the rear wagon wheel. "Can't I stay here? If she wakes up, she might get scared."

When Eleanore deferred to him, Jordon lifted Beth Anne back into the wagon and checked to make sure the brake was set. "You sit right there. We won't be long."

Beth Anne leaned over the back and whispered, "Okay."

The store was crowded with Saturday shoppers. While Eleanore picked up what she needed, Jordon chose a warm wool cloak for her. A clerk rushed to his side.

"May I help you?"

Jordon glanced over his shoulder. "Would you wrap this for me. It's a surprise."

"Of course, sir."

While the man wrapped the cloak in brown paper and tied it with string, Jordon stepped over to a small glass case displaying gold rings and broaches. There were four plain bands, two with stones and one the width of a ten-penny nail with fine etching.

The clerk set the package on the counter. "See something you fancy?"

"That ring on the end. How much are you asking?"

The clerk withdrew the one Jordon pointed to and handed it to him. "Only two dollars and fifteen cents, sir. Do you think that will fit the lady?"

Jordon held it up. "Her fingers are slender, but I just don't know."

"Is the lady with you?"

"Yes, but I planned on surprising her with it."

The clerk smiled knowingly. "If you'll point her out, I think I can handle the situation to your satisfaction."

Jordon peered over his shoulder. "The pretty one in the gold-and-brown calico with the boy and girl, by the yard goods."

"Why don't you look at our tools while I speak with her?"

Jordon wandered around on the opposite side of the store until the clerk returned to the counter. After making sure Eleanore's back was turned to him, he joined the clerk.

The clerk smiled. "Fits her like a glove."

"Good. I'll take it. And I'd be obliged if you could tell me where I can find a preacher." He paid the clerk.

"Go right on up the street till you come to the blacksmith. Take a left. Can't miss his house, right by the church."

Jordon tucked the ring in his trousers pocket. "Thank you very much." He carried the package out and put it under the seat of the wagon. He walked around back. "How're you doing?"

"Shh," Beth Anne whispered. "Are we going now?"

"Be a few more minutes. I'll hurry them up." He went back in the store and made his way to Eleanore's side. "Are you finding everything?"

"Yes, but it's too much. I'll—"

"Let me take those. Don't forget mittens and gloves for yourself, or the shoes for all of them. Oh, you'll need an extra pair for handling the team, too. While I keep the cows moving, you'll have to drive the wagon."

She nodded and handed him the clothes and material. She found yarn to make mittens and a pair of strong leather gloves for herself.

Amelia moved over to a table with a display of ladies cotton hose and picked up two pairs. She went over to Mr. Jordon and added them to the stack of goods. "Miss Eleanore needs them."

"Good girl." He smiled and bent down to her. "Remember, after the wedding, you can call her Mama."

"I won't forget." *Papa,* she said under her breath.

Jordon met Eleanore at the counter and paid for the merchandise. "Thanks, again."

The clerk smiled. "Good luck to you folks."

Eleanore glanced back. "Why did he wish us luck?"

Jordon shrugged. "Just friendly, I guess."

Everyone climbed back into the wagon, and Jordon followed the directions the clerk had given him. A few minutes later, he pulled up in front of a whitewashed house.

Amelia finished buttoning her good blue dress and hurried to change into her new shoes. If this wasn't the most special occasion, there wouldn't be one.

Eleanore stared at the cross in front of the church next

door. This was it. Now or never, but there was no choice to be made. She glanced at her sleeve. If she'd only had a good dress to wear . . . If he only loved her . . .

Jordon put his hand over hers. "Are you ready?"

She gazed into his misty green eyes and nodded.

He climbed down and lifted her to the ground. While she shook the dust from her clothes, he helped the children out of the wagon. "This's where we're going to be married."

Amelia joined hands with Beth Anne and Patrick. "We'll be good."

Jordon smiled. "I wasn't worried." He put Eleanore's hand on his arm and led the way to the door.

She curved her fingers around his arm. She looked to the children and noticed Amelia was wearing her good dress. Eleanore smiled, then walked at Jordon's side up to the front door of the house.

He was really going to marry her. She glanced over her shoulder at the children, again, and realized she'd never honestly thought it would happen. A man dressed in a black suit opened the door. She gripped Jordon's arm.

She didn't hear the preacher's name or what Jordon said. Bits and pieces of memories flittered around in her mind. Then she heard him say, "I do." She blinked.

The preacher glanced up from the book. "Do you, Eleanore Merrill, take this man . . ."

At some point she said, "I do." It felt as if Jordon raised her left hand a moment later and slipped a beautiful gold wedding band on her fourth finger. It was the same lovely ring the clerk had asked her to try on, telling her a customer wanted to purchase it if it fit a slim finger. She moistened her lips, feeling slightly dazed. Jordon had gone to such lengths.

"I now pronounce you man and wife." The small book in the preacher's hands closed with a snap. "You may kiss your bride, sir."

She felt Jordon's large, gentle hands turn her around to

face him. She saw a flash of an easy smile just before his lips caressed hers.

"Whoopee!" Patrick tried to break free of Amelia's grasp.

Amelia sent up a prayer of thanks and grinned so hard she thought her face might split, but she didn't care. All was right and Miss— No, Mama would be really happy.

Patrick broke free of Amelia. "We're all Stones now!"

The preacher nodded. "And you have a new papa."

"And mama," Amelia added proudly.

As Beth Anne stared at Eleanore and Jordon, she echoed Amelia.

"Papa," Patrick tugged on Jordon's sleeve, "will you be sleeping with Mama now?"

Jordon struggled to keep a serious expression on his face. "Yes."

"Don't snore too loud."

Eleanore sat with her hands resting on her lap in such a way that she could gaze at her wedding band. The idea of Jordon buying her a ring had never entered her mind. She moved her finger and watched the way the sunlight glistened on the delicately etched rosebuds.

"Eleanore . . ." Jordon glanced at her and chuckled. She seemed spellbound by the gold band. "Eleanore, I'd better show you how to handle this team before we get to the ranch. It's just up the road."

She dropped her hand to the bench, under a fold of her skirt. "Yes. I'll get the gloves." She climbed over the seat. If she'd been thinking straight, she would have put the heavy leather gloves where she could reach them. They were in the second bundle. She returned to the bench and sat by Jordon's side.

After pointing out the differences between a horse harness and the oxen yolk, he had her take the leather reins. He tried reaching over to give her suggestions, but he kept brushing her breast with his right arm, which was very distracting for both of them. "It'll be easier if I stand behind you."

She nodded. It couldn't be worse; her breast still tingled from his touch. When his arms came around her, she trembled, then his hands rested on hers. She tried to pay attention to what he was saying, but it wasn't easy to do in his embrace.

When he bent near her, a faint scent of roses drifted up from her neck. It was decidedly distracting, and he had a hell of a time concentrating on the task at hand and not kissing her. "That's good. Try to relax. You don't want your arms or back to cramp up." Great advice, he thought, if only he could follow it himself.

His arms were warm on hers, and his cheek grazed hers when the wagon jolted them. Each time he took a breath, she felt it, and every time he let one out, it fanned her jaw. How was she supposed to "relax"? It was impossible even to change positions without touching him. She glanced up as a hawk glided over the road. It didn't help. "Why don't you sit back down? I think I've got the hang of it."

He sat back down next to her and put his foot up on the jockey box. The scent of roses seemed to be everywhere. He shifted on the wooden bench. "I'll take the reins now."

She handed them over to him.

"Rest. This may be the last chance you have before we camp for the night." He tipped his hat down lower on his forehead and settled back. Even with gloves, handling the oxen day after day was going to be a hardship for her.

She stretched her back and changed positions. It would take a couple days to get used to handling the oxen but that was a small price to pay for a dream. As they made their way down the road, she felt like they were all alone in the middle of nowhere. She was glad Jordon was with her, and she began to understand why he had been worried about her setting out on her own with the children.

She peered sideways at him. "The oxen are slow, aren't they? Why didn't you want to use horses?"

"Oxen aren't that particular about what they eat. We have a couple high mountain ranges to cross. Oxen are hardier, stronger, will pull the weight better."

She nodded. "Ned wouldn't have lasted, not with this weight, anyway." She pulled her gloves off and idly flexed the leather fingers. In the many times she read her guide, she had envisioned the journey with a team of horses pulling the wagon much faster, covering so many more miles each day.

"If you're restless, you can walk."

She stared at the rutted road and wondered how many wagons had passed that way before them. "I think I will." While he brought the animals to a stop, she urged the children to get out and walk with her for a while.

The children enjoyed the opportunity to run around. Eleanore kept pace with the wagon at the side of the road. Amelia and Beth Anne ran through the prairie grass. Patrick tried to race a lark darting about above him. By the time Jordon called out that the ranch was just ahead, Eleanore was very grateful to him and determined to be as much help as she was able to be.

Jordon stopped the wagon a short distance from the house. A man came out from the barn and greeted him.

"How can I help you?"

Jordon held out his hand. "Jordon Stone. You're Mr. Dodd?"

"I am." Dodd shook hands with Jordon.

Jordon smiled and put his hand on Eleanore's back. "This is my wife and our children."

Mr. Dodd removed his hat and acknowledged Eleanore.

"Mr. Tucker in Myles Creek told me you sold cows. We're interested in five."

Dodd nodded again, as if he'd known what Jordon was going to say. "I still have fifty head here. Follow me."

Jordon looked at Eleanore. "Wait here."

Patrick ran over to him. "Can I go with you . . . Papa?"

Jordon grinned with pride. "You can."

Eleanore watched them go with Mr. Dodd and turned to the girls. "We better let Smidgen run around out here."

Later that night, she recalled Jordon's warning about rest and knew he hadn't been teasing her. After only two or three hours of handling the oxen, her arms, hands and bottom either hurt or felt numb, not to mention her aching back. Stopping by the side of the trail on their trip north from Kansas had been a picnic compared to this journey.

While Jordon tended the cows, she had said good night to the children. She quickly changed into her nightgown and wrapper before he came back. She was sore and exhausted. He had set up the two army tents he'd purchased for their quarters. She had put the mattress in, which was more difficult than she'd imagined, and made the beds. She'd have rather curled up in the wagon, but he insisted they use the tent.

She yawned and gave up waiting for him. He'd worked harder than she had and must be ready to fall asleep, too. She took off her wrapper, dropped it at the end of the mattresses and literally crawled into bed and collapsed.

Jordon finally finished tending the stock and returned to camp. The fire still burned, but no one stirred. He rinsed the trail dust off and crawled into bed beside Eleanore wearing only his drawers. She lay on her side. He reached out and felt her hair on the pillow. He combed his fingers through the silky strands and kissed her neck.

She didn't move. He trailed his hand along her arm to her elbow, dipped down to the curve of her hip and slid around to below her belly. Ever so gently he pulled her to him. Her breathing was steady. He caressed one breast and felt her nipple harden. She made a soft, contented sound but didn't awaken. He cuddled up and went to sleep with her back pressed firmly against his bare chest.

CHAPTER TWENTY-THREE

Four days out of Nebraska City, Eleanore was only beginning to fully understand how rugged the journey would be. Calluses were forming on her hands. Jordon said he liked the way her face tanned, and she was sure she was gaining muscles in her arms. The days were getting a bit cooler, and the measureless land inspired daydreams. Amelia and Beth Anne searched for flowers or pretty rocks. Patrick learned to ride Ned.

They broke camp shortly after sunrise each day, stopped for dinner around midday and made camp a while before sunset. A week later they had settled into the routine. One night Beth Anne had fallen asleep first, followed by Patrick. Amelia had joined them within a short time.

Eleanore poured more coffee into Jordon's cup and her own. He was staring at the western horizon. "Is something wrong?"

"No, just wondering how long the good weather's going to last. If we don't get bogged down by rain, we should make Fort Laramie before the end of October."

"That's a month from now. Is it really that far away?"

"According to the guidebook, a little over three hundred miles from Fort Kearny. We're still almost twelve days from there." He could see her calculating the long days ahead. "I'm hoping we can travel between the forts with supply wagons till we reach Fort Laramie."

She frowned. "What happens there?"

"That's were we'll stay until spring thaw. The next fort

along the trail is Hall, some five hundred and thirty-five miles west of there." He noticed the way she kept glancing at him and the way she held her arms over her chest, the set of her jaw. Would it take her all winter to thaw out as well? The damnedest thing was he didn't understand why she held herself apart from him.

She sat across from him fascinated by the way flames of the fire shifted light and shadows across his face and were reflected in his eyes. That familiar coil of nervousness tightened within. She sipped her coffee and added twigs to the fire.

It was time to go to bed, but she wasn't sleepy. A walk might help, but it was a moonless night, and she had more sense than to wander around in the dark. She could sew, but there wasn't enough light and she didn't want to waste kerosene. Confound it! That wasn't what she wanted.

She gripped the mug with both hands. "You could've made this trip much faster on horseback. Are you sorry we're slowing you down?"

He gazed at her and gave her a tentative smile. "No. If I'd been in a hurry, I would've taken off long ago." He swirled the coffee around in the cup.

She nodded. I'm married to a good Samaritan, she thought, and in love with a man who either can't voice his feelings or doesn't return my affection. She set her cup down. "I think I'd better go to bed. Good night." She couldn't ask him to love her, and it wasn't something she could make happen.

He steeled himself for the truth, but he had to ask. "Eleanore, are you sorry you gave up your home?"

She paused at his left, within arm's reach of him, and fingered her ring. "I may have regrets, but no, I'm not sorry."

He gazed at her folded hands at her waist. "Regrets about what?"

"What will never be . . . poor judgment on my part." She dropped her hands to her sides and met his pained gaze. "I'll try my best not to disappoint you and to make you a good home." She stepped into the tent and clamped her teeth down on her lips to thwart a cry.

He sat there by the fire grinding his teeth until the embers died. The sparkle had gone out of her eyes, and the only time she really smiled was with the children. What had he done to cause her such pain?

Eleanore swung Beth Anne around a third time and set her down on her feet.

Beth Anne giggled and dropped to her knees.

"Mama, I'm next." Patrick stood next to Beth Anne.

Eleanore imitated a frown. "You're getting awfully big."

"Oh, you can do it." He raised his arms to her.

Eleanore lifted him up and managed to swing him around once. "You are growing up, young man."

Patrick grinned and glanced at the girls. "Come on, let's find a mouse for Smidgen to play with."

"No." Beth Anne planted her hands on her hips. "She can play with a string."

Patrick kicked up a clod of dirt. "You're no fun."

"You could play leapfrog." Eleanore repacked the dishes and pot.

She saw Jordon returning and knew it was time to continue on until suppertime. He hadn't said a word since last night. She knew she had to talk with him again. They couldn't go on this way. Maybe wanting his love was asking too much of him. She was miserable and felt sure he was, too.

"Patrick . . . Amelia . . . Beth Anne, come on. We're leaving." They looked back, and Eleanore waved for them to come to the wagon.

Patrick won the race back. "We had to catch Smidgen. She's a fast runner."

Eleanore laughed. "I'm sure she is." Especially with the three of you chasing her, she thought. Patrick handed the cat to her, climbed into the wagon and held out his hands. She gave the kitten back to him before helping the girls up.

Jordon hung back, watching them laugh, primarily Eleanore. He stepped over, intending to lift her up, but she climbed to the seat before he could give her a hand. He veered away and mounted Nugget. They had perfected a wordless relationship. She started the oxen moving, he the cows.

Later that afternoon, as she stared at the deeply rutted track ahead, she thought she saw a building. She had to be mistaken. Jordon had said they wouldn't reach Fort Kearny for another three or four days. From time to time, she changed her position so her bottom wouldn't go numb. The prairie was beautiful, peaceful. An occasional hawk, owl or prairie dog sitting up on a small mound always made her smile.

Jordon rode up ahead a ways and circled back. "There's a station not too far away." She smiled at him for the first time in days, but it didn't make him feel any better.

Patrick poked his head around the edge of the canvas. "Are we gonna stop!?"

Amelia and Beth Anne joined him.

"Might as well. By the time we get there, it'll almost be time to make camp." He grinned at the children and went back to round up the wandering cows.

The children scrambled back and sat on the mattresses, all the while guessing about the station ahead. Eleanore laughed to herself over some of their ideas. If it would've done any good, she would have whipped the oxen to a run, but she didn't think them able to move any faster. Fortunately her daydreams helped her pass the miles.

Jordon rode alongside the wagon. "Pull up a ways on the other side of the station."

She nodded and halted the four yolk oxen where he had pointed. She set the brake and brushed the dust from her face. "Come on, children." She climbed down and helped them to the ground.

"Wipe as much dust off your clothes as you can. We can wash our faces and hands at the well." Eleanore shook her skirts and swiped at her sleeves. The grime seemed to have become imbedded in their clothes and skin.

Jordon tied Nugget to the back of the wagon. "Would you like to have supper here?" he asked.

"Yeah." Patrick grinned and started back to the station.

"Wait up! We'll go in together." Jordon didn't move until Patrick came back to his side. "Okay. Let's see what they're serving for supper."

Jordon walked with Beth Anne and Patrick. Eleanore was a pace behind with Amelia. Jordon had already given thanks for the station's location. They all needed to see and talk to people. He noticed two horses tied up outside but no other wagons. He held the door open for Eleanore and followed her inside.

A large brute of a man wearing a soiled apron greeted them. "Howdy, folks. Ya kin sit at this end of the table. Not so hot. What kin I get fer ya?"

Jordon left his hat on a peg by the door. "What have you got for supper?"

"Stew, biscuits and sweet potato pie."

"Sounds good. You'd better bring us five plates."

Eleanore watched the man amble toward the cooking area in the large room. There were four long tables with benches. Two men covered with dust and wearing guns were seated at the far end of one. Eleanore loosened her bonnet strings and slipped it back. To be honest, she was grateful for the hot meal and to eat inside at a table.

The man served their food, coffee for Jordon and Eleanore and milk for the children. Jordon thanked the man and started in on his stew. It was surprisingly good.

The man stepped over to the two men at the end of the table and picked up their empty plates. "You ridin' on to Omaha, now?"

"Yep." Each of the men handed the cook a coin. "See ya next week."

Patrick ate the last bite of his biscuit and finished his milk. "I'm full. Can I go look around?"

Jordon glanced at Eleanore, but again, she merely lifted one shoulder. "We'll be done soon. You'd better wait for us."

Patrick glared at Beth Anne. "Hurry up."

"I'm full." Beth Anne peered at Eleanore, then put two pieces of meat in each hand.

Eleanore laid her fork on the plate. "I think I'll pass on the pie."

Jordon eyed each one. They shook their heads. While Eleanore left with the children, Jordon settled up with the cook.

"Ya kin take this with ya." The man handed Jordon a pie tin more than half-full. "Them young'uns'll want it later."

"Thank you."

"There's a stream jist down a piece," the man said, pointing to the back of the station.

"Thanks, again." Jordon went out and walked around awhile with the children. When they returned to the wagon, he found Eleanore smiling at the kitten as it hopped stiff-legged through the grass. "The cook said there's a stream down there." Jordon glanced at her. "We can camp there."

She picked up the kitten and put it back in the wagon. "All right." Her gaze slid away from him, and she climbed back up to the bench seat.

Jordon turned on his heel and called the children. "Do you want to walk or ride down to the stream?" He pointed at some green bushes a couple hundred feet away.

Patrick looked to the girls, and they all nodded. "Can we go now?"

"Yes, but *do not go near that water* until I've seen how deep it is."

"Yes, sir!" Patrick led the way, with the girls in quick pursuit.

As usual, Jordon secured the animals and Eleanore set up camp. He joined her at sundown. "Patrick's quiet. What's he doing?" He looked around. "And where're the girls?"

"They just went to bed. They were worn out."

He nodded. "I'm going to walk back to the station. No need to wait up for me."

She glanced at the children's tent and spoke softly. "I want to talk with you."

He stiffened up. "That can wait. Right now I don't trust myself to be too polite."

She stared at him, and he walked away from her. She turned her back to him and balled her hands into fists. When the children went to bed early, she'd hoped to spend time with him, to settle whatever was between them. She stomped to the wagon, found a towel and soap, and marched down to the stream. A nice cool bath should calm her down.

Jordon was fed up with Eleanore's frosty disposition. They'd gotten along and made love before he mentioned marriage to her. Hellfire, what would it take to break through her proud bearing? He drank several glasses of what was supposed to be whiskey. By the time he returned to camp, he was feeling much better. In fact, he'd come to the conclusion that what she needed was to be made love to.

He pulled his boots off, and his socks, trousers, and shirt all landed in a pile just inside their tent. She was curled up on her side facing away from his side of the bed. He crawled under the covers and curved his body around hers. As his hand explored her thigh, he nuzzled her loose hair aside and nibbled on her neck. She smelled fresh and clean and must have dabbed more rosewater on.

She had heard him stumble into the tent. However, she was shocked when his hand started roaming over her body. She pushed it aside. In doing so, she realized he was completely naked. His hand fondled her bottom and she pushed it away again, but it was more difficult this time. He was breathing in her ear and kept kissing the tender nape of her neck.

She felt her body opening up to him. Dear Lord, she wanted him to make love to her. She ached for him. And they were married. Maybe afterward they could talk. She rolled onto her back and turned her face to him . . .

He snored in her face, then his forehead slid down and rested on her shoulder.

She would have screamed if not for the children. It wasn't fair! He had wanted her as much as she did him. She rolled back onto her side, drew her knees up to her chest and let the tears stream down her cheeks to the pillow. She had never felt so humiliated, embarrassed and frustrated in her life. She prayed she'd fall into a deep sleep and not have to face him the next day.

Jordon came awake slowly the next morning. He soon realized that he was curled up with Eleanore—and that her nightgown was hitched up to her waist. He sighed and smiled. His memory wasn't too clear about the night before, but he definitely felt much better and assumed she would, too.

Overcoming the pounding in his head, he eased out of bed and dressed. After a dip in the cold stream, he started breakfast.

Patrick crawled out of the tent first. "Smells good."

Jordon placed a finger across his lips, and Patrick nodded. "You can eat soon as you wash up," Jordon whispered.

Patrick quietly woke up the girls. "Come on, food's ready."

Jordon fed the children and ate, too. Eleanore was still asleep. "If you promise not to get wet, you can go fishing."

Patrick's eyes lit up. "Do you have a pole?"

"We can make one." Jordon rigged a crude fishing pole

using a sturdy twig, string and a pin he found in Eleanore's sewing basket. "Don't stick yourself with this." He watched the three of them hurry down to the water, then he poured a cup of coffee and went to wake Eleanore.

He stepped inside the tent and set the cup within her reach, then hunkered down and smoothed her hair back from her face. "Morning, Ellie."

She'd heard him come in but wasn't sure just what to say. She preferred not even facing him, but he seemed bent on waking her. Her eyes snapped open and she sat up . . . on her bare bottom. She gasped and glared at him.

His brows puckered. Now what was wrong? Before, when they made love, she'd been so happy the day after. "I hope I didn't . . . hurt you last night."

She came to her feet, and the gown dropped down to her ankles. She walked around him and picked up her clothes. "I would like to dress in private."

He stepped outside and snapped the flap down. Damnation, she'd gone too far. As he marched to the wagon, Smidgen jumped up and firmly planted her claws into his thigh. He yelped and lifted the kitten up to his face. "You, too? I'd like to know what the hell I've done to set you both against me." He held her on his shoulder, and she purred in contentment. If he could only calm Eleanore as easily.

Eleanore left their tent and peeked into the children's tent. "Where are they?"

"Fishing in the stream." He leaned against the wagon wheel and stroked the cat.

She refilled her cup and stared at it. She wanted to check on the children, but part of her knew she and Jordon might not have another private time for days. She took a sip, trying to decide what to do.

He put the kitten down and walked over to her. "I'd like to know why you're so dad-blamed mad at me."

She dodged the issue. "Because I wanted to dress in

private? I'm not used to taking my clothes off in your presence yet."

"I remember two, no three, times you weren't embarrassed. But that's not what I'm talking about. You've hardly looked at or spoken to me in more than a week. You act like you can't stand the sight of me." That got her attention. "After last night, I thought maybe you'd changed your mind."

"Why would last night change my mind?" He stood there watching her, and she began to wonder if he'd made love to her while she'd slept. No, it couldn't have happened. Surely she was too angry to have responded to him.

He gaped at her, his mind spinning. "We made love." He lowered his voice. "Don't *you* remember?" She couldn't have slept through it, though his memory of it was still a little hazy.

"You must have dreamt it. You were pixilated, swizzled, almost as bad off as Martin was that night you brought him home from the saloon." He looked better than he had last night, but his eyes were a little red, and he'd put his hand to his forehead a couple times, as if it hurt.

"I know I was feeling good, but I didn't imagine waking up this morning draped across you with your gown up around your waist." He was amazed how quickly her pale cheeks turned red. "Back to my question. Why have you been treating me as if I weren't here?"

"Me? You haven't been too friendly, either. I even began to wonder if I'd get more of your attention if I were a cow."

He sputtered and shook his head at her. "You laugh and play with the children; you won't even hold a conversation with me and you appear to suffer with my company. Damn it! Tell me what the hell's going on!"

"First let me tell you something else. You *did not* make love to me last night." He scowled at her, but before he could speak, she continued. "Oh, you came back and crawled in bed in a very friendly spirit and tried, but when I turned to you, *you* snored in my face!"

They were standing about three feet apart, and she stepped forward. "While you're so interested in questions and answers, you can answer one of mine. Why did you marry a woman you don't love?"

He felt his own face heat up. "I've taken about all I can stomach of your self-righteous attitude myself." He planted a hand on each side of her shoulders and held her almost toe to toe with him. "I wouldn't have married you if I didn't love you."

He kept her in his grasp, heart pounding and breathing like a steam engine, as he watched her face. Her brown eyes grew round and her lips parted. She tilted her head ever so slightly, then straightened up. Was she really smiling?

"You really love me?" Was he serious? Or only trying to appease her? She had to be sure. She couldn't go through this again.

He kissed the tip of her nose. "I really love you. You didn't know that?"

"You never said so."

He eased her into his embrace. "I thought you knew. Why else would I have stayed with you? Wanted to help you? Bought that wagon, all the provisions?" She wrapped her arms around him, and he felt his body respond to her touch.

"I thought you were just being kind," she mumbled into his chest, then gazed up at him. "That's why I made you agree to that condition."

He groaned. "And I was so sure I could make you forget about it." He eyed her. "If you didn't think I loved you, why did you accept? I would've seen you safely through this trip as a guide, if that's what you'd wanted."

"How was I to know that? Your reasons made sense when you proposed to me, though it was more like a business proposition."

"Is that the only reason you agreed to marry me?"

She shook her head. "I knew I loved you. I couldn't have married you if I hadn't." She grinned. "All I wanted was to know you loved me."

He moved one hand up and cupped the back of her head. "Why didn't you ask?"

"I was afraid you'd say no." She stood on tiptoe and pressed her lips to his. Lord, it felt wonderful at last to be where she wanted to be.

He grinned. "I had no idea how very strong-willed and stubborn you could be. Together we'll make your dream come true."

His dimple was there again on his cheek, and she smiled. "You already have. We'll have to work on a new one."

"Mama!" Patrick yelled as he raced back to the wagon. "See what I caught . . ."

"We helped!" Beth Anne called, running with Amelia after Patrick.

Eleanore turned around within Jordon's arms to see their children. "We have quite a family."

"That we do. But I'd still like to have a wedding night with my bride."

She grinned up at him. "We have a lot of miles to cover today, and I feel sure our children will be very sleepy by sundown."

Her back was to him and his arms crisscrossed her chest. He slipped his hand under his other arm and kneaded her breast. Brushing his lips over the velvet curve of her ear, he whispered, "I'm counting on it."